THE UNDEAD DAY ELEVEN

RR HAYWOOD

Copyright © 2017 by RR Haywood

All rights reserved.

No part of this book may be reproduced in any form or by any electronic or mechanical means, including information storage and retrieval systems, without written permission from the author, except for the use of brief quotations in a book review.

Cover design and artwork by Mark Swan

❦ Created with Vellum

THE UNDEAD
DAY ELEVEN

rrhaywood.com

CHAPTER ONE

D AY ELEVEN

MONDAY

We drive silently through the flatlands. Each of us, apart from Lani and Tom, remembering what happened here just a few of days ago. It's still night so the ground is featureless apart from the dark shapes of the mounds. We can't even see if the bodies have been cleared away but the air is tinged with the smell of burning. Whether that is coming from the fort ahead or the corpses that have been burnt we can't tell.

I smile at Lani to re-assure her. She has left everything she knows, the place she lived and any hope of seeing a familiar face again. She's one of us now though so I know she will have many pairs of eyes looking out for her. But for the rest of us, that sense of coming home is strong. So much has been invested in this place, so many lives laid down, so much suffering and loss. That has to stand for something.

The road is longer than I remember and it takes a few minutes to navigate the track leading to the outer doors.

'Feels like home,' Clarence says quietly from his position sat on a crate of heavy calibre ammunition in the back of the van.

Reaching the fort we see there are large fires lit along the top, like the castles of olden days when the knights would patrol the turrets and warm their hands on the naked flames, and make ready to unleash fire arrows into the dark perimeter. Only now it's high summer and the heat is sweltering. We're all bathed in sweat and even with the windows of the van open it feels like there is no movement in the air.

'Why are there fires lit? Doesn't that just advertise it to every passing zombie?' Lani asks quietly as she peers up and looks along the top of the fort.

'I was trying to figure that out,' I reply, 'but I think I know why he's done it.'

'Who?' She asks.

'Big Chris, he's sending a signal. Letting other survivors know this is a safe place and we're not going to hide away in the shadows.'

'Either that or he's forgot to put the things out when the sun went down,' Clarence adds.

'Well, we'll soon find out,' I say as I bring the van to a gradual stop a few metres back from the doors. The headlights pick the detail out on the heavy doors. The same doors we burst from snarling and growling as we charged the undead army.

We climb out, all of us stiff from sitting for so long after another few hours of running and fighting. Sweat drips from our faces and our clothes cling to our bodies. I stretch upwards and hear popping noises as my bones crack pleasurably.

'Did we need to phone ahead and book a room?' Cookey asks as he walks stiffly to the front of the vehicle.

'We'd have been spotted way back,' Clarence remarks.

'You were spotted way back you noisy fuckers,' a familiar voice comes from behind the door; making six of us break out in huge grins.

'We weren't exactly trying to sneak in, open up we've got some presents for you,' I say with a laugh. The single door opens and big Chris steps out holding a shotgun in hand. His white teeth showing in a huge grin through his dark beard.

'Mr Howie,' He nods in a mock serious manner.

'Mr Chris,' I nod back, he strides forward to pump my hand and clap me on the back. He gets engulfed as the lads swarm round him, shaking hands and smiling. Chris and Clarence grip each other in a bear hug that would crush any normal sized man.

'You did it then?' He turns to me smiling.

'They got back okay?'

'Yesterday morning, we were worried. We thought you'd be right behind them but then they said about the problem with Darren…' His voice trails off as he looks at each of us, 'you lost one,' he says quietly after counting our number.

'Steven, he was in the police with Tom,' I nod towards Tom as I explain.

'I'm sorry to hear that Tom,' Chris nods again at the young officer before turning to Lani.

'Chris this is Lani, Lani this is Chris.'

'Nice to meet you Lani, I heard about you from the others that got back yesterday.'

'You too,' she nods back and shakes his hand.

'It's late so we'll get you in as quick as we can but you've got to be checked for bites and scratches first. Doc Roberts is jacking a team up now.'

'Yeah fair one,' I reply with a yawn, 'mate the van is full of weapons and ammunition, take it in if you want, we'll wait here until the doc is ready.'

'Where did you get all that from?' Chris asks genuinely surprised.

'Navy supply ship in Portsmouth harbour,' I answer him.

'What were you doing on a supply ship?' He asks with a sweeping glance.

'Ah you know, thought we'd bring you a gift back from our travels. So how's it been here?'

'Hard like you wouldn't believe,' he replies quickly, 'clearing the bodies up and then when the women and children got back...of course they didn't know who had survived and who was dead. Awful,' he rubs his beard one handed while shaking his head, a far-away gaze in his eyes, 'just bloody awful...still...you're back now. I'll get that van in and get Doc Roberts to hurry up, you must be knackered.'

'Understatement,' Clarence rumbles while resting his frame against the front of the van, 'this heat! I am bloody melting,' he pulls his top away from his body and flaps it about to get the air circulating.

'Tell me about it, try being here and doing manual work instead of pissing about on ships getting new guns,' Chris calls out as he disappears through the single door and narrowly misses being struck by the water bottle thrown by Clarence.

'Are we getting the same rooms back? Cookey asks. I turn round to see him, Blowers and Nick all looking pensive.

'What's up with you three?' I ask concerned. They don't reply but look downcast and avoid eye contact. Then it hits me. The same thing I felt on the pier. Being together and on the road, going somewhere, having *a thing* to do. Now we've done it and got to the place we worked so hard for. We'll still be together in the fort, but not as a unit. We won't be working and fighting alongside of each other.

'Bloody hell, we've done it,' the thought sends me reeling. I push my hand through my hair, 'we've done it,' I repeat quietly.

'We have Mr Howie,' Blowers says. I glance up and the importance of this moment hits us all. Dave is staring hard at me, they all are. The same question on all their faces. What happens now?

'We got what we fought for boss,' Clarence says.

'It doesn't feel over,' I say quickly.

'It's not,' Dave cuts in, his voice flat. We all turn to stare at him; he just shrugs and looks off into the distance.

'How do you know that?' I ask him. He turns his head slowly and fixes me with a level gaze which becomes intense and uncomfortable after a few seconds.

'I think we all feel it boss,' Clarence adds.

'Lads?' I look to them stood there. The young army recruits from Salisbury. They've changed so much just in a few days. They were boys. They're men now. Hard men. Killers.

'This ain't done,' Nick whispers.

'We stick together then, inside here I mean,' I look round to see them nodding in agreement.

The double doors swing open as Chris and a couple of other people walk out. One of them heads towards the van.

'We'll sort the van out,' I call out and stop the man in his tracks.

'But Chris said...' he looks unsure.

'Yeah, change of plan. We'll sort it mate but thanks anyway.'

'Er...yeah okay.' He turns with a shrug and heads back through the doors, passing Chris as he strides out.

'Doc's ready, Lani do you want to go first?' Chris calls out.

'Er yeah, is that okay Mr Howie?' She asks with a quick smile.

'Yeah definitely…you should go first,' I nod back.

'Why is the van still there?' Chris asks pointing at the vehicle and turning towards the man walking back into the fort.

'I said we'll sort it out, it's got our kit and bags inside, it'll be easier.'

'Okay, makes sense. Right, follow me Lani; I'll lead you to the charming Doctor Roberts.' They disappear through the outer doors into the wide avenue that separates the two high walls of the fort. I can see some tent structures set up on one side, torch lights bobbing about and then the sound of a generator kicking in and more lights flood the area. Within a few minutes we're being led inside one by one and taken through an opening into a brightly lit tent. Trestle tables with equipment and a large dentist style magnifying glass on a swivel stand. Doctor Roberts stood there dressed in a long white lab coat, his intelligent eyes watching me under his bushy eyebrows.

'Howie,' he greets me with a firm handshake, 'good to see you,' his manner is brusque and he turns away to put a clipboard on the table. 'You've done this before so you know the drill, strip off and we'll check you over.'

'Yes Doc,' I sigh with tiredness and start peeling the sweaty layers off, using a chair to sit down and unlace my boots. My feet smell of sweat which causes the doctor to glance round. He comes over and peers down at my damp socks clinging to my feet.

'Heard of trench foot? In this weather your feet will rot if you don't keep them clean and dry. Get those boots off whenever you can, clean and dry your feet thoroughly. We've got some powder here for you to use.'

'Okay,' pulling my socks off and I can see the skin on my toes is crinkled like when I've been in the bath too long. The air feels nice on my feet. My pistol belt is removed and I lay it within reach on the table, then I strip the trousers off and stand ready for the inspection. The doc moves in and starts a close physical inspection of my skin, using a bright torch and checking every square inch. I'm covered in bruises from the falling about but fortunately there are no open cuts or scratches. He checks my eyes and tells me to look left, right, up and down while he shines the light into them.

'So have you made any progress with finding out more about the infection?' I ask him as he sticks something in my ears and leans in to have a look.

'Ssshh,' he replies and I go quiet and let him finish. The examination is very thorough and eventually he steps back and gives me a satisfied nod.

'Get dressed but put some clean socks on for god's sake, now what did you say?'

'Have you made any progress with the infection?'

'And when exactly would we do that Howie?' He answers in a sarcastic tone, 'we've been somewhat busy patching everyone up from the fight, you have no idea how many people cut themselves on their own weapons or trod on those bloody sharp things you put down.'

'Oh right...of course...'

'And we're still getting our equipment set up. We need power but the fuel supply is running low after you used all the fuel from that tanker and then of course you blew the tanker up.'

'Yeah true...'

'Chris lets us have power to treat the injured but we can't get our research equipment running without more power. We need solar energy, generators, fuel, we need medicines, bandages, anti-biotics, penicillin, we need nurses and clean water and then maybe we can start looking at this infection.'

'Okay doc…sorry I didn't mean to cause offence.'

'You did not cause offence. You asked a question and I answered it. Now you're back you can go and get supplies. We need the stock from the local hospitals. Chris is run off his feet here so you'll have to do it.'

'What now? Doc we've been non-stop for days. We need some sleep.'

'Of course you need sleep. Do you want me to sign you off for a week? You all need to rest and take a long holiday but that's not going to happen is it. So get some sleep now and be ready to go out in the morning.'

'Right,' I nod wearily, 'yeah no problem. We'll need lists of what to get and where the hospitals are.'

'Sergeant Hopewell has kindly agreed to sort the mapping out, as for lists you don't need them.'

'Why not,' I ask him as I pull the pistol belt round my waist and start fastening it up. He walks towards the back of the tent and uses a hose to wash his hands, scrubbing them with some kind of medical detergent.

'Because we need everything you can find that's why. Send the next one in please.' And that's me done. Exam over. I give my thanks and walk out the tent to find several of the others already stood nearby and waiting.

'Next one can go,' I motion to the tent behind me, Nick stubs a cigarette out and heads that direction, 'we've got our orders, the doc wants us to scavenge the local hospitals and chemists shops. He said they're running low on everything.'

'You said it wasn't over Dave,' Blowers says with a rueful grin.

'Psychic psycho,' Cookey quips and apologises instantly on getting a hard glare from Dave and a round of "oohh's" from the rest of us as we jokingly take steps back leaving

Cookey stood alone looking distinctly unhappy, 'I really didn't mean it Dave...' Cookey adds. Dave just stares at him unflinching, seconds pass as Cookey suddenly sees his future mapped out in pain and suffering. Dave steps forward causing Cookey to yelp and jump back, Dave simply drops down and starts to unfasten his bootlaces while the rest of us burst out laughing, especially Blowers who bends over double laughing hard. Dave glances up and I see that rare smile on his face that changes his features so much.

'What happened?' Nick bursts out from the tent holding his top, pistol belt, boots and trying to pull his trousers up, 'what did I miss?' He grins at the sight of Cookey red in the face and everyone else wetting themselves.

'Cookey picked a fight with Dave and lost big style,' Blowers explains between taking breaths.

'If you have finished pissing about perhaps you could send the next one in please,' Doc Roberts looms out of the tent with his white lab coat flapping around his legs.

'Sorry Doc,' Clarence chuckles as he walks over and stoops down to pass through the tent opening.

'Nick put your top on,' Dave says in his sergeant voice after a few minutes of chatting. I turn round to see Nick stood there smoking with his top off.

'Sorry Dave,' he replies quickly and starts shrugging his arms through the holes, 'it's really hot.'

'We are not thugs on the beach Nick, we have reputation and image to uphold,' Dave intones.

'Sorry Dave,' Nick repeats.

'We are back amongst other people now and we will show a standard of behaviour. We are a unit, a fighting unit and that makes us close,' Dave stares at Blowers, Nick, Cookey, Tom and even Lani, 'we have banter and jokes but in sight of other people we show a level of professionalism and respect.'

'Good advice,' I add, 'these people will be suffering and

grieving so take it easy with the pissing about, got it?' They nod back looking serious, sweaty and very tired.

'You all cleared yet?' Chris asks walking towards us from the inner gates.

'Almost,' I answer as Blowers darts in to be checked.

'We've got some rooms put by for you. Roger got some of the old stores emptied out so you got a bit more space but they're right at the back though, does that bother you?'

'No mate and we won't be here long by the sounds of it. Doc Roberts said he needs the local hospitals checked…'

'…I bloody knew he'd get that in quickly, I told him to give you a break and we'd sort it out,' Chris's spits in a flash of anger.

'Chris it's fine mate, really. We can go back out in the morning. We'll have the Saxon and maybe take a van or something.'

'You'll need more people with you then,' he goes back to rubbing his beard.

'We can take Ted or that Brian bloke that helped Clarence before the big fight.'

'Brian? He died in the battle.'

'Shit, did he? I'm so sorry I didn't realise…'

'Not your fault, leave it with me. Let's get you in and settled. You look fucked.'

'Understatement,' Clarence growls.

The inner doors are opened and we're once more back inside the fort proper. Nick drives the van slowly while the rest of us walk in front.

'It's big, a lot bigger than I thought it would be,' Lani says looking round.

'It can hold thousands of people,' I reply, 'we'll try and get you the guided tour in the morning.'

We stay to the far side, walking quickly and trying to get through to the back without disturbing too many people. Small fires burn throughout the interior. Figures walking round in the shadows. Children and adults crying. People calling out in pain. I'm glad it's night so we can get in quietly. I know Sarah and the others will be here and will want to see us but we're beat and need sleep more than anything.

We're led to the back, past the police office and the rooms we used the last time to an arched door set into lower wall. Gas lanterns are already lit inside and I see Sarah stood by the door smiling. So much for the quiet entry.

'Hey,' she calls out softly and rushes forward to embrace me in a tight hug, 'you made it...again.'

'Again,' I say at the same time and hold her closely, 'you got back okay then?'

'They kept their word,' she says, 'they argued all night because of what you did, leading them away like that but they took us to the harbour in the morning...'

'We saw the boats going over, we were up the pier,' I reply.

'We saw the smoke coming from the town...was it bad?'

'Bloody awful, we lost Steven.'

'Oh Christ!' Her hand covers her mouth as she breaks free and finds Tom standing nearby. She hugs him next as I remember Tom and Steven went with them when they fled the fort. They stand murmuring for a few minutes before she moves away to Clarence.

'Let's get in,' I say and head towards the door. Inside the room looks inviting with a soft glow from lanterns set on low. Doors lead off into other rooms and we move round checking inside each door and finding two beds set up in each. Just mattresses on the floor but at least they've got clean sheets and a lamp. Someone has put bottles of water in the rooms and snack food. There is a big table in the main room with wooden chairs set round it, several mugs of steaming coffee on the table filling the room with a nice aroma.

Checking the rooms gives me a flutter of panic. Eight of us and four rooms. Two beds in each room. Two sharing each room. Seven men and one woman. I can feel my face going red just from the thought of how this is worked out. Maybe Dave, Clarence and I can share and give Lani some privacy. Or better still Nick, Blowers and Cookey can share but no, that would leave Tom on his own and there's no point getting four of them to share one room. I start biting my fingernails as my exhausted mind tries to work out the best solution.

'Two per room, I'll share with you Mr Howie,' Lani brushes past me and puts her bag onto one of the beds. I glance round expecting there to be stares and giggles but no one bats an eyelid. Clarence and Dave have gone into one room, Nick and Tom and then the inseparable Blowers and Cookey into the last one.

'Right, yes...' I move away and grab a mug of coffee from the table and start gulping quickly.

'Weapons and kit bags first, wash then sleep,' Dave exits his room and crosses over to pick a mug of coffee up. Lanterns are brought into the main room and turned up as everyone starts checking kit bags and taking their assault rifles apart.

Exhaustion kicks in and the conversations become stilted and quiet. Eyes look heavy and movements become slow, cumbersome. Eventually the essential bit is done and we drift off in silence into the rooms and I hear bodies impacting on mattresses. Within minutes there are snores drifting through as I turn the lanterns off and leave one burning on low in the main room. Entering the room and I see Lani sitting on her mattress pulling her boots off. She smiles up at me. The room is small and square. The mattresses are next to each other with just enough room to stand in between them.

I sit down and unlace my boots before pulling them off. Socks too and then I go to take my top off and pause. I glance round and see her lying on one side with her head propped up by one hand smiling at me, she winks suggestively then laughs quietly.

'Not funny,' I murmur.

'Just take it off; you'll roast if you leave it on.'

'You're still dressed,' I say then have another little panic as I realise I might have sounded like I wanted her to get undressed. I hear rustling coming from her direction and then quietness again.

'Now I'm not,' she whispers, 'just strip off and relax, I'm too exhausted to attack you now.'

'Okay,' I chuckle at the thought of the fearless leader of the living army, having fought countless battles and now worried about the improper attire when sleeping in the same room as a beautiful woman. I shrug and take the top off then stretch out on the bed. The humidity feels so high and not having the top on makes no discernible difference.

I roll onto my side and my heart starts beating rapidly at the sight of Lani lying on her side facing me wearing tight shorts and a bra. The low light of the lantern casts her in a golden hue, and I can't help but run my eyes over the contours of her body. The gentle fall of her hips into her waist, gem stone glittering in her naval. The bra is white and plain but the soft mounds of her breasts stand out against the athletic leanness of her body. I look up and see her watching me, a gentle smile on her face. I smile back and extend a hand out. She meets it halfway, entwining her fingers into mine. Her eyes are drowsy and just watching them closing heavily makes my own feel the same.

We sleep hand in hand with the sweat dripping from our glistening bodies.

CHAPTER TWO

DAY ONE

The German Shepherd dog doesn't know days and nights. She has no concept of time. Only that the light and dark follow each other in an endless cycle. She has memory and knows her pack is gone. The images in her mind unsettle her. Fleeting images of the pack. Their hands rubbing her tummy and stroking her ears. The soft noises they made.

They were a close pack. The bond was unbreakable, or so it seemed. Every night she would lie at the top of the stairs and sleep with her ears pricked. Eyes opening and scanning at every sound. When the little one coughed or cried out she raised her head and listened intently. If the crying persisted she nosed the bedroom door open and roused the bigger ones, alerting the pack leader that something was wrong. They always responded kindly, praising her for waking them and giving a few strokes of her furry head.

In the mornings they would wake and she would watch

with interest as they moved quietly about the rooms, depositing their scent into the water and washing their bodies. While the pack leaders were doing this she would creep into the little one's bedroom and stare at the sleeping form. If the little one didn't wake she would gently nuzzle the face, giving small licks to the mouth and nose. The little one always woke up and showed his teeth. This was a good thing for them to do and she felt a sense of contentment as the little one threw his arms round her shaggy neck and pulled her in for a cuddle. Despite nearly always being uncomfortable, with a sharp elbow or knee poking in her side, she settled down and wagged her tail, showing she was happy while the little one made soft noises and played with her fur.

Then she would be allowed outside, and after depositing her own scent in the given area she would nose round the perimeter and check the grounds of the den. Scent trails put down in the night. Animals going through her territory while she guarded from the inside. She would find a corner of the grounds to defecate and then stroll back to the pack. Checking the position of each one. The little one up the hill making long noises and putting more covers on. The pack leaders in the place of the food, talking and moving quickly as they prepared to leave.

She knew the routine and moved between them, waiting for the little one to come down and knowing she would get a treat if she sat quietly under the flat thing.

Her own food would be put down, she didn't eat it straight away but left it until they were all gone and the den was hers. She would graze throughout the day, moving from room to room and nosing the net curtains aside to stare out of the front room window. When the pack returned she knew her special time was close when she would be taken out on patrol with the pack leader.

But then it changed.

The little one went to his den to sleep and the pack leaders stayed downstairs staring at the thing with the bright lights and loud noises. She heard it well before the rest of the pack; the noise from outside. A high pitched wail from further away. She cocked her head and strained to listen. More high pitched noises and even she knew they were sounds of distress and pain. Noises like the little one made when he fell down.

She didn't like the sounds and made a warning growl to alert the pack that something wasn't right. The pack leader made the thing with the bright lights go quiet as they all listened. The sounds got closer, other noises too. Things breaking and noises the pack made when they were angry. She was worried; this was too close, the noises were too close so she made sound to tell them she was here. This was her ground and they must not come here.

The pack leaders looked out the window and made noises to each other. She knew from the tone that they were worried and they spoke quietly. Then they opened the door and looked out. She didn't want this to happen and whined at them, urging them to seal the den. Danger was outside and she could smell blood, lots of blood. It was hanging in the air and tasted metallic in her mouth.

They went out and she waited, moving back to the stairs as she realised the little one was unprotected now. The pack leaders made loud noises. They were in pain and she wanted to go to them but knew the little one had to be defended. She was the main one in the den now and with the door open the danger could come in here.

Her ears twitched as she picked the sounds out, following the noises of her pack as they got louder and angrier. Then they were quiet. She moved up the stairs and turned to lie down with her front paws and nose over the top step.

Something was coming close to the den. She could hear

the steps being taken and the ragged course breathing. The doorway filled with something. She recognised the form as the pack leader. It still had the scent too but it was different now. It smelled of blood. It wasn't the pack leader anymore. She knew this and stood up; making herself look bigger and she showed the thing her teeth. The thing ignored the warning and came in anyway so she made noise. Loud noise. Angry noise. She stood her ground as the thing came faster up the hill.

The little one was alone now. She had to defend the little one. They were the pack. Defend the pack. Defend the ground. She lunged at the thing and used her sharp teeth to bite into the neck. She knew through instinct this was the weakest point and it was already bleeding.

Her weight took them both down and the normally gentle animal used every ounce of her strength as she tore it apart. Ripping and biting, feeling the blood pour in her mouth as she savaged it to death. She destroyed the enemy without mercy. This wasn't the pack leader she felled. It was an enemy, an attacker.

She knew the life went out of it. She could detect the heart beat ceasing and the lack of breath. The energy gone from the thing. She had defeated the attacker and defended her ground so she once more went back up the hill to lie down and watch the entrance.

More came. More entered the den and posed a threat to the little one. They were dealt with the same way. Killed and savaged as they tried to get past her. She moved quickly, jumping high and tearing flesh open. Ragging the bodies about and showing them she was strong and fierce. She didn't tire or feel bad. This was instinct. Throughout the night she killed and killed again until the downed bodies were a new level to walk on.

As the sun came up she sensed a difference. The energy of

the attackers was different. They were slow and weak now. She used this time to drink from the place where the pack deposited their scent.

She nosed the door open and walked to the little one, gently nosing his face and waiting as he opened his eyes and showed teeth. The little one gave her fuss and made soft noises. She whined and pulled away; trying to tell the little one they had to leave.

She watched as the little one moved noisily about and deposited his scent. The little one then went into the place the pack leaders slept. The pack leaders were gone so the little one started to move down the hill and stopped when he saw the enemies taken down during the night.

The little one made noises and kept making noises. She whined and stayed close, sensing the fear from him. She licked the salty liquid that fell from the little ones eyes and felt her neck being squeezed as he clung to her neck and made the noise she recognised as the sound they called her by.

'Bear....bear.....bear,' other sounds but that one was her sound.

They had to go. They had to leave this place. This wasn't a safe den anymore and the pack leaders were gone. She ran down the hill and whined for the little one to follow her. Noises were made and she knew the little one didn't want to follow, but she persisted and urged until finally he came down.

The little one made lots of noises as he walked on the bodies of the enemies taken down during the night. The dog watched as he pulled at the body of the one that was once the pack leader.

In the end she gently gripped the material of his coat and tugged him away. Pulling him and whining. The little one came with her and they walked outside into the open air.

The smell of blood was everywhere. Bodies were everywhere.

The little one made whining noises to show he was scared. She rubbed herself against his legs and ushered him away from the den. They had to find a safe place. This wasn't safe.

Another attacker was nearby, she could smell it. The stench of the thing was unmistakable. She growled to alert the little one as they walked out into the open grounds. There it was. Moving slowly but she could sense the hunger in it. The predatory nature of the thing. It wanted the little one who made noises at the thing and then ran towards it.

She ran in front of the little one, making more noise to tell him to stay away but he didn't listen. He ran towards the thing with his small arms held out. The thing kept coming closer and she tried blocking the little one but he ran round and kept going. The little one didn't know the danger. He was too young.

With a big jump she took the thing by the throat and dragged it away from the little one. Pulling with all her strength and shaking her head so her teeth would slash the wound open. The little one made a high pitched sound and kept making the noise as she felt the life end in the thing she gripped.

She released and looked to see the little one was down on the ground and making a long whining noise. She sensed the sadness and fear and tried to lick his face. She was pushed away but stayed close, whining and slinking with her ears and tail down. More coming. She lifted her nose and sniffed the air. The things made low sounds and she knew there was more than one. Another pack coming their way. A pack of the things. She growled and whined for the little one to move. She tugged at the material and felt the little one grab her neck and squeeze hard. She knew the he was scared and wanted the contact of the pack to feel safer but this was not the time. She waited for a few seconds and wriggled free, bouncing away and turning to face the pack of things now in view.

She positioned herself between the pack and the little one and made noise. Telling this pack she had killed many and would do again. The little one wouldn't move but stayed on the ground with liquid falling from his eyes.

The pack was closer now and she knew she had to act. She ran at them and stopped in front, making noise and showing her teeth. They paid no heed to her warning and came anyway. The smell of blood filled her nose, the smell of their scent, the way they moved. They were hungry and wanted to take the little one.

She moved quickly and took the first one down. Dragging it to the floor and shaking her head to damage the thing. They didn't react but kept going. She moved between them. Pulling them down and biting deep into their necks. She took fingers away from hands. Hands away from arms and an arm away from a body. She killed each one before they reached the little one who stayed on the ground covering his face and making noises.

It was hot here. No shade. She was thirsty and wanted to drink but the little one wouldn't move so she stayed thirsty. More came. More were killed. The little one stayed low on the ground with his face covered while she dealt with the attackers until all around were the bodies of the things she killed.

She laid down panting hard. Then a big thing came. She had been inside the big things before when the pack leaders took her somewhere different. She knew they would go the place with the big salty water and the soft ground and she would be able to jump in the salty water with the little one.

The big thing had to move slow as it couldn't go over the bodies she had killed. Then it was not moving and people were coming out of it. They made noises and went towards the little one. She watched them but sensed no danger. They didn't have the hunger of the things and the noises they made were soft and nice. She let them touch the little one and watched as the little one clutched at them and more liquid fell from his eyes.

One of them took the little one into the big thing. A man stayed and looked at the bodies then at her. The man seemed to know she had killed the things and he bent down and looked closely into her eyes, his face calm but he smelled of fear too. The man stroked her head and looked back at the big thing. She sensed he was unsure of something, she could feel his indecision. He looked back down at her and pulled some material out. He wiped her mouth and looked at the blood on the material then shook his head. He stroked her head and went over to the big thing. She knew they were taking the little one away. The male was the leader of another pack. They wanted the little one but not her. The little one needed a strong pack to survive so she sat down to show she accepted this.

The male stopped at the big thing and looked at her. She lay down to show she understood that they should take the little one into their pack. The little one needed to be with his own kind. He moved his face up and down a few times. He conveyed a message. He would protect now.

The big thing moved off and she was alone.

She went back inside the den simply because she knew there would be water. She drank. She drank all of the water and then ate the food that was left. Once she was finished she walked round the den, going into each room and savouring the scent of the pack. She lay down in the place the little one slept. She felt sadness and wanted to be close to the smell of him.

The dog was tired but this was not the place to sleep. She jumped down from the bed and moved to the door. Looking back and breathing in deeply. With a soft whine she went down the hill and walked over the bodies of the things she had killed.

Outside she moved away from the den, keeping to the shade and listening for the sounds of the things. She heard them often and scented them more.

She sensed the hunger, the predator in them. She knew if they found the little one, they would kill him. So she killed them first. She was strong and fast. She was almost as heavy as them too. She had power and speed, sharp teeth and a strong neck. They were no match for her and she took advantage of this.

By the end of that day she had killed many. Leaving a trail of savaged bodies behind her. She killed them in groups, in couples, hordes and on their own. She found water and drank and kept moving.

She saw people too. Running and hiding. She saw one fighting the things and attacking them with something in his hands. She helped the man and took several down with him.

Then one of the things bit him. She killed the thing and watched the man on the ground holding his neck. She sensed the life leave his body while he stared at her. His hand stretched out to touch her face. She let him ruffle the hair and his hand dropped down. Then his life came back but it wasn't *his* life. It was something else. He wasn't the same as he was. His eyes were those of the things. He smelled of them. He had that hunger. She killed him quickly.

As the light went and the dark came she heard them make noise. It made the hairs on her neck stand up. She cocked her head and listened as all around her the things howled into the darkness. She sensed the change before she saw them. That hunger was strong now. They moved quickly like they did before.

She heard them running. She waited in the shadows, watching a pack of them moving past her. They had prey in their sights and were chasing it. She was dark too. Her pack leaders used to call for her in the grounds of the den and she knew they couldn't see her. She used this as she ran alongside this pack with long easy strides and watching them. Then she moved out and took one down. Savaging its neck and tearing the life from it. She caught the pack up and took them down one by one.

She felt the tiredness slowing her down. She moved away from the area of the hard ground where the people lived and moved into the soft ground. She found water running in a stream. She drank the water. She pushed herself into bushes and found a hole to lie down.

The dog felt a different sensation inside her. A strange feeling that made her stomach gurgle and her heart beat faster. She felt hot and panted heavily as her eyes rolled in her head.

She closed her eyes and slept.

CHAPTER THREE

D AY ONE

'CUT! Paco that was brilliant, absolutely brilliant.'

'Say, was it okay? I mean was it good?'

'Paco it was pure art and perfectly executed.'

'I don't mind doing another take to make it perfect. I should have lifted the eyebrow more.'

'Paco are you crazy, it was perfect. The eyebrow was perfect.'

'Really? I'm not sure...can I see the playback?'

'Now? You wanna see it now?'

'I could have got more out of it; ...maybe the other eyebrow instead?'

'Okay, get the playback ready. Your angle was fine Paco.'

' I was walking in the street right? I was expecting something to happen, just not that. I wasn't expecting that to happen. So the show of surprise has to be mixed with one of expectancy right? Well that look always comes better from the other eyebrow.'

'Can you see the monitor Paco? There you are, walking through the town. Smoke and debris littered everywhere right? Your walking through and then bam! There it is, right in front of you. Now...here we go...close up and bam! The head tilts back...the eyebrow lifts... bam! its perfect, Paco it's perfect, you look perfect.'

'You think?'

'What? You're Paco Maguire; you look perfect in every scene.'

'Maybe I shouldn't look so perfect Bob, you know this is Armageddon so maybe I should look a bit less....you know....perfect.'

'Paco if we covered you in mud and shit you'd still shine; you're a star Paco, a gleaming star surrounded by the end of the world, death, suffering and disease...'

'I get it Bob, but hey if this is the end of the world then shouldn't I look a bit...you know...rougher...'

'Rougher?'

'Maybe tougher?'

'Tougher?'

'Rougher and tougher?'

'Oh rougher *and* tougher...I see what you mean Paco and you know what? I'm glad you raised it. But this is the start of the event so you get rougher and tougher as it goes on, you can't start off rough and tough...there'd be no transition.'

'Transition?'

'Yeah Paco, you need a transition. You're an everyday guy right? You're looking for your family right? So why would an all American everyday guy start off looking rough and tough. That comes later when you....well when you have the transition.'

'Transition. Right. So is that like a montage or something?'

'What?'

'The transition Bob, how are we doing the transition? I'm thinking a montage.'

'A montage?'

'Yeah, show the character transiting…'

'Transitioning.'

'Yeah transmissioning…you know, like old school Rocky.'

'Paco, did you read the script?'

'What? Of course I read the script, what are you saying Bob? This is a creative flow.'

'No, no Paco, the idea is great. I love it! It's great that you have these ideas. Isn't it great that Paco has these ideas? I said it was going to be great working with Paco cos he has these ideas, didn't I say that? See I said that. It's just that, you know…we have the script and everything is already in place. The studio might not like the idea of us moving away from the script.'

'I can talk to the studio Bob; you want me to get my people to speak with the studio?'

'No! I mean no Paco, you're in the creative flow right now and we need you focussed Paco, we want nothing distracting you from the creative genius you have. Why don't you get some rest and we'll prep for the next…'

'You sure Bob? It's a phone call; I get my people to speak with your people. If you want a montage then we get a montage.'

'I tell you what Paco, we'll speak to our people and get someone to get back to your people but hey buddy…Paco… We need you sharp and ready, you gonna be ready?'

'I'm ready Bob?'

'You sure Paco? The trailer okay? You got everything you need?'

'The trailer's fine Bob, I'll get ready.'

'You do that Paco...*jeesh*! Actors...I mean I know the guy is grossing big right now but did you hear him? A fucking montage? What is this the fucking eighties? Like the studio is gonna go for a fucking montage, *hey Bob...do you think I should have lifted the other eyebrow*...jeesh! Get ready for the next scene...where are my zombies? Hey where the fuck are my zombies?'

Paco walks through the film set casually nodding a greeting at the horde of zombies stood next to the catering truck, drinking coffee and smoking while taking care not to damage the make-up applied to their faces. Layers of latex twisting their features into gruesome bone exposing blood soaked undead.

'Hey guys, you look great,' Paco calls out with a thumbs up, getting a round of twisted macabre smiles in response.

'Damn it's hot,' he mutters as he reaches the trailer door. Leaving the door open behind him he pauses in front of the full length wall mirror. The mirror that he insisted was present so he could check his reflection before leaving the trailer every time. He casts an appreciative glance at his form. Solid upper body, bulging chest muscles and wide shoulders tapering down to a narrow waist. Huge beefy arms looking even bigger within the too tight stretch top. He smiles to show his perfect gleaming straight teeth and dark tussled hair giving him that all American appeal. Women loved him. Men loved him. Everyone loved him. He knew it. His agent knew it and the studio knew it better than all of them which is why they were more than happy to agree to any demand he had.

'Hey can I get costume in here?' Paco leans his head out of the trailer and shouts into the general bedlam of the set, knowing full well he would have been heard. Two minutes later a breathless but attractive young lady knocks on the open door.

'Mr Maguire? You called for costume sir?' the girl calls out.

'Hey yeah...wow yeah Hi,' Paco smiles down at the woman and held his hand out, helping her up into the vehicle, 'who are you?' Paco winks, tensing his bicep muscles as pulls the girl up.

'I'm Jenny,' the girl replies. She had been warned exactly what to expect from Paco but still felt herself becoming star struck in the presence of the man, she smiles back and stands there staring at his perfect teeth and dark sparkling eyes.

'Well I'm glad they sent you Jenny,' Paco beams knowing the effect he's having.

'Me too,' she murmurs quietly.

'Say Jenny, maybe you can help me with something...'

'Anything Mr Maguire.'

'Hey call me Paco, I'm one of you. Sure I'm the big name actor,' he smiles, making finger quote marks, 'but the cast and crew are the same Jenny, we're all in this together.'

'Er...okay Paco,' Jenny nods eagerly. Her first week on set of a major Hollywood financed movie and already she was in a luxury trailer with *The* Paco Maguire.

'Say Jenny,' Paco began, emphasising his American drawl knowing these English girls always fell for it, 'do you think this top is tight enough?' he steps in close and turns side on to the girl, straightening his arm to tense his triceps muscle. The rock hard horseshoe bulging under his skin, 'I'm not sure if it's showing the guns off enough, what do you think Jenny?'

'Oh...'Jenny replies, captivated by the size of the muscle and the carefully tanned skin.

'See here,' Paco pushes his finger up inside the sleeve, pulling it away from his skin, 'I think the sleeve is a little loose, they should be tighter yeah? Here you try.' He lifts her hand to push her slender finger under the material. She breathes heavily as she feels the hardness of his muscle. They told her he would do something like this, and wouldn't be able to keep his hands to himself but still...he was Paco Maguire...and he looked so good.

'Do you think it's too loose?' he asks softly.

'Yeah,' she whispers paying more attention to his arm muscles than the actual tightness of the material.

'I knew it,' he nods, promptly pulling the top off, exposing his rock hard abs and defined chest, 'can you get me a smaller size?'

'Oh my...'Jenny wheezes at the sight of one of the world's most famous six packs.

'What?' Paco says in surprise, 'oh you mean these,' he runs his hand down the washboard muscles.

'Wow,' Jenny stares at the smooth skin plunging down into the top of the trousers.

'You like them? Yeah they're pretty famous. More famous than me I think sometimes,' he laughs, 'here, wanna touch them?' Her hand shoots out faster than she intended to start feeling the warm rock hard muscles.

'Well that ain't fair,' Paco murmurs softly, 'you gotta let me have a turn too.' He slips his hands under her denim shirt, running his fingers up her not so defined stomach. Within a second his hands have pulled the front of her bra down, cupping her breasts. Jenny hardly notices as she strokes his stomach, barely believing that she was inside the trailer with Paco Maguire and getting her tits touched up.

Precisely two minutes later she's on her knees in front of him as he rests against the end of the sofa, pushing the back of her head firmer into his groin. Exploding with a grunt he holds her head in place for a few seconds until she pulls away coughing and spluttering.

'Wow Jenny... that was so good,' Paco smiles down at the

girl. He tenderly lifts her up and uses a tissue to wipe the mess from her face. He doesn't care for the girl but he knows from years of experience that he now has a regular supply of sex as long as he shows some kindness, 'now be a good girl and get Paco a new top hey,' he pats her behind as he steers her towards the door, Jenny still wiping her face and not quite believing what just happened.

Smiling to himself he closes the door and walks through to the back of the trailer. Using the power shower to rinse himself off and the soft Egyptian cotton towels to gently dry his perfect skin.

Friday night in England and he hadn't expected it to be this hot. No air and he hated the thought of looking sweaty and red faced, apart from when the time came to look sweaty and red faced but that would be carefully contrived from the make-up girls and not from any real physical exertion. He was fit, he had to be to have a physique like this but that was done in the privacy of a gym with a team of trainers and nutritionists.

He dresses into a clean pair of trousers that exactly matched those he had worn previously, then busies himself making a fresh latte from the brand new coffee machine.

'Hi Paco...I got your top for you,' Jenny knocks on the door, grinning up at the Adonis stood there holding a coffee cup.

'Well gee Jenny that's just great, you know I knew we'd get along well, here you want some coffee?' He asks taking the top from her and casually throwing it over one muscled shoulder.

'Er...well we've got the catering truck out here and the producer said we shouldn't....'

'Hey forget that producer, get in here and have a decent cup of java with me, I promise I won't rat you out,' he smiles and helps her inside, making a scene of squinting outside to make sure no one was looking and quickly closing the door. She giggles as he presses buttons on the coffee machine.

'So Jenny, tell me about you,' he asks handing her the cup and staring intently into her pale blue eyes that might as well have had hearts instead of pupils.

'Well, oh gosh...er...well I was at university studying fashion and then I got the degree and a friend of mine had this business and said I should come work for her...oh my god I'm babbling...'

'That is so interesting Jenny,' he nods, 'are you enjoying it?' Paco couldn't care less if she was enjoying it. He enjoyed sex with women and she was a woman. That was it. He had been through the days of arrogance and knew that a few kind words would have the girl dropping to her knees whenever he asked.

'Oh gosh well yes it's so exciting! This is the first movie I've worked on and everything is so fascinating. I really had no idea how all these things were done....' She drones on holding her cup in two hands with her feet crossed at the ankles. Paco nods and murmurs to show he's listening while eyeing her shapely legs and savouring the image of later when he would be naked between them.

'Paco, you're needed on set, they're ready for the next scene,' a voice calls from outside the trailer.

'Got it,' Paco calls back, 'hey Jenny I'm real sorry we got to cut this short but you know...duty calls,' he shrugs as though it's a bad thing while pushing his arms through the top and pulling it down over his torso. Jenny plonks her coffee cup down and rushes over to help him with the now far too tight top. They get it down and she stands back to look at the material clinging to his frame. He was right though. The tighter top did suit him. Without an ounce of fat on his body it was like a second layer of skin.

'Gosh you look so good Paco,' she purrs.

'Gee thanks Jenny,' he flashes her a big smile, 'now I'll go out first and you wait a couple of minutes and sneak out after. We don't want that producer getting all antsy now.'

'Okay,' she replies eagerly, desperate to impress him.

'Enjoy the coffee Jenny,' he winks, opening the door and walking out, leaving her swaying on the spot.

Paco strolls out of the trailer and across the concrete of the small town American film set. More and more filming was taking place in sets like these across Europe with lower costs and the average crew salary being far less than in the States.

He crosses the end of the set, stepping over snaking wires and rail tracks set up for the camera systems. Make-up units, lighting, sound engineers and a hundred other professionals all moving about and making ready. He steps a few more feet into the street, staring at a working set of mainstream American traffic lights, American road signs and American line markings on the road surface. Just the sight of it makes him feel a little homesick with a sudden longing to be back in his own country and away from the flat and weird tones of the English.

'Paco! You look great! Have you been pumping up?' The director yells loudly as he paces over the street towards him.

'Hey Bob, no it's just a tighter top,' Paco replies without any sense of shame.

'Okay Paco, this is the big scene. You're walking down the street and you've already seen the zombies turning the corner and coming towards you right?'

'Right,' Paco nods listening intently.

'So now, there is a few seconds of stand-off and then the woman comes running out from the side street, she's screaming and not watching where she goes. She runs straight into them...bam! And they set on her right?'

'Right Bob.'

'You Paco, you look at them hard, then you see her and you look confused, then you look scared for her safety and you try to yell a warning...'

'Hey lady?' Paco suggests.

'Yeah "hey lady" is great, you yell "hey lady" and you look terrified as she gets taken down.'

'Okay Bob, so I look hard then confused then I yell and then I look terrified.'

'That's it Paco.'

'Okay Bob and then what?'

'Paco are you sure you read the script? Never mind, then we'll get ready for the next scene which is you running at them and trying to save the woman.'

'Okay Bob. Hard, confused, yell out then terrified...got it Bob.'

'You're a trooper Paco, a real trooper. Places everyone....' Bob walks away waving his arms and shouting orders as the commotion suddenly ceases and perfect quiet descends. The horde of zombies are led out and put into position, a couple of them coughing and practising their groans while a few more jump up and down on the spot swinging their arms to limber themselves up.

'This is a hot set,' Bob bellows as he stalks backwards towards the camera equipment, 'I want quiet on set...anyone so much as farts and they'll be out of a job.'

Instant silence as everyone apart from the actors freezes in place. Anything that could rattle, jangle, shake or vibrate was gripped. Conversations ended abruptly. The atmosphere charged instantly as all eyes turn to Paco and the horde of zombies being quietly moved onto their exact spots. A long drawn out line of them with the most graphically created zombies at the front.

The unknown actress standing at the fake junction of the

fake side road takes deep breaths as she prepares for her fifteen seconds of fame. Paco runs through his facial reactions, quickly practising them, contorting his face, angling his head and deciding whether to stand face on or angled to the side. Hard. Confused. Yell. Terrified. Got it.

'Okay rolling camera...everyone ready....Action!' Bob shouts out as the person with the digital clipboard moves out from in front of the main camera.

An instant groaning commences from the zombies as they finally get to use their undead voices for the first time. The camera pans in close to the first zombie who bites down on the capsule within his mouth, pushing the thick bloody gunk out to slide down his chin. His eyes rolling as he staggers towards the camera which pulls back smoothly bringing the whole of the horde into view.

Paco gives his "hard" look. Narrowing his eyes and tilting his chin up. Setting his mouth firm and glaring from his eyes. He breaths in knowing it will flare his nostrils slightly and increase the intense look.

The actress, reacting to a prompt, screams and runs from the side street. Camera's swoop out to watch her progress. The zombies stumble and turn towards her, giving higher pitched growls. She flails her arms, windmilling wildly, her steps shorter than normal to give her that jerky out of control manner.

Paco takes his "hard" look and converts it smoothly into a look of "confusion". What is this? What is this woman doing here? Why is she running into the horde of zombies? He gives his best puzzled frown. Plunging his eyebrows down and slightly squinting one eye while gingerly lifting his top lip and tilting his head. The camera was some distance away but he knew it would be zoomed in completely on his face and he held the look for seconds while the girl runs across the road.

'Hey lady!' Paco yells in a deep voice, taking a step

forward and raising one muscled arm as though to pluck her away to safety.

The woman runs across the street straight into the midst of the horde. They grab out and take her down onto the pre-cushioned section of road surface.

Paco shifts his look, going from the "yell" to the "terrified" look seamlessly. He opens his mouth and makes his eyes go wide, again pushing the head back and off to one side. He knows he's good at this. The close up reactions are a strong point of his.

'My god...' he says deeply, adlibbing on the spot.

'CUT!' Bob yells, 'HOLD YOUR PLACES.' Everyone knows what to do. Paco holds his place, watching with mild interest as the make-up and prop department move in. The actress is lowered into a pre-set hole in the ground with just her arms, shoulders and head left above ground. A prosthetic body exactly matching her from the shoulders down is rushed in and laid out perfectly to resemble her own body. The dress material on the dummies stomach has been weakened to allow it to be ripped open easily. The smooth skin of the prosthetic mid-section has been made to be torn open and the harmless fake innards, already pre-coated in glistening crimson fluid, were ready to be pulled out and bitten into. The upper thigh of the right leg was also primed for the flesh to be bitten away.

The crew move quickly as the zombie actors hold their positions, chatting quietly. The whole process is done within a couple of minutes and they move away leaving what appears to be the actress still lying on the ground with a horde of undead above her.

'Paco, you wait a few seconds until you get the prompt. Then you yell out and run down towards them. Get your speed up and run straight past them, it's the run up and the action of zombies eating the woman we need. The fight scene comes after, got it?'

'Got it Bob,' Paco replies, bouncing up and down to stretch his leg muscles out.

'Zombie one, you go for the stomach, bite down and use your hands to tear the flesh open. Make it good because we get one shot at this. Zombie two, once zombie one has opened the flesh you get in and scoop some in the innards out, zombie three you go for the right thigh, zombie four you lean back and growl and thrash your head, zombie five you come and drop down to a crawl and start crawling towards them. I want you all into it, get the blood and gore on your faces and hands. Splay your fingers and show us the blood, Actress...' Bob explains, not knowing her name and not caring either, 'you scream and thrash your hands up and down, let the screaming go on but don't lift up too high otherwise we'll see the body is a dummy, keep screaming until they're all into the stomach and then you die, got it?' The zombies and actress nod back.

'Camera rolling...ready...ACTION!' Bob yells again. The growling starts instantly as the zombies sway and buck their way closer to the screaming woman. Paco keeps his terrified look for a few seconds, letting the zombies "eat" into the body.

Zombie one throws his head back dramatically and then lunges down to burrow his face into the skin of the dummies stomach which tears open easily as he pushes his hands in while thrashing his face side to side. He has done this before and is a well-known *zombie* actor, having worked on many films and television shows. He knows the exact amount of thrashing to be done and how to lift his elbows up high to make it look like he's digging down into the torso. His face disappears into the flesh as he seeks the big lump he knows is a couple of inches down. The actress lets rip with an ear shattering screech, shaking her head violently while drumming her hands on the road. Zombie one comes up with an almost triumphant look, like bobbing for apples. He holds the meaty chunk in his mouth and uses his hands to smear the fresh wet goo over his face. Zombie two drops in, using his hands to scoop out the long entrails that look like a string of sausages. He hungrily shovels these into his mouth while thrashing his head about. Zombie three, on cue, moves to the right thigh and after gripping the meaty *flesh* between his gnarled hands he bites down and tears a chunk away, the pre-loaded section bursting blood and gore out onto his face, an arterial spray pumps thick bright red liquid out.

On cue, Paco replaces his terrified look with one of determined action and starts moving towards the woman. He begins slow, allowing the camera to keep the zoom on his face as he shows the smooth move from terror to action. He picks his speed up, taking care to pump his powerful arms and lift his manly thighs high while maintaining a determined look on his face.

He gains speed as the zombies all sink down onto the dummy stomach and pull entrails, organs and props out in a frenzy of eating. The actress screams, thrashes and gradually grows silent to lie twitching in her final death act. She finishes with eyes open which she regrets, fearing her eyes will water from having to stare without blinking.

Precisely at this point, while Paco is doing his *action* run, another zombie appears from the back of the street. The third camera man, in a state of panic thinking he's missed a vital part of the script, pans in to film the late arrival. Everyone freezes. The make-up on this actor is brilliant; the fresh blood round his face, the torn clothing and the jerky staggering motion. The third camera man zooms in close on the red bloodshot eyes; giving thanks that he's captured the actor and hoping no one noticed he missed the entrance.

The new zombie jerks and staggers towards the horde on the ground. Paco, seeing the new arrival and also panicking thinking he had never read the script, keeps running while holding his *determined* face. Was he meant to arrive after this new one? Before? Shit. He curses himself for not getting someone to read the script and tell him what was expected. Jenny! He would get Jenny to check it and tell him in between dropping to her knees.

Bob, on seeing the new zombie actor quickly raises his clipboard and starts flicking through the notes, frowning at where this had come from.

The head of make-up crosses her arms as a look of thunder spreads across her face. This wasn't one of hers. So who had authorised this? Which union was he from? She wants to shout out but stops herself, knowing that nobody ever shouts out on a "hot-set".

The new zombie staggers towards the horde on the ground. They're unaware of the new arrival and are busy making noises, *eating* the innards of the dummy while smearing blood and howling into the sky.

Paco slows down and waits, sensing he should arrive just after the new zombie. He knows they will be able to edit the run so it looks seamless. For such an organised set there's a whole pause as everyone checks notes and looks to each other.

The horde feels the arrival of the new zombie as he shoulders his way through them towards the body. Zombie one glances at the late comer, inwardly cursing at the new one looking even better than he does and he's meant to be zombie one! His agent would be spoken to about this. The new zombie plunges its face into the dummies stomach and starts thrashing about. The howls turn to groans as it realises the flesh isn't flesh. It had seen the feeding frenzy and jumped in, hoping to quench the urge to bite and feed. This wasn't flesh. It was gunk. It turns slowly towards zombie one as Paco picks his running up again, starting the final sprint towards the horde.

Zombie one looks in horror as the new one lunges at him, pushing him to the floor and taking a chunk from his neck as Paco sprints past with a look of utter confusion on his face as he stares at the zombies. Are they meant to eat each other?

'CUT!' Bob yells, 'What the hell is going on here, who is that? Why is he attacking zombie one?'

A cacophony of voices bursts out as the head of make-up turns on everyone near her and starts yelling for "*who the hell did the new zombie?* Camera men shout for copies of the script, demanding to know why they hadn't been told about the new arrival. Paco eases his running and turns slowly to stand looking genuinely confused at the zombies still doing their feeding frenzy.

'YOU!' Bob shouts pointing his clipboard at the zombies on the ground, 'WHO ARE YOU? You will never work on any of my sets again, do you hear! You will be blacklisted and out of this industry, you'll be doing panto for the rest of your life buddy…Hey! Hey stop that now I am talking to you…'

Zombie one couldn't scream. His windpipe had been ripped out and he lay choking on his own blood. The real zombie turns and attacks zombie two frozen in terror at the sight of the angry director charging at them. Zombie one dies. Zombie two is savaged. The director runs into the fray and, in a fit of utter rage, drags the real zombie away from zombie two while screaming abuse and threats. Crew run in from all sides as the new zombie thrashes in the directors grip.

Bob, not believing that anyone on set would ever defy him, whacks the clipboard round the head of the zombie as it lunges up and bites deep into his neck. Bob goes down with a gurgled cry and a spray of blood bursting into the air. People scream. Paco screams.

'SECURITY,' someone yells. The burly black clad figures standing chatting in the distance of the catering truck ditch their coffee's and started running towards the noise.

Hands grab at the new zombie attacking Bob. Zombie two dies. Zombie one comes back to life as cast and crew look down at him. The poor actress, wedged into place and unable to move screams again and thrashes as zombie one surges up and bites into the face of one of the producers. The real zombie, gripped by hands and dragged from Bob, kicks and fights like the evil spawn he is. Biting and tearing flesh open. The deadly infection passes into the bloodstream of everyone cut and wounded.

Paco stands there rooted to the spot, screaming in terror. He ignores the look on Jenny's face as she runs towards the bedlam, staring at him with a look of disgust. The situation develops quickly with zombie one biting at will, zombie two turning and coming back to undead life to join in with the savage attacks.

Bob the director, bleeding heavily and having been dragged away by several members of the cast slumps down into unconsciousness. Cast and crew scream in horror as he becomes unresponsive, one of the producers yelling for the on-set medics to *get here now*. They arrive, carrying large padded bags and looking good in tight fitting uniforms specially designed for the television and movie industry. The bags are opened revealing a plethora of equipment as the paramedics rummage through the kit with shaky hands, applying dressing to the gushing neck wound and bending over to shine small pen torches into Bob's eyes.

'HE'S GONE,' the torch shining paramedic bellows very loudly, discarding the torch to tilt Bob's head back. He checks the airway is clear and disregarded the breathing apparatus supplied with the kit bags, preferring to use mouth to mouth and knowing that he'd be able to sell his story for thousands later. *The paramedic who gave the famous director mouth to mouth. Heroically struggling despite the violence erupting around him. Valiantly fighting to save his life despite the overwhelming odds.* The paramedic knows, regardless of the outcome, that he is now set for life and can milk this for years. His mind racing with thoughts of the television interviews, shaking hands with politicians and being famous for giving live on screen demonstrations for first aid.

'I NEED PADDLES...STAT!' he yells far louder than he needs for his assistant is already rigging the defibrillator up, having set it to pre-charge.

'COME ON BOB....BREATHE DAMN YOU... BREATHE FOR ME BOB,' the paramedic thumps the director's chest dramatically and plunges back down to press his open mouth against the directors lips, exhaling heroically while glancing up to make sure everyone is watching him. They cheer as the director twitches to life and wraps his arms round the paramedic's neck, pulling him in close. The paramedic feels a sudden searing pain as teeth clamp onto the soft tissue of his lips and tears them away with a savage shake. The paramedic reels back with blood pouring from his ruined mouth. More screams erupt as the director sits up, opens his red bloodshot eyes and lunges for the juicy calf muscle of the head of make-up standing there still holding her clip-board. She tries to jump back but Bob grips her ankle with his clawed hands and sinks his teeth in. The deadly saliva purging from his mouth, into the woman's bloodstream. She jerks away and hobbles off wailing in alarm.

The panic makes her heart beat faster and sends the infection into every cell of her body. She drops down within fifty paces to lie twitching on the floor. One by one the cast and crew are taken down.

The set was a closed set. Secret filming of the new Paco Maguire blockbuster being carried out late at night. Not one person on the set had any idea of the devastation sweeping the outside world and here, as with everywhere else, saw them running in all directions. The natural instinct to run towards other human beings in trouble, lying on the ground bleeding and injured. Medical assistance was given, hands pressed into wounds to stem the bleeding. Phones, that had been strictly controlled and turned off, were activated as trembling fingers dialled the emergency services.

Paco stays rooted to the spot as the devastation explodes all around him. He screams in terror at the sight of the real blood and gore being torn from real bodies of the real people. He backs away on shaky legs, gibbering and whimpering with utter blind panic.

'PACO! Help me...please help me...' the unknown actress buried in the hole screams in panic, holding her hand out to the movie star. He stares back in horror, willing her to shut up and not draw attention to him. The undead hear her screams and start towards her. She sees them coming, screaming louder, knowing that the strong actor can easily pull her from her position and give her a chance of survival. He doesn't. He backs away and watches in horror as they descend.

Jenny, who just a few minutes before had been taking a part of his body in her mouth, is now taking someone else's body in her mouth. Her red bloodshot eyes matched the colour of the glistening blood cascading down her chin. She turns her head slowly and fixes Paco with a baleful stare. An intense look of hunger in her eyes as she jerks to her feet and starts staggering towards him.

That was enough for Paco. He turns and runs. His strong legs pumping furiously as he pounds down the mock street and away from the lights of the set, into the darkness.

Paco runs through the movie set, passing through varying streets of international design. Each styled according to the scenes filmed. He runs through sixties London complete with vintage vehicles. An Italian *Sorrentine* piazza complete with café and working fountain. The building fronts were fakes. There was nowhere to go other than straight on. He knows that behind the buildings are snakes of wiring and electrical outlets and, more worryingly, deep shadows. The thought of running behind the buildings and into the darkness terrifies him even more.

He whimpers and twitches his head round, jumping at every sound. He follows the sets, not realising he's looping round in a giant circle and leading back to the point he started. He is fit and despite the muscle on his frame he is also athletic so keeping a constant jogging pace was easy. There's no rational thought process in his mind. Just utter panic. Seeing people being killed and ripped apart right in front of his eyes. He'd sue the studio for putting him danger like that, he'd sue the studio and the companies that provided the sets, the security, the catering, the cast…he'd sue everyone. He's Paco Maguire and they put him in danger. Even the security should have run to protect him first but they didn't, they ran into the fight and got themselves hurt and therefore unable to protect him. He'd sue them first.

He loops through a mock bombed out World War Two English street and turns a corner, coming to a sudden stop and staring back down at the lights of the set he had fled from. Frozen to the spot his eyes sweep across the set and the people still attacking each other. Blood everywhere, screams and shouts as the few survivors group together and back into a corner. They've armed themselves with bits of metal, chairs, tripods and anything they can grasp. Paco stares as the advancing horde takes them apart within seconds. A dark stain forms on his groin as he pisses himself through fear and a small dribble of shit exits his arse as his bowels void. He has no idea his bodily functions were doing this; such was the fear and panic that steals through his mind.

He turns round with his hands pressed to the top of his head, spinning and spinning as he desperately looks for an exit. His brain unable to cope with the situation and unwilling to process the information.

The service road. He needs the service road. He searches round in blind blithering hysteria, not realising he's still whimpering and uttering high pitched squeals. He sees the exit at last and starts towards it, intent on getting to the security gate and finding people who will protect him. Checking over his shoulder he observes the group of attackers leaving the bodies they had taken down and starting towards him. He screams and again starts running. His screams send a message to the horde that had already detected the stench of fear, shit and piss and started after him.

Paco runs fast. Sprinting down the service road towards the lights of the industrial hangars used for the indoor sets. The gate is ahead of him and he peers ahead trying to seek out the guards he knew will be there.

The gate is empty and hanging open. Paco doesn't hang around to find out why as he races through. He twists round to check behind him and feels a slight relief at the empty road behind him. Something snags his feet and he goes down, sprawling over a soft object. He splays his arms out, grazing his palms on the road surface. Scrabbling round he recoils at the remains of the guard spread out on the road, the entrails and innards strewn about and looking every bit as good as the prosthetic dummies used on set. He screams again and crabs backwards, gaining his feet and running towards the hangars.

Bodies strewn everywhere. Blood pooled and black in the

shadows. He jogs on uttering with fear at every corpse and swerving round them, desperate to avoid being anywhere near the bloodied things.

'HELP ME!' A voice pierces the air; he stops abruptly, spinning round trying to see into the gloom. The voice screams again, somewhere close but unseen. Someone in pain. A woman needing help.

He ignores it and runs on. He's an actor not a hero, not a cop, not a soldier. Sure he'd played all of them many times in his movies but he kept the thought in mind that he was depicting them, portraying them. They were professionals with training and equipment. They took those risks as part of their chosen careers. His was acting so why should he put himself at risk.

Groans and howls sound out, echoing through down the narrow alleys between the hangars. Not one living person to be seen. He wants to run inside the hangars and find someone, find a phone, find somewhere brightly lit and safe but most of them were locked up for the night. Those that were open were in darkness and looked too foreboding to enter.

In crazed fear he ploughs on, hurdling over bodies and swerving away from the noises in the shadows. He hears voices and whimpers, people crying in pain and suffering but his suffering is worse than theirs. He is world famous. People need him. He has to keep going and find someone to protect him.

He reaches the end of the hangars, sweat pouring from his face as he runs out into the lane that leads to the main road and the main entrance. There will be security at the main gate, always a whole team of them ready to search vehicles. Paco slows down, his chest heaving and the blood pounding past his ears. The front of his far too tight top now darkened with sweat and the piss stain still vivid on his tan coloured trousers. Glancing about nervously he creeps on down the bush lined road.

Howls come from behind him. He spins round, walking backwards as he watches the end of the hangars and the entrance to the road running between them. Shadows flitting and growing larger by the second. The high wall lights cast the silhouettes of the horde running after him onto the side of the hangar.

They stagger into view. Twisted, gruesome features ravaged by injury and blood soaked, all of them staring at him as they stagger faster now their prey is in sight.

He screams again and starts running, then stops at the sight of the undead guards running towards him from the direction of the main gate.

'Oh fuck...oh fuck...' he mutters as the panic rises higher in his stomach. He flicks his gaze between the horde coming from the hangars and the guards coming at him. All of them savaged and jerking. Rooted to the spot he spurts more shit out of his arse as he struggles to think.

Bursting away he surges through the thick bushes, scratching his skin and tearing his t shirt as the sharp branches fight against him. He struggles through to the other side, breaking free and plunging into the almost pitch blackness of the grounds bordering the road.

He staggers on, feet tripping over branches and making far too much noise. The horde reach the point of his disappearance and start after him, groaning with frustration as they too struggle to push through the thick bushes.

Paco races on, blundering through the undergrowth, running straight, then running left and then right. He sees a gap in the darkened hedgerow and aims straight for it, jumping through and landing on the road just a short distance up from where he went in. The now joined hordes are still trying to get through the thick bushes. Taking advantage of their backs being turned he runs on towards the gate.

Racing round the corner he can see the security hut brilliantly lit against the night sky. The security barriers are still down but he runs on, hoping against hope that someone living and normal will be there.

Reaching the hut he scrabbles round all sides of the building, staring in at the empty room. He finds the door and pushes his way inside, wrenching the phone handset and dialling 9-1-1 out of pure instinct. A loud beeping sounds at him from the receiver and it takes a few seconds to remember he's in England and the emergency number was 9-9-9. He presses the buttons and again gets the beeping sound. He tries again while peering out of the window. The beeping coming back at him.

A list of essential numbers pinned to the wall and starts with the first one for the head of security. It's engaged. They're all engaged. Pressing his face against the window he half screams when he sees the first of the undead staggering into the light just metres from the hut.

Ditching the phone he runs from the building and vaults the downed security barrier with ease. Running down the small access road and out onto the smooth surface of the main road, he sprints hard, desperate to make distance from the things behind him. With each step he waits for the hands to pull him back, expecting the twisted fingers of the monsters to take hold of his flesh and pull him to the ground. Tears pour down his red cheeks and mingle with the sweat that burns his eyes. His chest heaving for air, his arms and legs pumping furiously.

Five days a week he was in the gym being pushed by the best personal trainers money could buy. His diet was perfect and he avoided alcohol for months at a time in preparation for the roles he played. While many of his peers used recreational drugs, he lived on a diet of low fat, complex carbs and high protein. Steroids were used to give his muscles that extra pump in the weeks before filming, but they were strictly controlled and administered by well-paid doctors. He was fitter and healthier than the heroes he portrayed on film and he put every ounce of that fitness to use as he propelled himself away from the horde. Fear gave him extra stamina. A near hysterical belief that the things were right behind him; they were monsters and would keep going all night. Nothing would stop them. They wanted to eat him and take his brains.

His speed starts to ebb away, the adrenalin exhausted and leaving his muscles weak and powerless. Paco can feel his legs starting to feel rubbery and his breathing becomes uncontrolled. He knows he has to slow down but the fear keeps giving him extra spurts of energy. He whimpers and cries out, begging them to leave him, begging for forgiveness and crying out for his mother.

Gradually, step by faltering step he slows. Stumbling and wracking his body with heaving sobs and sucking air into his lungs. He windmills his arms trying to drive himself on. He berates himself, telling himself he's Paco Maguire, a star. His body gives up and he collapses to the ground. On all fours he crawls with snot dripping from his nose, vomit coming from his mouth. He tastes bile and tries to spit it away, his airwaves becoming clogged and his vision blurring.

He gives up and waits for the first hand to reach out and grab his ankle. Waiting for the teeth to sink into his skin.

He rolls onto his back and looks up through teary eyes at the stars in the clear night sky. He sobs, whimpering, flailing his arms pathetically against his own chest.

Nothing happens. Nothing grabs him. He glances up and looks down the long straight road that is completely devoid of life. The moon is high and bright; casting shadows from the tree's bordering the tarmac. Nothing moved. There's nothing coming after him. The whole of the road is empty.

Paco Maguire, Hollywood's most famous alpha male, laid flat out on a country road in southern England on a hot Friday summer evening. Soaked in tears, sweat, piss and shit he sobbed and wailed. Too terrified and too exhausted to move.

CHAPTER FOUR

DAY TWO

The dawn sun moves gradually across the wide stretch of undergrowth separating the urban sprawl. A steady trickle of water meanders over rocks and pebbles. Birds chirp in the branches. Within a clearing of the bushes a very large German Shepherd dog lies on her side. Her long pink tongue hanging from the side of her open mouth. Her chest rising and falling with each rapid breath. Her tail twitches listlessly. Her feet and legs make small running motions as she whimpers softly.

Her eyes open. Beautiful soft brown eyes with dark pupils and perfect white surrounds. She sits up and pants heavily, shaking her head from the dream. She looks about and sniffs at her own legs, deciding that the crusted blood and filth must go she commences an energetic cleaning session, twisting round and gnawing the dirt away. Her long rough tongue rubbing the dirt from her soft hair.

Finished and she stretches, letting her back legs dip down as she drives her front legs into the ground and elongates her back. Another shake and she is ready for the day, moving down to the stream and taking a long drink. She moves through the undergrowth and finds a spot to defecate and deposit her scent. With voided bowels she turns lazily and sniffs at the steaming pile of faeces. It smells normal. So does her scent.

Hungry. She works her way along the footpath and finds several of the black things left on the ground. She knew the black things. The pack leaders always kept them in the garden and then some people invaders would come and take them away. The black things always smelled good. She used to open them and eat the insides but the pack leaders made it known this was bad. But she was hungry and the pack leaders weren't here. Out of habit she looked round several times already feeling guilty for knowing what she wanted to do. She sniffed through them and found one that contained meat and quickly shredded the thin outer layer to rummage through and wolf the food down.

The strange sensation she had during the night left after a few hours and she barely registered the discomfort as she slept and recovered her muscles from the exertion of the previous day. Now, fed and watered she felt entirely normal, apart from a deep sense of loss from the little one being taken away and the pack leaders changing the way they did.

She left the soft ground and moved back into the hard ground where the people lived. The stench of death hung heavily in the air. Scent trails drifting low over the warm ground, as tangible to her incredible sense of smell as colours to the eyes of humans. She walked slowly, inhaling the odours and working out how many of the things moved through here, how long ago, the direction they went and the gender they were before they changed. The unique scent they left was one of decay, blood and a negative energy that screamed of a dangerous hunger.

She could smell fear too, fear from the people still living in the area and she knew without conscious thought that if she could smell it, they would too. It was a real thing accompanied by its own set of signals. The same as sadness, anger, happiness. She often sensed the fear in people when they met her for the first time. Her huge frame, dark face and intelligent eyes made many people very cautious. But those things didn't smell of fear. They were animalistic in their manner. Moving in pack but not working as a pack. They didn't react as a pack when one was threatened or taken down. They moved in numbers but not together. She maintained motion, trotting at an easy gait as she worked her way through the streets.

The loss of her pack weighed heavy inside her. She felt a need to belong, to find her position and work together. Being alone was hard and it made you weak.

Once more she scented them before she saw or heard them. Turning into the next street she spied a horde shuffling along. Their slow and jerky movements and the low growling noises they made. She tracked them quietly, gradually going lower as she fixed her eyes on the one at the rear. It was big with strong legs and a wide back. She recognised the size of the prey and knew it would be harder to take down. She judged her angle of approach and crept along. The thing jerked left and right, following a set pattern of movement.

Decision made and she ran forward, using the things solid back and the shelf of its arse to power herself up and take a big chunk from the neck as she bounced off. A bright spray of crimson blood spurted out as the bite severed the main artery. The thing kept going for a few steps then slowed, staggered and fell.

The others showed no reaction and kept with their

forward momentum. She tracked the next one and positioned herself once more behind it. Launching high she powered her front paws into the back and took the thing straight down, landing fully on the things back and tearing the neck open quickly. She leapt away and took the next one in the same way. A high jump and using her power and momentum to simply knock it over. The sharp teeth and quick shake of the head ripped the flesh open and they were dead.

It was easy.

As the morning wore on she perfected the technique. Tracking the scent of them on the street. Finding the horde and using her weight to take them down. She killed men, women and children. Simply knowing they were not men, women or children. They were things that would kill the little one if they found him.

The heat wore her out faster than the exertion and she kept having to stop and find water. Making her way into the open dens of other packs and finding the place they deposited their scent, drinking from ponds, streams and outside taps left dripping.

The taste of the things didn't bother her. She did not see them as a food source. They were prey to be killed. So she killed. With each kill she drank the blood as it spurted into her mouth and coated her tongue, some of the flesh was swallowed too.

The infection was ingested time and again. Infected cells raced through her blood stream, surging through her organs and desperately attempting to do what it was designed to do.

It failed as the anti-bodies in her system killed the infection. Despite the sustained ingestion and the constant attack she faced; it failed.

The pure blood of the dog was untainted by the foulness.

CHAPTER FIVE

DAY TWO

Paco woke with a start, yelling out and sitting bolt upright, sending the branches and debris flying off in all directions. He breathed heavily, not knowing where he was and squinting from the bright sunlight pouring through the trees. Slowly, he gained control and looked about. He was in a small clearing of a wooded copse. Nodding with small jerky motions he remembered the previous night and how he crawled from the road sobbing and losing more precious fluid as he cried and cried.

He crawled from the road, through ditches and bushes. Delving deeper into the woods and further away from the road. He knew those things would come for him. They were monsters born from the worst nightmare and they wanted to eat his flesh. Exhausted and petrified he crawled for what seemed like hours. He found a stream and remembered something from one of his movies when he played a fugitive on the run from an evil prison warder, his character had gone through water in an attempt to get rid of his scent and stop the prison dogs from tracking him. Paco wallowed in the shallow water, scrubbing at himself and rubbing the brackish water over every inch of his body. With a raging thirst after so much running, he even drank some of the foul water and instantly regretted it, spitting it out and making himself retch, bringing more bile up.

Soaking wet he crawled on and found a clearing with dead branches and foliage on the ground. He was beat, too exhausted to move another step. Covering himself with the branches and debris from the ground he lay silently, listening in terror at the sounds of the night animals creeping about. A fox calling for her cubs gave him palpitations and he screwed his eyes closed, praying someone would save him.

With body and mind exhausted he fell into a fitful sleep. Imagining that if the evil monsters didn't get him, then wolves or bears would sniff him out and start devouring his legs. He knew of the famous English weather too and expected to be dead from hypothermia or exposure within a few hours too.

But England doesn't have wolves or bears, and the weather was very warm, so warm in fact it dried his clothes out while he slept so he awoke to no more discomfort than feeling very thirsty and with a few cuts and bruises on his body.

His body may have only suffered minor discomfort but his mind was a mess and no sooner had he opened his eyes and remembered where he was than the fear once more gripped him. The images of everything he had seen the night before running through his mind.

The studio would be frantic with worry for him. There must be police and everyone out searching. This would be national news; no... it would be international news.

He stood up and patted his pockets down, then remembered he was still in costume for the movie so didn't have his phone with him. No wallet either. But he wouldn't need a wallet, anybody would recognise him.

The police must have got a grip of whatever happened by now. Some kind of chemical attack probably. Terrorists or something. Yeah, a terrorist attack with chemical agents that made everyone go crazy. Looking around he searched for the route he came in but everything looked the same. He had no tracking skills and couldn't recall the direction he'd came from. His t-shirt was ripped and his tan trousers were filthy but at least he wasn't cold.

He set off expecting his legs to be shaky and weak, but they weren't. The running had tired him out and he felt a little soreness in his thigh muscles but nothing more than that. He stretched his arms back and flexed his upper body as he walked. Getting the blood pumping and the muscles engorged just in case he bumped into any of the search teams out scouring the land for him.

Paco walked all morning. He walked through the woods, then more woods. He crossed fields and streams, meadows, rolling hills and pleasant undulating rural land. But no roads. His sense of direction was hopeless. The sun was hot and he worried about getting sunburnt, not wanting to suffer the redness or ruin his perfect flawless skin.

He was also thirsty, ragingly thirsty. So by the time he found the narrow country road and followed it for a few miles and saw the houses in the distance there was only thing on his mind. Water. Ice cold water and lots of it. It was all he could think off. It consumed his every thought. He imagined himself escaping enemy soldiers and running across the parched Sahara desert, finally seeing the dwellings and bursting in like a hero gasping for water. The home owners would be surprised to see Paco Maguire at their door and sure they'd sell their story for a good buck, but hey who can blame them. But he'd have to make sure they didn't take any pictures until he cleaned himself up, that much was fair.

He kept a close eye on the roofs of the houses in the distance and worked his way down the country lane. The birds were singing and it was a gorgeous day. Now the end was in sight he almost felt good. The feeling of escape, of being safe made him giddy. He would be a true hero now.

Shit, but he'd run away. The studios didn't have CCTV cameras anywhere near the filming lots, they were banned simply for the fact someone would sell the footage of the top movies being made. That meant, if he was the only survivor, that he could give an account of how he tried to fight them off but honestly believed they were sick and he didn't want to hurt them. No, that wouldn't work. They were killing each other and then chasing him. Got it! He'd say he led them away; he shouted and abused them to lure them away from the injured people on the set. They chased him and he kept them going so the others could get help. Yeah, perfect.

The hedgerow was high but he got fleeting views of the village he was approaching. It must be afternoon by now. No cars though, and he'd expected to see helicopters out searching for him. Maybe he'd wandered far away from the search radius by now.

He followed the gentle curve of the road and smiled as he saw the village just ahead. It looked small, just a few dozen houses all clustered together and stretching off down the road.

He reached the first house. An old stone built cottage with a grey slate roof and a pretty garden covered in colourful flowers. He opened the white picket gate and walked up the narrow path to the wooden door, extending his hand to knock. The door was slightly open. He smiled and pushed it carefully.

'Hi! Anyone home?' he called out and listened for a response, getting his best smile ready for when the person came to the door and saw the famous actor on the doorstep.

'Hi, anyone there?' he called again and frowned when there was still no response. He pushed the door open and peered into the small quaint hallway. Stepping in he called and banged on the door. Nothing. Whoever lived here had gone out and left the door unlocked. Still, this was the countryside and hardly the Bronx or South Central.

He walked into the hallway and through a lounge area with floral sofas and china plates on display above the fireplace.

'Say...anyone there?' he called again. He saw another door leading to a kitchen and the thirst took over. Striding through he found the faucet and turned it on. No, wait the English call it a tap. He smirked as he ran his hands under the icy cold water cascading noisily into the stainless steel basin.

A small china cup was upturned on the draining board; he rinsed it out, taking care not to catch someone else's germs despite the dryness of his mouth. He filled the cup and drank it down in three big gulps. The water was perfect. Cold and soaking into his parched mouth. He felt the chill as it ran down his throat and into his stomach. He drank more and kept drinking. Filling the tiny cup again and again, gulping it down. Turning his head he saw a pint glass inside a glass fronted cupboard and pulled it out, filling it up and then turned to lean against the sink as he sank it down in big noisy gulps.

The feeling was poetry. Pure poetry. He lifted the glass higher and higher, letting some of the water spill from his mouth and down his front. His head tilted back as the glass was pushed higher and the contents drained into his greedy mouth. Eyes closed in ecstasy he lowered the glass and gave a big belch.

'Oh hi,' he said startled as he opened his eyes and saw the figure standing in the doorway. Then he took in the details. The blood encrusted mouth and the red bloodshot eyes. The ragged wound in the neck and the head lolling from side to side. There was drool coming from the mouth and mixing with the blood, making little pink trails of spit drip from the chin.

Paco gripped the glass and froze in utter fear as the creature shuffled slowly towards him. An old lady dressed in a white gown now heavily stained with blood and filth. He couldn't back away. He was already pressed into the kitchen sink.

'Stay back,' he yelped in a high pitched voice, 'please... please stay back....'

The woman shuffled slowly towards him, her movements uncoordinated and jerky. Walking stiff legged and groaning like a sick dog.

Paco spun round, searching for a way out. The window. He leant over the sink and pulled the lever up and pushed the window open. He looked back and cried out as the woman kept coming towards him. Clambering on the sink he dropped the glass which smashed on the floor and then sent the draining rack and crockery flying as his large bulk forced itself towards the window. In his panic he tried to go head first but his wide shoulders jammed in the frame.

Crying in fear he turned and twisted sideways, squeezing through as the woman inched closer. He got his legs out and watched in horror as the woman's bare feet stepped onto the shards of glass. He heard the crunch and watched as blood started pouring from her feet. She didn't even flinch but kept coming. He cried out again and dropped out of the window, landing in the flower beds of the back garden and backing away from the building expecting her to be clambering out the window after him.

Paco ran onto the lawn and then round in circles as he realised the garden was fully enclosed with a solid high fence on all sides.

He was trapped and panicking. He ran back across the lawn and saw the patio doors leading into the dining room. He raced over and pulled them open. Knowing he had no choice he sobbed as he ran through the dining room and collided with the zombie woman now shuffling into the dining room. His solid frame sent the little old lady sprawling but he still screamed in utter terror as he hurdled the flailing body, running through the hallway and back out through the front door.

'HELP!' He bellowed as he ran through the gate and into the quiet street, 'SOMEONE HELP...' He saw figures in the distance and started towards them, then stopped as he saw the same jerky manner of their walking. The blood stains were clear as day on their pale skin and nightclothes. Old people. Lots of wrinkly old people all covered in blood and shuffling in his direction.

The fact that they were slow now didn't register with Paco. The mind numbing hysteria that gripped him held him rooted fast to the spot. A groan behind him and he twisted round to see the woman from the cottage now exiting the gate. She was in the road just metres from him. He backed away from her with a look of horror crawling across his face. Tears once more streaking down his cheeks.

He took several faltering steps before turning and seeing the group of monsters coming from the other direction. They were quite a distance away and shuffling along very slowly but that didn't matter. What mattered was that he was trapped. The old woman was one side and the other old people were the other side.

He couldn't escape. They would get him. They would lunge and leap, howling like demons and tear him apart.

He sobbed and wailed, stamped his feet and spun one way then the other. Then he saw the garden path of the next house and the front door standing open. Without further thought he ran through the garden and into the house. Slamming the door closed behind him. He ran through the rooms blubbering and knocking into furniture, expecting to see the demon monsters coming at him. He stumbled through to the back door and out into the garden. The same high fence but this time he jumped up to look over. It looked clear. He clambered the fence and ran from garden to garden, scaling high fences and brick built garden walls. Running an entire assault course with the speed of a Special Forces soldier. He didn't think to get tired. He was too scared.

He ran, vaulted and climbed. He ran past garden sheds full of good heavy weapons. Some of the houses had shotgun cabinets within them. Every house he passed held weapons and supplies. He ignored the lot and kept going. One thought pressing into his panic filled mind. Run away. Run away from the monsters.

Minutes later and breathing hard he scaled the last high fence and dropped deftly down onto the verge of another country road. He scurried about and found the junction of the road he had been on minutes before. The horde were still there, still shuffling slowly towards the point they last saw him.

A lucky escape. The monsters almost had him. He turned and ran. Heading back into the safety of the countryside.

CHAPTER SIX

DAY TWO

The dog followed the trail through the quiet residential streets. The stillness of the hot air served to enable her ears to hear better. The lack of breeze meant the scent trails stayed in situ for a long time.

There were many trails here, all of them heading the same way. She tracked and moved across the road, sweeping left and right and picking out the many different tracks. She knew the horde was big so when it came into view it posed no surprise to her.

Outside a den the things were gathered and waiting. There were people within the den.

She moved to the far side of the hard ground and stared from the shadows of a large tree. Movement from the den. High up. Faces peering out. A woman holding a little one. The things wanted the little one. She sensed their hunger.

A low growl sounded in her throat as she watched the

window. The dog could see the fear on the woman's face. She watched closely as another little one appeared next to the woman and looked down at the things. One pack leader with little ones. She couldn't go outside and fight the things or the little ones would be left undefended. The den entry was blocked. The things were many in number.

She trotted out into the sun and watched the woman show a reaction. The woman pointed at the dog and the little one waved.

Instinct kicked in and the dog made noise. She made loud noise and waited for the things to turn and look at her. They were slow so she made more noise. She wanted them to come for her and away from the den. They didn't move away from the den so she killed them. All of them.

She started with the closest and jumped up high to tear the throat out. Then she leapt from body to body and with each one she got quicker as the method became better practised. Bodies dropped with jugulars ripped out, blood pumping onto the ground in thick pools. She worked steadily and felt the heat bearing down on her. It took time but the work was done. They were killed and the entrance to the den was made clear.

She moved out from the street and across the hard ground into the shade of the tree. The smell of blood overwhelmed everything else. It coated her paws and the front of her coat. Her tongue was dry and swollen and her chest heaved as she fought for air to cool down. The woman looked down into the street. Still holding the little one but with one hand covering her mouth. The little one stood next to her was waving again.

The woman opened the window and made noise. The dog knew the tone was friendly so she went closer and looked up. The woman made more noise. So did the little one. She wagged her tail and sat down. She looked up and continued wagging her tail. The woman made more noise and went away. The dog moved back to the shade and rested. The woman came back and made something fall slowly from the window. It was big and the woman waved her hands over it. She went over to the den and watched as the thing came down through the air. It landed on the ground and she saw it had water inside. She drank the water. She drank deeply and felt the coolness of the clear liquid as it quenched the thirst and cooled her.

The dog moved to the den entry point where there was shade and rested out of the sunlight, lying down with her head resting on her paws.

She stayed there for the rest of the day, only moving out when the undead staggered into the street and then returning to drink the water and rest in the shade. She cleaned herself between kills, licking the blood and gore from her hair.

The single mother inside the house had watched with trepidation as the dog had first appeared and started attacking the things gathered outside. She thought the dog must be one of them. Infected with whatever disease that made everyone go mad. When the dog savaged them all she held her hand to her mouth and tried to cover her son's eyes while still holding the baby. As the dog leapt from body to body she realised it wasn't eating the things. It was simply killing them. As the last one fell the dog checked around before moving over to the shade of the front door. It wagged its tail and barked up at them. Despite being one floor up she could clearly see the dogs eyes were clear and normal and nothing like the eyes of the things that had been outside all morning. She found an old plastic bucket and filled it with water before lowering it down, watching with interest as the dog rushed over and noisily lapped the water down with a long pink and normal looking tongue.

All day she watched from the window as the dog moved out and took the undead down before quickly trotting back to the door and drinking from the bucket. She wanted so much to let the dog in but it was a huge dog, very powerfully built with massive paws and huge white teeth. They wouldn't stand a chance if the dog turned inside the house and she couldn't take that risk, so the door stayed closed.

The bodies were everywhere and the scene grew more gruesome as the day wore on with a seemingly endless supply of the undead shuffling down the road.

She had watched during the night as the street outside her house first became a warzone and then turned into something from a horror film. She bolted the door and pulled all the curtains closed in the downstairs rooms then taking her children she barricaded herself into her bedroom armed with a large kitchen knife and constantly dialling the emergency services.

By early evening the mother thoughts turned to escape. Low food stocks in the house and she knew that with two mouths to feed plus the baby they would soon run out. They needed to get out and find somewhere else. Find other survivors, or somewhere that had food. Her car was parked in the narrow lane at the back of the house. If she could quietly get to the car she could slip away and head away from the town. As the hordes gathered during the morning her hopes of getting away grew slimmer, simply through fear of opening any doors with such a large mob outside. But now, with the dog taking them down they could get away.

As the afternoon wore on she busied herself round the house, gathering essential items into rucksacks and bags. Clothes, sleeping bags, bottles of water and the measly items of food she had in the cupboards. Cleaning items, soap, toothbrushes all went into bags. Then she collected photographs and family treasures, jewellery and within a few hours she realised she'd packed enough bags for a long holiday. She had to do it one journey. Get from the house to the car with one baby and one small child plus the bags. She couldn't risk going back and forth. She could carry the baby and her son could walk, he could carry a small bag but that meant she only had one hand free. A rucksack and two other bags. That's all she could take from the house.

The bags were emptied and the three chosen ones were set aside. She wanted to take so much, not knowing when, or if, she would ever be able to come back to the house. The mother was so busy with the bags and taking care of the children she failed to realise the evening sky was darkening. The shadows lengthened and became deeper.

Walking into her dark bedroom she instinctively reached out to turn the light on. The room filled with an orange glow as she passed the still open window, brushing her hair back from her face while frantically thinking of how to fill three bags with everything they needed.

A sudden spine tingling howling noise snapped her back to reality. The air was filled with guttural whines of undead lifting their faces to the inky black sky and joining in verse. Realising the folly of her actions she scurried back and thumped the light switch, missing the first time and striking it again. The room plunged into darkness with just the glow from the street lights casting their sickly hue into the house.

The mother rushed to the window and looked out, the street was even more littered with bodies now. The dog had stayed there this whole time, killing every undead that shuffled into view. Now the ground was covered in corpses, blood, filth and twisted remains. She leant down and saw the dog standing up, it looked tense and was staring with its head cocked to one side, ears flicking and twitching, the hairs on its immensely broad back were standing up.

There wasn't a living thing in sight but the howls were coming from all directions. She'd left it too late. There was no way she could go now in the dark. She left the window and ran back into the house, gathering her children and hastily snatching snack food and bottles of water. She got back in the bedroom and closed the door, once more pushing the wardrobe and chests of drawers to block the entrance.

With her heart hammering in her chest she slumped down against the wall and held her baby tight. Her son cuddled up to her whimpering softly, she stroked his head and made low soothing sounds.

Then the baby woke up, opening his eyes and realising he was wet and hungry. He needed changing and a feed. The baby did what all babies do and let rip with an ear piercing scream. The mother's heart dropped into her stomach at the noise as she searched round feeling for the pacifier and trying to shove it into the baby's mouth. The baby was having none of it. He wanted food and the wet nappy taking off.

The mother quickly unbuttoned her shirt and pulled her bra down, exposing her breast and guiding the baby onto the nipple. It clamped on hungrily and thankfully went quiet. But the damage was done. As the howls had finished from outside, the baby had continued and all around the area undead ears pricked and turned at the sound of a succulent child screaming into the air.

The dog listened intently as the howls of the things split the air apart. Getting to her feet she sensed the change, the atmosphere became charged. Their energy was back, they would be fast again. Her acute hearing picked the individual voices out, pinpointing the closest ones and the direction they would be coming from.

Another sound joined the fray. The sound of a little one crying out inside the den. Not her little one, but another little one. Her own little one had once made noises like that when he was hungry or wet. The howling of the things ended but the noises from the little one continued.

She moved down the path and onto the street. They would hear the little one. They would be coming.

The dog glanced back up at the den and through the open window she could hear the little one eating. The sounds of contented gurgling and swallowing.

Sadness plucked at her heart. Her own little one gone now, gone far away with a new pack. Her pack leaders dead.

They came from the left first. A running horde coming straight towards the house. She heard them before she saw them. Sounds from further away to the right. They would come from both sides but the left would be first.

Her head lowered and she showed teeth. A deep bass growl sounding in her throat, it grew in pitch and volume as she pulled the lips back further. The wolf in her was ready. Her heart rate increased, flooding her muscles with adrenalin. Her eyes fixed, ears pricked.

The domestic pet snarled and made noise. She filled her lungs and made loud noise. This is my ground. Look at the ones I have killed already. Look around and see my destruction. See what waits for you.

As the horde came staggering into view she moved off with long fluid strides, a streak of darkness thundering through the street. Her eyes fixed on the thing in front. It was a male. Big and strong. It showed teeth. It growled as it charged at her. They all growled.

She growled back and leapt high into the air.

CHAPTER SEVEN

D AY TWO

Still snivelling, Paco kept a fast pace thundering through the English countryside, constantly glancing over his shoulder convinced that hordes of the monsters were chasing him or were lying in wait somewhere ahead.

Like many people from big countries, Paco had a preconceived idea that England was a small country and that translated that everything in it must be small. Small roads, small houses, small towns, small cars. So that meant the countryside must be small too. But now, after plodding aimlessly about for hours on end he realised just how large the rural areas really were.

By afternoon he found a road but having no idea what direction he was travelling, or if it was the same road he decided not to travel on it, but rather skulk alongside it keeping to the fields and bushes. Several times he had to come of the undergrowth when prevented from making headway by natural barriers such as thorny thicket hedges. When he did emerge he did so tentatively, almost tiptoeing on the tarmac to avoid making noise with his footsteps.

He grew thirsty again as the hot sun burned down onto his exposed head and arms. Hunger pangs kicked in, this being the first time in years that he hadn't been given exactly the right amount of food at exactly the right time.

Sticking with the road he wound further into the deep countryside, the thickets of trees grew thicker, the grass longer, the fields bigger. This was farming country proper with not a village or town in sight. He crested hills and dropped down into shallow valleys.

By early evening he was getting desperate, knowing that the night was only hours away. Staying on the road, Paco kept his eyes up and scanning. A pheasant bursting from the bushes in a flurry of wings and twigs sent him diving into a ditch with a loud yelp, only to emerge shaking and cursing himself for crying out and drawing attention to himself.

He almost missed the opening to the dirt road, having established a walking method of turning his head left then right, up then back over his shoulder. He was so focussed on listening and watching for the monsters he came to a startled stop on seeing the lane and the faded old sign post for *Willow Trees*.

'What the goddamn is Willow Trees?' He muttered quietly. Is it a place? A house? A village? Why can't the English put proper signs up and post boxes like normal countries?

It had to be something. A signpost always pointed at something. And right now, something was better than nothing so entered the shaded dirt road and gingerly made his way along.

The lane twisted and turned in true English style, with oppressive high hedgerows on both sides he felt hemmed in.

The heat was unbearable. His mouth was parched and his stomach made noises, demanding to be fed.

As with the village, Paco spied the roof for some time before actually gaining a view of the building. Winding his way through the lane he gradually came into sight of another stone built cottage standing alone in a clearing, outhouses and old sheds bordered a stony garden area.

He crept forward, slowly placing one foot in front of the other and viewed the house. It was more functional looking than the stone built houses in the village. They were pretty and decorative with nice flower beds and white net curtains in the windows. This was plain looking with weeds growing from the cracks where the bricks met the ground. The path to the front door looked clear and even in his panicked state he realised this meant someone lived here. Staying low he shuffled forward and frantically scanned the area, straining his ears for any noise. Nervously glancing at the sky and trying to guess the time and how long he had until the sun went down.

Making a decision to keep edging forward he moved out from the end of the lane into the open area, heading slowly towards the house. Halfway across he froze in terror and stifled a scream at the sight of a body lying half out of one of the outhouses, a pitchfork standing upright with the prongs buried deep in the corpses head.

Paco went to run back, then panicked and decided to run to the house. But whoever killed that man might be in the house so he turned and started back to the lane again. But that dead man would probably be one of the monsters, which meant someone brave was here, someone who could kill them with a pitchfork, someone who could protect him. He about turned and ran back towards the house. But what if they were a psycho? It could be like that film about the author man who got his legs chopped off by the crazy fan woman in the deep country. Gibbering with fear he once more about turned and started back towards the lane. But that would mean another night out in the open with those monsters roaming the land seeking him out to eat his brains. That was more than he could take so he once more stopped and headed back to the house, coming to a full stop at the sight of the woman stood in the doorway holding a shotgun.

'What the hell are you doing?' She called out, 'running back and forth like a madman!' Paco stayed still taking in the full bodied figure of the young woman. Blond hair pulled back into a loose ponytail and wearing tight jeans, an open checked shirt and a white vest top underneath which showed off her ample cleavage. She was beautiful but was also holding a shotgun, which was pointed right at him.

'Hi,' his voice quavered in fear so he coughed and took a breath, the consummate actor preparing to cover his nerves, 'sorry I had dust in my throat,' he smiled and stood up straight, 'I er….wasn't sure if anyone was here, then I saw the body and well….' He smiled sheepishly.

'You're that actor aren't you? She said suspiciously.

'Yes Ma'am, I am that man,' he bowed his head and held his hands away from his body.

'Well what the bloody hell are you doing here?' She asked.

'We were filming in the studios near here,' he took a step forward and stopped as the barrel of the shotgun lifted a few inches, 'whoa! Take it easy lady…the film set went crazy like everyone attacking each other…'

'How did you get away then?' She asked bluntly.

'Well I…I tried to lead them away, there were some injured people and survivors so I kind of made a hell of a lot of noise and made those…those things come after me…I left the studios and then kind of got lost in the countryside…'

'I see,' she replied, clearly thinking of what to do now.

'Ma'am may I ask, is this...this thing...is it just here or what?'

'Everywhere,' she replied instantly.

'What do you mean everywhere,' he took another step forward as his stomach dropped into his shoes, she didn't lift the shotgun again seeing the look of fear on his face and guessing he had no idea what was going on if he'd been lost since it began.

'It's everywhere,' her tone was softer now, 'the whole world probably.'

Paco reeled in shock, his hands going to his face. His legs felt rubbery and weak, 'how...how do you know that?' He asked quietly.

'It was on the news. It's everywhere. Then the telly stopped working. The phones are down, no television, no radio, nothing. Internet is gone too...the power is still on.'

'Jeesh,' Paco shook his head taking it in. Convinced that this was a localised event and truly believing he would be safely on a plane home within a couple of days. 'What about the States?'

'I don't know,' she said softly, 'it started in Europe and seemed to sweep across within a few hours. Then he turned up so I figured it was here too.'

'He?' Paco asked confused.

'Him,' she nodded at the outhouse and the body with the pitchfork through its head.

'Oh...him...was he one of the monst....er...things?'

'Yes, he came this morning and caught me off guard but he was moving slowly, not like the ones on the telly last night.'

'Yeah,' Paco nodded, 'they were fast last night but I saw some today who were all slow.'

'I thought you said you'd been lost in the woods all day?' She eyed him again.

'I am…I mean I was…I found a village some miles away but it was crawling with the…well the things I guess.'

'Village? Was it a long road with houses on both sides? Stone cottages…lots of flowers in the front garden?'

'Yeah that was it,' Paco nodded.

'Crawling was it?' She asked, 'I know that place, the youngest person living there must be seventy…'

'Hey lady, trust me it was packed with those things, like wall to wall…' Paco lied.

'Shit,' she spat, 'I was going to head for there.'

'Really? I wouldn't do that now if I were you, it's…well it's gone.'

'Figures,' she tutted and lowered the shotgun, 'well you look like you could do with a drink, come inside.' She turned and disappeared through the open door. Paco swallowed his nerves and started after her, entering the darkened hallway of the cottage and watching the back of the woman walk down the hall and into the kitchen at the back. He followed her into the kitchen and looked in amazement at the pots and pans all filled with water and covered with film. Every available receptacle had been used and were scattered over the worktops and large table in the middle of the floor.

'Is the water off?' He asked.

'Not yet but I thought I'd better get prepared in case it does,' she replied, 'help yourself,' she nodded to the sink and handed him a big ceramic mug. He nodded and reached the tap within a second, turning the flow on and filling the mug. He downed the contents and kept going, filling and drinking.

'Thirsty then?' She asked. He nodded back with the cup pressed to his

'Can I wash up?' He asked the woman who was stood the other side of the table watching him closely.

'Wash up? There's nothing to wash up.' She replied with a frown.

'What?' He asked.

'Why would you want to wash up? You've just got here?'

'Sorry I've been running all night and day, I feel filthy and the sweat has dried on my skin...' he explained feeling confused.

'Oh! You mean you want to wash? Like wash your face?'

'Yeah, wash up,' he shrugged.

'We call that washing here, washing up is when you clean the dishes after eating food,' she shook her head.

'Oh, my mistake,' he smiled his coy smile and looked down at the floor, giving it his best slightly embarrassed look.

'There's a bathroom upstairs if that's any better for you,' she smiled brief and quick, just a show of teeth and with no humour from the eyes but the gesture was there.

'Thanks, say what's your name?' Paco asked as he started towards the door.

'Lucy and yours?' She asked in return making him frown.

'Er...Paco, its Paco Maguire,' he replied.

'Course it is! Sorry I couldn't remember. Not really into the whole action movie thing. No offence,' she said plainly.

'No none taken,' he smiled and moved down the hallway. How can anyone not know my name? I'm the most famous man in Hollywood at the moment. Even if she didn't watch my movies she would have seen me in magazines and newspapers. He climbed the bare wooden staircase taking note of the ramshackle appearance of the house. The walls chipped with long faded paint, the bannister worn smooth with several sections missing. Reaching the top he walked slowly down the hall, peering into the bare rooms. Only one of them has furniture consisting of a large brass double bed and a chest of drawers. Suitcases and bags stacked along the wall, the tops open with the contents on display. Some clothes on the bed.

In the bathroom he stood in front of the stained sink and

turned the tap on. The water gushed out filling the room with noise. A single toothbrush in an old glass, a tube of toothpaste on the side. Stripping his torn, filthy and far too tight top off he body washed in the cold water, using a flannel and a bottle of shower crème found on side of the old bathtub. He soaked the sweat and dirt away from his skin, rubbing at his armpits and all over his upper body.

He toed the door closed and stripped his boots and trousers off. The water from the stream washed most of the shit away but they still smelled bad. He took the clothes to the bathtub and used the bigger taps to scrub the trousers and top, concentrating on the rear section and the brown stains left there.

Paco stripped his boxers off, repulsing from stench coming from them. Urine and shit mixed with days old sweat. He scrubbed his groin and arse, rubbing the flannel down his legs and washing between his toes.

Finished, he wrings the clothes out, his muscles bulging with exertion as he twists the material round and applies pressure before shaking them out to get rid of the creases.

He tried putting the clothes back on, but despite the heat of the day, the cold wetness of the clothes clinging feeling turned his stomach. Glancing round he saw a flimsy white cotton gown on the back of the door and squeezed his frame into it. The gown barely covering his modesty and the sleeves ending just below his elbows.

Taking his bundle of wet clothes he walked back down the stairs hoping the woman won't be offended at him washing his clothes and using her gown. Maybe he should have asked first?

'Say Lucy, I hope you don't mind but I rinsed my clothes out,' he called ahead.

'That's okay, you looked a state...' she stopped dead at

seeing his hulking frame squeezed into her gown, a mixed look of confusion and humour etching onto her face.

'Er...it's all I could find,' he lifted his eyebrows apologetically.

'No, that's fine,' she replied with a widening smile, 'I don't think I'll have anything that fits you.'

'These should dry quickly, can I put them somewhere?'

'Yeah, here let me,' she stepped forward taking the clothes from him and glancing at his heavily muscled chest. He noticed the look and smiled shyly, making a point of holding his head down so he could look up at her, knowing this particular look made him look sweet and vulnerable.

'Did you find everything you needed? I've got a spare toothbrush if you want it? It's new, still packed and everything.' She turned away cursing herself for getting caught looking at his chest like that. Being a buxom woman she knew what it felt like when men stared directly at her boobs and not her face and she'd effectively just done the same thing. Shit, she might as well have stared at his groin.

'Say that'll be great Lucy,' he replied sincerely, 'I used the flannel and shower crème, I rinsed it out though,' he added quickly.

'I've made you a coffee, thought we'd better make use while the power's still on.'

'Great! Er...you think the power will go soon?'

'No doubt about it Paco, if the phones are down, the telly stations and radio stations are off so we've got whatever is left in the pipe I should think.'

'The pipe?' He asked puzzled.

'Figure of speech, whatever juice is left flowing from the power stations...that's all we've got. They'll have shut down fail-safes with no personnel in them; I should think it'll be today or tomorrow at the latest.'

'Goddamn,' he sighed, 'what then?' He asked following

her through the kitchen and out the back door to watch as she pinned his clothes on a washing line.

'Then?' She replied without looking, 'we'll be without power,' she shrugged.

'What….well what'll we do?' He asked feeling the panic rising again and desperately trying to swallow it down.

'Do?' She said, repeating his last word back to him again, 'cope I guess. There's a wood stove here and enough food for a couple of days. The water supply doesn't rely on power so that will last a lot longer. The only problem I can foresee with that is if it gets infected.'

'Infected?' He stared at her back in horror.

'Yeah, if those things get into the water supply then it will get infected. It's mostly a closed system but there will be points that people can fall in or get into it.'

'Jesus,' he muttered, 'no power, no water…'

'Nope. Back in the dark ages but worse.'

'Worse? How can it be worse?'

'Zombies Paco, lots of zombies everywhere. Lots of scared people too, lots of guns and weapons and millions of people not having a clue how to survive without a microwave or oven.'

'Zombies? Seriously…you think those things are zombies?'

'What else would you call them?'

'Hell I don't know, terrorists or…diseased, or crazed savages but not zombies.'

'You say you saw them attacking other people? On your movie set right?'

'Well yeah but…'

'How were they attacking them Paco?'

'Well yeah but…' he repeated.

'They were biting the other people weren't they? They were biting them and then trying to find more people to bite.

And the ones that got bit, did they stay dead? No, I bet they didn't.'

'Lucy come on! Zombies? This is the twentieth century...'

'It's the twenty first century,' she said with a glance, 'call them what you want but I call a spade a spade.'

'Hey that's racist,' Paco replied quickly. Lucy stopped mid-stretch as she was about to pin his last trouser leg in place, shaking her head and not quite believing what she just heard.'

'No. The word spade used in an abusive term is racist; otherwise the word spade refers to the implement used to dig. The racist term dates from the 1920's, the original phrase of the saying dates from something like the fifteenth century.'

'Oh...'

'But anyway, whether you want to call them zombies or not is up to you, but either way I'd suggest they want to eat your flesh and make you one of them.'

'That's gross,' he shuddered, looking ridiculous stood there in the flimsy gown and having to hold it closed or risk showing his bits off.

'Reality,' she said brusquely.

'How do you know these things?' He asked meekly.

'How does anyone know things, they listen and take things in. I read books, watch documentaries...I don't know... I just kind of know.'

'Sure,' he realised how weak he was coming across and made of point of standing straight and affecting a serious, slightly hard look, which wasn't easily passed off in the feminine gown.

'Let's get that coffee before it gets cold. I didn't sugar it, I guessed with a body like that you wouldn't pollute it with sugar. Wasn't sure about milk either but we've only got powdered milk anyway.'

'Black is fine,' he said quickly following her back into the kitchen and feeling a bit better at the *body like that* compliment.

Inside the kitchen she handed the coffee over and sat down in a wooden hard backed chair at the table. Going to sit down too he realised that everything would be on show and quickly stood back up to back away and lean casually against the side.

'So you're here alone then?' He asked carefully, not trying to sound threatening in anyway but wanting to know her circumstances.

'Yes,' she nodded, 'I bought this place a few months ago. I worked in the city but had enough so I bought this to do up and live peacefully. Only moved in a few weeks ago, hadn't even started doing anything yet. So much for that great plan.'

'What did you do? In the city I mean?'

'Finance, it was a shitty job in a shitty world full of shitty people that were greedy, I hated the city, hated just about everything. Figured the change would be good.'

'I think it might have just saved your life, I mean if this is everywhere then the cities will be far worse than here.'

'True, that's what I've been saying to myself since yesterday anyway.'

'Family?' He asked and instantly regretted it seeing the dark look cross her face.

'Of course,' she replied flatly, 'and you?'

'In the States. Parents, brother...cousins...' his voice trailed off as he sought to absorb everything that was happening.

'It might get better,' she said kindly on seeing the emotions in him, 'you never know.'

'Guess so,' he said quietly, 'not likely though huh?'

'Not really,' she shrugged, taking a sip of the coffee and sighing.

'Is it okay me being here? I mean I was worried about the

night coming and being outdoors with those things everywhere.'

'Well you're here aren't you?'

'I just didn't want you to feel threatened by me.'

'Threatened? Of what? Are you going to rape me Paco? The shotgun is over there and it doesn't have any bullets anyway. I only grabbed it for show.'

'Rape you? God no Lucy, I wouldn't ever do something like that,' he spluttered.

'Slow down big guy, I wasn't saying you were going to rape me. Only that there isn't much I could do about it if you wanted to. Look at the size of you.'

'What?' He said struggling to keep up with the logic and how they got onto this subject, 'no Lucy I wouldn't do that.'

'Yeah you just said that,' she replied staring at him, 'well if you do feel like raping me then just ask, I'll probably give it to you willingly if it saves you beating me. Unless you're into beating women as well as raping them.'

'Hey can we stop this, I don't rape anyone. I'm not doing anything. Hang on...did you just say you wanted to have sex with me?' He asked.

'I said no such thing,' she protested.

'You said you'd give it willingly,' he said with a frown and rubbed his head with his palm. The stress was too much. He was alone in a country he didn't really understand, with no way of getting home and was now in a cottage in the middle of nowhere with a beautiful but strange woman talking about rape and beating.

'I said...' She explained, 'that if you want to rape me then just ask, I'll let you do it so you don't beat me.'

'Let me? Beat you? Lucy I...I don't want to rape or beat anyone, can we change the subject please.'

'Alright tetchy,' she sighed and shook her head, tutting noisily, 'honestly some people,' she muttered.

'Great coffee,' he said to change the subject, feeling very creeped out.

'Glad you like it,' she smiled suddenly, 'you making the next one? We might as well before the power goes.'

'Er...yeah sure, I can do that,' he replied, 'er...how?'

'The kettle is filled just switch it on and fill the cups. The coffee is in that jar.' He took her coffee mug from her outstretched hand and turned to figure his way through making instant coffee with a kettle for the first time in years.

Lucy watched his form as he worked, admiring his deeply bronzed and toned calf muscles and the shape of his narrow waist spreading up and out to his wide shoulders.

Should be an interesting night she mused to herself.

CHAPTER EIGHT

DAY TWO

She destroyed the first one quickly. Tearing its throat out and leaving the body still teetering on the spot as she landed amongst them. She bit into legs, shredding hamstrings and Achilles tendons and making the things fall to the ground. She jumped high and used her weight to drag the bodies to the ground and rip them apart.

She had to move fast. They were still heading towards the den. She worked with devastating speed and accuracy. Shredding their flesh and bringing them down. She knew she could disable them and make them go slower and then have time after to finish them off.

Snarls and deep growls filled the air, along with thumps after thump of bodies slamming into the ground and the dog jumping deftly away to find another victim.

The pack from the left were dealt with and she span round, cocking her head and listening to the drumming footsteps of the horde coming from the other direction. With a final savage bite at a crawling thing she moved off. Once more going low and becoming a streak of flattened ears and dark fur.

She caught them yards from the entrance to the den, more here than the last lot. They were frenzied and again she sensed the energy in them, the hunger, the desire to feed. She fought her way through their legs, lashing her big head left and right and biting deep into the backs of legs, shaking with each bite and tugging the bodies down.

The things were stumbling and tripping over their fallen kind. It slowed them down but it made her faster as she used the downed bodies as stepping stones to gain height to leap from. It worked well and added another tactic to her rapidly evolving method of killing.

Pure instinct drove her on. Kill after kill and as fast as they poured into the street they died. They didn't turn or try and attack her but instead sensed the feeding frenzy of the horde that there was food here. That incessant urge to feed, to bite and tear human flesh pushed them on.

The mother sat holding her sleeping baby with her free arm pushing the small boy's head into her stomach to block the sounds of death coming through the still open window. Tears streaked her face as she prayed over and over again that the dog would stay alive and defend them. She heard the growls, the snarls and the barks. She heard the thumps as the bodies hit the ground and she heard the wet tearing sound followed by the gurgling as blood poured into the open windpipes of the downed things.

The dog was alive. With a beating heart that pumped blood to her muscles and made her lungs suck air in. The night was hot but the sun was down and she took what opportunity she could to take water from the bucket. Her eyes fixed on the path, daring the things to enter her ground.

For every one that entered the street she made noise and urged them to see what she had done, see her destruction and come at their peril. She would not give up. She would not sleep or rest while these things came for the little ones in this den. For if they took these little ones they would find her little one, and for that she would kill them all or die trying.

All across the land, the country, the continent and the world brave men and women stood their ground and defended what was theirs. They defended their lives, their families; they took revenge for the ones they had lost. They chose not to run or flee but to stand the line and stare down the horror that came for them. The cost of freedom, to live how they chose, to die how they chose. With weapons and fighting with their bare hands, teeth snarling, eyes alive, anger coursing their systems they stood their ground and defended their packs.

She fought with pride and courage. A beast of strength and speed and with a mouth full of vicious teeth.

She stood her ground, and she didn't fail.

CHAPTER NINE

D AY ELEVEN

'Blowers and Cookey, you get the Saxon back down here and kitted up, show Tom and Lani round it so they're familiar. Dave will give you a hand to get the GPMG rigged up again,' in the main room of our quarters early morning and the sunlight is pouring through the open door. The few hours of solid sleep have refreshed all of us.

Lani had woken up before me and was out of the room by the time I stirred and roused my sleepy head, staggering out to find her brewing a load of coffee's up and she greeted me with a big smile.

Our privacy was short lived as we were joined by Blowers and Cookey. Cookey moaning noisily at the smell of Blowers' farts. Their noise soon woke the others and they drifted into the room scratching arses and yawning. Apart from Dave who looked as alert as ever, that man doesn't change.

With muted tones we drank the coffee and Nick soon

excused himself to head outside for a smoke and was quickly joined by the other lads. The sight of the sunlight drew us all outside and we stood about sipping from our mugs and looking at the inside of the fort.

Big Chris has worked fast. The interior had been damaged from the big battle, fires breaking out from the flaming bodies and debris sent over the walls from the housing estate going up. Many of the tents had been damaged but he's had them pulled down and new ones erected.

There are far less people here now, the losses we suffered from the fight has reduced the numbers drastically. But that gives more space and I can see he's kept to the method of keeping clusters of tents together around one structure used for cooking. The guest centre still stands in the middle and I wonder if there have been any changes made to that.

People move about quietly between the tents, children cry out, small groups stand talking. Soft plumes of smoke rising up from the cigarettes smoked. Moving away from the side of the fort I look up to the front walls and the Saxon still left in the same position we left it in. The memory of Tucker bringing the trays of food fills my mind, the last meal we all ate together, sat up there waiting for it to start.

Guards patrol now, armed with shotguns, rifles and several of the archers patrol with their bows held ready in their hands.

Re-fuelled with coffee we get ready for the coming day. All of us were worried about what the future held, if we would stay together, and for us – coming back to the fort was like the end for us. But in reality we had a short sharp shock as Doc Roberts made it clear we were needed to get urgent supplies. This isn't the end. Jesus, there will be something to do every day from now. This will never end.

'Howie, we're having a meeting in the police rooms in ten minutes,' Chris says walking towards us.

'And good morning to you too Chris,' Clarence mutters.

'Ah what's up? Has the big man not had his eggs and soldiers this morning?' Chris laughs.

'Have we got eggs?' Nick asks quickly, 'I'm starving.'

'You're always starving,' I reply, 'what's the meeting about? I thought we were heading straight out for supplies.'

'That's what the meetings about; hey this is the modern world. Nothing gets done without a meeting, bring a bean bag so we can sit round in a circle and hold hands,' he laughs striding off.

'We don't all have to go, do we?' Cookey asks, 'we'll get the Saxon and our stuff ready.'

'Yeah, makes sense. Dave and Clarence, you come with me, the rest crack on.'

'Thank god for that,' Cookey replies with a smile of victory.

'Or maybe you should go and the rest of us will get the Saxon ready,' I say with a smile.

'Oh no Mr Howie, they need the bosses not the grunts,' Cookey jokes.

'Grunts!' I laugh at the expression.

Leaving the lads and Lani to sort everything out, the three of us stroll down the camp towards the police offices.

'It's funny how we have to have names for things, like the rooms where the police officers worked from, they're now the police offices, like we still have a police force...or offices for that matter,' I give voice to my thoughts as we walk slowly along. People are waking up now, stepping out of their tents and watching us as we walk through.

'Human nature,' Clarence replies.

'Dave you alright mate? You're very quiet this morning.'

'I'm fine Mr Howie,' he replies staring back into the middle of the fort and the now large crowds of people watching us walk through.

'What are they all staring at?' I whisper through the side of my mouth.

'Us. You,' Dave says bluntly.

I make a point of nodding at a few of the people as we pass, they nod back and we get a few waves too. Reaching the office we find it already packed out and squeeze into the back of the room. Well Clarence squeezes and we just follow in his wake.

'Howie!' Ted's voice booms out and the crowded room melts back to show Ted striding forward with his hand held out.

'Ted!' I greet the man and grasp his hand; he pulls me in for a hug and pats my back in a manly fashion.

Looking round I see Sergeant Hopewell, Terri and Jayne are here too and I smile at them, genuinely pleased to see them. Then I remember Steven and a sudden feeling of guilt passes through me. Here I am walking in like a prick and smiling after they've lost one of their team. The look must have translated on my face because they move forward and surround us.

'I'm so sorry about Steven…' I start explaining, looking round at their faces.

'We heard,' Sergeant Hopewell cuts in, 'but he made a choice Howie. It was his choice to go with you.'

'I know but…'

'No buts, Steven was a wonderful man and he will be remembered. We will honour him and everyone else we've lost but now is not the time to dwell. We can't ever expect to get through something like this and not suffer loss,' she steps back and looks round at the room at large, 'we've all lost, and we'll lose more but now we have work to do, lots of work to do.'

Her tone sets the mood and makes it known this is about business. The lines on her face look deeper, bags under her eyes too. She still wears her police sergeant uniform; it even looks clean and pressed. Her shoes are shiny too. I glance over and see Ted is the same. Smart uniform and clean shoes. Clean shaven too. Maintaining standards in the face of such adversity but it's good to see.

'How's Tom?' Terri asks quietly.

'He's great, he's outside getting our gear prepped with the others. He fits in well, fights like a lion,' I reply.

'If we don't get to see him say hi from us,' the normally quiet Jane cuts in quickly.

'Yeah course I will, but you can see him once we're done here.'

'Hello Howie,' a strong female voice sounds from behind me. I turn to see Kelly stood there with a tight smile.

'Kelly, good to see you again,' she takes my hand in a grip as firm as Ted's.

'You too, glad you're back safely.'

'How's it been here?' I ask.

'ORDER PLEASE,' Sergeant Hopewell shouts from the end of the room. We look round to see her holding a clipboard and staring round at the room. The muted conversations die out just as Chris walks in.

'Sorry, have I missed anything,' he squeezes through to join Sergeant Hopewell at the end of the room.

'No, we're just starting,' Sergeant Hopewell replies.

'Make way please,' Doc Roberts walks in and instead of politely squeezing through he simply shouts and barks everyone to move. 'Right, let's get on with it shall we, got a lot to do.' He blusters.

'Right. Mr Howie and his group got back safely last night,' Sergeant Hopewell starts off and I wince inwardly at being called Mr Howie in a room full of people. Not just people but doctors, engineers and police officers.

'Chris has done a bloody hard job while we've all been

away and I understand you've appointed Kelly to sort the outside area out?' She asks, looking first to Chris and then to Kelly.

'I did,' Chris nods, seemingly comfortable in front of the people watching him.

'I think if everyone is in agreement, we'll have a quick round robin so we know where we all are, Chris do you want to start?' I catch a look on Dave's face. This is quite possibly the first meeting of this type that he has ever seen. Instead of just someone giving him a blunt spoon and telling him to invade another country.

'Well,' Chris steps forward, a gesture to make sure everyone is looking at him, 'Kelly has taken over getting the flatlands sorted out, and she's also stepped up to head the engineering contingent amongst us. New structures, buildings, anything of that nature will go to Kelly and her team. Doctor Roberts who you all know, he heads the medical facilities. Roger – you all know Roger, he was the curator here before…well…before it happened. Roger has given them the best rooms to use. The cleanest and driest and I think we all agree the medical people should have those rooms. We'll also be sorting out a hospital area but we need supplies…'

'Yes,' Doc Roberts interrupts, 'we need medicines, antibiotics, bandages…'

'Doc, we'll come to that in a minute, please just hang on,' Chris smoothly moves on, 'We've got tent city out there at the moment which is fine now while the weather is good…'

'It's not good, it's bloody sweltering,' a voice calls out to a few chuckles.

'Well at least it's not cold and raining,' Chris keeps going, 'we can use the tents for now but eventually we'll have to look for more permanent structures. Inside the fort, we've got fresh running water and we're bottling what we can in case it runs dry. Food, we've got plenty at the moment but we also have a lot of people to feed and more turning up every day so we need more food supplies. Weapons, we've still got shotguns and plenty of ammunition for them but they're no good for range. Howie brought us back some ammunition and assault rifles so that secures us for a while, but as with the food, we'll need more. Briefly that covers it, Kelly?' He hands over to the engineer.

'Thanks Chris, starting with the outside. The grounds are ruined. I know there was talk of using them to plant crops but with the amount of blood and bits of bodies soaked into the ground it's just not feasible. The infected blood from those things is in the ground, now I'm not a doctor and maybe Doctor Roberts can say otherwise, but I'm not comfortable with eating food grown in soil soaked with so much infected blood,' murmurs of agreement sound out, 'but that is something we'll have to look at when we can. The bodies are still being cleared away but we need more fuel to burn them. We've been stacking them in the housing estate for now but they need burning before they spread disease. As for the inside, my team will help with whatever is needed. We've got engineers, mechanics, electricians and plumbers; we've got all sorts so between us we should muddle through for now.'

'Thank you Kelly,' Sergeant Hopewell speaks up, 'Doctor Roberts?'

'Thank you Sergeant. We can function as basic field triage at this stage. We can perform basic surgical operations but that's about it. Howie and Chris managed to get some of my research equipment from my hospital in London and that's still waiting to be set up. But we need power, fuel, generators, we need everything we can get out hands on. We need nurses too, or anyone with more than a basic knowledge of first aid...'

'You'll have to make do with basic first aid,' Sergeant

Hopewell cuts in, 'we've checked everyone and already sent the medically trained people to you.'

'It's not enough,' the doctor retorts.

'Then train them because we don't have anymore,' the sergeant snaps back.

'Well we don't have any choice do we. Right, well send me the basic first aiders then. They'll have to learn as we go. Supplies. I spoke to Howie last night and told him what we need. My team have drawn a list up of the essentials but we need everything. Find a hospital and strip it clean...'

'You said about chemists too,' I inquire.

'That's my bag,' a smart looking man steps forward, neatly trimmed hair and moustache. 'I'm a pharmacist, so I agreed to deal with that. But it's the same as Doctor Roberts said; we need everything you can get. If you find a chemist then bring everything back with you.'

'Okay,' I reply wondering just how much stuff they think we can carry.

'Guards and fort security is being handled by Ted,' Sergeant Hopewell carries straight on.

'Yep,' Ted nods, 'we got enough guards and we're going to do weapons training every day. There's a few ex-army folks still with us so we're getting it sorted. We got a full rota of guards on the walls and the gates, those archers are bloody good. We're getting some training done with them too and they asked me to tell you they need more bows and arrows,' he looks at me.

'Of course they do,' I nod back.

'Don't worry Mr Howie, we've got lists prepared in order of priority,' the Sergeant smiles fleetingly. 'Right, well I think it's your turn now anyway...' she looks at me.

'Right...well bloody hell. What do you want to know?' Caught off guard a little as I was so absorbed in the things being said.

I start off giving a brief outline of what happened once we left the women and children on the Isle of Wight. The fight we had overnight leading up to Dave shooting Darren with our last remaining bullet,' cheering breaks out in the room at the news of Darren being killed and questions get thrown in before Sergeant Hopewell brings them back to order. I run through the naval supply ship and mention that might be worth a re-visit. Then I explain about the council estate and the compound full of youths run by Maddox. That elicits more questions and between Clarence and I we try to answer everyone. We even ask Doctor Roberts to spare someone to send over so they can be checked medically.

As I finish I look round at the looks of awe coming towards the three of us stood in the middle of the room. One giant, one small quiet man and a supermarket manager.

'So your team is happy to go back out?' Kelly asks, breaking the silence.

'Of course, but how are we going to bring all that stuff back? We'll need lorries, vans, drivers, directions and maps…'

'We can get those,' Sergeant Hopewell says quickly, 'we've been preparing this morning. We've plenty of big vans ready to go out and we've got volunteers to drive them too.'

'Quick runs with less people will be safer and easier,' Clarence says, 'we should go for one place, get the goods and bring it back then go back out…too many vehicles and too many people will make it far harder and slow it down.'

'Good point,' I nod, 'we can have the Saxon out front and then on guard action, the lads can secure the entrance which leaves a few of us to clear the building and get loaded. Ted… we'll need some more people to help us, can you spare anyone?'

'We'll sort that,' Chris answers for him, 'Ted can get a few of his guards so you have people with weapons experience and we'll get a few able bodies to help move the gear.'

'Good, as soon as you're ready then,' I nod round at the faces.

'One more quick thing,' Sergeant Hopewell adds, stopping everyone as they turn to leave, 'we've got questions coming in about the burials and ceremonies to honour those we've lost.'

'Right?' I ask slightly confused.

'We've got many different religions within the fort, Christians, Muslims, Hindu, Sikh and they all lost people, we have to consider how we're going to do it.'

'Do what?' I ask.

'Well how are they going to worship? Do we have separate places for each religion? We've got Muslims asking about prayer times and Christians wanting to bury their dead. There's all sorts of religious implications if the bodies aren't dealt with within certain time frames.'

'Dealt with? What do you mean dealt with? We burn them. We burn all of them together. Frankly, and I don't care who this offends, but I couldn't give a shit about religion right now. People can worship how they want, they can pray to whoever they want but survival comes first. We're not giving any ground to any religion.'

'Who are you to say that?' A man steps forward and asks the question bluntly.

'What?'

'I said who are you to say that? England is a multi-cultural society that prides itself on the acceptance of all faiths. We must adhere to those principles. It's the basis of any fair and decent society.' He says with a fixed gaze. I take him in, a middle aged man, portly and serious looking. He looks intelligent and is wearing a short sleeve shirt with pens in the top pocket and sweat marks on the armpits.

'What about food? Will religion feed everyone? Will it provide medicine and security too? Will it give us lights at night time? Will it fend off the next attack we get? Or do you think this is over and we can go back to normal living? That infection, or disease or whatever it is…it's mutating. The infected are getting smarter. They can speak and act like we do. They'll come again, they need to eat and find humans to carry their infection on. Do what you want but if you give any of our essential ground to religion I will tear it down. Burn the bodies and burn them quickly.'

'Faith gives hope Mr Howie,' the man continues and I feel Dave bristling at my side.

'Faith gives hope, religion pits man against man. We can deal with those things later but for now we carry on as before. We give no ground for any religious buildings.'

'What about a multi-faith area, they were common in many places. A quiet area for reflection and for people to worship how they see fit.'

'No! Is this meeting over? Good, we've got work to do.'

'Meeting adjourned, Mr Howie will get his team ready at the front and we'll send the people down there.'

CHAPTER TEN

DAY TWO

'So Mr Maguire...is the food okay for you?' Lucy asks watching him tuck into the plate of pasta and chicken cooked in a creamy sauce, topped off with a mound of grated cheese and served with two garlic bread baguettes.

'Wonderful,' Paco mutters with a mouthful of food. The worry in him had increased as Lucy prepared the food, watching the calories mount up and when he saw the white bread going in the oven he felt another mild state of panic settling in. However, he was hungry and despite most of the foods being banned by his nutritionist he soon tucked in and started devouring the lot.

'I haven't eaten anything for hours, not since last evening on set and that was just a salad.'

'You said you were on set, what were you filming?' Lucy asks sipping from her glass of wine.

'Ha! You wouldn't believe it but a zombie film,' he winced at the memory.

'No way? Now that is ironic.'

'Uh-huh, definitely. We were filming a scene where this woman gets taken down by zombies, that's when it started, only one of the zombies turns out to be real.'

'Oh my god,' she leans forward staring in horror, 'is that true?'

'Yeah, as I sit here now. One of the zombies was real. It ate another zombie, one of the actor zombies…'

'Bloody hell, you couldn't make it up could you.'

'Why would I make it up?' Paco asks.

'Eh? No it's a saying, like when something is too weird then it must be true because you wouldn't make anything that weird up.'

'Oh I get it…I think,' he replies forking another load of pasta into his mouth.

'Listen Paco, we can't leave the lights on tonight. We'll have to stay in the dark and use candles. We can't risk anything seeing the lights through the windows. Only two of the rooms have curtains and they're threadbare.' She stared off to the window and the darkening sky outside while Paco felt yet another state of panic course through him at the prospect of being in the dark.

'Okay,' he nods, not wanting to show the fear, 'makes sense I guess. Do we need to keep watch or anything like that? Like you know…one stays awake while the other…'

'Yeah I know what keeping watch means, we're pretty isolated here. The nearest house is a few miles away, the nearest village is the one you went through and that's quite a distance. I don't think anything will come here.'

'What about that one out there?'

'Him? Oh he lives in that house a few miles away so he's accounted for,' she shrugs, taking another sip of wine.

'Did he live alone?' Paco asks.

'I don't know I've only been here a couple of weeks. I only met him once to say hi, I never went to his house.'

'Well didn't he say if he had a wife or anything?'

'Nope, he was too busy looking at my tits to mention if he was married…Paco? Are you okay?'

'Yeah fine,' he sputters on the food going down the wrong hole at the casual way she mentioned the man looking at her breasts.

'And don't think I haven't caught you looking at them either,' she adds quickly.

'What? I haven't looked at them,' Paco protests with the fork hovering an inch from his mouth.

'No?…well why not? What's wrong with them?'

'What? Say Lucy I don't mean to be rude, you have a great rack and all, but the whole end of the world thing has kinda distracted me.'

'Oh yeah…that,' she says glumly making him frown, 'so you think I've got a great rack eh?'

'Er…yeah, really nice,' he shoves the food in, concentrating on munching, preparing the next forkful and avoiding looking over at her. Having got this attention a lot from women he wasn't unduly surprised but right now, after everything that's happened…it's just a bit much.

'So, we'll go by candle light tonight and then tomorrow we'll have to think about going out for supplies,' she switches instantly back to serious mode.

'Supplies? Where from?'

'My car is in the garage; we can take that and check that village or maybe go into one of the other towns.'

'But that village was overrun, those things were everywhere,' Paco replies, both relieved at the change of topic but also slightly alarmed at the way she flits so quickly.

'But there's two of us, one to watch and the other to go

inside and get stuff. If it's too dangerous we'll go somewhere else.'

'Yeah,' he nods again. The thought of going out anywhere is terrifying but she's right. They'll need supplies.

'Maybe you should have a bath tonight; the power won't last so we should make use of it.'

'Er, yeah that'd be great Lucy, what about you?'

'That an invite is it?' She quips quickly.

'No I meant you should have one too,' he answers.

'I know what you meant, yeah I'll go first but no sneaking around trying to see my tits okay?'

'Huh? Yeah sure...'

'I mean I know they're pretty good right, not fake like those American girls.'

'Yeah sure Lucy,' he says staring down at the food again.

'Oh you're going to try and look at me in the bath aren't you? I know it. Bloody hell Paco if it's that hard for you then you might as well just say something.'

'What?' He says for the umpteenth time.

'I'll be up there soaking my body, naked and vulnerable and you'll be hanging about outside with your todger in your hand trying to look at my tits.'

'Todger? What's a todger?'

'Your John Thomas, the old wedding tackle...your cock Paco! You'll be stood with your cock in your hand banging one out.'

'What the fuck? Lucy I don't get half of what you're saying but I won't be hanging round masturbating if that's what you mean.'

'Okay, fair enough. No need to get all shirty about it. Christ Paco, they're only tits! Bloody hell do you want me to just get them out now or something?'

'Lucy please stop this, I'm in shock right now. I've been chased through the woods by monsters and seen my friends getting killed. I don't want to rape you or feel your tits and I won't be hanging around outside the bathroom.'

'Okay. Well I'll go and run a bath now and let you finish up down here. Make coffee if you want. We'll give it another half hour and get some candles on. There's more food in the fridge if you're still hungry,' she says lightly, taking her glass and heading out of the room. Paco stays seated, stunned and confused by the way she seems so normal and intelligent one minute then going on about her boobs the next.

'This is fucked up,' he mutters pushing the plate away with a sudden loss of appetite. He's Paco Maguire and this shouldn't be happening. He should be in a shelter with the other important people. His studio or agents should have seen this coming and got him to safety. Feeling angry and frustrated that there's no one to blame he starts clearing the table. Shovelling the leftover food into the bin and stacking the dirty plates by the sink.

He makes coffee, thinking furiously. The situation is bad. But weigh it up Paco, outside there are monsters that want to eat you, inside there is a very strange woman who keeps mentioning her tits and being raped. She is beautiful and I guess the old Paco charm has worked quicker than normal. Hell, out here in the middle of nowhere, a lone woman, then a big movie star turns up. Who can blame her for being like that? Women throw themselves at me all the time, why should it be any different now?

She must be scared and frustrated and all those hints, well she obviously wants a bit of Paco inside her. If I want to stay here then I need to give her what she obviously wants and it's not like she's some ugly broad is it?

Nodding with firm resolution he pushes himself away from the kitchen side and walks slowly down the hall, stopping at the bottom of the stairs.

'Say Lucy, is it okay if I come up a second?' He calls out.

'Yeah sure, what's up?' She shouts down. He climbs the stairs, hearing the sound of running water and the bath being filled. The bathroom door closed but not shut properly and he smiles to himself. Left the door open for me eh?

'I was kinda thinking about what you said.'

'Sorry love, hang on I can't hear you...' she opens the door with a towel wrapped round her torso, covering her breasts and the tops of her thighs.

'Hey,' he smiles his best wooing smile.

'Er...hi? What did you say?' She asks in a normal tone.

'Well Lucy, seeing as you're up here alone and that water sounds nice and hot...I was thinking maybe we should save water and share the bath?' His voice trails off softly at the end as he pushes one hand out to lean against the wall, knowing it will show the muscles in his biceps.

'I beg your pardon?' She replies with a look of distaste.

'What?' He pulls the arm back and stares at her confused, not expecting this response.

'You want to have a bath with me? You dirty bloody pervert! I knew you'd be hanging around at here trying to perv over me.'

'Lucy, hey I'm sorry but I thought....'

'You thought what? That I'd just drop my towel and let you shag me? Piss off and let me have a bath in peace,' she steps back, slamming the door closed, leaving Paco stood there with an open mouth and a look of sheer confusion on his face. The signals weren't wrong, he never gets it wrong. She was hinting at him, hinting heavily and now she's slamming the door in his face.

'Broads,' he mutters and walks slowly back down the stairs. In the kitchen he continues shaking his head and wondering what just happened as he drinks coffee and continues clearing the table.

Looking out the window he realises it's now full dark and

finds the box of candles left on the table. Using a box of matches he lights one of the candles and lets some wax drip onto a plate to secure the base of the candle. He switches the light off and sighs deeply.

'Paco?' Lucy calls out from upstairs, 'bathroom is free love, I've emptied my water and started filling it up for you.' She sounds perfectly normal again.

'That's great Lucy, thank you,' he calls back keeping his tone normal. He climbs the stairs holding his plate and candle, reaching the top to see a smiling Lucy walking out of the bathroom, her skin looking pink and flushed and the now wet towel once more wrapped round her torso.

'Say Lucy, I'm sorry about that, I didn't mean to…'

'What? Ah think nothing of it, waters running and I've left that gown for you to use if you want,' she replies and slinks past him into the bedroom.

He enters the steamy bathroom and rests the candle next to the sink before going over and checking the bathtub. Pushing the door closed he strips off and climbs into the almost scalding water. Sinking back gently and letting the heat of the water soak into his muscles he sighs deeply with a tight knot of fear deep inside his stomach.

Everyone is gone, the world is over and life will never be the same again. No hope of getting home, no phones, television, no internet. All that money and fame and for what? So he can die from being eaten by monsters or scratch around to survive and eek out an existence.

The back of his throat gets tight, tears sting his eyes as he rubs his face with worry. Shaking his head he rubs the tears away, feeling helpless, alone and very homesick.

He'd had the choice between a cop thriller and the zombie action movie. With zombies grossing theatres out everywhere his agents had convinced him to go for the zombie flick, telling him there was potential for a lucrative series. If only he'd gone with the cop thriller. He would be safely in LA now, surrounded by armed security and helicopters ready to whisk him away somewhere safe amongst his own kind.

His brother lived in the city and would undoubtedly be dead by now. Their parents lived on a ranch in Wyoming, wide open country and far from anywhere. He'd bought it for them a few years ago and got it refurbished. If only he'd been with them. Fuck the brother, he was a dick anyway. A religious nut always devoting himself to the poor and needy. Sanctimonious douchebag. His folks would be safe on the ranch. They had horses, fresh running water and guns, lots of guns.

The thought of home, of the States, of his family and more than anything of being alone and feeling scared brought the tears on fully.

Sobbing quietly into his hands he didn't hear the door being opened and the footsteps of Lucy as she walked into the room and coughed, making him jump and rub his face quickly, pretending to be washing.

'What the fuck?' he stammers with blurred vision from the tears and sudden hot water he was splashing into face, 'Lucy, is that you?'

'Oh yes,' she replies quietly.

'What's up?' He answers, trying to cover his privates with one hand while rubbing the water from his eyes with the other.

As his vision clears he looks over to the woman stood above him. The black shiny PVC tight trousers and the black shiny PVC studded jacket. Stood there tapping a riding whip against her leg. Her eyes dark with black make-up and bright red lipstick. Her hair pulled back into a tight ponytail and a black shiny PVC cop's hat on her head.

'Lucy! What the fuck...' He tries to shuffle backwards,

forgetting he's in the bath. He sits bolt upright using both hands to cover his bits while staring open mouthed at the black clad woman.

'Lucy…What…What…' he stutters in panic. She stands there with a serious face, staring hard at him. The whip giving tiny thuds as it bounces from her leg. She shifts position, her outfit creaking. Without uttering a sound she reaches up and starts pulling the zip down on her black shiny PVC top. The rubberised zip making a loud slow buzzing noise as it clicks slowly down her chest and stomach. The jacket falls open to show her black PVC bra underneath, the huge soft mounds of her breasts spilling over the top and barely covering the nipples. Paco took the sight in with a dumb frown, fixing on the glittering silver skull fixed in her belly button.

'So Mr big shot movie man…trying to watch me in the bath were you?' She says slowly, her voice low and menacing.

'What?' Paco stammers once again.

'Trying to take advantage of me were you? Little me all alone in this big farmhouse and you come along, all big and strapping with your movie teeth and movie hair.'

'My movie hair?' He asks incredulous.

'Well Paco…you were caught. Caught being a bad boy. A naughty boy. A naughty boy that needs punishing…'

'Lucy, I…but…hey now,' he yelps in alarm as she hits the whip harder against her leg, stepping closer to the bath.

'Don't talk back you naughty boy,' she orders, looking lasciviously down the length of his naked body.

'But…' he yelps again as the whip lashes out catching him on the shoulder with the soft tasselled end of the whip. There was no pain, just the action of being struck while naked in the bath.

'Don't talk back to me you naughty boy, now have you washed properly?'

'Lucy...what the fuck?' She hits him again making him yelp with fright.

'Have you washed properly?' She demands.

'Er...'

'Don't speak!' she strikes him again, 'just nod or shake your head. Have you washed properly?'

Paco nods quickly, his head bobbing up and down.

'I don't believe you. You're a dirty boy that needs to wash. Now wash and do it properly.'

'Hey come on...ow! Hey don't hit me...ow! Lucy stop it... Ow...okay okay...ow!'

'Have you finished speaking you bad boy? Yes? Good. Now wash for Mistress Lucy. Wash your feet...yes your feet... I want clean feet. Go on, wash them toes, oh yeah get in between them, that's it...right in between them...yeah you bad boy you wash them feet. Now your legs, good boy...all the way up and clean them big thighs...that's it...give them a good hard scrub....you been a bad boy, a dirty boy that needs cleaning and washing all that dirty naughtiness away....now clean your stomach....come on lift them elbows up and show Mistress Lucy what you've got...oh wow! There's a big boy, a big dirty boy! Clean that stomach...now the chest....and get under those armpits, yeah get right in there and clean them pits my boy....Now the face, clean that face...scrub it! Scrub it harder! Good boy... now...what's left?'

'Lucy I don't think....Ow!'

'No speaking! Now what's left...oh yes...the todger you were playing with....clean it. Clean it movie boy....you clean that tackle for me...come on...'

'Ow!'

'Clean it then...clean it! That's a good boy...come on... scrub it harder. Scrub it! Scrub it!'

'Ow!'

'Then scrub it properly...that's it...nice and hard... come

on scrub it you dirty little man! Scrub that todger…good boy! You scrub that todger for me you dirty little man.'

'Ow…why're you hitting me…'

'Shut up and scrub it…come on scrub it!'

'Ow…hey…I'm scrubbing ain't I…'

'Scrub it…harder! Stop! Stop touching yourself right now you filthy deviant.'

'But…Ow…for the love of god…stop hitting me woman…Ow.'

'I never said you could make it get bigger…did I tell you to make it grow? You think you can just have a five knuckle shuffle when I'm telling you to wash?'

'Sorry…I didn't mean to…it just happened!'

'Now stand up…come on stand up.'

'Okay okay….Ow! I'm doing it already.'

'Good boy now let's have a proper look at you shall we… why is that thing still getting big? Make it go down…'

'I can't just make it go down…Ow! Please stop…Ow!…'

'You make that thing go down…It's getting bigger. Do you like being whipped? Is that it? You dirty boy getting all turned on at being whipped.'

'No I'm not it's…Ow.'

'It's what? What is it? Come on spit it out.'

'I don't know! It's just getting bigger on its own.'

'On its own! Got a consciousness has it? Got a brain has it? Or have you been staring at my tits again?'

'Lucy come on…this is fucked up…Ow! Please stop…'

'Right follow me my dirty little man…'

'Ow! Oh god Lucy don't grab that…Hey now come on lady…okay okay I'm coming just don't grip so hard…hey take it easy…'

'Well seeing as it's getting all big I might as well make use of it shouldn't I you naughty little man…'

With a firm grip, she marches him from the bathroom,

across the hall and into the bedroom. A single candle flickers in the corner of the room, casting shadows and a soft orange light.

Paco, having been a world famous movie star for many years had enjoyed far more than his fair share of sexual experiences and had dabbled with one tentative toe in the murky world of BDSM, preferring the straight and normal experiences of pliable women willing to relieve him at the twitch of a smile. Now, with Lucy literally manhandling him into the room he feels panicked and scared but strangely excited. The intelligence and bravery of the woman was clear. She knew things about what was going on and seemed a good strong person to be with. She was beautiful too with a figure to die for. Full breasted, narrow waist and long legs. Dressed to thrill in the PVC outfit and he couldn't help but get a natural reaction to the situation.

She was dominant and he was weak. Despite being a hulk of a man he knew he was truly terrified and her power was clear, plus it was her house, and she knew the area, and was braver than him.

He went with it. Playing along simply because he was too scared of doing anything else. She made him go on all fours and straddled his wide back, riding him like a donkey and whipping his bare backside. She made him undress her slowly, deliberately giving him instruction he would get wrong so she could whip him with the soft tassels.

Eventually, she was naked and the candle extinguished. What followed wasn't really that abnormal and Paco took the lead to do the other thing he was famous for.

If nothing else, it served to release the tension.

CHAPTER ELEVEN

D AY THREE

She stands on tired legs. Her head hanging low. Eyes alert and watchful, ears pricked. A sentinel holding post, sturdy, unmoving and unbeaten.

All through the night she has fought and killed. The bodies lay mangled and deep. Flies and insects buzz around the corpses. The street is covered with her vanquished enemies. The flow of them didn't stop all during the hours of darkness.

They came in ones, twos, groups and hordes. At times they reached the house and threw their bodies against the doors. The windows were smashed but she fought hard and only one gained the window ledge to clamber through and he was dragged back out by his trailing foot and savaged to death within seconds.

During the frantic battle the water bucket was knocked over, spilling the precious liquid away. She managed a few licks of the pooled water before it drained into the thirsty earth. After that she suffered with the high heat and constant action. Still she didn't fail.

A foul taste in her mouth from the infected flesh torn apart by her teeth. The sticky blood round her muzzle and dripping from her chin onto her filth encrusted paws.

Now, as the birds herald the start of a new day she checks both ends of the street, looking over the multitude of bodies and searching for any new threats. Turning slowly she walks to the water bucket and noses the thing aside, pawing and whining with thirst.

A voice from above, she moves back and looks up to see the woman making noise. The water bucket lifts slowly and she waits patiently for it to be filled and put back down. When it does come her tails wags softly, showing her pleasure and she drinks deeply. The water turning pink from the blood in her mouth. The water is cool and she drinks until her belly feels swollen and her tongue rids of the disgusting taste of the things.

She desperately needs sleep and moves over to the door but the ground is too littered with the dead and she can't find space to lie down. She moves off to the far corner, to the only patch of ground not covered by a corpse. She turns a few times and lies down. Gradually her breathing slows and her eyes close but her ears remain alert and listening.

In the house, the mother stares down at the huge dog and gives another prayer, this one of thanks and gratitude. Throughout the long hours of the night she listened to the sounds of the battle raging outside. She heard the thumps against her door and gripped the knife blade ready to end her children lives to prevent them becoming those things. She prayed it wouldn't happen that they wouldn't breach the house.

The window smashing brought the knife up and the sharp blade hovering inches above the baby's throat. Her toddler son asleep with his head on her lap. First the baby, then the son, then herself. It would be murder but it would be done with love and she would stop them becoming whatever they were outside.

Her ears strained as she heard the dog growling and snarling, the sounds of bodies being dragged over broken glass. No further sounds from inside the house and she wept with tears of fear and relief when the first tender rays of sunlight started to pour into the room.

On checking the view she stood rooted to the spot, staggered by the sheer numbers of cadavers littering the street. Two, three deep in places. The blood and gore was indescribable. Nothing on earth could prepare her for that sight and one which would stay with her until her dying day. Bodies twisted and mangled, hacked apart by teeth, flesh torn and gnashed and the dog stood on the path ready for more.

A sudden feeling of guilt. She had left the defence of her family to this one poor animal and looking down she saw the water bucket was knocked over and dry. She quickly re-filled it and lowered it down, seeing the dog wag its tail as it hurried to quench its thirst. She called down many thankyou's to the dog, telling it she would never forget what it had done.

The dog had saved them. Given them a chance of survival. She took that chance and quickly gathered the essentials into the three bags and after rousing her sleeping son she dragged them down the stairs and out the back door, crossing the garden and finding the car safe in the back lane.

She didn't heed the law of child seats and shoved the bags

and children into the vehicle, desperate to be inside and moving.

Reversing out of her lane she thought about the dog, how she wanted to take it with her. But surely it must turn. It must have been injured and the blood must have got into its system. But it was still normal, seemingly unaffected.

She drove to the end of the lane and pulled out onto her street. The bodies were less here and she paused, looking down the road and watching as the dog came into view.

The dog slept for a few minutes before hearing the noises coming from inside the house. She heard the little ones waking up and the hurried movements as they went from the top to the back of the house. She heard the sound of one of the big things and then listened as it came closer. Rising up on her exhausted legs she walked down the path and over the bodies to stare down the street at the big thing parked at the end. The woman was sat inside. The little ones must be with her. The big thing was hard and moved faster than she could run. They could get away and find a new den with the big thing. She understood this and sat down.

The woman made noise from the big thing, she waved her arm and then the big thing moved away. She watched and listened until it was gone from both sight and hearing.

She went back to the water bucket and drank again. She sat next to the water bucket and cleaned herself, removing the blood and gore from her coat. She walked from the street and kept walking until she found soft ground covered in trees. She moved through the soft ground, pleased to be rid of the stench of the things.

She found bushes and pushed her way inside. She made the ground flat and lay down.

She slept.

CHAPTER TWELVE

DAY ELEVEN

'Ha, now that is a nice sight!' I call out as Clarence, Dave and I walk back to our area and see the Saxon parked outside, the doors open and our kit being loaded. Nick stands in the central hole cleaning the GPMG with a cigarette hanging from his lips.

'She's back Mr Howie,' Blowers steps out from the rear and greets us with a big smile.

'She's part of the team,' I reply and move round to peer into the back, at the bench seats and cupboards. The memories are strong and stir a reaction within my stomach and again I give thoughts to the lads we lost.

'There's still bits of zombie brain on the front, it's all dried on and stuck,' Cookey winces with a disgusted face.

'Nice,' I wince back, 'can't we hose it off or something?'

'Tom's gone to find a stiff brush, water ain't shifting it.'

'Oh well, don't worry too much, I'm sure we'll be adding some more on there soon.'

'I fucking hope so,' Nick mutters from the top.

'Language,' Dave immediately chides him.

'Sorry Dave, I meant I jolly well hope so,' he smiles down, his face twisted to one side so the smoke doesn't go in his eyes.

'So if Dave is like the sergeant and Mr Howie the officer then what about Clarence? Is he a grunt like us?' Cookey says with a wicked grin and starts backing away from the glare sent his way from the big man.

'What did you say?' Clarence growls.

'Ha, you might be a big man but can you run?' Cookey dares him with a laugh and yelps as Clarence moves faster than anyone of us expected. Cookey tries to sprint off but is caught within a few easy strides and gets pinned to the floor as Clarence calls for the hose.

'I'll get it,' Blowers says laughing and runs round the front to pull it free.

'No...I was joking...no...Blowers don't you dare,' Cookey yells between laughing as Clarence pins him down.

'Ever heard of water boarding?' Clarence asks with a chuckle. Tom walks back with a brush and stops at the sight of Cookey pinned and the rest of us laughing.

'Blowers don't you dare,' Cookey yelps as the cold water starts sloshing his face with Blowers taking care not to aim directly for his mouth, 'you fucker...I thought we were mates.'

'Hold him Clarence,' Nicks shouts down.

'He's a wriggler,' Clarence laughs at Cookey bucking about and giggling between splutters.

'Lads,' Dave's voice cuts through the laughter. Clarence glances up and his face drops instantly at the sight of the crowds of people in the camp standing and staring at the horseplay. Cookey bends his neck up and looks about, the giggling dying off quickly as Blowers pulls the hose back.

I turn round to see the glum faces watching us. A few smiles here and there but mostly downcast people clearly thinking how we can piss about at such a time.

'Sorry,' Clarence says loud enough for most to hear him. He extends a hand and helps Cookey to his feet who wipes his face and nods respectfully at the people watching.

'Me too, I didn't mean to cause any offence,' he says earnestly.

'Let's get loaded,' I say and turn back towards the Saxon with a mixed reaction of feeling bad about the lads laughing and joking when everyone has lost so much, but then we've lost too. We've all lost someone. We've seen our mates die by our side. I shot one of our team just a couple of nights ago. They've got the right to blow off a little steam especially after everything they've been through, but maybe not here.

'Mr Howie, can we get some tools to carry? Wire cutters and strippers, set of drivers? That kind of thing?' Nick asks pulling me away from my thoughts.

'See that woman,' I point to Kelly stood talking outside the police office, 'she's in charge of the engineering here now, go and ask her for what you need.'

'On it,' Nick drops down and scuttles out the back, jogging away towards the woman.

'Nick,' I call after him.

'Yes Mr Howie,' he stops and looks back.

'Politely with no swearing.'

'Of course Mr Howie,' he grins and starts off again.

'We've sorted the spare rifles and ammunition out; we got them down to the armoury while you were in your meeting. The other GPMG is down there too,' Blowers explains as he hands my kit bag and axe over.

'Well done mate, good work.'

'Lani got all our bags loaded with full clips and water bottles. She stuck some snack food in them too. The shotguns I put in the Saxon, I didn't want to give them up to the armoury but I figured we've got enough kit with the assault rifles, pistols and hand weapons.'

'We checked our radios too and Nick got them onto the same frequency as they're using here.'

'Good work Blowers,' Dave adds one of his rare compliments making the hard faced youth smile.

'Cheers Dave,' he replies.

'What's he grinning about?' Clarence says at the sight of Nick running back holding a small bag in his hands.

'You got some stuff then?' I ask.

'Fucking right I did,' Nick grins, 'shit, sorry Dave,' he adds quietly, 'I didn't swear when I asked her,' he says quickly.

'Okay mate, what did you get?'

'She gave me her own tool kit! Can you believe it! It's got like everything in it, snips, wire cutters, drivers...everything... here look at this.' He drops down and starts pulling rubber handled things out of the bag. Tom and Clarence both kneel down and admire the collection of tools which he shows of proudly.

'And she said this was her own kit, she said it was a gift for everything we've done for everyone. She's so cool,' Nick says quickly.

'You've done well mate,' Clarence pats him manfully on the shoulder, almost sprawling him into the ground but he still grins up reminding me just how young these lads are.

'So we know where you'll be working if we ever get time back at the fort,' I say with a smile.

'Yeah bloody right...er...if that's okay with you Mr Howie, I'm with this team first though,' he says with a sudden seriousness.

'Right, everyone here? Gather round...we're going for the

local hospitals for supplies. They've got lists prepared for things they need. Hospitals, chemists…and no doubt a million other things too. We'll be taking others out with us in vans to bring the stuff back. Our job is to find the place and make it safe. We go point and secure the area then guard while they get loaded up. We need to stay focussed and work together. This will be fluid and not only have we got each other to watch but others too. Ted said he's sending people with weapons experience but that's out job. We keep them safe, get them in and out and get the stuff back here. Got it?' They nod back, intense looks and taking the information in.

'Nick, show Tom how to use the GPMG and then he's on it first, that okay with you Tom?'

'No problem Mr Howie,' he nods seriously.

'Dave, if we get somewhere that needs inside clearance that will be down to you to lead, do you want to run through the hand signals you showed me before?' I ask him, remembering back at the farmyard when he was waving his hands at me.

'Listen in,' he barks, 'this means hold,' he makes a clenched fist and holds it up next to his head, 'if I extend one finger and point in a given direction it means there is one target in that direction, clear? Good. Two fingers means two targets and so on. An open hand being closed and opened means multiple targets. Watch for the points to see where they will be. If there is no point then it means I don't know where they are. I prefer pistols in confined spaces and room clearance. Two handed grip like this,' he pulls his pistol out and grips it with both hands, 'sweep and keep the pistol pointing where you are looking. Step surely and if you see a subject then fire twice, a double tap. We'll practise today as we go round. Each of you will work with me in turn, got it?' They stare back in awe at his instructions, 'now if I make a motion like this,' Dave opens his hand and dribbles an imaginary basketball, 'that means go low, if the hand is down and to the side it's an instruction to do something. Two people go that way, two go this way, one to hold here...understand? Watch Clarence, he knows this as well as I do so follow his instruction too.' He finishes off and looks to me.

'Done, right, load up,' I clamber into the driver's seat and give a slight smile at being back inside the vehicle. Clarence comes up front with me, taking the passenger seat which makes sense instead of being crammed into the back.

'Alright boss,' he smiles, 'that was an interesting meeting.'

'Yeah,' I agree and start the engine. She fires up first time with a loud roar that elicits a low cheer from Blowers, Nick and Cookey.

'Who was that bloke asking about the religious stuff?' I ask gently pulling away.

'No idea, I see where he's coming from but maybe his timing was a bit out.'

'Really? I don't see where he's coming from. Religion is a pain in the arse.'

'You think?' He asks, 'religion or faith?'

'I've got no issue with faith, but religion? I don't know... just makes me uncomfortable. I think it's divisive.'

'Chris is no fool, despite what he looks like the bloke is an amazing diplomat.'

'Oh no doubt, maybe I shouldn't have sounded off then.'

'You've got every right to say what you said, you more than anyone boss.'

'Aye, well...here we are,' I change the subject as we reach the inner gates and wait as they're pulled open. We trundle through straight through the already open outer gates. Ted standing there in full uniform complete with police flat cap, Sergeant Hopewell stood next to him holding her beloved clipboard and also wearing a hat.

'Good work,' Clarence mutters at the sight of them. I

know what he means, just the sight of the uniformed officers gives a sense of control and organisation and I notice Ted now has a pistol strapped to his belt. Three large vans are parked off to one side, the drivers and guards armed with shotguns standing nearby.

'Two minutes,' I call out and jump down from the vehicle, 'Ted, we all set?'

'Yes, we've got a driver and two guards for each van. The guards will help load up.'

'Okay, can I speak to them quickly?'

'By all means,' he leads me over and introduces me to the group. I recognise most of the faces from the fort, men that have survived the battle.

'Right, we'll be out front in our vehicle. If we get a contact just stay in your vehicles and we'll do our best to sort it. We've got the GPMG up there,' I point to Tom standing through the hole in the Saxon, 'so we'll cut down most things. When we get to our destination, we'll secure the area and start clearing inside. Once clear we'll form a guard while you load up, it'll be fluid so we'll see how it goes and adapt as we go along, everyone okay with that?' I get a round of nods and replies of "yes" and "yes Mr Howie" which still makes me feel weird.

'Howie, this is the map of the local area. The route to the hospital is marked in red,' Sergeant Hopewell hands me a local map book.

'This route goes north, wouldn't Portsmouth be closer?'

'We worked on the basis that it'll be looted by now, big city and all that.'

'Those buggers would have looted it the first day' Ted moans.

'Oi, I'm from Portsmouth,' one of the guards grins.

'I bloody know you are Pete, my point exactly,' Ted retorts to a chuckle from Pete.

'You nicked me enough times to know that Ted,' Pete quips back to my amazement, Ted sees my look and cuts in quickly.

'Pete's a good lad, just had sticky fingers in his day. He got me out the shit once though. Remember that Pete?'

'I do Ted, that was a bad night.'

'What happened?' I can't help but ask and I can see the others are looking with interest.

'Pub fight, first on the scene and the crowd turned on me,' Pete says with a glint in his eye, 'then Pete here steps out and stands back to back with me until help arrived.'

'Bloody hell,' I say.

'He was on bail at the time too, I'd nicked him just a few days before,' Ted adds.

'You were decent though Ted,' Pete says seriously, 'always decent every time you dealt with me and I wasn't gonna stand by and let you get cut up.'

'Finished reminiscing have we?' Sergeant Hopewell joins us, flicking through the papers on her clipboard, 'have we got everyone's details? Howie how about your lot, are they recorded anywhere?'

'Recorded? What for?'

'We keep records of everyone coming in and going out. Give me five minutes and I'll get everyone's names and details,' she rushes off towards the Saxon.

'It's frantic now,' Ted explains, 'but with more people turning up every day we got to keep track of everyone. It helps when people ask if we've heard or seen from so and so.'

'Yeah, figures.'

Five minutes later and we're pulling out down the lane heading towards the housing estate with the vans tucked in behind us.

Passing through the estate now in the daytime we can see the mounds of bodies piled up. Grotesque human remains all twisted and broken, human and zombie shoved away from the fort and ready to be burnt.

'We need a theme tune,' Cookey says suddenly, breaking the uneasy silence.

'Have we got a sound system then?' Lani asks.

'We got the loudspeaker system, could rig something up to it easy enough,' Nick replies.

'Ride of the Valkyries,' Clarence says twisting round to look down the back.

'What's that?' Cookey asks.

'Wagner,' Dave says.

'What's that!' Clarence scoffs, 'the Para's song is what that is.'

'Hmmm, I think we need something more modern,' Cookey muses with a sly grin.

'Modern,' Clarence tuts.

'Barbie Girl?' Nick offers to a few chuckles.

'Yeah I can see us blasting out Barbie Girl as we thunder into action,' Blowers says.

'How about the music from the Old Spice advert?' Tom shouts down.

'Carmina Burana,' Dave adds.

'Yeah that one,' Tom shouts.

'Nah that's old, we need something modern and good,' Cookey shouts up.

'Bonkers by Dizzee Rascal,' Nick offers again.

'Nope, got to be something tough, like the music from Rocky or something,' Cookey replies.

'Eye of the tiger,' Dave says.

'What about Metallica, the opening bit from Sad but True?' Tom shouts.

'That's more like it,' Cookey grins.

'Paradise City?' Lani adds.

'Guns N Roses,' Dave says.

'Classic,' Blowers says.

'I know...' Lani laughs, 'Missy Elliott...We Run This.'

'Oh yes!' Cookey shouts, 'that's it. It's perfect...blasting into battle, we run this shit!'

'Brilliant Lani,' Blowers laughs at Cookey's impression.

'Mr Howie, can we have Missy Elliott for our theme song?'

'I like it,' I laugh at the thought of playing it through the sound system, 'Dave, Clarence?'

'I'm sticking with Wagner,' Clarence replies.

'Dave?'

'I don't know it,' he says.

'What? How can you not know it?' Lani says.

'I don't know it, how does it go?' He asks and I get the sudden impression just from his voice that he does know it.

Cookey immediately launches into the opening music with loud dum de dums, the others join in noisily. Dave knows exactly what he's doing. They're wound up tight and need a release, he was mindful of the other people in the fort but then Dave is never normally mindful of other people. Respect and professionalism. That's what he thinks about. Us playing about in front of others, it's not about those people feeling sad; it's about the lads not acting the part. But here, he can get them to release in the safety of the vehicle. That bloke is switched on, very switched on.

'Mr Howie, we need a CD player and a CD so I can rig it up,' Nick calls out.

'I got it on my IPod,' Lani says.

'You can't rig and IPod to the sound system,' Cookey says.

'Bet I bloody can,' Nick replies already opening his new tool bag.

'This will be interesting,' I say quietly to a grinning Clarence.

CHAPTER THIRTEEN

DAY THREE

'You go and I'll keep watch, if anything happens I'll sound the horn, okay?' Lucy asks from behind the steering wheel. Paco leans forward and stares at the first cottage, remembering the old woman he found inside. Despite his protests Lucy insisted on trying the village first and they drove in to find the main street deserted.

'But...' Paco thinks furiously, not wanting to come across like a complete coward but dreading the thought of going back inside the houses.

'But what?' Lucy asks staring at his chiselled features. They had slept late, the fear and exhaustion of the previous days dragging Paco down into a deep and troubled sleep. On waking they found the power was still on and sat quietly chatting in the kitchen, drinking coffee and eating the food from the freezer.

Nothing about the previous night was mentioned. Lucy

was as straight talking as before with no reference to her breasts or him being a bad boy. Paco went along with it, content to just be in someone else's company, and someone who was intelligent and as self-assured as Lucy.

'Say, I was just thinking that if they turn up out here I could hold them off, that would be safer than maybe one inside the house,' he offers knowing it's an awful suggestion but he put it across with lustre and meaning.

'Yeah, that does make sense,' she replies biting her bottom lip and staring out of the windscreen, 'yeah, okay then I'll go in the first house and you keep watch, sound the horn if any of them turn up.'

'Yeah sure,' he nods, inwardly breathing a sigh of relief. She climbs out of the small blue car, making her way slowly to the first cottage. Paco steps out and stands scanning up and down the street. She turns back on reaching the door and gives him a thumbs up; he returns the gesture as she disappears from view.

Alone with the car he is tempted to drive off and find somewhere else, but he doesn't know where to go, where to get fuel or even how to drive the funny little English car with the manual gear stick in the middle. No, he'd be better waiting for Lucy, she seems to know what she's doing and the sex thing last night was weird as hell but painless. He can put up with that if it keeps him safe.

Where did the monsters go? They were all in the street yesterday. Unless they followed him through the woods and were still on his trail. He glances round expecting them to be coming up behind him, but the view is clear. Just a sultry hot summer afternoon in a quaint little English village. Flowers in the gardens, white fences and stone built walls. Idyllic really. He hums nervously to himself, trying to fight the temptation to lock himself in the car or drive off. The feeling of panic was still there, of being unsafe with eyes watching him from every window. It was quiet. Too quiet. The kind of quiet that precedes something bad. If this was a movie the camera would be panning out to show him stood in the empty street, no soundtrack or music playing, just quiet. Then it would happen. The monster would reveal itself behind him. He spins round expecting the worse and found the view the same as it was thirty seconds ago.

'Hey I got some good stuff,' Lucy calls, splitting the quiet with her monstrous voice.

'Ssshh,' he says fiercely waving his hands to quieten her. She freezes on the spot expecting there to be something nearby.

'What is it?' She whispers.

'They'll hear you yelling like that,' he complains.

'Oh for goodness sake Paco,' she sighs, 'I thought there was someone there. I got some tinned stuff, ham, cheese and some milk that hasn't gone off.'

'That's great but will you stop shouting,' he pleads.

'Okay okay, keep your shirt on,' she tuts, lifting the carrier bags into the boot and slamming it down making him wince visibly.

'Oh god, they've heard us,' he whimpers staring down the road at the sight of the geriatric horde shuffling into view from a junction. 'We'd better go.'

'Hang on,' she stares down the road at them. She waits for long agonising seconds just staring at their slow movements, 'Paco, they're going to take at least half an hour to get here, look at the pace they're going at. We'll do another couple,' she says brusquely walking off towards the next house.

'Are you crazy?'

'They're not running are they?'

'Lucy! What if they start running?'

'Sound the bloody horn then, I won't be long,' she walks quickly to the next cottage and pushes the door open, checking inside before disappearing from view. Paco stands transfixed at the site of the group hundreds of metres away. The slow jerky shuffle. They're going to start running, they're going to just let rip and sprint at me. They'll get me, they'll eat my flesh. Why was she taking so long? Couldn't she see the danger they were in?

Whimpering softly to himself he spins round checking all sides before looking back down the road at the barely moving horde. Christ they were getting close now.

'See, we've got more food now,' Lucy says holding more bulging carrier bags, 'oh they haven't even moved,' she adds with a glance down the road.

'They have, they're getting closer. We really should go.'

'No no, we're alright for a minute,' she says after loading the car up and walking off to the next house, 'bring the car down for me.'

The car? How was he meant to drive that thing? He stares with horror at the horde then down at the small car. He opens the driver's door and clambers in, scratching round for the seat lever and yanking it back with a crunch. He stares at the dials and feels the unfamiliar three pedals under his feet.

Staring at the group he twists the ignition causing the car to shoot forward a few feet with a violent lurch, he gives a gurgled scream at the sudden unexpected motion and gets ready to flee on foot then remembers the clutch, hold the clutch down.

Pressing his left foot on the pedal he tries again and listens as the car fires up. The noise of the engine far too loud in the quiet street. He eases the clutch up and feels the car starting to move, he lifts too fast and the car shoots forward, stalling again.

'Stupid mother fucker,' he mutters and tries again, this time easing his left foot up while pushing his right down harder. The vehicle rolls forward a few metres, stopping outside the third house. He keeps the engine running and drums on the steering wheel, staring intently at the horde and praying they don't start sprinting. Sighing with relief at the sight of Lucy exiting the cottage with more bulging plastic bags.

'I love old people, they've always got loads of tinned food. We got prunes here, that'll help keep us regular.'

'Great can we go now?'

'What? They're bloody miles away, just be patient and move the car down.' She walks off again leaving his heart racing and the knot in his stomach getting tighter.

Great. This is just great. I'm driving the car closer to the monsters while she looks for tinned prunes in some old ladies pantry. This is the last one. We've got to go. If they start running we'll be in danger. He moved the car down to the next house and waited with baited breath until she came out carrying two large knives.

'No food, but I found these, here you have one, it'll make you feel better, right driver move on to the next one please,' she commands after passing the long bladed kitchen knife through the window. He dumps it straight on the passenger seat vowing to never be close enough to need one.

Fingers drumming, breathing shallow and sweat forming on his forehead he keeps a constant watch on the shuffling horde. They were close enough to see the gore on them now, the blood stained night clothes. In varying states of undress with ragged wounds clearly visible to the naked eye. Heads lolling as the feet shuffled in a straight legged walk. Drool pouring from mouths and he imagined the noises they would be making, groaning and snarling with venomous evil.

'Say this is enough now Lucy,' he snaps as she walks back to the car carrying more bags to dump in the back.

'I think you might just be right my dear,' she says looking at the approaching group of undead, 'right, drive down to that junction,' she adds climbing into the passenger seat. Paco eases the car forward, taking care with the weird pedals. He grinds up to second gear as they pass the horde, too busy watching them turn and stare with their red bloodshot eyes and saliva dripping mouths.

'If you can't find 'em...grind 'em,' Lucy quips.

'Who has a manual shift these days?' he moans.

'Hey, ease up and pull in here,' she points to the side of the road, leaning over him and wagging her fingers.

'What? Why?'

'We'll start at this end now while the old biddies are shuffling round,' she explains waiting to open the door as he coasts to a stop. Paco cranes his head round to look out the rear window at the horde as they slowly turn and start back down the road.

'I think we've got enough, we should head back,' he stares at her blue eyes, willing her to agree.

'Nah, big man like you! You'll eat all that lot within a couple of days and it's mainly prunes and pilchards anyway. I'll do these houses and you keep watch again,' she replies cheerfully hopping out of the car and jogging round the front.

Paco felt his stomach drop, the tension was too much. They needed to go and get back to the safety of the house. Being out here was inviting trouble. Sure, these monsters might be slow and doddery but what if some more came along? Faster ones with sharp teeth and clawed hands?

He shivers at the macabre thoughts coursing through his mind, telling himself to keep calm, breathe deeply and just keep watch.

'Paco, this door is locked, come and give it a kick for me,' Lucy yells over. He spins round to find she hasn't even got in the first house yet and is stood there rattling the front door.

'Someone could be in there Lucy,' He shouts back stretching his tall frame out from the car.

'I don't think so, it looks empty. I think the door just closed and locked.'

'Lucy I don't think we should do that, what if someone is inside and armed with a gun.'

'A gun? This isn't Los bloody Angeles Paco...who'd have a gun round here?'

'You had a gun.'

'Yeah but no bullets, besides the thing's an antique and I doubt it would fire anyway.'

'I just think...'

'HELLO? ANYONE IN THERE?' She bellows through the letterbox.

'For the love of god what are you doing?' He seethes; glancing round to check nothing was creeping up on him.

'Checking if anyone is inside of course,' she says as though it was the most obvious thing ever.

'Well they're not gonna answer you are they?'

'Why not? I'd answer if another survivor was at my door, HELLO? I'VE GOT PACO MAGUIRE OUT HERE...'

'Oh my,' he groans rubbing his forehead.

'Nope, no one home, come and give it a kick for me.'

'But...'

'Come on, stop your bleating and kick this door in. You must have done it a hundred times in your movies.'

'They're prop doors, rigged to burst open. Not real doors,' he moans walking through the gate.

'Yeah well you're still a big lad so come on, give it a whack for me.'

'Jesus Mary and everything else!' He mutters taking stock of the door. He takes a wide legged stance and eyes the middle section near the lock. Exploding out and ramming the door with the bottom of his shoe. It thuds and creaks but otherwise doesn't move.

'What was that? I could have kicked it harder,' she berates him. He gives it another kick, harder but not hard enough.

'Paco, if you don't kick it properly I'll get my bloody whip out!' she snaps, making the first reference to last night's activity. He sucks a breath in and slams his foot into the door, his powerful thighs driving the leg forward. The door wrenches open with a sound of splintering wood, destroying the lock and hanging limply from the hinges.

'I did it!' He stares in shock at the open doorway, 'did you see that? I kicked the door in!'

'Well done, now you keep watch.'

'I did it! I kicked a real door in, a real wooden door. You know the prop guys always said you'd break your foot trying it for real.'

'Did they?' She shouts from somewhere inside the house.

'Yeah for sure, they always said it was the quickest way to injure yourself and shouldn't be done unless you had really strong knees and ankles.'

'Well I guess that means you have strong knees and ankles then.'

'Yeah I do!' He shouts back and whoops for good measure then realises where he is and what they're doing. Spinning round with a look of intense fear. At the end of the path he checks the progress of the horde and looks in every direction, cursing himself for being so stupid as to look away for even just a few minutes.

The knot in his gut tightens into a hard ball, his hands shake and palms become sweaty. They going to kill me, they going to kill me in a horrific slow and painful way, eating me bit by bit while I scream and beg for mercy. I'm too good for this, too beautiful. I'm an actor, an artist who reflects life and gives pleasure to ordinary people, I make them feel good about themselves.

Wringing his hands he switches his gaze between the

horde and the cottage that Lucy went in. His foot taps nervously as he drops his arms and beats his fists against the side of his legs.

'PACO!' Lucy screams from inside the house, his stomach flips at the piercing scream that follows. He takes a step towards the house, stopping and almost crying with panic.

'LUCY?' He yells, glancing round at the horde then back to the house.

'Paco,' he looks up to see her opening an upstairs window, 'there's two of them here,' she shouts.

'What? Where?' He stays rooted to the spot.

'They were in a bedroom, they're outside the door...do something!'

'Do what? What can I do?'

'Use the knife, there's only two of them!'

'I...But...'

'There's no weapons in here, I'm in a spare room. Just a bed and nothing else, she shouts looing round at the room behind her, 'use the knife.'

'Lucy...I can't,' he stammers.

'Paco, just man up and use the bloody knife, you can't leave me in here like this...that bloody lot are getting closer too.' He spins round checking the hordes progress, they're closer now.

'Lucy...' he backs away towards the car. The thought of entering the house with the monsters, all red eyed and sharp teeth, clawed hands just waiting to tear his flesh open. It's too much, the fear consumes him. Utter terrifying fear that grips his stomach and makes his legs shake.

'Paco, get the bloody knife and get up here,' she commands turning to look back in the room, 'they're at the bloody door Paco, they're trying to get in...'

'Lucy, I'm so sorry...I...I just can't,' he sobs.

'Paco for god's sake man up and get in here!'

'I just can't,' tears stream down his face as he moves to the car, feeling for the open driver's door and glancing round at the group. They're so close now and the blood looks stark against their pale skin, the wounds festering with bits of skin flapping open.

'Paco…' she shouts in a warning voice, 'don't you fucking leave me…give me a knife, get me a weapon…Paco, this room is empty, my knife is downstairs…I can't fight them with my bare hands.'

Crying hard he climbs into the car and starts the engine, firing it up and grinding through the gears in a muddled attempt at finding first.

'Paco…please…fucking don't do this Paco…I took you in…' her voice is desperate, she can see exactly what he's doing, the state he's in and the panic showing from his body language.

'Lucy,' he sobs staring up at her through the open window. He hears the first low groan from the horde several metres back from the car and it sets him off with a yelp, slamming his foot down on the pedal and tyre spinning away, leaving Lucy leaning out the window and screaming after him.

'DON'T YOU LEAVE ME HERE…I SWEAR I'LL FIND YOU PACO MAGUIRE…DON'T LEAVE ME…I WILL HUNT YOU DOWN….'

Through tear filled misted eyes he watches the rear view mirror, watching Lucy leaning out the window and waving her arms at the retreating car. Loud sobs wrack his body, his chest heaves as he beats the steering wheel and dashboard.

CHAPTER FOURTEEN

DAY THREE

She needs rest. The night's constant exertions have exhausted her muscles and left her weary. Sleeping in the bushes stretched out she slowly recovers. Waking every so often to shift position and pant the heat of the day away. The dog stretches her limbs out regularly, straightening her legs and groaning softly at the pleasure it gives.

She senses the day drawing on and the high heat of the afternoon. The bushes are shaded which provides relief from the scorching sun but the air is still super charged and humid.

By late afternoon she is unable to sleep anymore. Thirsty and hungry she moves out from her position and finds a suitable spot to deposit her scent. Moving off and searching through the soft ground for food or water.

A shallow stream, shaded by tall trees provides a perfect spot to cool down and she wades into the water, drinking first and then lying down and letting the water flow past her. The running water turns a pale shade of pink from the blood stains as the dried gore softens and comes away from her fur. She drinks more and savours the chill feeling on her stomach and hind quarters. Still the sense of sadness burns within. She knew there was another pack in that den and she protected the little ones but they're gone now too. Images flash through her memory, fleeting glimpses of her pack laughing and stroking her belly. The pack leader taking her out for a patrol and throwing things for her to chase and catch.

Soft brown eyes blink as she whines softly and her ears dip down. Alone and hungry. She can find food and keep going but without a pack she feels desolate and aimless.

Cooled and watered she rises from the stream and walks gently through the soft ground, using her nose to head back towards the hard ground. Keeping to the shadows she slinks down streets and roads until she finds a pile of the black things. Again she glances round out of habit, checking no one will tell her off and make noise. Her nose picks out the best choices and she rips the bags open, devouring any food left inside them. The wasteful nature of society means she again eats well and fills her stomach with left over meals and discarded food.

The smell of the things is everywhere. The stench of them permeates the air and it's already getting worse. Decay and dying flesh, rancid, awful and sweet.

With nothing else to do she puts nose to ground and starts tracking their movements. Using that foul stench to hunt them down. She's alone but she knows that her little one still lives somewhere, those things will kill her little one.

She must kill them first.

CHAPTER FIFTEEN

DAY ELEVEN

'Try that,' Nick says flat on his back between Clarence and me with his arms stretched into the inner working of the Saxon's electrical wiring system.

'It hasn't worked the last five times Nick,' Cookey moans.

'Just press play and try Cookey,' Nick's muffled voice calls out. The headphones of the IPod dangle just above his head as he cuts and splices things, his new tool bag open on his chest and a pair of wire cutters gripped between his teeth. 'Have you pressed play yet?'

'Yes mate,' Cookey replies.

'It should be working,' Nick says, 'Clarence is the PA system on?'

'Hang on,' he leans forward and checks the switches on the dashboard, 'er...no it wasn't, do you want it on?'

'Yes please,' Nick says frustrated but retaining a polite tone remembering who he's talking to.

'It's on,' Clarence flicks the switch and the sound of Missy Elliot booms out from the loudspeaker attached to the outside of the vehicle. Cheers erupt from the back and even Clarence's face splits in a wide grin.

'Fucking yes!' Nick slides out and grins up at everyone.

'Well done,' I shout down over the sound of We Run This belting out.

'What else you got on here?' Cookey asks and fiddles with the IPod. The song ends abruptly as the opening for Eternal Flame by The Bangles starts up.

'What the fuck?' Cookey laughs.

'I like it,' Lani says defiantly.

'You got some good stuff Lani,' Cookey flicks through her playlists.

'Only problem is we can't really use it too much,' I break the bad news, 'we'd draw them for miles around if they hear it.'

'Is that a bad thing?' Blowers shouts up.

'It is if we're trying to keep a low profile and do a quick raiding mission.'

'Since when have we kept a low profile?' Clarence chuckles.

'True,' I nod and smile, 'where now mate?' Following the map we've headed north away from the coast. Going through villages and towns, all of them looking more torn apart and destroyed than the last. Burnt out vehicles and bodies littering streets, pavements and road. Signs of intense fighting everywhere and we see small groups of undead gathered in central places, turning to shuffle slowly as we drive past. Tom shouted if he should fire on them, the temptation was great but we decided to conserve our ammunition and just concentrate on getting to the first hospital.

'Take a right, about a mile up the road now,' Clarence

advises as he examines the map and looks up to check local landmarks and road names. We're in a built up area now. I've no idea what the town is and to be honest, it doesn't make any difference to me. The area is built up and urban which means there was a high population density here. That means there will be undead aplenty and also that the hospital will most likely be overrun or looted already. It would only take one infected to get taken there by ambulance when the outbreak started.

'Music off,' I call out. Cookey switches the IPod off quickly and pushes it onto the dashboard. 'Almost there, we'll slow down for the last quarter of a mile. Switch on a keep a good look out.'

I hear rustling and slight clanging noises as the lads get their rifles ready, checking magazines, pulling bolts back. Taking pistols out, ejecting the smaller clips and ramming them back home. Clarence twists round to watch them, looking at me with an impressed nod.

'There it is,' he points ahead to a modern looking building set back from the road. A big sign board indicates the route in for the various departments. We take the access road for the Accident and Emergency department knowing it will be big enough for ambulances and there-fore big enough for our vehicles.

'There's been some contact here,' Tom shouts down.

'Got it,' I call back looking at the corpses in the mostly deserted car park. Several of them scattered about.

'Looks like they were run over...several times,' Tom commentates as we drive slowly down the access road.

'Right outside a hospital too,' Cookey mutters to a few sniggers.

'Alex, you're with me for the first clearance when we go in, make sure your rifle can fit on your back with the strap. We'll be using pistols.'

'Okay Dave,' Cookey instantly switches to a respectful tone of voice.

'Here we are,' I slow to a crawl for the last short distance. Approaching the wide front of the hospital emergency department. Two sets of double doors stand open, the building looks huge. Really long and at two stories high we're going to have our work cut out clearing it.

'Have you got your radio's on?' I ask.

'Yep, yours is clipped to your bag Mr Howie,' Blowers answers, proving I didn't need to ask.

'Looks clear, there's an ambulance over there…we'll have that if the we can find the keys,' Clarence points further down the road to wide parking bays marked up with Ambulances Only.

'Right, Tom you stay on the GPMG. The rest spread out and check this area first.' Bringing the Saxon to a stop I hear the back doors opening and sounds of feet jumping down onto the concrete. Blowers hands me my kit bag and rifle as I climb down and feel the heat of the morning hitting me like a brick wall.

'Jesus, it's fucking hot,' I moan quietly. It feels like hot air from an oven.

'This has got to be the hottest summer this country has ever seen,' Clarence says shrugging his bag on and picking his rifle up, 'I've known deserts cooler than this.'

'Humid too,' Blowers adds wiping sweat from his forehead. Walking away I see Cookey, Nick and Lani have already taken steps away from the building and are facing away, checking the view all around and holding their weapons at the ready. The vans have stopped a short distance away and I wave at them to stay put.

'Howie to the vans, are you receiving me over?'

'Lead van to Mr Howie, this is Pete, yeah we're receiving you loud and clear.'

'Howie to Pete and the other vans, hold your position. We'll leave someone on the GPMG and start checking inside over.'

'Pete to Mr Howie, okay, we'll hold here over.'

I nod at Dave who signals Cookey to head over. We start walking slowly to the entrance as Cookey pushes his rifle round and draws his pistol. Entering through the main doors we fan out into a line and look at the devastation. Blood everywhere, corpses mangled and rotten. Furniture upended, a wheelchair lying on its side, blankets and sheets scattered over the floor. To the right is a large waiting room with chairs bolted to the floor and a long reception desk. The corridor leads on into the emergency treatment rooms, and the curtained sections used by the triage nurses.

Dave steps out front and motions Cookey to move by his side. Both of them have their pistols drawn and held out in front in a double handed grip. Dave turns and signals Clarence to watch the rear, the big man nods back and steps back a few paces half turning so he can maintain a clear view.

The two men lead the way slowly progressing down the corridor, taking steady steps until they reach the first side rooms. Dave holds his hand up, fist clenched and we pause. He indicates the rest to keep eyes on the front and signals that he's going to clear the room on the left.

Heavy double swing doors with a solid metal strip across the middle section to protect the wood from being battered by beds rammed into them at speed. Dave pushes one side with his foot and indicates Cookey to push the other side open. They step in, holding the doors open with their feet and sweeping the pistols round the room. The doors swing close behind them with shushing noise. Two loud shots ring out and we grip our weapons tighter as the tension ramps up a notch.

The doors swing open as they walk out, Dave motioning that one was inside and was taken down by Cookey. They cross the corridor and repeat the movements, pushing the door open and disappearing for a few seconds.

Ten minutes later and we've only cleared the first main corridor and reached a crossroads with large corridors leading off left, right and ahead.

'This is going to take too long,' I whisper to everyone, 'Dave you take Cookey and Lani left, Blowers you and Nick with me to the right, Clarence holds here.' They nod back and we move off. Pistols drawn. We keep to the same method of room clearance of two going in to each room and the other remaining outside.

We rotate round the pairings round, taking it in turns. Some of the rooms lead into offices and administration areas, those are cleared quickly. Other doors lead into smaller waiting rooms with more corridors going off to yet more smaller examination and consultation rooms.

Bloody footsteps and smears indicate there has been undead here and most of the doors are simple swing doors without handles or locks, meaning they could be anywhere. The air smells stale and hot, tinged with the stench of decaying, rancid meat. We find corpses throughout the rooms. The bodies hacked apart by dozens of mouths and destroyed beyond possibility of coming back.

Halfway down our corridor and we pause to pull water bottles from each-others packs and swig the rapidly warming liquid down. It does little to cool us and I can tell Blowers and Nick are as uncomfortable as I am. My back feels like there's a hot water bottle trapped between my skin and the material of the bag. My face drips sweat from my chin and my top is sodden.

Nick and I push into the next room; an undead turns slowly on seeing us. A doctor still dressed in a white lab coat but half his face torn off. He groans audibly as Nick fires a single shot into his head. Blood and brains splatter the wall behind him as the round takes the back of his skull off.

'Shot mate,' I whisper.

'Thanks Mr Howie,' he whispers back. Just a single room and we back out just as Blowers fires down the corridor at another undead exiting a side room, pushing the door open with his body and shuffling into view.

'I think they know we're here,' he comments and exhales sharply blowing a spray of sweat from his upper lip.

We move down and I hold while they take the next room. Another shot rings out and I hear more muffled shots coming from further down the corridor. I glance back to see Clarence aiming down the corridor ahead of him and taking a shot.

'Hang on lads,' I say as they walk out, '*Howie to Pete, you receiving me?*'

'*Loud and clear Mr Howie.*'

'*We've got multiple contacts here, might take some time, over.*'

'*Yeah we heard the shots, do you need a hand? Over.*'

'*No mate, just bear with us.*'

'*Roger that.*'

'Okay, crack on,' I clip the radio back onto my bag strap. A squeaking noise comes from further down the corridor. We hold position with pistols raised and waiting as the noise draws closer. A door starts swinging open ahead of us, a few rooms down. An undead female dressed in a hospital gown and pulling a wheeled stand holding a now empty drip behind her. The fact that the wheeled stand is still attached and upright causes us to pause for a second. The wheels squeak annoyingly as she slowly ambles towards us.

'We should put some blood in that drip bag, she'd be happy for hours,' Nick comments then fires a single shot taking her in the throat. She spins back and slams into the wall, slumping down as fresh blood pours from her throat. The drip stand remains upright.

We clear the rest of the corridor, getting frequent contacts until we're satisfied the rooms are all clear. Strolling back down we swig water and change magazines. Dave reaches the main junction just ahead of us, Cookey and Lani both red faced and sweating heavily. Even Dave looks a little flushed, but only a little.

'There's loads of them,' Lani remarks as we move down the corridor, stepping over the body that Clarence shot.

'More than I thought there would be,' I smile at her and she grins back showing her white teeth. She looks so beautiful with her glowing face and I can't help but stare for a second.

'More rooms,' Dave mutters. 'We'll do the left you do the right?'

'Okay mate, Nick you swap with Clarence for a few minutes.' They swap round and we keep going.

'Dave, Clarence, you okay if they start getting the equipment from the sections we've cleared?'

'Makes sense boss,' Clarence nods. I can see Dave would prefer to have the whole building cleared before they enter but that will take valuable time.

'Howie to Pete.'

'Pete receiving you Mr Howie, go ahead.'

'Mate, we've cleared the A and E department and the main corridors up to the signs that lead to the x-ray section. Do you want to start in behind us while we press on?'

'Yeah got it, we'll come in now and get working.'

'Roger that, take care, there's bodies everywhere and it's hot as hell in here. Tom you receiving me?'

'Tom to Mr Howie, receiving you loud and clear, go ahead over,' his training as a police officer shows clearly as his confident voice comes through the radio.

'Tom did you hear the last? They'll be coming in to start unloading. You stay put and keep watch there.'

'Roger that Mr Howie, acknowledged the last, remaining in position until further notice.'

'Right, who wants an X-Ray?' I ask. Another set of double doors ahead of us and the more double doors to the right leading to the X-Ray section. You lot crack on, I'll hold here.'

Clarence nods back and goes to push the swing door open. It hits something the other side and bounces back at him. He frowns as the door starts swinging towards him, a clear groaning coming from the other side.

'I'm too hot to piss about,' he growls and slams one hand into the door. It bursts open with a loud thud as the body on the other side is sent flying backwards. He strides in and kicks the undead hard in the head, breaking the neck. Cookey stares in awe and looks back at Nick and Blowers both grinning like idiots.

'Nick, chuck us a smoke mate,' I call out before he disappears. He drops back and hands me his packet and a lighter. I stick one in my mouth and light the end, savouring the smoke as I pull it back. 'You having one?' I ask him.

'Is that alright?' he replies and lights one up. Dave might not be very happy with us smoking on the job but hey, it's hotter than a hot place on a hot day and it stinks too.

'Good job with that IPod Nick,' I breathe the smoke out and feel the pleasant tingle as the nicotine receptors get a hit.

'Thanks Mr Howie,' he nods back blowing smoke downwards and tapping the ash on the floor. I'm suddenly reminded of McKinney. We stood and smoked in a hospital in London a few hours before he got killed.

'You okay Mr Howie?' Nick asks as an involuntary shiver goes through me.

'Yeah,' I smile back, 'fine mate. You okay?'

'Starving,' he says quickly.

'You're always bloody starving; I don't know where you put it all.'

'Nervous energy, I burn it off...that's what I was told anyway.'

'Boring in there,' Cookey says coming back through the doors, 'we were going to X-Ray Blowers to see how thick his head was but the powers off.'

'Very funny,' Blowers replies drily.

'You two take the rear and have a smoke if you want,' I stub my cigarette out on the tiled floor.

'Thanks,' Cookey pulls a packet from his pocket and hands one to Blowers as Nick and I push through the next double doors.

'Well hello!' Nick smirks at the sight. A wide open main reception area with stairs leading up. A café and newsagents on the far side and the hospital pharmacy off to the left. The metal shutters still firm and locked in place across the counter. The area doesn't look looted but then I guess the horde of zombies here have kept everyone at bay.

Patients and medical staff clustered together at the base of the stairs, blood soaked and covered in gore. Their skin looks drawn and tight, a sickly pale colour with sunken cheeks and almost hollow eye sockets. Hands clawed and tight, all moisture drawn from their skin and flesh. The clothes hang from their frames, hair limp and filthy. Flies and insects buzzing in and around the festering sores.

Almost gagging from the stench we fan out into a line and watch as they slowly turn and start the ungainly shuffle towards us.

'Rifles?' I ask.

'Okay,' Dave replies. We holster the pistols and pull the assault rifles round, taking aim and holding for a second. Everyone waiting for everyone else to fire first. After a few seconds we all look at each other and start laughing, triggers get squeezed and the noise of the weapons deafens us in the enclosed space.

It takes just seconds to slaughter them down. Rounds ripping into heads and blowing skulls apart. Brains and hair matted cranial bits flying off everywhere. We use single shots, picking them off until the area is clear. Magazines are changed and we re-draw the pistols.

'Dave you go right and check the café and shop with Clarence, we'll take the pharmacy. Lani, you hold at the bottom of the stairs.'

We split up again as Lani strides to the base of the stairs and aims her assault rifle up, then sweeping round to aim at the main entrance doors a few metres away.

'Cookey, get some food from that café,' Nick calls out. We head towards the pharmacy. A small waiting with the same bolted to the floor chairs. Low tables with old faded magazines on them. Signs and display notices pinned to walls telling visitors to wash their hands and use the gel dispenser on the walls.

I check the metal shuttering to find it's fixed in place, seemingly locked from the inside. We head down the side to find a single door marked up with AUTHORISED PERSONNEL ONLY.

'Oh fuck it, we're not authorised,' Blowers mutters.

'Mr Howie, can you authorise us to enter the pharmacy?'

'I can and you are,' I reply.

'Ah that's good then,' Blowers adds and pushes the door handle down, 'locked,' he says.

'We're fucked then,' Nick eyes the door.

'Blowers, you stand next to me, we'll kick it together. Aim for the middle, ready?' He nods back and we each launch a foot at the door, striking it mid-section and bouncing off with jarred knees.

'Shit that bloody hurt,' Blowers winces as we rub our knees and Nick chuckles.

'Howie to Clarence.'

'Clarence to Mr Howie, receiving you, go ahead.'

'We've got an obstacle here, can you pop down to the pharmacy please?'

'Big door is it?'

'Yep.'

'On my way.'

'Defeated by a door,' I moan.

'I bet he gets it first kick,' Blowers says.

'Probably just punch it in,' Nick adds.

'Boss, lads, is that it?' Clarence walks up and stares at the door then grins at us still rubbing our knees.

'Yeah, it's fucking solid,' Blowers stands upright, 'and it called you a wanker.'

'Did it now?' He steps up to the door and first pushes the top, then the bottom.

'What are you doing?' Nick asks inquisitively.

'Checking to see if there are locks at the top or bottom, or just in the middle. Being a pharmacy they would have used a decent door with a decent lock. See, it doesn't budge when I push the top or bottom which means it has three locks in place.'

'How would they do that from the outside?' Blowers asks.

'Not bolts, locks. Activated from the main keyhole.'

'Oh I see,' Nick says.

'Yeah, so on a door like this a kick to the middle will just hurt your knees,' he glances round with a wry smile as the others walk round to join us.

'Café and shop clear,' Dave reports.

'So how do we get in then?' Blowers asks.

'You either get an enforcer, you know...those big metal things the police use, or...' He steps back and first extends a foot to the door gently. Checking range and adjusting the distance a little. He focuses hard and takes a deep breath, exploding out with a low roar and slamming his gigantic foot into the door, splintering the frame and sending the thing flying in several feet to smash into the shelving units behind.

'Fuck me,' Cookey says with shake of his head, 'I want to be Clarence when I grow up.'

'That'll never happen,' Lani shouts from round the corner.

'Ha! Nice one Lani,' Blowers laughs.

'It's clear,' Dave peers his head inside.

'That should cheer Doc Roberts up a bit,' I say.

'Have they got Viagra?' Cookey asks to a torrent of abuse from Nick and Blowers, I can hear Lani laughing too.

'Do you need it then?' Blowers asks.

'No I was going to slip it in your water bottle for the next time we have a big scrap, it'd be funny as fuck watching you trying to fight with a boner,' he laughs.

'You want to watch me with a boner?' Blowers asks in a serious tone.

'Fuck yeah,' Cookey laughs again missing the point, 'no! Not like that...don't be disgusting,' he adds quickly.

'Come on, where next?' I lead back round to the stairs. One corridor runs off at the back of the room with a large collection of signs indicating every possible type of medical department. More signs are attached to the wall next to the stairs, indicating yet more departments.

'Alright to come through?' Pete shouts from the door we came through a minute ago.

'Yeah it's all clear mate,' I yell back.

'Bloody hell I can see that,' he says striding over with his shotgun held in one hand.

'Pharmacy is there mate,' I nod towards the shuttered counter.

'Yeah we got the door open, it had the old top middle and bottom locks but we er, well we bypassed them with our advanced door opening technique,' Cookey says.

'Big bloke kicked it open did he?' Pete smiles and winks,

'we've started loading from A and E and I'll get the pharmacy done next, you checking the rest?'

'I don't know...do we need to? What else should we take?' I ask around.

'The doc just said to take everything, but I guess medicines, bandages and equipment are the priority,' Pete answers.

'Surgical stuff then I guess,' I say, 'where's the surgery section? Operating rooms or whatever they're called.'

'Upstairs, but equipment covers pretty much everything that's not medicine and bandages,' Clarence says.

'We should have brought one of the medical people with us,' Lani suggests.

'Yeah, we'll do that next time. Right, let's go for the surgery place and get what we can. We'll have to leave a guard down here though as that corridor isn't clear. Blowers, you and Cookey hold here.'

'Got it,' Blowers nods as they both move away to take position facing the double doors

'Shall we?' I start up the stairs, holding my pistol double handed as Dave joins me at the front. We reach the top and start down another long corridor with more doors leading off left and right. Splitting into teams we work our way down, taking shots at the undead stood drooling in some of the rooms.

'Shit, look at this,' Nick calls out from inside a room. We push inside to see a row of beds. All of them surrounded by monitors and banks of equipment. Dead bodies lie in the beds. Normal dead bodies not turned or infected.

'Life support machines,' I say softly, 'they must have died when the power went out.'

'Why didn't the zombies get them?' Lani asks, 'maybe they were already dead...like no signs of life or something.'

'Just luck I think, fucking poor luck...missed by the zombies and dying when the machines went off,' I reply. The room is a stark difference to everywhere else. Clean and free from any blood or debris. The smell of death hangs in the warm air, but not the rancid stench of the undead. Just normal death smell, still nasty but not *as* nasty.

'We should take some of this equipment,' Nick says softly.

'Yeah I guess,' I say and move to the first bed. The wires lead to small sticky pads stuck to the corpses chest and arms. More lines lead into veins via cannulas held in place by sticky tape. Oxygen masks cover the mouths. The corpse looks mottled with sunken yellowing skin. Lifeless and sobering. After so much gore the sight of an unharmed dead body is weird, looking round I can see the others must feel the same too as they're all staring quietly at the bodies.

'Poor buggers,' Nick says.

'Why? They died without pain,' Lani replies, 'no suffering, just slipped away quietly.'

'So I reckon we just pull those sticky pads off and the cannulas...can't see anything else,' I look round the bed. Reaching out I grip the first sticky pad and pull it away, it breaks free with a small section of flesh from the decaying skin. 'Well that ain't working,' I stare down at the patch shaped hole in the corpses chest.

'Er, hang on...I saw this on television,' Lani says and leans over the body. She pushes one finger onto the patch and yanks the wire free from it, leaving the patch in situ.

'Oh so we just find more patches?' I ask.

'Got them, they're on shelves under the machines,' Dave holds a box up. We work quickly, pulling the wires out and then rolling the machines out of the room into the corridor. Once done we keep going, clearing rooms and marking bits of equipment we think would be useful, moving them out into corridor.

Breathless and sweating like crazy we keep going, radioing down to Pete and updated him of the things we find. The drivers and guards work harder than we do, carrying and wheeling equipment down the long corridors and having to negotiate the manky bodies. With little choice we have to keep stopping to take water on. We run out within a couple of hours and end up raiding the café and shop. The vans crews foolishly didn't bring extra water with them and get a stern warning from Dave to prepare better next time.

Eventually we're done. Well the vans are filled anyway but the hospital is still filled with equipment. Clarence finds the body of a paramedic in the corridor and checks through the pockets, coming up trumps with a set of keys for the ambulance. Pete allocates one of the drivers and our convoy heads off. Poor Tom taking a break from his position on the GPMG and sitting in the cooler back of the Saxon with a red face and drinking warm bottles of coke.

Our convoy moves off. A whole morning with no disasters, nothing too uneventful either. A first successful mission completed.

CHAPTER SIXTEEN

DAY THREE

Sat at the kitchen table, clutching a lukewarm mug of coffee the tears pour down his tanned cheeks. His eyes swivel round the room that now feels so empty and hollow. He found his way back more by luck than judgement. His subconscious taking over and guiding his hands to steer the wheel and navigate back to the only safe place he now knows.

Self-loathing isn't strong enough to describe the feeling inside his soul. But one other emotion blots that out, an emotion so powerful that it drives all other thought and reason away.

Pity.

Now he's alone and even more frightened than before. His mind filling with images of Lucy stuck in the house surrounded by the monsters and just a flimsy English ply board bedroom door holding them back. How long can she survive? Hours at the most before their combined weight forces the door open. Even if they move slowly she'll have the choice of jumping out of a first floor window into a group of them or trying to fend off the monsters coming through the house.

The anxiety increases by the second. He bends over the table clutching his gurgling stomach. The nerves and fear turning his insides to jelly.

What now? Stay here and try to survive I guess. There's plenty of food now, and the water is still running. Use the candles and keep a low profile. No, keep a non-existence profile. One candle at night and only in the back bedroom when the curtains are drawn. Yeah, do that. But the thought of being alone in the dark house terrifies him even more. Lucy's words replay in his head over and over. *I will hunt you down.* She was scared and panicking, knowing she was trapped as he fled in her car. But those words, those final words, they spin round and round, twisting his mind.

Clutching his griping stomach he heads up the stairs and sits on the toilet. His insides have liquefied and pour out his arse, filling the room with the fetid smell of shit. He gags at his own stench, reviling in his demise and crying loud sobs at the sorry state he's in.

Cleaned up he heads back downstairs, moving slowly from room to room, spying out the windows and constantly checking the perimeter. He keeps looking over to the outbuilding, at the corpse still in situ with the pitchfork driven through its head. Imagination in overdrive he imagines the corpse has shifted position the next time he checks it. Surely it has, it's further out now. Someone is out there playing mind games with him. He looks away and rubs his sore eyes, checks again but the corpse is still in the same place.

The seconds tick by slowly. With no sound other than his own breathing and the footsteps his boots make as he creeps from room to room he flinches at every noise coming from outside.

Birds singing, foxes running through the yard and barking for their cubs, the house creaking as it heats up from the scorching summer sun.

Afternoon turns to evening turns to dusk turns to night and still he moves from room to room, checking the view, checking the perimeter. The constant pattern soothes his troubled mind; the repeated action serves to ease the knot in his stomach. Then, as darkness hits fully the tension ramps up as he loses sight of the corpse in the farmyard and is no longer able to see the perimeter. A cloudless night and a bright moon but the area is heavily wooded, casting deeper shadows everywhere.

He drinks water and forgets to eat. Collecting the candle and matches he feels his way through the hallway to the bottom of the stairs. Pausing behind the door and straining his ears for any sounds.

The stairs creak loudly as he climbs up, wincing and inwardly cursing the loose wooden boards and Lucy for not having the house fixed up properly. The thought of her catches in his throat and he whimpers softly, gripping the worn handrail and forcing himself to climb to the top. *I will hunt you down Paco Maguire.* He should leave but he doesn't know anywhere else and it's dark now, too late to be outside. *I will hunt you down.*

In the bathroom he pee's sitting down, afraid the sound of his urinating standing up will be too loud and could be heard from outside. Groping his way into the bedroom he goes to the far corner and sits down, resting his back against the wall. He slides a match out and softly strikes it along the course strip. The light flares and even that soft noise sends a feeling of panic shooting up inside him. He lights the candle and blows the match out, sitting back and trying to work out if the paltry flickering light can be seen through the curtains.

Thinking of outside his mind goes to Lucy again. Images of her fighting for her life, screaming in panic as the door slowly drives inwards and the clawed hands reach through the gap to rake her skin. Being slowly pushed back, inch by inch, knowing she's doomed. The terror she must have felt and the horror of knowing she's going to die at the hands of those things. The feeling of the teeth as they bite into her flesh, the blood pouring into her system. Turning her. Paco draws his knees up to his chest, his own body heat making him sweat in the sultry evening air.

Lucy, torn and bloodied, stumbling towards the cottage, her red bloodshot eyes fixed ahead as she makes her way through the lanes, *I will hunt you down*. She will come for me; she said she will hunt me down. I left her to die alone and afraid. She will come here to seek revenge.

His mind races with ever increasing grotesque pictures of Lucy with clawed hands and sharpened teeth, her skin pale and drawn.

As time goes by he tries to think of the distance, knowing she must be close. He imagines her coming into the yard with her eyes fixed on the front door. She must be halfway across the yard by now. She will be at the door any second. His mind races, waiting for the imagined bang of the front door. When it doesn't happen he convinces himself that she's chosen to walk round the house and probe for weakness. The twisted blood encrusted fingers feeling at windows and fingering the back door handle. She'll find a way in, remember a hidden key or just somehow open the door. His mind fills with the thoughts of the Lucy creeping through the house, course ragged breaths and soft footsteps. He knows that at some point the door will creak open and she will be there, dripping blood and staring at him with baleful eyes.

Gibbering with low moans he gently rocks back and forth, his heavily muscled arms bulging as he grips his thighs.

He prays to God, to Allah, to Jehovah and to Buddha. He panics thinking there will be a vengeful left out god slighted by his wrong prayers so he prays to every god ever known or thought off. He prays for the baby Jesus to show mercy, for Mary and Joseph to keep him safe. He prays for the prophet Mohammed to give him strength and see him through this ordeal.

He doesn't sleep. Sleep would mean death. Lucy is outside the door now, waiting and listening for the sound of his sleeping form. He won't give in to it. He won't give her what she wants. He fights fatigue and thirst. The sweat continues to seep from his brow and soak into already sodden clothes.

The candle burns down to a low nub, barely flickering as it fights for fuel. He curses himself for not bringing another candle up. But it's too late now. It can't be that long until dawn. The candle burns bright, flickers and fades out, plunging him into blackness and the absolute worse state of terror he has ever known.

Paco squeezes his eyes closed then as the first tugs of sleep threaten to pull him under he opens them wide and stares into the darkness. Colours and lights flash as he searches for anything other than darkness. He stares at the window and finds the tiniest flicker of moonlight coming through a bare patch in the material. He seizes on it and stares until his eyes sting and water. Still he doesn't blink but makes himself feel that pain, knowing it will keep him awake.

Hours go by, fear filled hours until eventually and achingly slowly he finds the room gradually getting lighter. The shadows seem less now, the black blurring to grey until he can make the outline of the bed out. Then the door. He can see the door and more importantly that it's still closed. He waits longer until the light is strong and slowly stretches his aching legs out.

Rubbing his thighs and kneading his calf muscles he rolls onto all fours and crabs over to the window. Rising up inch by inch and gently pulling the curtain back. He gains the view of outside, it all looks normal, everything is the same. But this is the back of the house. He needs to see the front and be sure she isn't coming for him.

He edges over to the door and eases it open, it creaks too much so he slows down and moves it millimetre by millimetre. Lucy isn't there. Leaning out he checks both ends of the short corridor. All clear. He moves out and creeps gently towards the front bedroom. The door is half open and he can squeeze through without having to touch it and make noise. He crouches down once inside the room and starts heading towards the window. No curtain here and he waits until he's right below the sill before he starts to lift up. The movement has caused him to sweat and he can hear the drops of liquid falling from his chin and hitting the bare floorboards under his feet.

His forehead crests the windowsill; he lifts higher until he can see the tops of the trees. He keeps going until he gets a full view of the yard. He breathes a huge sigh of relief at the sight of the clear open ground. The corpse is still there with the pitchfork still jammed in its head. Everything is the same.

Paco rubs his eyes and feels the fatigue crashing through his system. He survived the night and now it's daylight, he can sleep for a few hours and rest.

He stands up and leans his sweating forehead against the cool glass, opening his eyes he slowly scans his eyes across the yard to the entrance of the lane and Lucy stood there staring up at him. Her pale skin covered in red glistening blood, her arms hanging limply at her sides. The rest of the horde behind her.

CHAPTER SEVENTEEN

D AY ELEVEN

'How was it?' Chris asks striding out from the gates with a number of men and women behind him. They head straight to the vans and start unloading the equipment and supplies.

'Straightforward, which worries me as nothing bad happened,' I reply.

'Yeah I know what you mean, every half hour right?'

'Fact Chris, we had contact, the hospital was crawling with them but it kind of served a purpose as it kept everyone else away by the looks of it. Not sure if what we got was any good as none of us really know anything about medical equipment but we got the contents of the pharmacy and some surgical stuff from some store rooms near the operating rooms.'

'That should keep Doc Roberts happy for maybe an hour,' he says drily, 'this heat is too much Howie. They're wilting in there. We've had to open the back gate so the kids can go in the sea and cool off.'

'That's not a bad thing is it?

'Not really, it feels like there's no air...'

'Clarence said he'd been in cooler deserts than this.'

'Deserts are different, they got dry heat. This is humid, sticky and making everyone snap,' he pours water onto a piece of cloth and rubs his neck and face.

'Howie, are you okay to go back out once we've unloaded?' Sergeant Hopewell walks from the gate, her hat is now gone and her hair is plastered to her red forehead. Terri walks behind her swigging from a bottle of water.

'Straight to the point Debbie,' Chris grimaces.

'Sorry,' she frowns and visibly slows her walking pace down as if that will also slow her fast moving mind, 'it's this heat, unbearable,' she mutters. 'Everything alright?' she offers me a smile.

'I was just saying to Chris it was an easy run really, lot of contact but they were all slow.'

'Well that's good then, so the next trip?' She prompts.

'No worries, the van crews didn't take any water with them, but other than that yeah we're ready to go.'

'Good, next on the priority is this little town marked on the map. I'm reliably informed there are two well stocked chemists there plus a supermarket, a cash and carry warehouse and a DIY store.'

'Christ, do you want all of them done?' I step back to shake the beads of sweat off my head.

'Well yes, that's the general idea,' she replies, 'oh and there's a medical centre used for out-patients. They want that done too.'

'Right,' I sigh as Clarence walks over to join me. He takes the map and the looks at the attached bit of paper listing the various stores. 'Debbie, we struggled at the hospital not knowing what to take exactly. Can you spare anyone to come with us?'

'These aren't hospitals Howie,' she remarks in a rather patronising tone, 'empty the chemists, get whatever food you can from the supermarket and the cash and carry and then the DIY store.'

'And the medical centre?'

'Yes that too, just grab what you can,' she adds.

'That hospital was full of equipment, grabbing what we can might not be the right thing. There could be vital things we're missing.'

'That was a hospital Howie, this is a medical centre therefore it will be smaller with less stock.'

'You said it was used by out-patients so it will still have supplies.'

'And you take them,' she says too quickly. I take a breath and bite my tongue while Clarence clears his throat.

'Tell you what,' Chris interjects, 'get this run done and if we have another hospital then we'll make sure we've got someone from the medical team with you.'

'Fine,' I reply.

'The medical team are too valuable to be put at risk like that,' Debbie argues, 'we shouldn't be sending them anywhere.'

'And we aren't valuable then?' Clarence bridles.

'You're not a bloody doctor are you?' Debbie snaps back.

'Okay okay,' Chris steps forward, 'it's hot, everyone is snapping. The lads will get this run done and we'll see where we go from there. Happy?' He looks round at everyone.

'S'fine,' Clarence mutters.

'Good, I'm glad we understand each other,' Debbie adds stiffly and walks off leaving Terri staring at her retreating form and looking back at us with an apologetic expression.

'Nick!' I call out, 'You got a spare cigarette?' I turn and

walk off, quietly seething from her abrupt and patronising tone. Cookey pops out from the back of the Saxon and hands me a pack of cigarettes and a lighter. His plain expression makes it clear they've all heard the conversation.

'Cheers mate,' I light one up and inhale.

'You okay?' Lani appears holding two bottles of water out for me and Clarence.

'Yeah, it's this heat,' I make an excuse for the way she spoke.

'And we're expendable,' Clarence mutters, 'story of my bloody life that is.'

'We can't be The Expendables,' Cookey says quietly, 'it's already been done.'

'Good movie,' Clarence nods before swigging from his bottle of water.

'You could have been in that film,' Cookey says to him, 'you look like one of them.'

'You're not the first to say that,' Chris cuts in.

'She was rude,' Clarence turns on big Chris.

'Yes she was,' he says plainly, 'what do you expect? Tea and medals? She's worth her weight in gold and with everything going on a bit of rudeness is the least of our worries.' His tone brings our egos back down to size and we nod back feeling a little humbled.

'The vans are ready and I heard what you said, Kelly is getting someone from the engineering lot to go with you for when you do the DIY store....'

'Are we going to have enough room in the vans Chris? Supermarkets, chemists and the warehouse place...'

'It's taken care off; you got two more vans going with you.'

'Fucking hell Chris,' Clarence flares up again, 'there's only eight of us. How the hell are we supposed to guard five bloody vans and crews and clear the buildings too?'

'The vans have armed guards, they can protect their own vehicles and you focus on the buildings.'

'They've got shotguns Chris, double barrelled shotguns that take time to re-load.'

'What do you want Clarence? We're keeping the other assault rifles here. You've just got to do the best you can. Everyone has to.'

'If we get a heavy contact those guards will be fucked,' Clarence seethes, his already flushed face going a deeper shade of red.

'And you've got a fucking great big machine gun on your armoured fucking vehicle and the best fighters this fort have are with you. Cope!' Chris snarls back.

'Clarence,' I say in a low tone and surprisingly he backs down. Glancing at me with a single nod.

'Sorry boss,' he growls.

'We'll do the best we can Chris,' I try my hand at diplomacy.

'I've told the vans crews that if it goes bent they're to just focus on getting back here with whatever they've got,' Chris explains in a calm voice but his face still looks angry.

'Sounds good mate, have many more turned up here today?'

'A few, we get a steady trickle all the time. Word must be spreading or something.'

'Ah that's us, we're putting posters up and leaving flyers on car windscreens,' I say with a smile.

'Well can you stop it please, zombies can read you know,' he smiles back easing the tension.

'Come on then,' I speak up so everyone can hear me, 'load up.' I take the driving position again this time with Dave up front and Clarence squeezing his frame into the hole to man the heavy machine gun.

'Right, we're off,' the engine starts with a roar and we pull out, going past the vans to the front. They pull out behind us and I glance round quickly to see the others sat quietly in the back. Heads dropping as they doze in the hot air. Lani in the corner with her feet stretched out and her head resting on a bundled up jacket.

'Has anyone got a hat? My head is going to burn.' Clarence calls down to a few low sniggers.

They rummage about until Dave pulls an old camouflage wide brimmed sun hat from a dusty cupboard. He bangs the material against his leg a few times to get the muck and grime off before handing it up.

'Christ, I haven't seen one of these for years,' Clarence chuckles. Climbing back into the passenger seat Dave settles back and takes a long drink from a bottle of Lucozade. He bends over his bag and drags another one out, unscrewing the cap and handing it to me.'

'Cheers Dave,' I gulp at the warm syrupy liquid.

'Simon, get those back doors open. There will be a catch to hold them in place, get some airflow in here,' Dave calls out and twists back round to face the front.

'Why do call them Simon and Alex?' I ask him quietly.

'That's their names Mr Howie,' he replies.

'Everyone else calls them Blowers and Cookey.'

'They do but the lads need to have that different regard for me which is maintained by using a different more formal manner of addressing them.'

'So if we all called them Simon and Alex you'd be calling them by their surnames?'

'Yes Mr Howie.'

'Oh, okay. You do fit into the sergeant's role very well.'

'I know Mr Howie,' he says bluntly.

'The room clearances went well I thought.'

'They did, they need more practise though.'

'We all do! But I think we'll get that by the looks of the list they've given us.'

'Maybe we could it with just knives next time?'

'Just knives? That sounds a bit dangerous mate.'

'More dangerous than charging a horde of the undead with one magazine and a bayonet?' He replies quickly and I know full well he's referring to the service station when I exited from the back to reach the Saxon.

'That was an act of necessity, what you're proposing isn't.'

'Knife skills are a necessity; they won't always have guns with bullets.'

'True, so what…just with their bayonets then?'

'Yes, but held free hand and not fixed on. I'll be with them to make sure nothing bad happens,' his tone isn't bragging, just matter of fact.

'They've had plenty of practise with the axes and Lani is already brilliant with a knife.'

'Axes have range Mr Howie and they are also easy to drop or slip from wet hands. Nothing beats a knife.'

'A gun.'

'Sorry Mr Howie?'

'A gun beats a knife.'

'Only if it has bullets.'

'A sword then that beats a knife.'

'Swords take years to learn how to use, plus there are many different types of swords.'

'Same with knives.'

'To an extent yes, but a knife either slashes or cuts. Swords parry, thrust, block, sweep…'

'Okay okay, so nothing beats a knife?'

'No. Quiet, easily hidden, you can open a vein or penetrate the heart. Instant death, slow death, disable the target without killing it.'

'Jesus Dave, so what is your favourite type of knife?'

'Oh I don't have a favourite,' he suddenly looks animated and turns to face me, something he rarely does when we converse, normally choosing to watch the area around us, 'I have often thought what would be my favourite one but I don't think I could choose. There are some great knives out there, perfectly balanced for throwing, or long and thin for thrusting, then you get the big ones which are good for hacking...'

'If you had to choose one?'

'I couldn't Mr Howie. I like the variety of them. So many different styles, weights, handles and grips. Chefs knives are very good, and butchers knives too.'

'Right...I see. So we know what to get for your birthday then?'

'What?'

'Eh?' I glance at him.

'What will you get for my birthday?' he asks seriously.

'Knives Dave, we'll get you some knives.'

'I've got loads already.'

'Yeah I know, it was a...'

'Can I choose them? I know birthday presents are meant to be a surprise but firstly I don't like surprises,' an image of Dave walking into a darkened room that suddenly fills with light and everyone shouting *surprise* flits through my mind, followed by Dave slaughtering half of them before they've got halfway through the word, 'and also Mr Howie, I might already have the same knives you would get, plus I might not like the ones you get which could lead to you being offended when I tell you I don't want it.'

'Would you say that then?'

'Say what?'

'If I gave you a present and you didn't like it would you say you didn't like it.'

'Yes.'

'But…right…yeah I guess that's the best thing.'

'So can I choose my own birthday knife please?'

'Yes mate…I didn't actually mean…no, no of course we can do that, we'll go knife shopping.'

'Okay.'

'When is your birthday? That might help.'

'Today,' he replies.

'What? Are you bloody joking? Why didn't you say something?'

'Yes.'

'Yes what?'

'Sorry, Yes Mr Howie.'

'No I wasn't correcting the way you replied, I meant what are you saying yes to?'

'Oh, that it was a joke.'

'What? So it's not your birthday?'

'No.'

'Fuck's sake,' I shake my head with a chuckle, 'so when is your birthday? And how old are you?'

'I'm…'

'Mr Howie,' Blowers calls out quickly, 'I think you just missed the turn off.'

'Eh? Did I? Shit, is there another one?'

'Not for a few miles,' he replies. I glance round to see him holding the map and wonder why he's doing it instead of Dave.

'Right, bollocks. I'll turn round and head back,' I slow the Saxon down and start to turn round in the wide motorway. The Saxon has the turning circle of an oil tanker and it takes several attempts to get it facing back the other way. Five big vans all wait with grinning drivers and guards waving at us as we slowly head back past them. I keep the speed low until they've all turned and behind us then move down to the junction, bouncing over the rough surface to turn onto the slip road.

'If any of the guards have infantry training they could man the GPMG while we do room clearance,' Dave suggests once we're back on the right road.

'Good idea,' I reply.

'Gives us two teams of four then,' he adds.

'Take the next left,' Blowers shouts from the back. I take the turn; leaning forward and trying to let the intense heat between my back and seat dissipate. This is oppressively hot, I feel lethargic and de-motivated, which is a dangerous state of mind with what we're now doing.

'You got any more Lucozade Dave?' I think I'm going to need it.

CHAPTER EIGHTEEN

D^{AY SIX}

The small town in the south of England is being gradually purged. Bodies litter nearly every street. The decaying corpses left to rot in the sun and eaten by rats before they too turned and headed off deep into the sewers, urged on to Howie and his group in the service station.

Now, after six long days of unbroken hot weather the bodies are diseased and infested with maggots.

She moves down the street, sticking to the shadows. Her bulk slightly diminished from the constant action, food growing scarcer by the day. The streams that ran through the soft ground have dwindled to a trickle but they serve he purpose to provide water and a place to cool down.

Every day she searches the town, seeking the things and destroying them quickly. Her skills now honed to an almost perfect pattern. She sizes the things up, working out the best angle of approach. The bigger ones are taken down by a leap to the chest or back as she uses her body weight to slam them down and rip their throats out. The smaller ones are simply ragged about until the life leaves them.

Every street has signs of her battles. Every corpse has her teeth marks on them. She patrols and still feels the sense of loss from her pack being gone.

She's met other people here and there, skulking through the roads during the daytime, packs together and single ones trying to escape. When she sees them she makes noise and runs. But now the people panic and run away from her. They throw things and make loud noise.

She senses their fear and wags her tail to show she's happy, not aggressive. They don't see the signs and keep her at bay. She senses these packs don't want her and keeps her distance.

The dog picks out where the dens are that still have people inside, they don't show themselves but she can smell them.

By late afternoon on the sixth day she's following a new scent trail that clings to the ground. Someone moving through here just a short time ago. The path she follows is jerky, seemingly going left and right between the big things left on the road. The scent smells of the living but there is a strong smell of fear here too. Fear and terror that pours from the trail. It must be a little one. Only a little one would leave a trail of fear like this.

A little one alone in the open. She follows the trail weaving back and forth across the street. The trail leads to the entrance doors of the dens but never goes across the threshold. It swerves and deviates between the big things.

Closer now, the smell is stronger, fresher and not yet contaminated by the overriding stench of death and decay.

She pauses and feels the sudden change in air pressure. The sky darkens with thick cloud. Fat drops of water splatter the ground and she looks up as a torrential downpour commences.

Within seconds her coat is soaked and surface water is running everywhere. She laps at the fresh sweet tasting water and savours the cooling effect of the liquid soaking her fur. Dropping her nose she can just make the scent trail out and starts off trying to follow it but loses it when the water becomes too powerful and washes all grounds smells away.

Sheets of rain lash the road, drumming on the cars and vehicles as the dog shakes her body, sending thick splatters of rain high up and to the sides. The sky is grey and overcast, the heat gone for just a few minutes.

The little one must be here somewhere. The scent trail was recent and judging by the erratic route already taken it could be just a little further ahead.

Her sense of smell is ruined for a short time, hearing diminished too from the percussion of raindrops all around. Left with just eye sight she moves on, moving over to walk down the middle of the road. Her eyes are not as sharp or clear as humans but they are excellent motion detectors. The predator using her nose to find the smell, then her ears to find the direction and finally her eyes to look for flight of the prey.

She pushes on, pausing every few minutes to lap at the water and shake her coat. At the end of the road she holds still, waiting in the middle of the junction and looking down each side in turn. The cadavers left here are pelted with rain. The congealed and dried blood loosens from the incessant action of the raindrops causing little pink streams and tributaries to flow along.

She sits down in the flowing water and waits. Checking each side and looking for any signs of where the little one went.

CHAPTER NINETEEN

DAY SIX

'Damn that's a big dog,' Paco mutters to himself. A trait he has developed after spending the last few days alone. After seeing Lucy stood outside he panicked and ran screaming down the stairs. Such was the fear and tension that exploded from him and warped his mind he ran straight out of the front door and froze on the spot at the sight of them all. They must have been moving all night to have got there so quickly.

Paco simply ran away. Not taking into account their slow daytime shuffle or stopping to get supplies. He ran. Round the back of the house and deep into the woods. He kept running. Fear driving him. Terror propelling his legs. Panic pumping his lungs and heart. Without sleeping all night he still maintained a steady few miles before slowing to a fast walk and getting his breathing back under control.

After that he kept moving, not wanting to stay anywhere

for more than a few hours. He kept to the woods for the rest of that day, drinking water from streams and refusing to listen to his starving stomach.

By evening he realised he had a choice of staying in the open or finding somewhere to hole up. But both options presented terrifying scenarios that whipped up gruesome images in his mind. Out in the open where they could get to him with ease, or somewhere inside where he could get trapped.

By dusk he was on the outskirts of a town, watching fields give way to streets and roads and the rural slowly change to the suburban and then the urban. Finding some shops on the main town access road he hunkered down and watched the front for any movement. He needed food, any food. Having not eaten the previous day or during the night and after the many hours of nervous energy, staying awake and then running all day he knew he wouldn't be able to keep going without sustenance.

The shops looked looted, windows smashed and doors ripped off. He edged closer and closer, moving between abandoned vehicles and dropping down every few metres to listen and watch. Finally satisfied he sprinted the last few metres to the first door and crept inside.

The floor was littered with debris but fortunately no blood or monsters. Rummaging through the litter he found a bottle of cola, a few chocolate bars and bags of potato chips. Scooping them up he retreated to a corner and with both eyes fixed in the front door he devoured it all within a couple of minutes.

The sugary drink felt wonderful and he felt his limbs shaking from the rush of quick fix energy. He checked along the floor and quickly peered under the shelving units, finding more bottles of fizzy drink and junk food. Snatching them up he ran outside, not wanting to push his luck too far and risk getting trapped.

Round the back of the shops he found a long row of flat roofed garages and lock up units. A ladder lying on its side propped against a wall. He took the ladder and used it to climb onto the concrete roof of the garages, pulling the ladder up behind him. He skirted the edge, checking all the sides were too high for anyone to jump or climb up without using something. It was the best he could do so he went to the front and lay down behind the low wall. The rest of the food was gone quickly and he lay stretched out on his back, knowing he couldn't be seen from the ground.

It took less than ten minutes for his eyes to start drooping, and another five minutes before he submitted to the lure of sleep.

As the night fell properly he heard the howls for the first time. The song of the undead as they faced the moon and roared their hunger out. Coming awake instantly with wide eyes he felt the hairs on his arms and neck standing up. The howls were coming from every direction but none of them were that close. They went on for ages, freezing his stomach and sending his blood pounding through his ears. When they ended suddenly he stayed completely stock still, repeating the prayers he practised so well the night before. With his lips moving silently his heart rate gradually slowed down to a steady rhythm and once more his eyes fell closed.

Since then he'd kept moving during the day, not knowing where he was going and finding different places to hide. He rested for only a few hours at a time, believing that if stayed anywhere for longer than that the monsters would find him.

In his mind Lucy was stalking him with the pitchfork monster. They led a horde of monsters intent on finding him and devouring his living flesh. Revenge for leaving her trapped and causing her death.

Because of that very fact, that Lucy had become trapped so easily, he avoided going in any houses unless he was either absolutely desperate for water or food and there was no other choice. Even then, the very houses he did enter were checked quickly, food and drink was snatched up and taken somewhere else to consume.

Six days in and when he felt the first drops of rain he smiled for the first time in days. Beautiful, life giving fresh clean water pouring from the sky. He stopped moving for a few minutes and stood with his face turned up, savouring the feeling of the cool water drenching his face. Mouth open and drinking it down, he scrubbed at his face feeling the grease and grime that coated his skin.

Then he saw the dog walking out of the junction a couple of hundred metres away. He hunkered down quickly, using a car to shield him from view. He tried using the windows to peer through but the rain was cascading down them and obscuring his view.

'What you doin' boy?' He murmured to himself poking his head round the corner and glimpsing the dog just sat there. The rain was sheeting down, reducing visibility. With his heart hammering in fright at the size of the beast and the way it was just sat there looking up and down the road. Was it tracking him? Looking for a tasty meal? The thought suddenly hit him making his stomach drop and his blood run cold. A monster dog. It was a monster dog searching for him. Lucy and the pitchfork man must be following it somewhere. Shit! How did he let them get so close?

The sight of all the bodies had already unnerved him, corpses littering every street and road. Body after body with their throats ripped out, blood, gore, bits of flesh everywhere. He'd only ventured this far into the town to look for more food and he terrified himself with images of whatever had done this amount of killing. But all the dead bodies were monsters; he could see that much was clear from the open eyes staring out lifeless but still red and bloodshot and their mouths covered in blood and old festering wounds.

He had to move now and use the noise of the rain to cover his retreat. If it stopped raining the dog would find him easily. Moving backwards he crept along the side of the next car, feeling with his hands for the end of the vehicle and quickly tucking in behind it.

Eyes fixed up the street where the dog was still sat he retreated one car length at a time, beating a hasty withdrawal. Clothes sodden and clinging to his frame, the muscles of his arms bulging against the wet material, his shoulders flexed as he stretched his arm back feeling for the end of the car, his big thighs tensed from holding a crouched position.

He was getting further away, just a bit further and he could turn and run. Find somewhere to hide and wait for the dog to go. It might not be able to track him with all this water on the ground.

Easing round the front of the next car he kept his left arm flexed back, feeling along the metal side. Past the first door and he felt for the rubber edging of the window on the next door. Sliding his hand along the smooth glass and feeling the edge. Now the rear panel and he lowered his hand to gently rub along the side as it curved in. He was there, at the back of the next car. One more to go and he could run. The rain was still coming down with such fury that he couldn't see the end of the street where the dog was but prayed that it wouldn't come bounding towards him.

Creeping back with his hand still stretched out he groped and made small circular motions, feeling for the next vehicle. His fingertips brushed something, he moved back and extended his hand. With his focus firmly on the road he failed to register the soft yielding nature of the thing he was groping.

Eyes suddenly wide, mouth dropping open he twisted his upper body slowly round, his hand still pressing against the softness. It moved and he yelped, staggering out into the street and tripping over a corpse. Sprawled out he stared back in utter horror at the monster shuffling towards him. The red eyes clear through the rain and blood washed from its face to reveal sunken cheeks and pale dirty yellowing skin.

Whimpering in alarm Paco crabbed backwards, his hands groping and plunging into the decaying chest of another corpse. He scrabbled his feet which slipped on the wet surface. Bringing his hand up he looked in horror at the entrails hanging from his fingers. Screaming he backed away, hands and feet whirling like crazy but his body refused to work in harmony, the monster kept coming. Lips pulled back to show filthy teeth and the drooling saliva pouring out to mix with the water cascading down its face.

Paco crabbed and slithered, tripping over more bodies and landing heavily. Screaming in terror, this was it, this was the end. The monster had him. The head was lowering, the upper body bending as it prepared for the final lunge that would see his flesh stripped from his body.

Frozen in the grip of fear he clenched his eyes shut and gave a final prayer. The monster barked and snarled and came at him with a drumming noise. The drums of death coming for him. The monster barked again, louder and closer. Paco opened his eyes as the dog sprinted through the sheeting rain, puddles splashing as its feet pounded over the road. The monster came in for the lunge and was gone. A flash of black and was Paco staring up at the grey sky.

A ferocious snarling snapped him back, the dog had the thing between its teeth ragging it up and down the street. Gripping the neck and shaking with violent fury. Paco sat there mesmerised at the power of the beast, the strength it had was awesome, flinging the monster about like a rag doll.

The dog ripped the throat out and sank its teeth back into the wound, gnashing and tearing with almighty snarls emanating from its throat.

The dog stepped back and stared down at the corpse of the monster as though willing it get back up and try again. It stepped back again and shook its head, sending bloodied water spraying off in all directions. Then it turned its huge head and fixed its gaze on Paco. Soft beautiful brown eyes surrounded by black hair with flecks of brown. White teeth clear from its open mouth, long pink tongue hanging out.

The dog padded slowly towards Paco who remained frozen to the spot on his arse with his hands holding his upper body up, legs slightly bent. He might be fit but even he couldn't outrun a dog and the animal was huge with a thick coat, long legs and solid shoulders. Its big head was held high, it paused to drop down and lap at the puddled water then kept coming.

He'd survived the monster to die from a dog. Paco Maguire, the world's most successful action movie star, survivor of Armageddon, killed by a wild dog in some shitty English street. Only there would be no one to report this, no worldwide press coverage or people rushing out to buy his movies. No star on Hollywood Boulevard. No one would miss him. Dying alone and forgotten. He missed home, he missed his family. Tears poured from his eyes as he gave a final prayer. The dog was so close now. Moving slowly and willing its prey to run or do something. But Paco couldn't move, the fear crippled him.

The rain was coming down like arrows, straight from the sky to the ground but behind the dog there was water flying up to the left and right. His eyes stared at the phenomenon as his brain slowly registered that the dog was wagging its tail. The black bushy tail was moving from side to side, definitely wagging. Was that something they did before a kill? He thought back to the nature programmes he'd watched but couldn't recall ever seeing anything like it. It must be happy to have found a nice juicy meal.

The dog stopped moving. They locked eyes. Paco on his arse in the pouring rain and the dog stood within arm's reach staring across at him. Seconds passed. Neither of them moved, apart from the tail which wagged slowly.

The dog sat down and Paco looked down its belly at the lack of male genitalia.

'A girl?' he muttered to himself, 'you're a girl dog.' The dog's ears pricked and rotated forward. They stared at each other. It didn't look like it was about to eat him.

'Hi,' Paco whispered so quietly but the dog's ears pricked again and it stared hard at him. 'Good girl,' Paco tried the ultimate dog greeting and watched as the animal cocked its head to one side, the tail moving decidedly faster now.

'Good girl,' Paco said it again, louder this time and got the same reaction. It was sure not looking like it was about to rip his throat out, but those teeth…they were so big and sharp.

The dog whimpered and edged closer, dipping her head. She lowered down onto her tummy and whined again, edging closer, tail still going.

'Good girl,' Paco repeated and watched as the dog whined again and shuffled closer almost touching him. He stared at the dogs face, at her pleading brown eyes, she whined again softly.

He gently lifted his arm from behind him and brought it across his chest. The fingers stretched out and ever so slowly moving towards the dog's head. It saw the movement and shuffled closer, its paws now brushing the side of his leg.

Holding his breath and expecting the dog to lunge and remove his fingers before leaping to rip his throat out. His heart still hammering, thud thud thud in his chest. The world stopped spinning, time froze. Everything became still as his fingertips brushed the dogs face. It didn't savage him but stayed still. He brushed again, firmer this time, still it didn't attack him. He pressed his palm onto the top of the dog's broad head and stroked along its soft wet fur. The tail wagged faster and she whined again.

'Good girl!' Paco said. The dog lifted up quickly and pushed into him, rubbing her head against his chest, whining in soft tones. 'Hey beautiful,' Paco muttered and rubbed the dog's head harder, bringing his other hand up to stroke along her back. It was too much for Paco, too surreal. He laughed loud and hugged the dog, holding her soaking wet body close. She didn't pull away but lowered down until her upper body was resting on his legs, her head thrown up as he stroked her soft muzzle. She pushed into him harder, her weight and strength knocking him back onto the ground. He laughed with delight as the dog stood over him and started licking his neck and ears. He ruffled her fur, stroked her ears and laughed with abandoned glee.

She whined louder and moved round him, taking care not to tread on his body. He laughing, her with tail going crazy and they relished in the first contact that either of them had experienced in days.

Paco rubbed her shoulders, feeling the solid muscle packed in, he rubbed her tummy and stroked her thick neck. She moved to the side, dropping down as he bent over her. Laughing and fussing her. She rolled onto her side, letting him rub her tummy and boxing out with her paws. Paco got to his feet, took two steps back and patted his thighs. She responded instantly, jumping up and walking quickly towards him, holding a paw out and whining. Laughter came from his throat as he bent over and fussed her again. She snaked round his legs, weaving round his body and pressing herself against him.

'Boy am I glad to meet you,' Paco laughed, 'I thought you

were a monster dog, I did! I thought you were going to eat Paco but you didn't did you? No, you saved Paco and was a very good girl,' the sound of his own voice was pleasant and he kept the baby talk up as they fussed and moved with each other.

The dog sensed the fear in him. After hearing him scream she ran through the rain and took the thing down. She knew it was going to kill the man so she killed it first. The man stayed down and she could tell he was cowering in terror. He was a big man, much bigger than most other men but liquid fell from his eyes like the little one did. He seemed like a little one, the nerves and fear in him was just like a little one.

She stayed low, showing him she was not a threat. When he touched her head the connection was made and she felt a flood of chemicals coursing through her system as he stroked and patted her. The noises he made were soft and pleasant. She licked his neck and pushed against him enjoying the feel of another body.

Then he laughed, she remembered the sound of it from the pack. He laughed like the little one used to laugh only deeper and louder, but it was a nice sound and she knew it meant he was happy.

The fear was still there, inside him. She could sense it and it made her protective instinct that much stronger.

CHAPTER TWENTY

While most of the undead pour from the towns and cities to join Darren on his quest south to the fort, some remain. There are other threats than the one posed by Howie and Dave. More killers of the host bodies that have to be dealt with.

The infection knows this and it also knows it has suffered too many losses from the one that hasn't turned. The infection knows this is an animal and from the collective conscious of the hosts it controls it can understand everything there is to know about the dog. What it cannot comprehend is why it has not turned.

Through the many eyes of the host bodies it knows the dog has taken in the blood and juices from its victims and that blood carries the infection onwards. From that collective conscious and the amassed intelligence it has knowledge of anti-bodies, of genetic mutations, DNA, cell structure so it can accept the dog could be a fluke. A one off that carries a gene that produces a chemical that renders it immune to the infection. What it cannot accept is why the domestic pet is killing so many hosts.

The dog can't be turned so it is there-fore irrelevant to the infection. It does not have human intelligence and cannot communicate. The dog is a pack animal with a life span far less than the humans and without food and water it will surely die soon. So why is it killing the hosts? The infection could accept if the dog was taking a few host bodies for food, but it doesn't eat them.

The dog hunts the host bodies, tracks them down and kills them. The numbers are mounting and with the infection drawing on resources to join Darren it knows it cannot withstand such losses.

The dog must be destroyed. Hosts will have to be left back from the exodus to join Darren so they can find the dog and destroy it.

This is fact and it must be done soon.

CHAPTER TWENTY-ONE

D<small>AY ELEVEN</small>

The mother sits in the back of the van, her baby clasped in her arms and her toddler son sat next to her on the wheel arch.

'Water?' The Polish man asks with a heavy accent and waves a bottle at her.

'Thank you,' she replies wearily, taking the water and first giving some to her son then herself. The occupants of the van talk quietly amongst themselves, men women and children and all of them Polish. Some speak English and they make an effort to include her.

Bangs sound out from the front and a muted exchange of Polish words takes places, a message is passed which seems to revive them all from flagging in the oppressive heat of the vehicle.

The mother already knows what has been said, she can

tell from the reactions that they must be close to their destination.

'We close now yes?' A woman leans forward and touches her arm, smiling through tired looking eyes and holding her own baby close.

'Thank you,' the mother says. Since leaving her house the going has been hard. Far harder than she could ever imagined life could be. The fuel in the car was gone within a day of aimlessly driving about, trying to find something but not knowing what or where.

On foot they moved from village to village. During the day she had to risk entering houses and searching for food and drink, knowing she had to eat to produce milk for her baby and provide for her son. At night she found places and secured them into one of the upstairs back rooms, urging and threatening her son not to make a sound during the hours of darkness.

Several times the baby woke her, gurgling and making ready to wail. She pacified her quickly, giving the breast and feeding whenever she cried in a desperate attempt to keep her quiet. Sod the instruction of the midwife and the lessons she learnt with her son, *don't always give the baby a feed when it cries or you'll make a rod for yourself.* Yeah right, try doing that when your surrounded by undead things.

The mother saw other survivors here and there, families that were polite but didn't want the added responsibility of more mouths to feed, or a screaming baby to take care off. The Polish were different though. They had stayed all together in one house, the men going out to find whatever meagre supplies they could and eking them out to make sure everyone ate.

They took her in readily enough and she in turn helped with the other children and babies. The men came back yesterday, saying they'd heard from other survivors of a fort on the coast, one that was filled with doctors, soldiers and police officers. It was already late in the day, too late to travel and risk being outside so they stayed put for the night and prepared to leave.

Now, after being in the intense heat of the van for several hours while they drove around the south coast they finally found the road leading to the fort. Passing through the ruined housing estate and looking at the people working to pile the bodies into mounds.

They passed over the flatlands, the driver eyeing the fort in the distance and praying it would be all they hoped for.

A man with a shotgun waved them down and indicated for them to pull up on the side. Other people and cars were in front of them, being asked questions from people holding clipboards and dressed like police officers.

He relayed what he could see through the bulkhead, shouting that there was order here, a queue and people with guns and clipboards.

'We open the back yes?' The driver asked the guard.

'Do what mate?' The guard came closer to the window and cupped one ear, indicating the man to repeat what he said.

'The back? We open it yes? It very hot.'

'Eh? Oh you got people in there 'ave ya? Yeah mate, open it up they'll bleedin' melt in that oven.'

'I open yes?' The man asked with a confused look on his face, not understanding much of what was just said.

'Yes mate, that's what I said didn't I?'

The driver, still not fully sure of the answer, climbed down and walked slowly to the rear doors, pointing and gesturing, nodding the whole time. The doors were opened to the relieved sounds of the occupants clambering out looking red faced and very flushed.

'Is good yes?' The driver asked the guard.

'Yeah very good,' the guard replied slightly shocked at how many people were in the back. 'Right me old mate, you gotta wait here to be checked, shouldn't be too long, you want some water?'

'I not understand,' the driver replied with a puzzled expression. Words were exchanged between the group and the driver's faced to one of understanding.

'Sorry his English is not good, we understand to wait here?' Another man explains.

'Yep, wait here and someone will come and get you.'

'You say there is water?'

'Yep, I'll get you some, hang on.'

'This is the fort yes?' A woman asks.

'Yep, nice and safe here, we got plenty of space and some food, we got doctors too,' the guard replies before walking off. His words are translated, smiles spread across faces as the relief washes through them.

The mother sits down on the side of the path, little realising the blood shed that took place there just a few days ago. Her son, on finally being free from the van, runs about excitedly with the other children.

'Ere Terri, got some for ya?' The guard shouts as he walks to the big umbrella giving shade to the boxes of water bottles left there for the new people arriving.

'Cheers,' Terri shouts back and glances down the line. People queuing quietly and drinking from the water bottles. They all look a state, sunburnt, clothes filthy and faces gaunt. Hair greasy and plastered to their heads. Some of them still in pyjamas and god only knows how they've survived so many days in nightclothes.

All morning and afternoon she's been out here, processing the new arrivals, recording details of names, dates of birth, former addresses and any skills they possess. She asks each one if they've had contact with the things, if they have been exposed to any blood, saliva or other bodily fluids. Most of them answer no, having simply hid from the undead and only moving during the daytime. Those that do admit to having contact are marked on the sheets, ready for Doctor Roberts and his team to examine them thoroughly.

She explains the same thing over and over, 'when you go through you will be examined in medical tents, after that you will be taken to an area where you can have a wash and get some food and water. After that you'll be allocated a space, if you have any food with you, please hand it over so we can stockpile everything we have.'

Questions are thrown at her, desperate survivors asking about relatives and being told there are lists inside of all the refugees and people known to have not survived.

Hard work but each one is rewarding. The look of relief the survivors show her, the outpouring of emotion at finally being in a safe place with proper people holding clipboards.

'New lot are Polish,' the guard remarks as he passes by carrying a box of water bottles.

'Do they speak English?'

'Some do,' he shouts back. She keeps on, moving from group to group, taking details and recording all the vital information.

'Ready for the next ones,' a teenage boy runs over to pass the message.

'Okay,' Terri smiles at the small group at the front of the queue, 'follow Joe here and he'll take you through,' she passes the sheets with the groups details to the smiling boy before he leads them to the outer gates.

'This heat,' she takes a drink of water and wipes the sweat from her forehead with the back of her hand. She wishes she didn't have to wear her black police top but Sergeant

Hopewell was adamant that new arrivals should see someone in uniform so they understand straight away that this is an organised place with rules.

Terri moves to the next group, repeating the process and answering the questions they have with patience and empathy. Steadily she works her way down the line, handing sheets to Joe as he comes out for the next admissions.

She reaches the long white van at the rear and takes a long swig of water before heading to the back and the crowd of people sat about.

'Hi, I'm Terri, one of the officers here at the fort,' Terri introduces herself, speaking slow and clear so they can understand her. She explains the process that's already been repeated so many times. Her trained eyes easily see the ones that understand her and the ones that struggle to keep up and she waits patiently for the translations to be given.

She rests one knee on the hard earth, using it to steady the clipboard while working her way through the group, recording the names which takes longer because of the language barrier.

Reaching the mother she takes her name and those of her children and runs through the question and answer session, listening intently as the woman explains how she came to be with the Polish people.

'And before that, where were you?' Terri asks.

'We were on foot for a few days, just going from house to house for food,' the mother explains, 'that was after the car ran out of petrol, before that we were driving about but we didn't know where to go or anything.'

'Oh dear, that sounds awful,' Terri says softly.

'You've no idea,' the mother replies with fresh tears spilling from her eyes, 'I was so scared the baby would cry at night, or they'd hear us. I had a knife but I was going to use it on us if they found us,' she sobs.

'I understand,' Terri squeezes the woman's arm, not in the least bit shocked at the admission made by the woman after hearing so many awful tales of survival. 'It's safe here; we've got guards with weapons, soldiers, doctors, food...'

'I...I just didn't think we'd get through it,' the woman breaks down, two of the Polish women come over and rub her back, one taking the baby while the woman releases her frustration and fears.

'Hey it's okay,' Terri says.

'It was so bad, so bad,' the woman sobs, 'all that killing and I thought they were going to get inside the house...'

'But you're safe now,' Terri maintains the soft tone.

'All night they were going, banging and killing....I was so terrified...I held that bloody knife to my baby's throat....the window smashed and I thought they were coming in, there was so many, so many of them...'

'But they didn't get in?' Terri asks trying to draw the details out, hoping it will soothe the exhausted looking woman.

'No,' she sniffs and gives thanks to a tissue handed from one of the Polish women.

'See, that's a good thing,' Terri says, 'you made it safely.'

'Poor dog,' the woman sobs quietly.

'Oh you left your dog at home?' Terri asks with sympathy.

'Not my dog, the dog from outside...'

'What about the dog?' Terri probes.

'The dog that killed them all, we had to leave it...poor thing just sat there as we drove off, I felt bloody terrible...'

'Hang on love, a dog killed what?' Terri leant forward confused.

'Those things, it killed them things outside the house. They were trying to get in and the dog stayed out there all day and all night killing 'em, I put water down for it,' she adds quickly as if that will ease the guilt she feels, 'but the noise, the noise as it killed 'em.'

'The dog killed the undead?' Terri asked, avoiding using the zombie word.

'Yeah, loads of them. All bloody day and all bloody night too…'

'What kind of dog was it?'

'An Alsatian, a bloody big one too. Huge it was.'

'You said it was there all day and all night? When was this love?' Terri asked feeling a prickle on the back of her neck.

'I don't know, er…maybe the second or third night…I don't know it's all a blur.'

'It was when it just happened then?'

'Yeah, we we're still in the house.'

'Love this is really important, did you see the dog attacking the things in the day?'

'Loads of them, they kept coming and the dog kept killing 'em.'

'And it bit them? Made them bleed?'

'Course it bloody did, it tore half their throats out…'

'And then all night too?'

'Oh the night,' the woman burst into a fresh bout of tears, 'so many, when I looked out the next day the ground was just covered in bodies.'

'The dog didn't turn?' Terri finally asks the million dollar question.

'No miss, it was fine when we left, is…is that normal? I don't know?' She asked with a shrug but Terri was already off, running to the outer gates and calling for Joe.

CHAPTER TWENTY-TWO

D^{AY ELEVEN}

'Supermarket,' I say needlessly as we pull into the huge empty car park and drive towards the main entrance, 'just like being back at work eh Dave?'

'This isn't a Tesco store Mr Howie.'

'Well yeah apart from that.'

'And it's smaller than our store too.'

'Right fine, then it's nothing like being back at work,' the heat is getting to me. It's getting to all of us. Even the lads in the back have stopped their constant banter.

'Looks looted,' Clarence calls down.

'No shit,' I mutter under my breath. All the windows along the front are smashed in and the main doors have been obliterated by a car driven into them at speed. The car is still wedged in the entrance way. A few corpses in the car park but nothing like we've seen elsewhere.

'We'll have a quick look, might be something left,' I grab

my bag and assault rifle and climb down onto the glaring concrete surface of the car park. The heat seems to be coming back up off the ground as well as from the sky.

'Nick, you cover the GPMG mate, Clarence you better come with us...Lads...Lads what's going on?' Reaching the back I hear a heated exchange of words between Cookey and Blowers, both of them red faced and looking angry.

'Nothing,' Blowers looks away.

'Sorry Mr Howie,' Cookey murmurs and shoulders his bag before picking up his assault rifle. They both walk off, heading opposite directions.

'What happened there?' I ask Lani as she steps down from the back.

'Nothing, just the heat,' she answers quietly.

'You sure?' I don't want any ill feeling between the lads.

'Cookey made some funny comment and Blowers bit, Cookey bit back, that was all,' Tom explains.

'Fair enough,' and it is fair enough. I can't expect them to be perfectly behaved happy chaps all the time. 'Dave, you take lead with Lani.'

The rest of us hold back a little as Dave and Lani move towards the main doors. I signal to the van drivers to stay put, Pete's in the first van and waves back, acknowledging my request.

We climb through the debris, kicking bits of metal framework out of the way. Once inside we can see the place has been emptied and left in a complete mess. We walk down the main central aisle peering down each secondary aisle. The food has all gone; just the toiletries section has any stock left.

'Dave, you check the back store room...*Howie to Pete, you receiving me?*'

'Pete to Mr Howie, loud and clear.'

'Food has all gone, just some bits left in the toiletries section, we might as well have it...there's some nappies and baby stuff here.'

'Yep, we'll get some people in now.'

'Not much blood,' Tom remarks, 'no bodies inside either.'

'It's not a twenty four hours store so it would have been closed when it happened,' I wipe my sweating hand down my trouser leg as Dave walks back towards us with Blowers and Lani.

'Clear,' he shakes his head.

'We'll have this lot anyway, might come in useful.' We grab trolleys and help the van crews load them up. It's done within a few minutes and we head back out, stopping to force a path for the trolleys through the debris at the front door.

Outside we spread out and keep watch while the crews load one of the vans up.

'Done,' Pete shouts. Even the crews and guards are silent. Everyone is silent. I've never known heat this before.

'Load up,' I call out and head back to the Saxon. 'Where next?' I ask once we're all inside.

'Er...we'll go for the chemists in the town centre, then the medical place and finally the cash and carry on the exit road,' Clarence says back in the front and examining the map book.

'Which way?' I ask bluntly.

'Out the car park and right onto the main road.' Without another word I pull away, easing the Saxon along and waiting for the vans to loop round and get behind us.

'How's the fuel? Clarence asks.

'Halfway, keep an eye out for somewhere to fill up.'

'Roger that,' he says equally as bluntly and we drive on in silence.

CHAPTER TWENTY-THREE

DAY SIX

'I gotta eat something,' Paco tells the dog as they walk down the rain drenched street. His stomach gurgling with a feeling of hollow emptiness. Feeling slightly safer now but still checking behind him and to the sides every few seconds. He looks to the houses either side of the residential street and thinks of the food that could be inside. Mouth-watering at the thoughts of eating decent food he stops and looks about, checking for signs of the monsters.

One lesson he'd learnt for sure was to avoid houses that had the doors closed and locked, Lucy had gone into one such house and look what happened to her. No, he'd stick with the ones that had the doors already open, hoping and praying the monsters would have found their way out in their search for flesh and brains.

'You hungry girl?' Paco asks. The dog stared up at him,

ears pricked, eyes watchful and intent. 'I'm hungry, I'm starving hungry...what say we get some food?'

The fear starts to build as soon as he enters the garden path leading to house. The same fear that had gripped him since that first night. He stops halfway along the path, straining his ears for any sounds of movement in the house. Nothing. He examines the windows. The drapes are open but with net curtains so he couldn't get a good view of inside.

Terror started to build quickly, his legs feeling rubbery and weak. Stomach flipping over as he wrings his hands. He watches with surprise as the dog trots straight past him walking into the house, heading straight down the hall to the back. Paco moves forward, stopping at the threshold and examining the inside. No blood or signs of death here, it even smelled fairly normal.

'Dog? Hey dog?' Paco calls out, breathing a sigh of relief as the dog walks out of a doorway staring at him.

'Is it safe?' He asks, half expecting the dog to reply. He ventures in carefully, one step at a time. The dog walks straight past him and through another door, then re-appears a few seconds later panting.

'What about up there?' Paco asks pointing to the stairs. He takes a tentative step towards the stairs and reaches his arm out to grip the handrail. The dog takes the lead again, moving ahead and bounding up the stairs, disappearing into the rooms. Re-appearing as Paco gets to the top.

'All clear?' Paco asks quietly. He moves carefully from room to room, grimacing as the dog sticks her head into the toilet bowl and laps at the water.

Back downstairs he again checks every room with the dog trailing closely after him. In the kitchen he makes sure the back door can be opened and there was an escape route before going back to the hallway and closing the front door.

In the kitchen he opens the fridge, gagging at the stench

and warm stale air. Pulling tins from the cupboards he hardly glances at the foreign looking labels and gets them opened quickly. Using a spoon to shovel the contents into his mouth. Cold baked beans never tasted so good, the tomato sauce was so rich and juicy. Groaning with pleasure he wolfs the lot before opening the next tin to find small fat hot dog sausages inside.

'Want some?' The dog sat staring at him expectantly, *I've saved your life so feed me*. Fingers covered in brine he fished the meaty sausages out and gingerly held one out, she leans forward and takes it gently before swallowing it whole.

'Hungry huh?' He finds a bowl, filling it with the sausages and more beans from another tin. He places the bowl on the floor and steps back. The dog needs no further invitation and noisily shoves her nose in, shuffling the bowl along the floor as she gobbled the food down. Paco finds tinned fruit, vegetables, spaghetti. He re-fills the bowl with a tin of ravioli, thinking it will be better for the dog as it contains meat.

He finds eggs that were only a day or so out of date but with no power on he can't cook them up. Instead they're cracked open, put in the bowl and whisked up before being put down for the dog. Her appetite was as big as his as they munched and chomped their way through the edible contents of the kitchen.

Paco turns the cold faucet on and runs the water for a minute before filling a glass and another bowl for the dog. Fed, watered and feeling just slightly not so terrified he leans back against the kitchen top and watches as she starts cleaning herself. Front paws, sides then her privates. The sound is disgusting, like a greedy slurping noise of a child eating a milkshake.

Having eaten and on a come down from the adrenalin of almost being killed he feels exhausted and drained. Snatching a few hours sleep here and there over the last few days left him almost dizzy with tiredness. Stay here or find somewhere else? He considers the options carefully. They are in a locked house with two escape routes; one front and one rear. The rain might have served to cover their tracks too. He needed sleep that was for sure, and if not here then where?

After another circuit of the house, checking each door and window was secured he wearily climbs the stairs, stopping at the top and remembering how Lucy got trapped in a bedroom. The stairs were the only viable route of escape. Sofa, he would use the sofa in the lounge. That was midway between the front and back door.

Stretching out on the soft cushions he felt the pull of fatigue hitting him almost instantly. Turning on his side he looked over at the dog, sat on the floor and watching him with interest. Not only was she huge but she looked intelligent too, her eyes watching his every move, tomato sauce still round her muzzle but at least it wasn't blood, and better yet it wasn't his blood.

She watched as the man's eyes grew heavy and closed, his breathing changed and she knew he was sleeping. The fear radiated off him and he smelled too strong too. The things would be able to track him easily. She eased herself down, taking a position so she could see him and the door.

His signals were confusing. He gave her food and spoke to her in a soft voice which was what the pack leaders did, but he seems more like a little one in his actions and manner.

At least he didn't throw things and force her away. He wasn't her pack but he was somebody, and somebody was better nobody.

CHAPTER TWENTY-FOUR

DAY ELEVEN

'This doesn't look good either,' I say negotiating the debris littering the road. In the town centre now and it looks like the infection spread fast here. Friday night and the pubs would have been packed. Just one bite is all it would have taken and it would have spread so quickly. The shops are mostly smashed in with doors ripped off. Vehicles left dumped in the middle of the road get nudged out the way by the Saxon.

'There it is,' Clarence leans forward pointing to the left at the green cross sign attached to the wall. I drive the Saxon over, bringing it to a stop just past the shop front so the first van can park up outside.

We're out and scanning the area quickly. The lads moving out to stand in a rough circle and watch the many shops entrances and junctions. Dave and I head over to the building, examining the wreckage of the door and the bodies slumped just outside. I turn one over with my foot, bite marks to the neck. Dave nods and takes point heading through the doorway.

'Looks clear,' he says quietly, 'I'll check the back.' He heads off towards the counter and the shelving units behind it. They look mostly cleared out, Eleven days in and this is a sign of things to come. The best stuff already looted and taken. Survivors rummaging about amongst the crap left on the floor.

'Another body here, got a knife stuck in its chest,' Dave shouts back, 'not one of mine either before you say anything.'

I can't help but laugh at the comment which is so unlike him. Leaning over the counter I look down at the decaying mess of a middle aged men with a kitchen knife buried to the hilt in his chest.

'He looks normal dead,' I say to Dave, 'a knife to the chest doesn't normally stop them.'

'He is normal dead,' Dave replies leaning down and pulling one of the eyelids back.

'Jesus, killed by another survivor...'

'The back room is still locked.'

'Is it?' I walk round and head past the high shelves to a locked door. Trying the technique Clarence taught us I press the top and bottom to find they yield. One lock in the middle. I stand back and aim a boot hard at the middle. It gives a little with a splintering noise but holds closed.

'Together,' Dave says. He stands next to me as I count to three. Our combined weight forces the door open and we shoulder our way in.

'Happy days,' I mutter at the well-stocked store room. Boxes of medicines and cases of general stock left unlooted.

'Howie to Pete, we got a result in here.'

'Roger that, on way now.'

'CONTACT,' Blowers yells from the front, 'COMING

FROM THE JUNCTION.' We both run through the shop and out into the front. Blowers and Cookey stood a short distance off aiming at a horde of undead emerging slowly from a junction a hundred metres or so away.

'Can I have them?' Nick shouts from his position on the machine gun.

'Crack on mate,' I shout back, the last bit of my sentence cut off by the retort of the GPMG thudding to life. We watch as the horde are cut to pieces, blown apart by the large calibre bullets.

'OTHER SIDE,' Tom shouts aiming to a shop front at an undead staggering out. He opens fire, using single shots. The first couple miss, striking the front of the building and tearing a chunk of masonry away. The zombies are killed within seconds. More stagger out from the junction, but they're slow and spread out. Nick fires intermittently, letting a few come out together before he takes them down.

Pete leads the van crews into the chemist shop, grabbing every bit of stock from the store room and moving quickly to load up.

Shouting from further up the street sends us all spinning round and raising our assault rifles. A man waving his arms running towards us. He stops on seeing the rifles pointing at him, shouting but too far away to hear him clearly.

'Dave, tell him to come down but slowly,' I call behind me.

'COME DOWN SLOWLY, KEEP YOUR HANDS UP,' Dave bellows down the road. The man starts forward again, walking quickly and keeping his arms held straight as arrows above his head.

'Watch him, he might be one of them,' Dave warns as I start walking towards the man. He steps in beside me, assault rifle held at the ready.

'Hello? Are you the army?' The man calls out. He looks

dreadful, filthy and gaunt, clothes hanging from his once stocky frame.

'No mate, not quite…who are you?'

'My family are living up there,' he waves back up the street, 'we saw you lot and thought help was here.'

'Stay there, we need to check you before you get any closer. My mate Dave here is going to come and have a look at you, please just stay still.'

'Okay, we've not been bitten, honestly…we've kept our kids inside. It's only me that's been outside for food…if that means I'm infected then just take them,' he pleads, tears falling down his cheeks.

'It's okay mate, just hang on a second,' I say softly. Dave approaches the man holding his pistol in one hand down to the side.

'Open your eyes wide and look at me,' Dave orders. The man complies, widening his eyes and staring comically at Dave.

'Have you been bitten or scratched by the undead?' Dave interrogates him.

'No…god no…not even touched one of them…' the man says quickly.

'He looks alright as far as I can tell Mr Howie,' Dave steps away, turning to me with a shrug.

'Thanks, mate, we're from a fort on the coast a few miles down the road. We've got a whole set up going, food, doctors, security. You're welcome to come back with us if you don't mind riding in the back of a van…'

'Oh god…' the man sinks to his knees sobbing loudly, 'we prayed every day, we kept praying…we didn't think anyone would ever come.'

'You're safe now,' I step closer to him speaking softly, 'couple of my team will come with you to get your family then we'll get you out of here, okay?'

'Okay? More than okay…thank you…thank you so much…'

'Just be quick please, Dave take Blowers with you. BLOWERS, GO WITH DAVE TO BRING THIS CHAPS FAMILY OUT HERE.'

'On it,' Blowers shouts already jogging towards us.

'Are there anymore survivors here?' I ask the man.

'Probably, we hear people moving about, voices and things…we keep away from the windows though.'

'Wise move, any idea where they live? The survivors I mean?'

'No, sorry…'

'Okay, go with these two but be quick and just grab what you can carry especially medicines and any tinned food.'

The three of them jog away as I turn back and watch the crews moving between the chemist and the first van. An idea hits me and I wonder back towards the Saxon.

'Nick, when Dave and Blowers get back with that family, get the IPod going with some music. Anything will do, just make it nice and loud.'

'Okay Mr Howie…er…why?'

'Why's that boss?' Clarence turns from staring down the road.

'We'll draw any undead out and kill 'em, but also any survivors too. Just be careful who you shoot. Cookey, you get on the GPMG while Nick sorts our music out.'

'I can do that if you want Mr Howie,' Cookey says.

'Can you? Oh…sorry mate, I just figured Nick was our electrical man.'

'He is, but he's already rigged it up, just need to press play now.'

'Fair one, yeah do that then mate.'

'Any requests?' Cookey grins as he heads towards the front of the vehicle.

'Nothing too aggressive, we don't want to scare the survivors into thinking we're a bunch of wankers.'

'But we are a bunch of wankers,' Lani adds quick as a flash to a few laughs.

'Yeah but they don't know that,' Tom shouts over.

'Dave's back,' Nick shouts a few minutes later. I watch as Dave leads the family of four towards us, the same man with a woman and two small children. Dave brings up the rear, turning every few seconds to scan round.

'Pete,' I call out as he walks back towards the chemist, 'we've got survivors here, can you put them into one of the vans mate?'

'Yeah course, where are they? Oh…yeah I see 'em, leave it with me,' he nods and walks off towards the survivors, greeting them warmly and shaking hands.

'He seems a good bloke,' Clarence mutters from nearby.

'He does,' I agree. He speaks to the family for a few minutes, waving at Blowers and Dave to say he's got them. The look of relief on their faces is clear even from this distance. The children look terrified and stay quiet, staring up at the adults talking and nervously glancing round at the men with guns.

'Pete, sorry to keep calling you, we're going to put some loud music on to draw anymore survivors out but we'll probably get the things coming too, just so you know if we open up and start firing.'

'Yeah no probs Mr Howie, I'll let that family know and keep 'em safe in my van with me.'

'Music is going on, might be more survivors out here… stay alert, crack on Cookey,' I shout to my group all stood nearby.

The PA speakers crackle for a second with a low hiss. A second later and we're listening to Take That belting out a song, I couldn't tell which one not being an avid Take That fan. Smiles spread across faces, laughing and nodding at Lani who grins back and turns to watch the road.

The music blares out, a loud beat thumping down the road as they sing about someone re-lighting a fire. Despite music and the grins we all have the tension increases, knowing we'll get an influx of undead coming our way.

It doesn't take long. Zombies shuffle from many different places, exiting shops, walking into view from the end of the roads on both sides, coming from junctions and side streets. Shots ring out as the assault rifles open fire, each one being carefully aimed and making sure they're not firing on survivors.

'WE'RE DONE,' Pete yells at me, pointing to the chemist shop. I nod to Cookey to turn the music off. A deafening silence drops down as the music ends abruptly with just the occasional shot ringing out.

'Oh well, we got a few...load up for the next exciting trip,' I call out. At least the music and contact has lifted the lethargy but the heat is still as evil as before with an utterly scorching sun.

'Next?' I ask Clarence as he turns the map the right way round and holds it out to avoid the drips of sweat falling from his head.

'Further down this road, not far.'

We pull out and move slowly down the road, the GPMG firing every now and then as Nick spots undead shuffling into view. Another green cross and we pile back out, repeating the same actions as before. This one is completely looted and smashed up. Even some of the shelving has been taken judging by the large gaps on the shop floor and outline on the faded carpet.

No store room this time; a smaller family run pharmacy with the stock held behind the counter. Five minutes later and we're back on the road, heading towards the cash and carry with Cookey standing behind the front seats choosing the next playlist.

'Sorry Blowers, Lani doesn't have it,' he calls back.

'Have what?' Blowers asks.

'The Village People.'

'Get fucked.'

'I think that should be our theme song, YMCA…now that would be funny,' Cookey carries on. How he can keep the banter up in this stagnant humid air is beyond me. Glancing across I see Clarence looking strained and tired, his face bright red and sweating heavily. Tom hands warm sugary drinks round which we down quickly with more water.

'We could put signs up,' Clarence breaks the silence.

'For the fort?' I ask, thinking the same thing.

'But then Darren retained intelligence so it would just advertise our location,' he continues.

'That's what I thought.'

'After today we need a rest and some decent food,' he changes subject quickly.

'We're not likely to get it though, it's this heat mate… sapping everyone, it can't stay like this can it?'

'Fuck knows boss,' he shrugs. He seems drained and withdrawn which worries me, his strength and presence has seen us through some of the worst times. Mind you, we're all drained and withdrawn, apart from Cookey who is trying his best to keep our spirits up.

CHAPTER TWENTY-FIVE

D AY SEVEN

'What the...' Paco woke with a start, the fleeting images of his nightmare already ebbing away. It was dark and for a few seconds he couldn't place where he was. A heavy breathing noise from nearby sent his pulse racing until he remembered it was the dog and he was in the house.

Striding across the room he gently pulls the curtain back to see the last tendrils of daylight fading.

'It'll happen soon,' he muttered. He checked up and down the darkened street for movement. Nothing. A clock above the fireplace counted the seconds of his life away, penetrating the silence. He felt better, far better for having eaten food and sleeping solidly for several hours.

A low quick hissing sound knotted his forehead in confusion. Then the smell of the dogs fart reached him, a dirty foul smell of rotten eggs that filled every inch of the room.

'Damn beans.' He waved the air in front of his nose trying

to waft the stench away. Another low hiss and a gurgling noise coming from her stomach, he looked down sternly. She stared back with a big grin and long pink tongue hanging out and gave another low hiss, turning to stare at her own backside as if wondering where the noise was coming from.

'Shit,' he whispered gagging quietly and pulling a fistful of curtain over his mouth and nose. His own stomach was gurgling with a pressing sensation deep inside his gut. Leaning forward slightly he lifted one foot an inch from the ground, grimacing as he added to the smell with his own flatulence. A look of relief on his face while the dog cocked her head to one side staring towards his backside. He groaned as another one came out louder than the first, a long wet sound that spluttered and tailed off. She hissed again. He gave another one. They farted in unison with a big grin spreading across his face and the dog seemingly panting harder from the lack of oxygen.

The howling began and it sent his stomach plummeting, cutting off the farting and laughter. Instantly she was on her feet, staring intently towards the front of the house, ears pricked, head cocked and a low growl coming from her throat.

Paco backed away from the window, looking left and right. The howling was all about but not close. A distant wailing that drifted on the currents of warm air and brought utter terror into his soul. Backing away he fumbled to the sofa, sitting at the end and drawing his knees up to his chest. The howling ceased abruptly, filling the room with the sound of the second hand ticking round the clock face.

Eyes fixed on the window he failed to hear the dog padding over to him and pushing her wet nose against his hand, making him yelp in fright. Patting the seat next to him he urged the dog up onto the sofa, stroking her broad back and moving closer to her simply for the comfort of the contact. She allowed the fuss and stayed sitting up for a long time, enjoying being fussed for the first time in a week. With a sigh she lowered her body down to lie next to him, ears still pricked and twitching at sounds Paco couldn't hear.

They stayed there for hours, man and dog staying close together and both farting every few minutes.

Her growling brought him round, coming to quickly and this time knowing exactly where he was. Her growling was different, deeper somehow. He could sense the tension in her body as stirred and lifted her head from her paws. A noise from outside. A shuffling coming closer. Fully awake now he rested one head on the dog's head and felt the vibration of her growl coming through her skull.

Groaning from directly outside, something being dragged. The front door reverberated with a loud bang causing the dog to leap from the sofa making noise. Paco followed behind, trying to shush the dog but the damage was done. The front door rattled with the impact of bodies slamming into it from the other side. He heard them outside the window too, the unmistakable low growling noise as they staggered about.

She made more noise, telling them she was here and she wasn't afraid of them. She'd killed them before and she would again. She felt the presence of the man behind her, the fear was pouring from him. She could smell it and so could the things outside the den.

She made noise at the man, telling him to open the den and let her kill them. They wouldn't go now so she should attack them. The man was just like the little one, consumed with fear and not doing anything. He just stood there staring with his mouth open and his legs knocking together.

She threw herself at the door knowing they were on the

other side. Many of them and more coming, she wanted to destroy them, to end them.

The door held fast as the sworn enemies slammed and slammed again. Paco, once more rooted to the spot with fear watched as the dog barked, snarled and threw herself against the door. He moved to the kitchen, heading towards the kitchen. Reaching the back door he jumped back as something heavy hit the door from the other side. Groans and snarls coming through clearly. He leant over the sink and pulled the curtain back; the monsters were at the back door, slamming their evil bodies into it. They wanted his flesh and they'd found him.

Gibbering, whimpering, tears falling down his cheeks he moved away from the back door and stood in the hallway. His head jerking to stare at the doors as the monsters banged and thudded into them. His body convulsing and jumping in a never ending series of spasms.

A different sound penetrated the fear and reached his ears, a splintering noise. His eyes slowly looked to the back door that was slowly being battered inwards. The lock splintering in the frame with a loud crunching from the repeated strikes.

He could have moved quickly and thrown his substantial weight and strength against the door. He could have grabbed one of the many large kitchen knives from the drawer and stabbed out, making a brave stand. He could have done many things but he didn't. He backed away from the opening door, imagining the clawed hands reaching round to rake at his flesh. The dog was still barking at the front door, launching at the things beyond.

The air was thick with the stench of them. They were charged up, angry and hungry. She felt their thirst for flesh. A noise from behind, she glanced round to see them coming in from the other entrance. The man was screaming and running up the hill. They were through, in the den. She left the front door and bounded towards the big one at the front. He was different. The ones behind him were different too. They weren't staring past her this time.

They were looking at her.

CHAPTER TWENTY-SIX

D AY ELEVEN

'This doesn't look right Mr Howie,' Dave voiced out thoughts from his position stood behind the front seats of the Saxon. The cash and carry warehouse is further up this road, set on an industrial estate just outside the town centre.

There's more bodies here, far more than we'd expect on the outskirts of the town centre. Some attempt has been made to pile them up in big heaps of grotesque once human remains of twisted arms, legs and heads hanging down.

The ground is heavily blood stained with many more bodies littering the roads and pavement. The ones that we pass close enough are undead with horrific head injuries from blunt trauma and sharp implements.

'You two been here before?' I joke at Clarence and Dave; neither of them sees the funny side but just stare out at the morbid sight.

'Fuck me...' Clarence growls at the sight of the densely

packed horde all facing away from us. Slowing down I can see they're all on the approach road to the cash and carry warehouse. The tops of high metal gates can be seen over their heads, blocking them from entering the warehouse car park.

I bring the Saxon to a stop and reach for the radio clipped to my bag beside the seat.

'Howie to Pete and the vans, are you receiving me?'

'Pete to Mr Howie, we can see them...large contact right?'

'Yes mate, to the other vans further back; we've got a huge crowd of them ahead of us. We'll pull up here until we can clear the route. Stay in your vehicles.'

'Can I shoot them?' Nick shouts.

'Not yet mate, there might be people on the other side of the gates. We need to draw them out first,' I shout back.

'How do you work this thing Cookey?' Clarence asks holding the IPod in his hand, making it look like a postage stamp clutched between his huge fingers.

'Can I do it,' Cookey takes the device offered him by Clarence, his fingers quickly swiping across the screen. 'Got to be time for our theme tune,' he smiles, beads of sweat forming on his forehead.

The music blasts out from the speaker system, the opening beats of We Run This booming into the otherwise fairly peaceful area. Well, peaceful other than the hundreds of undead gathered here, and the mounds of bodies, and the other bodies lying about that is.

'Oh yes!' Nick laughs from over our heads, 'this is fucking brilliant!' The undead react as one as soon as the music blares out. Turning round to see the Saxon sat there holding several nice juicy bodies for them to munch on.

'COME ON YOU HUNGRY FUCKERS,' Nick bellows.

'Pull over onto that bit of ground, we can fire across them and avoid hitting the gates,' Dave points off to the side. I nod back and engage the engine to mount the high kerb and bounce onto the patch of sun scorched dirt.

'Are we getting out to fire?' Blowers asks from the back.

'Yeah, why not,' I shout back and reach down for my assault rifle. We clamber out, gulping the charged heated air, like walking into a furnace. Gathered on the passenger side of the Saxon sticking close to the vehicle we wait for them to slowly shuffle our way, turning across the pavement to head towards us.

'Head shots?' I ask.

'You're on' Clarence replies, 'and no cheating Cookey.'

'As if I would,' he replies indignantly.

'Am I excluded again?' Dave asks flatly to a chorus of "yes" from the rest of us, even Nick shouts the answer down. 'Nick, I'm taking that gun,' he adds in a something I can only describe as a sulky tone.

'Ah what? That's not fair…you'll kill 'em all,' Nick whines but does as he's told, dropping down the hole and swapping over with Dave. Nick takes his assault rifle and joins us on the side.

'Head shots is it?' Dave asks once through the hole and clutching the heavy machine gun.

'Oh he's done that before,' Cookey says in alarm at all the undead being killed and leaving nothing for the rest of us.

'What with that thing?' Lani asks with a puzzled face.

'Yep, on the way back from London, or going into London…something to do with London anyway,' Cookey answers wiping the sweat from his face with the back of his hand.

'And we were moving at the time,' Blowers adds.

'He got head shots with a big machine gun on top of a moving vehicle?' Tom asks in awe.

'Yeah, Dave do the headshots thing,' Cookey urges him. Dave doesn't need much temptation at the best of times. He settles himself in, face blank and devoid of expression. Aiming down the sights he takes a practise run, sweeping the gun across the crowd. Nodding once he lets rip, the air splitting apart from the solid recoil of the weapon. We watch as he sweeps the gun across the crowd.

'Oh....my....god,' Lani's mouth drops open, as does the rest of ours at the sight of undead heads popping open like exploding melons. Pink mist after pink mist, puffing into the air. One second the undead has a head, the next it doesn't as the heavy calibre round bursts the skull apart, blowing the brain into smithereens. Not every one is a head shot, the horde is made up off many different sizes and heights, but the effect is awesome and it looks like they're all headshots.

The competition is forgotten as Dave rakes the gun back and forth across them, it's as mesmerising to watch the heads pop as it to watch the look of utter concentration on Dave's face as he aims down the sights. A grand master displaying his incredible talent, which just happens to be killing other people. The thought skewers my perspective and for a second I'm not watching undead zombies being killed but people, men women and children. The sight suddenly sickens me and I have to turn away and squeeze my eyes closed. Thoughts race through my mind and I will myself to think of my mother and father, of Jamie, Tucker, Curtis and McKinney. Thinking of them and the blackness starts. Then Darren and Marcy fill my head, the image of Steven under me, screaming as I blow his brains out on the stairs of the church tower.

Fuck 'em. They're undead. They're all undead. I lift the assault rifle and fire into the ranks. The others join me a split second later, our small arms fire adding to the cacophony of noise. We change magazines and keep firing, picking them off but the GPMG does most of the work. Within a couple of minutes were looking at a vista of broken bodies. Dave picking the odd one off here and there from his advantage of being higher up.

'That was incredible,' Tom says quietly at the same time as Dave shouting "clear". We climb back into the vehicle and start driving back onto the road, the massive wheels crushing the bodies as we bounce over the corpses.

Gaining the access road to the cash and carry warehouse we look down at the metal gates, locked and secure with a man stood the other side holding a long barrelled weapon.

'Someone's already here,' Clarence says. The others clamber forward to view out the front at the gates and the person behind.

'Someone take over from Dave,' I call out and listen to the shuffling going on as Dave drops down and gets to the front.

'Game plan?' Clarence asks.

'Let's see who's here first,' I reply.

'Just remember boss, we got a lot of mouths to feed and the pickings will just get harder.'

'Okay mate, you and Dave with me, Blowers you're in charge.'

'Got it,' he says from somewhere behind me. Leaving the Saxon a respectable distance back the three of us drop down, leaving our rifles in the vehicle and walking towards the gates with our open hands held away from our bodies.

We walk slowly, trying to show the man we're not a threat to him, which will be hard seeing as we've just slaughtered all his zombies with our big machine gun stuck on the top of our army vehicle.

He stands fast, holding the shotgun across the centre mass of his body, resting in the crooks of his arms like soldiers hold their rifles. Feet planted shoulder width below a stocky frame. As we get closer I can see his face is weathered and hard looking with very short greying hair.

'Hi,' I call out from a few metres back, staring at him through the links of the metal gates. He nods back but stays silent and I can imagine his gaze flicking between the odd looking characters that have just strolled up to his gate.

'Er, we killed your zombies for you,' the joke falls flat and he stares with a barely perceptible nod.

'We've got a commune on the coast…we're out for supplies and well…we were going to try this place, cash and carry warehouse isn't it?'

'It is,' he replies with a deep voice.

'But obviously you're in there, have you got a large group?'

'Enough,' he answers.

'Is that your handy work on the road? All the bodies piled up?'

'It was, we we're gonna burn up…more showed up.'

'Yeah, they kind of keep doing that don't they, can I approach the gate? We're not here to threaten you or anything like that.'

'Can't really stop you now can I, what with my shotgun and your Saxon behind you.'

'We're not going to use it to force our way in, that's not what we're here for but we've got several thousand people in our fort…'

'Fort?' He interrupts me as I walk closer to the gates.

'Fort Spitbank, you know it?'

'I know it.'

'We've taken it over, got thousands of people there, doctors, medical facilities, security and police officers…we've got food but obviously we'll need more.'

'S'good fort that is, good move getting it,' he nods.

'There was a radio broadcast…the first or second day, it said to head for the forts but I guess not that many people heard it.'

'No,' he shakes his head, again just a small movement.

Closer now and I can see his face looks tired and drawn with large bags under his eyes.

'We've got more people turning up every day; it's a good location, defendable and secure. How many did you say you had in here?'

'I didn't.'

'No you didn't did you? Well I'm glad this conversation is going so well. Really it's not enough that we're fucking about in this heat but we just removed the gigantic horde of undead from your gates and now I'm in a conversation with a mono-syllabic man holding a shotgun,' I wipe my forehead with my shirt sleeve which comes away sodden.

'What would you do if a bloody great big armoured truck pulled up and a load of soldiers started shooting their assault rifles about?' He asks with a lift of his chin.

'Fair one,' I sigh and feel suddenly very weary.

'What's your name?' He asks quickly.

'Howie, this is Dave and Clarence.'

'Mr Howie and Dave is it?' he asks with a slow grin spreading on his face.

'Eh? What? Well....everyone keeps calling me Mr Howie but yeah that's me and he's Dave...how the...what...?'

'You're the ones that killed that nasty fella in Portsmouth, the one holding everyone hostage and making 'em his slaves...'

'Well it wasn't quite like that but...'

'And you saved all the people in the petrol station on the London road, blew up a petrol station too I heard.'

'Bloody hell, yeah that was us...but we didn't just blow it up, well no we did blow it up but you know...we kind of had a reason for blowing it up.'

'You fella's responsible for that big explosion a few days back too? That must have been down near the coast, bloody great mushroom cloud went up it did.'

'Er, yep...that was us, well Dave actually and it was a housing estate...'

'A housing estate? Why d'you blow up a housing estate?'

'To kill the zombies that were in it.'

'Oh...'

'Long story, how the hell do you know all that though?'

'News travels,' he shrugs, 'we've had people coming and going from here since it started, everyone keeps going on about this Mr Howie and Dave.'

'This is all we bloody need; this is your fault Dave.'

'Why me?' Dave looks at me with a slightly startled expression.

'For calling me Mr bloody Howie all the time in front of people.'

'Sorry Mr Howie,' he actually looks a little sheepish.

'You wanna come in then? It's too bloody hot out here,' the man says.

'Yeah, if that's alright with you...er we got a load of vans down the road too.'

'Got a big car park Mr Howie, get 'em in here for a bit,' he takes a key from his trouser pocket and unlocks the padlock, pulling the chain back and tugging the gate open.

'Howie to Blowers, drive through mate and park up...Howie to Pete, come down through the gates and park up too mate.'

'Blowers to Mr Howie, roger that.'

'Pete to Mr Howie, on our way.'

Mr bloody Howie. Bloody Dave that is, why can't he be Mr Dave and I be just Howie? And Clarence, he's a bloody giant, he should be Mr Clarence.

Clarence, standing quietly with a wry grin on his face up till now helps the man with the second gate, lifting it from the floor and pushing it over to one side and getting a shocked glance from the shotgun man at the same time.

'Sorry, you didn't say your name,' I hold my hand out which he shakes.

'Geoff.'

'Nice to meet you Geoff.'

'Clarence,' the big man steps up, holding his hand out for the obligatory shake.

'You're Dave then?' Geoff asks holding his hand out to Dave who gives a slight grimace and shakes it quickly before wiping his hand down the back of his trousers. Serves him right, I'm going to get everyone to shake his hand from now on.

The car park is wide and baking hot, we walk slowly waiting for the Saxon to inch through with a grinning Tom behind the wheel and getting a thumbs up from Cookey sat in the passenger seat. The vans come through as the lads pile out from the Saxon, slurping water and holding their assault rifles. Lani jumps down nimbly and catches me admiring her again, giving me a big smile.

'This isn't a trap is it Geoff?' I joke, which again falls flat as he stares back at me without expression.

'No,' he replies.

'Yeah…I was er…just joking.'

The vans pull through the gates and park up behind the Saxon, the drivers, guards and crews piling out into the sunshine, lighting cigarettes. Pete goes round the back of his van, opening the rear doors and speaking to the family inside. They too jump down and stand about looking scared and uneasy. Pete hands them water bottles and chats amiable.

'Do you know them?' I ask Geoff nodding towards the family, 'we met 'em in the town centre, they were holed up in a flat. We're taking them back with us.'

'No, I don't recognise them, you got room for more people then?'

'Yeah, we er…' I was about to explain about how we lost so

many in the fight but my voice trails off, 'yeah, we got plenty of space.'

'Geoff? Why the hell did you open the gates?' Another man comes charging from the door of the warehouse.

'Norman,' Geoff nods at the approaching man, 'this is Mr Howie and Dave, and that big chap is Clarence.'

'What?' Norman's face instantly glances to me, then Dave and back to Geoff.'

'Nice to meet you, I'm Howie, this is Dave and Clarence,' I take a couple of steps towards him holding my hand.

'Christ mother and Mary! *The* Mr Howie and Dave?' He asks still glancing between us.

'Er...well yes...' I reply, not sure on how to answer that.

'What? Well....he stutters and shakes my hand, 'Mr Howie right?...Er...I'm Norman.'

'Nice to meet you, that's Dave and Clarence.' Again we repeat the procedure of Clarence stepping in and offering a handshake which leaves Dave kind of forced to offer his. Which makes me grin, which he sees and passes me a quick dark look which just makes me snort with a suppressed chuckle.

'Oh god,' Norman pales as he looks beyond us at the lads stood their dressed like mercenaries and holding assault rifles. I'm guessing Lani must have said something to the other four as they're smiling nicely and not twatting about like normal.

'It's okay Norman,' Geoff says quickly, 'they've got that Fort Spitbank, taken it over they have, got doctors and hospitals and police stations and everything they have...thousands living there like a proper town.'

'Eh? No wait...we got doctors and police officers, and yeah a few thousand people there but not quite like that,' I add quickly. That'll be the next thing. Mr Howie and Dave have a super city where everyone gets a free TV when they arrive.

'Have you?' Norman asks quickly, 'I've heard of it, have you got space then?'

'Well yeah we have, how many you got here?'

'Erm...well we had a couple leave last night, and then that Thompson chap turned up didn't he Geoff...'

'He did Norman, and don't forget that family yesterday that went.'

'Christ mother and Mary! Of course, you know I'd forgotten all about them...so they left yesterday and that couple and then Mr Thompson turned up...' he counts silently holding his fingers out.

'Roughly...just roughly...we don't need to know exactly,' I prompt him.

'Er...Fifty six,' he answers with a smile, 'no, fifty seven with Mr Thompson.'

'Oh quite a few then,' I reply.

'Is there any food left?' Clarence asks with a concerned tone.

'Oh lots, we've been rationing very carefully you see, which has caused some arguments let me tell you that much for free but we said we'd have to be careful as we didn't know how long it would be till help arrived.'

'Help? What help?' I ask him.

'Well you know got to give the government time to get something worked out haven't we?'

'Government? Norman there is no government, there's nothing. The whole country's gone, Europe, the whole world...'

'Yeah that's what people keep telling me, but this is Great Britain...this is the United Kingdom! They'll have a plan somewhere, just got to let the boffins work it out, and anyway...you're here now, Mr Howie and Dave eh?'

'We need to cut to the chase,' Clarence steps forward looking very hot, 'we need food, you've got food. You need somewhere safe and we have somewhere safe, so how about it?'

'How about what?' Norman pales slightly looking up at Clarence.

'Er,' I step in before Clarence pulls his head off, 'as Clarence said we've got a safe place with doctors and medicines, it's early days but we're getting a good set up going… but we need food. You've got a whole warehouse of food here. So maybe you come to our fort and bring your food with you?'

'Christ mother and Mary! That's an idea…but well I'll have to put it to the committee…'

'The committee?' Clarence growls.

'Of course the committee, this country is a democracy not some tinpot autocratic dictatorship…oh no….we've got committee's on rationing, guards…er…toilet cleaning duties…'

'Entertainment,' Geoff adds helpfully.

'Oh yes the entertainment committee, they do marvellous things with keeping the little ones entertained you know.'

'Okay! Er…well you could go and ask them or…'

'I'll get everyone together and maybe you can say a few words, you know…Mr Howie and Dave coming to the rescue, I think they'll buy it,' Norman smiles.

'Buy it? I'm not asking anyone to buy anything. We're offering people a secure place to live so the zombies don't eat them…and you've got a warehouse full of food too.'

'Yes well…you know how tricky committees can be, I'll go and get them ready, I'll bring them out for you,' he walks off chatting excitedly with Geoff. Leaving the armed strangers alone in their car park.

'How the fuck have they survived this long?' Clarence asks.

'They got committees,' I reply, 'bored the zombies to death probably.'

'We need this food boss,' Clarence urges.

'I know mate, we'll talk to them and convince them to come with us.'

'Make it sound bad, really bad,' he prompts me.

'What 'cos it isn't already then? The whole end of the world, everyone's a zombie thing not bad enough?'

'You know what I mean,' he replies with a slight grin which is nice to see instead of his angry flushed face.

'Lads,' Dave turns and barks at the rest gathered by the Saxon, 'when that strange man comes back he's bringing everyone out with him. I want you lot over there chatting and being nice, tell them how good our fort is, don't let them touch the guns but smile and show them how professional you are,' he orders, leaving me and Clarence staring at each other in amazement. The lads buck up instantly getting what we're trying to accomplish, walking past quickly towards the front of the building and trying to look casual.

'And Nick...' Dave shouts.

'Yes Dave?' Nick turns with a grin.

'No swearing.'

'Yes Dave,' he nods still grinning.

'Bloody hell Dave that was good thinking,' I say.

'But aren't they all going come out and see a bunch of armed people now?' Clarence asks.

'No the lads will do good, they're good at this,' I reply confidently.

'Can I play in the headshots game now?' Dave asks suddenly. We both reply no.

Within a couple of minutes the warehouse people are coming out, tentatively poking heads out then taking a few steps into the bright glare of the daylight. The lads smile and nod, waving at the people and strolling towards them.

'See,' I say. More people come out and we watch as our lads separate and move amongst them chatting to groups and smiling the whole time. Lani looks amazing with her beautiful smile and stood there holding a bloody great big machine gun. It takes time for everyone to exit the building, a few of them look very worried and scared at the sight of the army truck, the vans and the men stood round but we give it time and let the lads get some good words in.

'Win their hearts and minds...' Clarence says quietly.

'Definitely,' I reply, 'come on, let's get in there too. Dave needs to practise his handshakes.' I grin at the small man taking a couple of steps towards the crowd.

'Hang on,' Clarence says, 'they keep looking over at us, at you and Dave...you'll have more effect if you stay back and talk to them as one.'

'You reckon?' I ask, but he's right. Looking at the crowd and many of them are staring over, glancing at Dave and me, chatting and whispering to themselves.

They look all look tired and scared but I do notice at least their well-fed and clean, something most survivors can't achieve. The crowd fractures into smaller groups, these then grow larger as more people join them, the groups congregate and a natural order ensues ending up with one large crowd with several key people in the middle talking loudly.

Norman appears from the building, carrying a plastic beer crate which he upends and stands on, clapping his hands to draw the attention of the crowd.

'Now settle down, settle down please...come on everyone just quiet down for a minute, thank you. Now, as you can see we've been visited by Mr Howie and Dave and the rest of their group.' Heads all turn to stare again, I raise one hand and nod back whispering for Dave to do the same, which he does woodenly.

'They've got a community down on the coast in the old Spitbank Fort, thousands of them and by all accounts its growing every day, they've got law and order with fully uniformed police officers, doctors, hospitals, people in charge and they've got security,' I wince as he relays the description, shaking my head slightly. 'They're here looking for food and supplies to take back with them...but they've invited us to go along with them and live in their fort, the question is do we stay here and hope for the best or take the invitation and go with them. I've spoken to Mr Howie and he's happy to field any questions you may have and say a few words...Mr Howie?' He looks over at me and I nod back, starting towards the beer crate.

'We need that food,' Clarence whispers as I pass in front of him.

'Hi, my name is Howie, that is Dave and the big chap is Clarence. The armed people amongst you are part of our group from Fort Spitbank, we've been together for quite a few days now,' standing on the beer crate and looking out I can see just how tired and exhausted they look. Scared people gathering together and not knowing what to do, so they cling to the lessons life has taught them. Form committees, form think-tank groups, discuss the options and wait for help. If they didn't have this pile of food it would be a far different story.

'The fort is on the coast, on a spit of land surrounded by flatlands and the sea so we've got a good defensible position. We've had one major fight with those things when they tried to take the fort but we fought them back. We lost a lot of good people but we've shown we can defend our home and in doing so we inflicted massive losses on them. I won't lie or tell you anything that isn't plain fact...they might come back, the chances are that they will come back. But that goes for everyone, not just us in our fort. They need to eat and find more people. We're already getting scarcer now so they'll up their game to do what it takes. We've killed the ones outside your gates but they will come back. Yes, you have big metal gates but from I can see here you've only got a few small arms with you,' I point to the few men in the crowd holding shotguns, 'also, you've got a big stockpile of food in here and this building is just a warehouse, it's not built to withstand a concerted attack. There will be other groups out there who want that food and will also do anything to get it. We've got plenty of space for you and you can join our fort, be a part of our community. We need people with skills, nurses, engineers, mechanics, plumbers, carpenters, we need fit and healthy people who are willing to work and muck in, anyone with medical training or who can sew, stitch and repair clothing. We need teachers for our children. Our food is split evenly amongst everyone too. Sounds idyllic doesn't it? A veritable utopia yeah?' I can from their faces that I've pretty much convinced most of them already, which just shows how desperate they are.

'Well it isn't,' I add firmly, 'but neither is this,' I wave my arm at the warehouse and car park, 'We've got a lot of work to do to get our fort up and running so it can house so many people, there is a hell of a lot of work to do and everyone has to play their part but there is safety in numbers and like Norman said, we have organisation and order. We don't have hospitals yet but we will have, we've been out today getting supplies from hospitals and pharmacies and as time goes on things will get more desperate. You are welcome to join us, we'll lead you back to the fort and you'll be admitted...'

'What's the cost?' Someone shouts.

'Cost?' I ask staring in the general direction of the shout.

'Oh shut up Frank,' someone else shouts in an irritated tone.

'No it's a fair question, we came here for the food and supplies, we won't take it from you by force, that won't happen. But we do need more food and supplies...'

'So you want our food then?' Frank shouts.

'Yes of course we do,' I answer bluntly, 'and we won't be the only ones that figure out where the depots are now the shops are all gone.'

'So we come with you but only if you have our food, is that right?' Frank asks.

'Unless you want to leave it here with a big sign up saying help yourself, yeah I think that's about right. We take the food with us, not us not you but we…because it will be all of us eating it…'

'Bloody hell Frank that was a stupid thing to say,' the other voice calls out.

'Is it true about you saving them people in Portsmouth from being slaves?' A plump woman at the front asks.

'Well…we…er…yeah we kind of met the people in the barricade and there was an issue of sorts.'

'And the people on the motorway?

'Yeah them too, we met them on the way to London.'

'London?' She asks, 'you been to London?'

'Yes, had to get my sister,' I explain quickly.

'Was it bad?'

'Very bad, completely overrun. Everywhere is overrun.'

'Have you heard from the government?' More people shout questions.

'No mate, there is no government, well no sign of them anyway.'

'Are you from the army?'

'Some of us are yes,' I don't give the full explanation.

'How do we know you won't do somefin' nasty to us then? Like make us slaves or sommit?'

'Why would we make you slaves? What for? And how would we organise a slave trade in the Eleven days since this thing began? We're the same as you, just doing what we can to survive but we've been lucky in that we got a good base with good people inside it…'

'Norman?' The plum lady calls out, 'do we all have to go or what? Like can some of us go and some stay?'

'Er...well we've always said no one is a prisoner here, you can come and go as you wish.'

'I want to go then,' she replies quickly, more people nod in agreement, some argue against the idea and voices start rising.

'Now come on, everyone just come on please,' Norman shouts taking his place on the beer crate I've vacated, 'I think we should have a vote and we go with the majority, yes? Everyone in agreement with that? We'll put it to the vote and all agree we'll abide by the decision...'

'But you just said people can do what they want?' Frank shouts.

'Well yes I know and they can, but we are a group and we should stick together.'

'Shut up Frank.'

'So I can stay here if I want to then?' Frank presses the point.

'Yes of course you can,' Norman appeases him.

'With the food?' He adds quickly.

'Well now that depends on how many want to leave, we can't leave all the food can we, so...well I don't really know about that...'

'So there ain't no bloody choice is there, if the majority say to go then the food goes too,' Frank shouts above the rising clamour of voices.

'Right come on, let's have the vote,' Norman carries on, ignoring Frank. 'All those in favour of going to the new fort with Mr Howie and Dave, raise your hands...' The air above the crowd is suddenly filled with hands waving and stretching high. No doubt about it, only a few don't raise their hands. I look back to Clarence to who smiles and nods.

'Vote passed,' Norman grins, 'right...well er...how do we do this?' He looks to me suddenly unsure.

'May I?' I motion towards the crate.

'Please do,' he says gladly and steps off.

'Go Howie,' Lani mutters as I walk past her, I glance at her grinning, not realising she was so close.

'Okay, have you got any vehicles?' I call out to the sea of excited faces.

'We put them all in round the back and the other side out of view from the gates,' Norman replies.

'We need to move quickly and get loaded up, do you have anything big like vans or...'

'Use the arctic,' a man shouts from the middle.

'You have a lorry?' I reply to nods and people shouting the types of vehicles they have, vans, cars and other things I don't hear.

'Get them all round the front, open those shutters up and get them loaded as quickly as possible. Form a chain and pass the goods out, my lot will help and we can use our vans too.'

Chaos descends as everyone tries to do everything at once. Clarence wades in, using his size and voice to cajole people into order. Pete and the van crews are soon amongst them as we try to organise over a hundred people into doing some fairly basic tasks. As normal, we start off with too many managers trying to take control and shout the others down.

But we get there slowly. The vehicles are driven round including one big lorry that certainly looks like it's seen many better days but hopefully it will do the job.

I call my group to me, using the radio instead of trying to shout and find them all, we meet by the Saxon, moving out of earshot from the melee going on outside the warehouse.

'Clarence, I want you to take the Saxon and go back down the road with Nick, Blowers, Cookey, Tom and Lani. We passed a load of used car sale places, find anything that will drive and get them back here, the bigger the better, Dave and I will stay here on guard. We've got fifty six people to get back to the fort...'

'Fifty seven with Mr Thompson,' Dave corrects me.

'We've got a fifty seven people to shift plus the stuff in the warehouse.'

'Boss, get Norman to send some people with us, we'll be able to do it in one go then,' Clarence adds.

'Good idea mate.' We break up as I work my way through the crowd, finding Norman and Geoff stood to one side talking. I relay my idea which he accepts and sends Geoff off to select some drivers. A few minutes later and they're off, the Saxon driving out of the main gate and heading down the road. I can hear the crunching of bodies being crushed under the wheels from here.

Dave and I stand towards the back, watching the main gate and the work being carried out now in some semblance of order.

'We got a few hours till dark,' I remark.

'We have Mr Howie.'

'Need a long cold shower when we get back, I might just sit under the hose for an hour or two.'

'Could go for a swim in the sea,' he suggests.

'That sounds like heaven mate, cool sea and a cold beer.'

'Shouldn't drink and swim.'

'Or drive.'

'I can't drive.'

'You should learn, I'll teach you.'

'I don't have a licence.'

'I don't think that matters now Dave.'

'Okay.'

'Really? You'll let me teach you to drive?'

'Yes Mr Howie.'

'We'll need one of them instructor cars with the dual pedals and leaner plates, we should find one.'

'Okay Mr Howie.'

'Or should we just go straight for the Saxon?'

'I don't mind.'

'Didn't the army ever teach you to drive?'

'No.'

'Why not? They taught you just about everything else.'

'I don't know, I never asked them.'

'Fair enough...'

CHAPTER TWENTY-SEVEN

D^{AY SIX}

Two beasts, one of foul blood and the other pure, running at each other, lips pulled back, teeth bared. They do what must be done. There is no thought other than primal instinct. The predator seeing its prey and charging with violence unknown to human kind.

The thing drop down, neck stretched showing the gristle and veins bulging under the pale decaying skin. The dog starts to lift, using her powerful back legs to drive her up, her front legs extended ready for the impact.

Within a split second she has taken in the change, absorbed the difference and now knows the things are here for her. She does not wilt or flee but charges with unrestrained aggression.

The thing doesn't stand a chance. Days of constant killing have honed her skill finely. She locks her jaws either side of the things mouth and drops her weight, dragging it down at the same time as she gives a violent shake of her neck. Flesh, teeth and jaw bone are shorn away. The next one is lunging in, she whips round and drives forward. Ploughing her body weight and driving it back. Teeth savaging any piece of the things body she can get at.

Two down and more coming. She uses the tricks she's learnt and bounds on the downed bodies, launching herself at the exposed necks of the oncoming attackers. In the open she is deadly, using her speed and agility to take them down.

In this confined space she is worse. Utter brute force and power driving a mouth full of sharp teeth that can generate enough pressure to break human bone, and she does. Ragging the things up and down the hallway, they drop down, lunging in ready for the bite. She takes this change of behaviour and uses it to her advantage, staying low and whipping in amongst their legs and biting up at the faces as they come down.

She climbs over the bodies and backs away to foot of the stairs, snarling and making noise. Daring them to come at her. Lips pulled up and eyes fixed. Deep growls emanating from her throat. Hair standing on end. They keep coming, launching themselves over the bodies, tripping, falling and dying.

The corpses mount up and she gives ground inch by inch, backing away to the stairs. She starts to rise, using the height of the stairs to lunge at their necks and drive them back down.

The front door yields under the sustained battering, splintering open as more of the things surge through. But the stairs are narrow and only two can fit abreast. She dominates them. Taunts them. Beckons them on.

Driving forward again and again she rips through flesh like butter, tearing throats out, destroying jugulars and opening arteries. Blood soaks the steps, making the slippery and causing the following things to slip and slide. With four legs she bounds up and down destroying anything that comes at her.

Upstairs, in the back bedroom. The strong muscular form of Paco Maguire, action hero of more than twenty blockbuster movies sits in the corner, knees drawn to chest and sobbing with unrestrained terror. Hearing the snarls, the growls, the killing he wills the dog to survive. Prays that she holds her ground and defeats the evil monsters.

Thoughts race through his mind. Images of the pitchfork monster and Lucy defeating the dog and tearing her open, pouncing on the stairs and lunging at the bedroom door. He prays to his mother, father, he prays to the name of every god and angel he's ever heard. He pleads for his life, making unremitting promises to live a wholesome life, to do good and help others.

But not once does he consider going to her aid.

CHAPTER TWENTY-EIGHT

D AY SEVEN

The sun rises on the seventh day of the new world. While Howie prepares the fort for battle, the dog finally kills the last undead.

The fallen bodies became so dense the things had to fight and crawl their way through and over them. But they just added to the pile. A spark of intelligence remained as they started tugging and pulling the bodies away, opening gaps to find a mouthful of teeth waiting for them.

The suns golden rays slowed the things to a shuffle which she detected instantly. The animal instinct not questioning the change but accepting it and adapting. She finished them off, her movements slow and almost cumbersome now. A few times she'd left the stairs to drink water from the toilet bowl and it was just enough to sustain her.

As the last one falls she feels an overwhelming sense of

tiredness come over her. Legs feeling wooden and shaky. Her coat matted with blood and gore.

Slowly she walks back into the den, clambering over the bodies and stopping when she's sees Paco stood at the top of the stairs. His mouth hanging open at the sight of the corpses and blood spatters high on the walls. His eyes take the view in, moving slowly over the scene until they finally rest on her.

'Damn,' he whispers but seeing the daylight and dog still alive gives him a sense of enormous relief. Taking great care he makes his way down the stairs, pausing to make sure the dog has finished her killing spree and isn't about to launch at him. She looks normal, apart from the blood and filth on her fur. Her head is hanging lower than before and she keeps yawning, showing the back of her mouth and her blood stained tongue.

With no other choice Paco is forced to step on the bodies, using them as stepping stones to gain a view of the street outside, shocked at seeing yet more cadavers strewn about.

'God damn,' he turns back to her. She stands with her tail wagging slowly.

'Good girl!' He says louder now, her tail beats faster as he makes his way down the hallway into the kitchen. Checking the back garden for monsters before he finds a bowl and fills it with cold water.

She's there instantly, drinking noisily and gulping it down. The bowl is licked dry and filled again. Pink water dripping from her muzzle, tainting the bowl. She doesn't stop but keeps lapping with her tongue, in and out, in and out. Rapid movements that drains the water surprisingly fast.

His brow knots and a grimace spreads across his face at the sight of her matted coat. Heading outside he finds a hose and calls the dog to him. She comes readily enough and even stands still while he jets the water on her body, using a dustpan brush to work at the bits stuck in her hair.

Finished he stands back just in time for her to shake her coat and soak everything within a six foot radius.

'You look beat,' he says softly, 'but we can't stay here, we gotta move.' He heads back into the kitchen and drinks more water before stomping over the bodies and leaving the house.

In the street he looks up and down, checking for signs of movement. The dog stands by his side, head still hanging low and still panting heavily.

'Come on,' he taps his leg and moves off. She follows a few feet behind, her ears still pricked and eyes watchful but just happy to follow the man where he leads.

Paco leads the dog through street after street. Knowing she needs a rest but wanting to create distance from their last house. Finally, just as she looks ready to drop he selects a house with a door slightly ajar and tentatively makes his way up the path. Shoeing the door open he stands still, listening for any noise and watching the dog. She senses his fear once more and walks past him, making her way slowly through the house and up the stairs. Only when she re-appears does he close and lock the door and start his checks, making sure there's an escape route through the back garden.

He stops in the hallway, staring up at the dog asleep on the top landing. Her paws hanging over the top step by a few inches. Her eyes closed but ears still pricked.

From having spent the night cowering in the bedroom, he too feels drained and exhausted. Finding the sofa in the lounge he stretches out and listens as the dog gently patters down the stairs and walks into the room, lying down on her side facing the door.

'Good girl,' he yawns watching her tail flicker at the praise.

Despite the sheer exhaustion it takes time for Paco to

drift off, his mind ablaze with thoughts and images of where to go and how to survive.

The town is too dangerous; they tracked him yesterday despite the rain washing the scent from the road. They knew where he was so they'll find him again. In his mind there is no choice, they'll have to leave the town and find some desolate house in the country. Lucy only found him because she knew where the house was. If he could find another house like that they could hide away.

He sits up, thinking it would be safer to go now before they rally and find them again, but the dog looks beat. She's been fighting all night and must be drained. Weighing up the options in his head he considers just going anyway and hoping the dog will follow. But then just look at how many of the monsters she's killed already, no, she is his best chance of survival and that means she needs to be rested to fight again. A few hours will do it. Dogs recover quickly right. Get some food and water in her and they can be off.

He rests back with his hands behind his head, flexing his biceps and rubbing the thick beard on his face. Sleep gently dulls his mind, drawing him down into slumber in the warm summer air.

CHAPTER TWENTY-NINE

D AY ELEVEN

'Terri, slow down! Who are you talking about? What dog?' Sergeant Hopewell looks at the flustered woman with confusion. Terri breaths out slowly, gathering her thoughts and getting her breathing back under control from sprinting through the compound to the police offices.

'A woman, she just arrived outside with some Polish families. She's not Polish though, English,' Terri nods trying to get her point across.

'English...right...keep going,' Sergeant Hopewell prompts as Ted looks on with interest.

'She said there was a dog outside her house, it was killing the undead...it was there all day and all night, she felt the dog was protecting her and her children...'

'Okay, keep going.'

'Well, the dog didn't turn! She said it was there all day, you see? The dog was killing the undead and taking in their blood and flesh but it didn't turn. She said it was still the same the next morning, like a normal dog with normal eyes and wagging its tail!' Terri watches as Sergeant Hopewell's eyes go wide as she grasps the implication.

'Where was it?' Ted asks stepping forward and staring closely at Terry.

'Er...it's on the form, hang on,' Terri replies flicking through the sheets of paper on her clipboard.

'She's outside?' Sergeant Hopewell asks.

'Yes Sarge, still waiting to be processed.'

'Ted, find Chris and meet me outside.'

'Will do,' Ted calls already heading for the door as he pushes his flat cap on and adjusts his utility belt.

'Tell me again what she said?' Sergeant Hopewell asks as they walk through the compound towards the front gates. Terri relays it her account again, slightly breathless from the fast walking.

'What kind of dog was it?'

'Er...I don't know...maybe she said but I can't remember,' Terri replies.

'Must be a big one to be able to kill them so easily.'

'Alsatian! She said it was a big Alsatian.'

'Was it one of ours? It would make sense if it was trained to take people down, but no...the police dogs go for the arms don't they?'

'Yes Sarge, they use the bite sleeves.'

'Well it doesn't matter, I suppose we can't exactly ask it can we, open the gates please,' she barks in advance of reaching the inner gate. The guards jump at her command, quickly wrenching the door back watching as the two officers stride through.

'Debbie?' Chris shouts from behind her. She turns round to see him striding through the gate behind her, his face looking very red and flushed.

'Chris, did Ted bring you up to speed?'

'Kind of, something about a dog killing the zombies but not turning,' Chris glances back at Ted following in his wake.

'Terri said a woman just turned up outside saying there was a dog outside her house all day and all night, it was killing the things but it didn't turn.'

'How many did it kill? How did it kill them? What was the time difference between the first kill and the last time she saw it?' Chris barks the question as Debbie waves her hands to slow him down.

'You missed your calling Chris, you should have been a detective...we don't know that yet, we're going out to speak to her now.'

'I'll get Doc Roberts and meet you out there,' he walks off towards the vetting tents, walking straight into an examination being conducted by two of the medical staff on a man stood there naked with his hands over his privates. 'Where's the Doc?' He asks in an urgent tone.

'Which one?' The older of the two medics asks pointedly.

'*The* Doc, Doc Roberts...where is he?'

'Having a break out the back but...' he gets cut off by Chris walking past them, nodding at the naked man and pulling the curtain back to find Doctor Roberts sat in a chair in the sun a few metres away.

'What now for the love of god?' Doctor Roberts groans at the big bearded man walking towards him with a look of focus on his face.

'Doc we got a woman just turned up outside...'

'Another one?' He replies sarcastically.

'No listen, she said there was a dog outside her house before she got here, it was killing the things...'

'I'm a Doctor Chris, not a vet...'

'Just listen!' Chris growls getting a hard look from the

doctor, 'the dog was outside all day and all night, killing the things…she told Terri it didn't turn…Hey…hang on…'

'Where is she? Come on man don't stand there catching flies!'

Swallowing a curt reply Chris takes off after the Doctor, rolling his eyes and muttering under his breath.

'Is he all clear?' Doctor Roberts demands of the two medics stood talking to the naked man.

'Yes Doctor,' they reply in unison.

'Then what the hell is he still doing here? Get dressed man! This isn't a nudist club.' He strides past, the long tails of his white lab coat billowing behind him. Chris passes through the tent, nodding once more at the very confused looking naked man. 'Open the gates please, come on I haven't got all day…get them open! Well done, now where is she? Chris what are you doing back there? Keep up man, I thought you were in the army?'

'Yes Doctor,' Chris bites his tongue, 'good god,' he blanches in surprise at the long queue of people waiting to come into the fort.

'Well? Are you going to stand there gawping all day?'

'Sorry Doc, er…down there with the police officers,' he leads the way. Walking past the filthy refugees sat in the shade of vehicles and drinking water handed to them by the guards walking up and down.

'Debbie, is this the woman? Hi, I'm Chris and this is Doctor Roberts,' Chris turns to the woman at a nod from Sergeant Hopewell, extending his hand at the terrified woman clutching a baby to her chest.'

'Have I done something wrong?' She asks worried at the sudden attention and feeling a sense of panic that maybe they'll refuse her from going inside.

'No, nothing like that love,' Chris switches to a soft tone, crouching down and smiling gently, 'you told Terri something about a dog?'

'The dog? Yeah but he didn't bite any of us, it was outside the whole time, we didn't go near it I promise.'

'That's great, you've done nothing wrong love, really. We'll get you inside very quickly I promise, we've got baby formula inside, clean water so you can get cleaned up and get some sleep. You must be exhausted?'

'I'm okay, really I am…I can work and do things.'

'It's okay love, we just want to ask about the dog, tell us what you told Terri.'

'Er…well it just turned up and stayed outside,' she shrugs clearly very scared.

'Chris, may I?' Terri touches his broad shoulder gently motioning him to budge over so she can take over. He concedes, accepting that his big bearded face being thrust at her might be causing her more alarm.

'This man is Chris, he kind of runs the fort, that man is Doctor Roberts, he's in charge of the medical teams here. This lady is Sergeant Hopewell, she's my boss and in charge of the police. The other man is Ted, he's in charge of all the guards here. You've done nothing wrong, really. But what you told me about the dog is vitally important, do you understand? There is nothing you can tell us that will mean bad things will happen to you. Unless you've been bitten or scratched and you've already told me you've had no contact…'

'No we haven't,' she replies quietly staring at Terri.

'So you can go in the fort, but what you told me about the dog, I need you to tell all of us again? Be as detailed as you can and don't leave anything out.

'Okay, it was an Alsatian, I know them cos my uncle had one when I was younger. We was at home, me and the kids and those things were outside, all round the house and trying to get in. I thought we were done for, I really did. My car was out the back but I was too scared to go outside…I didn't know if they was by the car or not as I couldn't see the car from the house…'

'Okay, that's great,' Terri nods in earnest.

'It was sat in the shade on the other side of the road, opposite the house. It was big, really big, biggest dog I've ever seen. It started killing the things, jumping up and biting them in the throat…it did all of 'em…one after the other until they was all dead.'

'What happened next?' Terri asks.

'It came over to the house and I could see it were normal, you know, like a normal dog. It was hot and pantin' so I put some water down in a bucket…'

'Did it drink the water?' Doc Roberts asks in an impatient tone and earning a very stern look from Sergeant Hopewell.

'It drank all of it, I put more down then more things kept comin' and it went out and killed them too, stayed there all day it did.'

'You said it was there in the night too?' Terri prompts, not wanting to lead the woman but aware that the impatient Doctor Roberts was stood right behind her tapping his foot.

'The night was bleedin' awful, they all got fast and howled they did. Started chargin' the house and banging at the doors and windows. I was in the bedroom with my kids but I left the window open and heard everything,' she sobs suddenly, the memory of her own actions still racking her with guilt. 'I had a knife, I thought they was gonna get in and I…I was gonna kill my kids so them things couldn't get 'em. I could hear the dog outside, snarling and barking all night. I could hear it ripping them apart…I could hear the bodies as they hit the ground. Then the front room window got smashed and I held that knife to my baby's throat,' she cries harder, tears free falling down her cheeks. 'That dog though, it must have kept 'em out…I didn't look until the morning and by then there was just dead bodies everywhere and blood, just blood and bits of body…'

'Was the dog still there?' Doctor Roberts asks, his tone softer now after hearing the awful account and seeing the grief pouring from the woman.

'It was Sir, I put more water down and it drank again. It was covered in blood it was. We left then, in the car…I couldn't stand another day in that house…'

'Was that the last time you saw it?' Terri asks.

'No, I drove down the side road and stopped at the junction, it was still outside my house, just sat there wagging its tail, I shouted thank you and we went off. I wanted to take it with us but I was worried in case it turned or somethin'.

'That's great,' Terri says softly, 'did you see the dog's eyes?'

'Yeah it was right below the window, could see them clear as anything.'

'What colour were they?' Doctor Roberts asks as Terri rolls her eyes.

'Brown, just normal dog colour.'

'Not red? Did you see any red colour in the eyes?'

'No,' she shakes her head.

'And that was in the daytime and the morning after the night, yes? You saw the dog's eyes both times?'

'Yeah like I said, I kept putting water down for it; it stared up and wagged its tail.'

'You said the dog was killing the things, how exactly was it doing that?' The Doctor probes.

'What do you mean? It bit them, with its mouth…and was like shaking its head when it got 'em down on the floor.'

'So you saw the dog biting into the things, it made them bleed yes?'

'Blood everywhere.'

'Was there any blood on the dog? In or on its mouth?'

'Course there was, the dog was covered in it…all over its

mouth, down its chest, on its paws, dripping from its tongue it was.'

'Thank you, we'll get you through very quickly...just wait here please,' Doctor Roberts nods at Chris and Sergeant Hopewell. They step away, going across the dirt lane with Ted and Terri and speaking quietly.

'What do you think?' Chris asks the doctor.

'What do I think? I think you need to find that bloody dog and get it back here.'

'Could a dog be immune to...whatever this is?' Ted asks seriously.

'No idea Ted,' the doctor knots his bushy eyebrows in deep thought, 'anything is possible. It could be that breed, a genetic mutation or that particular dog having some kind of anti-body that is resistant. When was this?' He snaps back to attention directing the question at Terri.

'She wasn't sure, maybe the second or third day.

'Could be dead by now, might have just been a delayed reaction...Chris, we need that dog here and I need fuel for the bloody generators so I can get my equipment running.'

'If we find that dog you can have all the fuel, I promise you that much Doc.'

'We need search teams...' Sergeant Hopewell cuts in.

'We need Howie and his lot,' Ted replies, 'they'll find that dog.'

'They're out on scavenging runs,' Chris says. 'Doc, you tell me how much of a priority this is and I'll get some teams out now...'

'Without knowing more I couldn't say, but based on that terrified woman's account that is already a week old...'

'But she said the dog was biting the things, that means it must have been taking their blood in...and it didn't turn all night,' Terri says quickly.

'True,' the doctor nods, 'you're right, Chris this is the

biggest chance we've got right now. Find that dog. Bring any Alsatians you find back here. If they find that dog get it back alive at all costs.'

'What if it's dead?' Chris asks.

'Bring the body here, we can still examine it but we need it alive. If that dog is immune to the virus this is the best chance we've got at finding a vaccine or a cure. Find it Chris, find it and get it back here.'

CHAPTER THIRTY

D AY ELEVEN

'How did you get on?' I ask Clarence as he jumps down from the Saxon. A convoy of vehicles drives through the gates behind him. Estate cars mostly and a couple of vans. 'Don't answer that mate, I can see. Any contacts?'

'A few shufflers but that was it, how's it going here?'

'Slowly getting there,' I reply, 'Norman was trying to get them to load everything self by shelf but I said to concentrate on the food first, then toiletries and finally everything else.'

The vehicles pull up in the car park, doors opening and slamming as the lads and Lani drift back towards the Saxon. They all look so hot and bothered with sluggish movements.

Loading the goods takes a while, first the lorry is filled up and moved out the way before the vans and cars get stacked with every type of food in the building. We'll never fit everything in but we do well and vastly increase our stock. We can always come back tomorrow and take the rest.

As the days drifts into evening we're finished. Having to leave enough free vehicles and space in vans to transport the people. It's a tight fit as we're forced to squeeze them into every nook and cranny we've got. The vans are seriously overloaded, as are the cars but I don't think the police will be out too much today so as long as we take it relatively easy we should be okay.

Surprisingly, Norman and Geoff are extremely effective at getting everyone where they should be. Geoff was one word answers when we first arrived but then I guess anybody would be faced with what he saw coming down the road, but they're both exceptionally polite and friendly. Listening to people while still getting them to do what's needed. I can already see they're going to fit in well at the fort.

The Saxon leads them out of the car park, using our radios to acknowledge when the last one leaves so we can pause while they lock the gates. Then we're off. Slowly driving a very long convoy back through the town and onto the motorway.

'Everyone okay?' I call out once we're settled in.

'Hot,' Cookey answers quickly.

'Fucking hot,' Nick adds just as quick.

'Damn hot,' Lani then says.

'What? You want the heating up? Okay, I'll put it on,' I reach out for the controls, not actually knowing which one to press or twist, the gesture is enough and I get a series of moans and groans in reply. 'I think we've earned an evening off, maybe a swim, a couple of cold drinks...we'll see if there's any beer anywhere, what do you reckon?'

'Is that a promise?' Lani asks in a suspicious voice.

'To the best of my ability I promise.'

'We'll hold you to that boss,' Clarence joins in, 'if anything else happens tonight I will...I will...'

'What? What will you do?'

'Cry probably,' he grins ruefully.

'Are we back out tomorrow Mr Howie?' Cookey shouts up.

'Probably mate, if not then I'm sure they'll have something else planned for us.'

'It's not been a bad day though, considering,' Tom adds.

'True, on the grand scale of how our days normally seem to go this one has been quite good, apart from the heat.'

'Is this heat from what's happening?' Cookey asks.

'How the fuck would that happen you twat,' Blowers snorts.

'Well I've never known it this hot before and I've also never known a zombie apocalypse either...'

'How can they be related?' Blowers asks.

'Actually, I was thinking about this,' I call out, 'with the sudden cessation of…'

'With the what?' Cookey interrupts.

'The cessation…with all the vehicles suddenly stopping, the factories, the airplanes, no fuels being burnt off. Less gasses in the atmosphere or air? Maybe some kind of connection.'

'Ha, in your face Blowers,' Cookey yells gleefully, 'Mr Howie said it might be so get fucked.'

'But then again it also might just be a freak summer, global warming or the polar ice caps…'

'Eat shit Cookey,' Blowers retorts as Cookey groans. Lani laughs wickedly at the banter, giggling away in the corner at the back.

'Was it hot in Thailand?' Nick asks.

'I don't know, I was a baby when we moved here,' she replies, 'no that's not true, I have been there with my family and yes it's hot.'

'Hot like this?'

'I guess so, it's very humid and this is humid and sticky too, yeah I think it is.'

'Can you cook Thai food?' Nick asks hopefully.

'That's racist,' Cookey blurts out.

'What? No it's not,' Nick responds.

'Just coz she's from Thailand you think she can cook Thai food, what like every Chinese person can do egg fried rice.'

'Piss off fuckwit, I asked if she could cook Thai food, I didn't just think she could.'

'Well can you cook English food then?'

'Er...yeah,' Nick replies sarcastically, 'I can do a full English.'

'A full English doesn't count,' Cookey retorts.

'What other English food is there then?' Nick demands.

'Well, other English food, you know...'

'Toad in the hole?' Blowers suggests.

'Fish and chips,' Tom adds.

'Isn't Beef Wellington an English dish?' Cookey asks.

'I don't think England is that famous for our cooking,' Nick says thoughtfully, 'anyway, ignore that retard, can you cook Thai food?'

'Yes Nick I can cook Thai food,' she replies laughing at the arguments.

'Wow! I'm starving...I wish we could have a take-away tonight,' he groans.

'I think they're closed,' Clarence says.

'Fucking zombies ruin everything,' Nick moans, 'I could murder a pizza.'

'I thought you wanted Thai food?' Lani asks.

'Well yeah but...yeah okay I could murder a Thai take-away, a Chinese, an Indian....anything really.'

'KFC?' Blowers asks.

'Shit chips at KFC,' Cookey replies.

'MacDonald's do the best chips,' Tom says.

'Nah, my local chippie does the best ones,' Nick sighs wistfully.

'Ah well, I'm sure we can have some baked beans and tinned veggies served with instant mash potato,' Blowers says.

'You remember that meal Tucker did before the fight?' Nick says quietly.

'Fucking right, Tucker was a legend,' Cookey adds.

'You'd have loved him Lani, he always had loads of food in his bag,' Nick explains, 'carried snack bars and made sure we always had stuff to eat.'

'He sounds amazing,' Lani says quietly.

'Fuck me we're going soooo slowly,' Cookey groans with a glance out the front.

'Can't speed up mate, those vans are seriously overloaded,' I shout back.

'Did you see those girls in the crowd outside the warehouse?' Nick says after a pause.

'I did,' Tom replies quickly, 'the blond and brunette yeah?'

'Yeah, they were fit,' Nick says.

'The one with the dark hair had massive ti...'

'Alex!' Dave shouts down from the GPMG, 'I can hear you and there is a lady present.'

'Sorry,' Cookey winces, apologising to Lani.

'It doesn't bother me, I worked in a nightclub for long enough,' she laughs.

'She said she doesn't mind Dave,' Cookey shouts up cheekily.

'I do,' Dave replies making me and Clarence grin.

'Can I say she was busty?' He calls up.

'Yes you can say that.'

'How about melons?' Cookey shouts to a round of low oooh's from everyone else.

'No.'

'Bazungas?'

'No.'

'Airbags?'

'No.'

'Hooters?'

'No.'

'Gob stoppers?' He keeps going, knowing he's getting laughs from everyone else.

'No.'

'Tits?'

'No.'

'Titties?'

'No.'

'Love pillows?'

'No.'

'Love pillows?' Lani laughs.

'Norks?'

'No.'

'Knockers?'

'No.'

'Gazongas?'

'No.'

'Babylons?'

'No.'

'Boobies.'

'No.'

'What? Boobies isn't offensive.'

'No.'

'Boobs?'

'Yes.'

'So busty and boobs, how about breasts?'

'Yes.'

'Okay.'

'Anymore Alex?'

'No Dave.'

'Good.'

'Yeah so the dark haired girl with the big boobs, yeah I saw her,' Cookey continues. I glance round to see Blowers clutching his sides with laughter, Nick and Tom almost crying from the quick exchange.

'He's a character,' Clarence chuckles next to me.

'He is,' I laugh back.

'Did you get their names?' Cookey asks.

'Nah, didn't really think it was the right time for my chat up lines,' Nick replies.

'Kate and Julie,' Tom says.

'How the fuck did you do that?' Nick asks stunned.

'I asked them, introduced myself while you were talking to the others.'

'You sly bastard,' Cookey laughs.

'Which one is which?' Blowers asks in an interested tone.

'Ah now that is sensitive information which I cannot divulge,' Tom replies.

'Tom! Come on mate, you got to tell us which is which,' Nick shouts.

'Do I?' Tom laughs.

'Tom, is Kate the blond one?' Cookey asks.

'I can't say,' he replies.

'Yes you can! Kate is the blond one isn't she? I know it.'

'Not saying, I've got an advantage at the moment so I can't give you any help.'

'Oh that's not fair,' Nick cuts in, 'you'll be like walking about in the fort giving it large and saying oh hi Kate or hey there Julie…stroking your gun and…'

'Stroking my gun?' Tom laughs.

'Ah this isn't fair, we're a team so we should share everything,' Cookey whines.

'Not everything,' Tom chuckles again.

'As soon as we get back I'm running down the vehicles to find them and ask,' Cookey says.

'Yeah that'll go down well,' Blowers replies.

'Bribe Doc Roberts and get them in first,' Nick jokes.

'We could if we knew their names…Tom…' Cookey adds.

'The dark haired girl is Julie,' I shout back.

'Ah Mr Howie,' Tom moans.

'Sorry Tom, I couldn't stand Cookey moaning the entire way back.'

'How do you know that?' Lani asks.

'Oh Mr Howie is in trouble,' Nick jokes to a few laughs.

'I heard someone calling her,' I shout back, twisting round to smile at her. She grins back to a few more 'oooh's' from everyone. I turn back to the road shaking my head at the absurdity of it all.

'Sun's going down, it'll be dark soon,' Clarence says after a few minutes of general chat.

'I won't miss not hearing the howls tonight,' I reply.

'Just keep thinking of that cool swim,' he says.

'Oh I am mate, a cool swim and a proper bed…sounds perfect.'

CHAPTER THIRTY-ONE

DAY SEVEN

Standing at the turnstile Paco looks back towards the town. Having left the house mid-afternoon and making his way through the residential streets, following the route of suburbia as it transitioned from terraced to semi-detached to the affluent outer reaches of detached houses with long driveways.

Carrying a gym bag filled with tinned food and water on his back he pauses and thinks if this is the right thing to do. Leave the town where there are houses with thick walls and doors. But that didn't stop them last night, so yes it is the right thing to do. Find somewhere remote and hide away. He nods and looks down at the dog sat next to him. An image floods of his mind of the DVD cover for *I Am Legend* with Will Smith stood next to a big Alsatian dog.

Paco auditioned for that role but he was told he lacked the emotional range so he missed out. This was his first zombie film and it was already billed to be the biggest zombie blockbuster ever. Well it was. Not now.

Cursing his luck he pushes the turnstile open, waiting for the dog to squeeze through. They walk into the footpath, shaded by overhanging trees and head away from the town into the countryside.

Here he is, the biggest action movie star of all time, walking through a post-apocalyptic land devastated by infected monsters with a huge dog and no one to see it. Mind you, he muses, all they would see is me blubbing in the corner of rooms while the dog does all the work. Emotional range? Damn he'd give them emotional range now. If this ever fixes he knows he'll spend the rest of his life in the counsellor's chair.

He thought being away from the town would make him feel safer and settled, but despite the recent bout of rain, the ground is hard and compacted. His boots crunch with each step, the only real sound other than the dogs faint panting. He moves over to the side, walking on the grass verge and swerving back onto the path checking which is the quieter route to walk. The grass, definitely the grass. A dry stick snaps underfoot making him jump. His already shot nerves feeling even more strained.

They press on, moving steadily away from the town and deeper into the countryside. Following signed footpaths, crossing fields and scrambling through bushes and copses. Sweat drips down his face, soaking his beard and drenching his t-shirt. Wiping it with the back of his forearm he catches the smell emanating from his armpits, grimacing in disgust and realising how easy it was for them to track him.

He stinks. Not just smells but he stinks. Shitting himself, pee escaping with fright, sweat, food, grime and filth coat his skin. The rain refreshed him but didn't budge the grease locking the dirt onto his skin.

Wash and stay clean, remove all traces of scent as often as possible. Muttering quietly to himself with an occasional glance from the dog he makes plans, creates lists and forms strategies for survival. The steady motion takes his mind back to the filming of *Man on the Run*. Playing an ex-special forces soldier accused of a crime he didn't commit and using his skills to survive in the wilds while being tracked by an increasingly growing army of police and military. A large portion of the film was showing Paco's characters using survival skills, testing for clean water, making a fire from sticks, making traps for animals. With audiences becoming ever more discerning he'd insisted on being shown the correct methods for each of the tasks he was set. A genuine survivalist was brought in to coach Paco through the close up stuff. Who was that guy? Paco frowns trying to remember his name, something all American, Chuck or Chad. Maybe Buck. He could picture the quietly spoken man now, showing him the techniques and talking him through the movements. Paco studied him closely, adopting his mannerisms and he'd scored a big hit with the audiences. But right now, at the point where he needed those skills more than ever he'd be damned if he could remember a single thing he was taught.

His mind was too full to think straight. Stuck on an endless loop of horrific images of what the monsters will do to him if they ever catch him. In his mind the sole purpose of the monsters, their sole intent was to track him down and eat him. Nothing else mattered. None of these normal little people that were killed to actually become the monsters of his nightmares. They didn't factor in his egotistical mind.

He'd fed and watered the dog before they set off, but that was simply to keep it strong and healthy as it seemed intent on sticking with him.

Looking down at the dog now, trotting along happily in the bright sunlight with her long pink tongue lolling out the side of her mouth he thinks back to how she killed that first monster in the road. Tearing its throat out with utter viciousness. And last night, listening to her kill and kill again. He shakes his head, reaching down to stroke the top of her head. She looks up, big brown eyes and gives her tail a quick wag.

'Good girl,' he says softly rubbing her head harder. Keep the dog fed, watered and happy he thinks.

A few hours of walking brings them to the side of a shallow valley. Looking down at a collection of farm buildings surrounded by cultivated fields. He drops down low, hugging the ground and staring for signs of movement.

'Too obvious,' he whispers to the dog lying next to him, 'that farmstead'll be full of good old boys toting shotguns and rifles. No sir, not for us, come on,' he scoots backwards dropping down the hill before standing up and walking away to skirt miles round the valley and deeper into the country.

They find an unmade track, rutted with potholes and two distinct lanes used by vehicle wheels with grass growing in the middle. A collection of buildings starts to show in the distance. Flashes of blue, green, yellow all in pastel shades. The land flattens out abruptly at the edge of a wooded copse. In front of him stands the stone built detached chalets. Built in a large circle around a central green. Still some distance away and he stands in the shades of the trees scanning and watching. No movement. No cars. No noise drifting over either.

They break free from the cover of the trees, edging closer to the buildings, puzzled at the display of colour so deep in the countryside. Each chalet is a different pastel shade with large sun windows. A gravel lane leads round the edge of the green giving access to the buildings. In the middle stands a brick built barbeque area and fire pit with old style wooden carved bench seats dotted about.

The lane leading in has a small car park and reception hut

made of wood. Stopping every few minutes he listens and watches. Only moving off when satisfied.

Reaching the reception hut he stops to read the welcome sign. *Table Top Holiday Chalets Are Currently Closed For Refurbishment*. His forehead knots with puzzlement at the strange name, then glancing round he nods with realisation at the unusually flat area.

'Table top,' he whispers to the dog knowingly, 'no cars, no people, miles from anywhere, what do you think dog?' He asks. She doesn't answer but sniffs the ground. He watches her for a while, checking that she's seems happy with the smells she finds.

She looks completely normal, scooting about with her nose to the ground and checking round to check he's still there every few minutes.

'Okay, let's do this,' he nods bravely and ventures past the reception building. The nerves start straight away with something new that needs checking and it sends his terror levels soaring.

They loop round the back of the buildings first, checking each window and moving from chalet to chalet. Back at the start he enters the circle again, this time to the front of the buildings and again going to each to look through the windows. With the doors and windows all locked and secured he feels satisfied that no one else is here.

At the reception building he peers through the window at the office facilities inside. An alarm box fitted to the side of the building gives him a momentary minute of worry but with no power the alarm can't go off. Finding a rock he gently taps at the pane of glass above the door lock. Wincing at the sound of smashing glass that cascades down onto the hard floor.

Inside he finds the key cupboard and thumbs through the fobs, each one tagged with a colour. Stepping outside he picks the one facing the entrance lane, pocketing the pastel blue fob and heading across the green.

Paco stands back after opening the door, staring down at the dog and watching her closely. She sniffs about and walks in without a care in the world. He holds position, waiting expectantly for her to bark, snarl or launch into an attack on monsters hiding in the rooms. It doesn't happen; instead she sniffs around the rooms and trots about. Single story, no stairs.

He closes the door behind him and walks through the small building. Two bedrooms, bathroom, kitchen and lounge. Sparsely furnished with bare essentials, some kind of idea that being in the countryside means you don't need home comforts.

In the kitchen he tests the cold tap, finding it still running with cool fresh water. With the dog watered he remembers his plans and strategies, stripping off in the kitchen and scrubbing his body down with cold water. No soap in the bathroom so he uses washing up liquid from a kitchen cupboard, foaming it up to remove the film of grease clogging his skin. Standing naked in the kitchen he soaks his clothes, using the washing up liquid and a stiff brush to scrub at the stains.

The dog watches him closely, lying next to the bowl of water and panting noisily as he wrings the clothes out and heads outside the back door to swing them round and round, sending the excess water spraying off onto the lush green grass.

With the clothes laid across a patio chair in the strong sun he potters about in his birthday suit, opening tins and feeling his skin tightening from the sudden removal of the grime.

He sits outside in the sun, feeling the warmth on his bare skin and eating cold beans, feeding the dog more ravioli and chuckling at the thought of the coming farting contest. As the sun sets he shrugs his now dry clothes on and stands at the front door, straining his ears. He waits for a long time, well past nightfall but no noises of the monsters howling reach him. He studies the dog closely, her ears prick and twitch as she detects slight noises in the bushes from animals but nothing more than that. When she lies down and rests her chin on her paws he knows they must be safe and gently calls her inside, locking the door and collapsing exhausted on the bed in the back bedroom.

The dog jumps up, walking round in a tight circle for a few seconds before lying down. Paco, laying on top of the covers with his boots on, moves his leg to rest against her back, feeling the comfort of the warmth from her body.

The following morning Paco woke from the sunlight streaming across his eyes. Blinking the sleep away he sat up, marvelling at having slept for so many hours undisturbed. The dog was already at the front door, scratching and whining. Stepping outside he stretched and yawned, checking the perimeter with a smile at the unchanged view.

'Perfect,' he whispered quietly as the dog took a piss on the grass. She turned round, sniffing her urine before moving off and taking a big steaming crap.

'Nice,' Paco said, 'maybe I should take a crap on the lawn,' he suggested heading inside to find a bag to clear the dog mess away before the smell attracted unwanted company. Failing to find a bag he used toilet tissue. The shit was half runny and still warm, soaking the paper which split as his fingers pressed into the gooey faeces. Gagging he stood up, turning round to glare at the dog. He stopped mid-turn, staring off into the distance at a thick column of smoke drifting high into the sky.

The sight brought him back to reality. Whatever it was that was burning was big, the smoke cloud was huge. Glancing around nervously he chided himself for being in a relaxed state before rushing off back into the house.

The rest of day was spent in a state of near bliss. No noises, no movement. Just peace and quiet.

He went outside periodically, making himself examine the view and memorise how everything was. If anything was moved or altered he'd know.

They drank water, lots of water and ate tinned food. The dog slept, sniffed about, pissed more and slept again. She seemed happy and content to just be which pleased Paco as he couldn't think of anywhere better to be right now. Other than in Wyoming on his ranch with his parents and all their big guns.

The day passed peacefully with Paco content to sit with his back to the front door and his legs stretched out across the gravel path. The sun was hot, the humidity was high. He dozed on and off, gently waking up every now and then. The dog did the same, shifting position to stay in the shade of the house.

By nightfall they two were rested and feeling secure for the first time in days. Nothing had happened. Not one sound other than natural animal and bird noises. Before the sun went down, Paco walked the edge of the gravel path checking the view one last time and making sure everything was still the same.

As darkness descended he retired to the bedroom, stretching out on the covers with the dog at his feet again. He thought of home, of his family and the life he had. He remembered the girl in his trailer giving him the blowjob before it all went so terribly wrong. What was her name? Hell, what was any of their names? Lucy was a strange cookie he mused in the darkness. Shame she got herself trapped, could have had some more fun with that one.

His breathing slowed, his heart rate relaxed as his unconscious slowly steals the light from his mind.

'Ssshh,' he nudges the dog with his leg, rolling onto his side. She growls again, louder this time snapping him awake instantly.

He sits up, the moonlight creeping in through the window and offering some illumination. Head cocked to one side listening intently. His heart already going like the clappers. He scoots off the bed, standing up slowly and creeping round to the other side. He rests his hand on the dog's head quietly shushing her so he can listen. She ignores him, eyes fixed on the window and staring hard into the night. He moves over to the side of the window, slowly poking his head round and peering out into the darkness. Nothing there, no movement. The moon is bright and his eyes well-adjusted to the gloom. He sweeps his gaze along the perimeter. All the houses are the same, he can see out beyond them to the surrounding area.

'What is it?' He whispers to the dog. There must be a reason why she's growling. He eases himself through the small chalet, checking out of windows and examining the view he'd already committed to memory. Everything looked the same.

He cracks the front door open and listens. Again nothing. He opens it wider, peering out but keeping his hands firmly on the handle ready to slam it closed.

The dog squeezes past his legs, standing in front of him and growling at the entrance lane. Something must be out there. The monsters, they must be coming down the lane after following his stinky armpits and fetid arse across the valleys and hills.

He tenses up, ready to flee. Monsters are coming; they're coming to eat the flesh from my bones. Monsters carrying flashlights. No, that's not right. They don't carry flashlights, do they?

He stares harder, watching the pinpricks of light getting larger; a dull roar reaches his ears. An engine. Vehicle headlamps shining down the lane. The relief is palpable, other people, other survivors. But it's the middle of the night, why are they driving in the night when it's most dangerous? Unless something is chasing them.

With the thoughts whirling through his mind he urges the dog back inside and closes the door quickly, dropping down and crawling into the bedroom to watch through the window. The dog, recognising the sound of the vehicle felt it could relax but the man's fear went up. He's scared and hiding. She stays alert watching Paco as he gradually lifts up to poke his head above the windowsill and watch the lights coming in.

The vehicle pulls into the gravel lane, the lights sweeping across the houses until it does a full loop, stopping by the entrance.

After ducking down and hiding from the lights going past, Paco again peers out the window and watches as the mini-van comes to a stop. Two people get out, both male by the looks of their size and build. They stand talking and looking about, the moonlight bathing them in an eerie glow which just increases the tension Paco feels.

One of the men lights a cigarette, causing Paco to break out in panic at the smell it will produce. Knowing the monsters can smell and track them from a great distance. One of the men says something, the other laughs. The sound is weird, not just laughing but drunken guffawing. They both laugh as one lifts a bottle to his lips and takes a big swig. The one without the bottle goes to the back of the van, opening the doors and leaning inside. He drags another person out. A woman with her hands tied behind her back. She screams and cries out, both the men laugh again and push her roughly to the floor.

Between them, the men manhandle the woman to the centre of the grass, near the fire pit. After dumping the woman on the ground they stand talking and sharing the bottle, passing it between them and tilting their heads back taking long gulps.

Paco watches with a feeling of dread growing in his stomach at the sight of the woman writhing on the ground. These men must have known this place was here. He curses himself softly, knowing it was too good to be true. Why can't they go somewhere else? Everyone has been turned into goddamn monsters, there's loads of empty houses. Why here?

The men laugh noisily, the sounds easily drifting over to Paco and the dog. He watches as they start breaking up a wooden chair, smashing into smaller pieces and piling the bits into the fire pit. Great, Paco thinks, they're settling in for a sing-song round the campfire, fucking toasting marshmallows.

One of the men goes back to the van, coming back with another bottle. He screws the lid off and pours some of the contents over the broken wood, lighting a match and flicking it down. The liquor ignites instantly, showering them in the golden glow from the flames.

One is big and fat. Standing over six feet in height with a great big gut straining against some kind of English football shirt. The other is skinny, wearing a vest and shorts and covered in tattoos. They both look like tough men as they stand there smoking and laughing.

Watching them, Paco almost forgets about the girl until the fat guy reaches down and drags her to her feet. She tries to pull away but he grabs at a length of rope dangling from her bound wrists, laughing as she tries to pull away and yanking her round in circles until she falls to the floor. Both men find this hilarious and quickly get the woman back to her feet and make her do it again, running round and round until she falls down crying and sobbing.

The fat man pulls her up again, this time he doesn't spin her round but pulls her into him. Turning her round so her back is pressed against his fat stomach. Paco's own stomach drops as his hands come round her front, roughly squeezing her breasts. The skinny guys laughs, egging him on. The fat man carries on for a few seconds, the girl writhing and begging them to stop. He laughs as he takes both his hands and rips her top off, tearing the material and exposing her breasts.

The atmosphere charges instantly. Paco's heart sinks as he realises what they're going to do. Right in front of him too. She screams as the fat man grabs at her naked breasts, squeezing them harder and harder until her knees give out and she drops down. He laughs and pulls her head into his groin, bucking back and forth as the skinny guy clutches his sides laughing at the sight.

An image of the girl in the trailer flashes through Paco's mind. On her knees in front of him. Just like that girl. The thought makes him feel sick. Overwhelmingly disgusted at himself and mankind for what they do.

The fat man pushes her away violently. Taking the bottle from the other guy he takes a long glug and spits it down onto her face.

'Oi you cunt, don't fuckin' waste it,' the skinny man shouts.

'She's thirsty ain't she? 'Ere love, you thirsty are ya?' The fat man leers, taking another mouthful and spraying it down onto her.

'I'll get another one if you're spittin' it about,' skinny man shouts.

'Go on then, not like we ain't got enough is it,' the fat man roars back, clearly showing who the leader of the pair is. The skinny man walks off, heading back to the van. 'Take ya pants off darlin', things are gonna get interestin,' the fat man nudges the woman with his foot.

'She's got her fuckin' hands tied ain't she,' the skinny man shouts, walking back with another bottle.

'Oh yeah,' the fat man laughs, 'she still looks thirsty to me, she look thirsty to you?'

'I reckon she does yeah,' the skinny man replies.

'Hold her 'ead, we'll give her a drink…go on take her fackin' 'ead will ya, fackin' 'ell, that's it, hold her tight, 'ere are love, go on have a drink on me,' they both laugh as the fat man holds the lip of the bottle to her mouth and gently upends it. The liquid pouring into her mouth as she chokes and gasps. They keep going, giving her a second to breath before doing it again. After a few minutes they get bored as the fat man's hand drops to her breasts, kneading and rubbing away, forgetting about the bottle.

'You gonna do her?' The skinny man asks excitedly.

'Course I fackin' am, get her pants off will ya,' the fat man staggers back, drunkenly pulling his football shirt off and shrugging his shorts down. His erect penis looks tiny against the bulk off his stomach and fat thighs.

'Oh no,' Paco whispers, his heart breaking at the sight. He wants to turn away but he remains rooted to the spot. Cursing himself for being a coward and not doing something.

Skinny man twists the girl round and starts pulling her jeans off, she tries to wriggle but he pushes one foot down onto her stomach, lifting her feet up and laughing as he tugs the material at her ankles. She tries fighting but the jeans come off.

'She ain't got no knickers on,' the skinny guy shouts, 'you 'ear that? The slag ain't got no knickers on.'

'She fackin' wants it she does,' the fat man shouts, his voice now low and hoarse with the flush of excitement at the naked woman lying in front of him.

'Please...' she says the first clear word since arriving, her voice soft and terrified. Paco winces at the sound, his eyes screwing shut, his hands gripping the windowsill. The dog senses his anguish and growls softly.

'Please...no....please...don't do this to me....'

'Shut up you fackin' slut, you want some cock don't ya? Yeah that's why you got no panties on' the fat man drops down onto his knees, his stomach wobbling with the impact sent juddering up through his legs. He grabs her ankles and draws her towards him. Skinny guy half laughing and watching with clear excitement.

'I'm begging you, please...oh my god! Please...' She screams in pain as the fat man thrusts into her. The muscles in Paco's arms bulge from his grip on the windowsill. Dropping his head he prays this is a nightmare, end this now. Please end this now.

'Oh god please no!...' She screams out as the fat man ruts away, his swollen gut crushing her as he props his props his body up on his arms, sweat dripping from his chin onto her writhing face.

'Please...Mummy...' she yells in such terror that something in Paco snaps. The poor girl calling for her mother is too much, and he stands up, striding towards the front door.

'Get your hands off her,' he bellows, wrenching the door open and striding outside. Skinny guy turns stunned as the fat man slowly twists his head round, poised mid thrust.

'Who the fuck are you?' the fat man asks belligerently. The fear hits Paco again, suddenly realising what he's doing. Standing and confronting two tough looking men. This isn't the movies Paco; they don't just stop when you yell something.

'I said...get off her,' he yells again but the power has drained from his voice, his legs feeling suddenly weak and shaky.

'Fack off,' the fat man shouts, 'wait ya turn, fackin yank cunt, sort him out Steve.' He carries on thrusting away, laughing at the look on Paco's face as he stands there bewildered and clearly shitting himself.

The sound of glass smashing snaps Paco's head to the skinny guy, stood there holding the remains of the bottle by the neck. The jagged ends facing towards Paco as he starts advancing.

'You want some yank do ya? Come on then...come on you fuckin' yank cunt...'

'Hey guy just take it easy,' Paco steps back raising one hand to wave at the man. Steve speeds up, waving the bottle left to right as he shouts goadingly at Paco.

'Big cunt like you backin' away like a pussy, come on you fucker,' the skinny man shouts louder, his voice harsh and brutal.

A black shadow flits past Paco's legs as the dog charges the man down. Hearing the aggression in his voice she doesn't hesitate, crossing the grass within seconds and using the same method she learnt with the things. Slamming her body weight into his chest, knocking him flat over before sinking her teeth into his throat and ragging her neck violently, tearing his jugular to pieces. Skinny guy's screams end abruptly as his windpipe is severed.

'Jesus,' Paco says stunned.

'Fack me,' the fat man shouts, rolling off the girl and crawling away towards his shorts. The dog releases the skinny man after shaking him about like a rag doll. She backs away growling at the body as though daring it to get back up. She turns slowly, fixing her eyes on the fat man crawling away.

'Ere mate, sort your fackin' dog out will ya,' he screams in alarm, getting to his feet to pull his shorts on, his penis already flaccid from the sudden turn of events.

Paco walks forward as though in a dream. Looking down at the remains of the skinny guy and the dog stalking towards the fat man.

'Have her for fuck's sake, we's only 'aving a laugh...Jesus mate...call your fackin' dog off will ya.'

'It's not my dog,' Paco replies stupidly, 'I don't know her name.'

'Well whose fackin' dog is it then?' The fat man shouts.

'I don't know,' Paco can't believe he's having this conversation. His eyes flicking back to the wound in Steve's neck. He'd seen the bodies in the house and the one the dog took down in the street but they were monsters with red eyes. This was a normal man; he was speaking just a few seconds ago. His eyes fall on the girl, lying there naked and staring at him in shock. Her legs still bent from the position the fat man forced her into. She looks young, maybe seventeen or eighteen years old at the most. Her fingers twitch as though reaching out for him. His mind flushes with the very recent memory of her screaming for her mother, the instinctive calling for the protection of the one person who has always cared for her.

His eyes rise slowly, settling on the fat man. Something on Paco's face sends a signal, causing the fat men to freeze.

For days now he's been living with fear. Terror has consumed him, driven all other thoughts from his mind. He's been unable to function apart from the one urgent pressing need to survive and flee, believing he was just an actor and not capable of defending himself or fighting. But all those action films and every one of them had instructors showing him what to do, how to fight, how to drop a man, break his arm, break his legs, snap bones. He was taught how to punch, how to kick, what strikes to use. Pre-filming training kept him in the gym for hours every day, sparring with experts. He became adept at the close quarters fighting techniques so valued by the studios these days. His trademark moves used in nearly every film. He was strong, fit and despite the fear that ate him up, he was skilled.

Paco strides forward, his long legs eating the ground as he crossed the grass towards the fat man, the dog pacing with him at his side.

'Ease up mate...fackin' 'ell mate...no hard feelings eh? 'Ere, you're that fackin' actor ain't ya, what is it? Paco Maguire, yeah...fackin' hell.' The fat man stops backing away, grinning like an idiot before clocking the intense look on Paco's face. He tensed up, full of alcohol and bravado. A veteran of many pub fights and football ground melees. Waiting for Paco to get closer he suddenly lunges forward, yelling loudly and flailing his fists towards Paco's head.

Paco's guard is up, blocking the punches, striding in close he delivers several snappy punches to the fat stomach, driving the man back. Paco lashes out, hammering his fists into the man's face. Stepping round his training kicks in as he goes for the trademark move of so many of his films. Slamming his foot down on the back of a knee, forcing the man down. Paco quickly wraps his left arm round the man's head pulling him in close. With every ounce of strength he grips the head, twisting to the side while pushing down. The spinal column snaps, breaking his neck.

With anger driving his actions he thinks something is wrong, the man is still moving. He heard the bone break, why is he still moving? He twists the head again, back the other way and roaring with power as he wrenches it back and forth, killing the man over and again.

He drops the body, realising the dog has a firm grip of one fat calf and is busy tearing it to shreds, jerking the body round. As it drops to the ground the dog drives in, going for the throat and ripping it out before dropping back low and growling.

He just killed a man. Killed him with his bare hands. He looks down at his arms in horror and awe at what he's done. The instant conflict raging through his mind. Murder. He wanted to kill the man and he did. That's murder. He intended it to be done; he wanted to end the life of this man.

Staggering round he spots the woman sat up, holding her knees to her chest and staring at the ground. He remembers what the fat man did and the guilt goes as quickly as it came.

He walks over to her, unsure of what to do. Hesitating and flapping his arms. She stares motionless at the ground, seemingly unaware of his presence.

'Hey, you okay?' He asks, cursing himself for another stupid question. She's naked, having just been raped. Do you think she's okay?

He drops down, edging closer to the girl. She doesn't flinch or shy away like they do in the movies. She just sits there, staring with wide eyes, unblinking, unmoving.

'We need to get you inside,' he says softly. She doesn't move, not a flutter. 'Listen, I'm gonna carry you okay? I'll take you inside so you can clean up…I promise I won't hurt you.' He gently pushes one arm under her knees and wraps her other round her back, lifting her easily and carrying her across the grass to the house.

Inside he takes her to the bedroom, gently lowering her down onto the covers and pulling them over her. She doesn't speak, doesn't whimper. Not a single reaction.

'I'll get you some water okay?' He moves into the kitchen, filling a glass and finding the washing up bowl, he fills it with water and grabs a cloth from the side. Rushing back into the room he puts the bowl down and gently lifts the girl up, pressing the glass into her hands.

'Come on honey, have some water,' he urges softly. She responds, grasping the glass and pulling it to her mouth, drinking quickly while staring at him with the same wide eyes.

'You're gonna be okay kid, they're gone now…you need to clean up, there's water and a cloth here…I'll be right outside if you need me,' his deep American voice seems to sooth the girl. Her hand reaching out as he goes to leave.

'Don't leave me,' she whimpers in a quiet voice.

'Sure kid, I'll stay right here,' he sits back down, smoothing her hair from her forehead. He wrings the cloth out and wipes her face, gently removing the fat man's sweat from her skin. 'What's your name honey?'

'Meredith,' she whispers.

'Well hey Meredith, I'm Paco…listen honey, you take this cloth and clean yourself, you know what I mean?' She nods back clearly terrified and shaking like a leaf.

'Get yourself cleaned up, I'll be right outside.'

'No,' she whispers urgently her hand gripping his wrist.

'Okay, I'll stay, I'm gonna turn this way okay? See, I can't see you kid, you get yourself cleaned up and I'll stay right here.' He listens to the rustling as the girl rubs herself with the cloth. Whimpering with pain she rubs harder and harder, whimpering louder as she tries to rid herself of the every trace of the fat man.

'Take it easy honey,' Paco says still looking away. She ceases at his deep tones and hands the cloth over. He takes it from her, his eyes squeezing closed for a second at the sight of the dark patches on the white cloth.

'Hey, see that's better,' he turns back, her face shining from the moonlight. A tear rolls down her cheek, followed by another. Her bottom lip trembling before she bursts in tears, loud sobs that wrack her body. She reaches out for him, he responds by shuffling closer and wrapping his arms round her shoulders. She buries her head onto his chest, her body heaving as she cries violently. Paco rubs her shoulders gently, his heart breaking at the grief and terror she went through. He should have moved quicker. If he'd moved quicker this wouldn't have happened. The dog, sensing the distress of the girl jumps onto the bed, pushing her nose into the girls face and licking her cheeks. She loops an arm round its neck, holding it tightly.

They stay there for hours, the girl sobbing and crying herself to sleep until Paco gently lays her down. She grips his arm as he goes to leave and he lies down next to her. The dog settles next to her legs, the two of them offering a protective shield to the young girl.

He wakes several times during the night to feel her crying next to him. He soothes her with quiet words, stroking her head until they both go quiet and he drifts back off to sleep.

The next morning, he wakes with a start at the dog nosing his face and whimpering urgently. Sitting bolt upright and staring at the empty space next to him. He scrabbles off the bed, glancing down at the bloodied water in the bucket and the cloth now stained pink.

He staggers into the hallway, crying out at the sight of the girl's body hanging from the inside of the front door. He runs over, yelling out and lifting her up, desperately trying to take the pressure from her neck. Fumbling he opens the door and holds her body up, blood stains still marking the white skin between her naked legs. He tugs the rope from the top of the door and lowers her body down. His strong fingers working at the ligature round her throat. The skin tight and misshapen from the downwards pressure of her body.

Crying with frustration he runs into the kitchen, wrenching drawers open and emptying the contents onto the side. With a sharp knife in hand he rushes back, dropping down and gently cutting into the rope. He gets through it, pulling the length away from her skin. Drool hangs from her mouth dried spittle coats her lips. Her eyes open and lifeless.

'Her kid, come on,' he yells and drops his ear down to her mouth, listening for breath. He pushes his ear against her chest, no heartbeat. He works quickly, pulling her head back and clamping his mouth over hers and exhaling. Her chest rises as her lungs inflate; he repeats the action before pushing his palms into her breast bone and starting compression. Ribs snap and break under the pressure. He keeps going; tears of his own streaming down his cheeks. The dog sat watching.

'Come on kid,' he yells in sheer frustration, 'don't do this...come on!' He keeps breathing for her, pushing at her chest. Sweat forms and drips from his head. Seconds go by, minutes tick away. She remains the same.

He sinks back onto the floor next to her. Crying with grief. Remorse flooding through his system, his hands shake as he rubs his face roughly. Pushing his hair back, rocking back and forth and wailing. Not caring if every monster in the country came for him. He wouldn't run. He'd offer himself to them. He deserved it. He deserved to die for what he'd done. He should have acted faster, he should have gone straight outside, he should have stayed awake during the night, he should never have left Lucy, he should have gone into the cottage and tried to get her out. Stinking dirty yellow coward. He beats himself in the head with his palms. The dog whimpering and lying down to stare at him forlornly.

The tears ease, the fear gone. A seed of numbness takes root in his soul, spreading its roots throughout his body. He stares at the ground between his legs, examining the minute details of the flooring.

He knows he has to do something with her body, that she's lying there naked and dead after being horrifically abused.

With a heavy heart he carried the dead girl into the spare bedroom, laying her on the bed to wrap her in the bed sheets. Leaving the corpse he ventures outside into the bright light and heat of the day. The ruined body of Steve inert on the grass, the fat man further away. He walks with purpose across the green, bending down to grasp Steve by an ankle, dragging him easily across the lawn to the fat man. Without pause he leans down and takes a firm grip of the fat man's ankle, the muscles in his upper body and legs straining as he drags the dead weight towards the van.

Paco dumps the corpses by the still open back doors and climbs in, looking for tools. He finds cases of booze, whiskey and vodka and cartons of cigarettes. A few items of snack food but no tools other than a tyre iron, which won't do for the task he has in mind.

He heads over to the reception building, reaching his hand through the broken pane of glass, opening the door and checking inside. A cabinet at the rear full of gardening tools, he nods in satisfaction grabbing a shovel and heading back outside.

Staring at the central grass area he thinks of where to dig. Not here, not where she suffered so much. That would be wrong.

Instead he heads inside the house and hoists the body gently over his shoulder, taking the shovel he heads backs down the lane, taking care to walk gently as though fearful of causing her discomfort.

Away from the houses he finds a grassed meadow bordered by a row of trees to one side. A peaceful and tranquil setting. Paco opens the gate and walks deep into the field, gently resting the body on the ground before spitting on his hands and driving the edge of the shovel into the earth.

The hard packed soil yields slowly but years of solid training, eating well and taking care of himself have made him strong. His mind now set and he digs, digs hard, relentless. The sun beats down as he drives that shovel into the soil again and again. Heaving the heavy loads to the side, the dog lying close by watching him silently.

Paco doesn't rest or cease, sweat pours from his body. The too tight top is too tight and is discarded quickly. Shoulders bulging, arms straining he digs the grave. Driving deep into the ground. Standing back he looks at his work. The sadness creeping up and threatening to pull him down into the open grave.

He lifts the body gently, carrying it over and down into the earth. He lays Meredith to rest, smoothing the bed sheets over her body. Finally, he tugs the sheet clear of her face. Staring down at her young face. Tears fall free now, she looks so young. A whole life ahead of her. He kisses his fingertips and gently touches them to her forehead before covering her face. The act of covering in the dirty soil upsets him more than anything. She was too good for this, too good to be left in an unmarked grave in an unknown field. This shouldn't happen this way. He forces himself to lift that first shovel full of soil, pausing before gently laying it onto her body. The soil crumbs tumbling across the sheet.

A sob breaks out from his throat, a dry sound that plunges him into despair. He works harder, shovelling the earth quickly. He doesn't look down into the grave now, but drives the shovel back and forth, slowly covering the body and filling the grave. He cries non-stop throughout the ordeal, berating himself, cursing himself, self-loathing bursting from every atom of his being.

Finally it's done, a mound of bare earth marking the spot of the taken girl. He stands back leaning on the shovel, his torso gleaming in sweat. Eyes red and puffy. One day this mound will seed with grass and flowers and become a feature of the meadow. Maybe in the distant future a young girl will venture to sit with a young boy, hold hands and plan their lives, never knowing of the poor Meredith that lies beneath them.

'Lord, I don't know if you're there, I guess not after what you've done to us,' Paco speaks out, standing at the foot of the grave, the shovel held over one shoulder, 'but this girl didn't deserve what happened and I will never forgive you for that, but if you're there…if you can hear me…please take this girl into your arms. Accept her into heaven, if she's sinned before she died then I'll take those sins, you hear me? I'll take the sins she committed, you send me to damnation a thousand times over and I'll live in the eternal fires for ever more but you take her into heaven and end her pain. He turns quickly, picking his top up and wiping the stinging sweat and tears from his eyes.

'Come on dog.'

The dog follows him from the field. Sensing his change. The fear in him has completely gone now. No longer a little one but a man. They walk down the lane only stopping as he climbs into the back of the van, coming back out with a bottle of whiskey. Throwing the shovel down he twists the lid off and holds the bottle to his lips.

'For Meredith,' he drinks deep, glugging the harsh liquid down his throat. They cross the lawn, entering the house. The door slamming shut behind them.

CHAPTER THIRTY-TWO

D AY ELEVEN

'There it is,' I shout out. The drive did speed up for the last few miles. Using the radio we checked the vans were okay, pushing just a bit faster to try and get back before dark. Driving down the lane towards the housing estate and the end is in sight. Spirits lift and the banter becomes louder, everyone chatting about the swim we're going to have, getting cleaned up and putting fresh clothes on.

Dave does interject and reminds the younger ones of their responsibility to cleaning their weapons and sorting their kit out first, and then goes on to mention about being back in the fort in front of others. Clarence and I smile like old timers at the mini lecture he gives which, to be fair, they listen to readily enough and promise to get everything sorted.

'Fo...M...Wie....' Our radios crackle with static and a broken transmission.

'This is Howie, you're not coming through, say again.'

'Fort to Mr Howie, is that you?'

'Howie to the fort, yeah this is me, who's that?'

'Howie its Ted, Chris has gone out on an urgent search, we need you straight back here.'

'We're on our way into the estate now Ted, what's happened?'

'I'll explain when you get here but be ready to go straight back out.'

'Yeah okay mate, just a few minutes.'

'What was that about Mr Howie?' Blowers calls out.

'No idea mate sounds bad though.'

'Speed up boss, the convoy'll be safe enough now,' Clarence urges. The light-hearted chat ends with the transmission, everyone leaning forward and staring out the front window. All thoughts of a peaceful evening and a cooling swim gone from our minds as I accelerate through the estate into the flatlands.

'Must be bad if they've sent Chris out,' I say out loud.

'Check your weapons and ammunition and make sure you've got plenty of water too,' Dave calls down.

'Doing it now,' Blowers replies. We speed down the access road, the night sky coming down faster now. The fort already showing lights to the front.

As we pull up we see Ted, Sergeant Hopewell and Terri stood with others talking animatedly, they look focussed and intense.

'Howie, where the hell have you been?' Sergeant Hopewell snaps as we climb stiffly down from the vehicle.

'We got the cash and carry, well all the stock from it anyway...there were survivors there too, they're behind us coming in, what's happened?'

'How many?' Terri cuts in quickly.

'Er...just under sixty or so, plus vehicles and food.'

'I'll get some more people to sort them out Sarge,' she says quickly, walking off towards the gate.

'Howie, Chris has gone straight out into a town north of here, a family arrived earlier, the woman said there was a dog outside her house for a period of over twelve hours. The dog was killing the things, but it didn't turn. It was there from the afternoon through to the following morning...'

'It didn't turn?' I ask quickly, the others crowding round behind me, listening intently.

'No, she saw it killing them. A normal dog, normal eyes, wagging its bloody tail and drinking water...Doctor Roberts said...'

'Yeah I know what he would have said, where is it? How long ago? What type of dog is it?'

'An Alsatian, very very big. Mostly black, a female dog she thinks. It was here on this map. We've got her to mark where her house was and the last place she saw it.'

'How long ago?' Clarence repeats my question.

'That's the bad thing,' she grimaces, 'maybe a week or so, all she can remember is that it was only a few days after it started.'

'German Shepherd,' Dave says as we all turn to look at him, 'the correct name is German Shepherd, Alsatian was a name they gave the breed during the war...'

'Yeah cheers for that Dave,' I nod at him before turning back to sergeant Hopewell, 'so she definitely saw it killing them? Taking their blood into its mouth and it didn't turn for twelve hours, is that right?'

'That's it, listen I know it's been a long day but Chris is already out and we...'

'We're going straight back out, we need fuel, water and food, we'll eat on the way.'

'Leave that to me,' Ted says curtly.

'Debbie, is there a hose near the front? We're desperate for a quick wash, we'll be five minutes while Ted gets what we need.'

'There's one just inside the inner gate.'

'That'll do, Lani you're the fastest, run to our rooms and get any clean tops you can find in there, Blowers I want you to speak to Ted and get us some torches and make sure he gets us spare batteries, the rest of you go inside and use the hose. Stay close to the front, we'll be moving off as soon as we've got fuelled up.' They head off without a word of argument, no moaning about being hot or tired, no mention of the swim we should have had. Dave goes with Lani, the two of them sprinting easily into the fort. Blowers grabs Ted who nods back at him and uses his radio to order torches and batteries to be brought down.

'What did the doc say?' Clarence asks the sergeant.

'Just that we've got to find it and get it back here, he needs fuel for his equipment but the most important thing is the dog.'

'Is it just that dog? That breed? All dogs? What more do we know?' I ask.

'We don't know, but I can tell you that the people in the camp recall seeing cats and rats infected like the people but no dogs, not one account of a dog being turned or being infected.'

'That doesn't mean they're immune,' Clarence says.

'We know that, Doc Roberts said the same thing. He said he'd bet no one had seen an infected cow or chicken either but that doesn't mean they're immune to...the infection, virus...whatever it is seems to target humans, maybe because of the intelligence and ability to communicate, the dominant species of the planet or the species that seems to live the longest...anyway it seems that other than the rats no other species have been noted as having turned. Now this dog could be many things, it could be a delayed reaction and it could have turned the minute she left it, or it could be the breed of dog, or it could be all dogs. We simply don't know but we can't take that chance. If there is an animal out there that holds something in its blood that prevents the virus from taking it over…'

'Then we need it here,' I finish her sentence for her, my mind buzzing with the possibilities this brings. It might be nothing, just a false lead or something a terrified woman recalls wrong, but they're right, if there is one slim minute chance of it being immune we have to find it.

'Won't we need a vet?' Clarence asks.

'We've got one, a student vet anyway, but she was in her last year and not far of qualifying. She's one of the female medics checking the new people over before they go in. But they both said, the vet and Doc Roberts that the blood is the important thing, we need that dogs blood here for testing… and fuel so he can run the equipment.'

'Shut everything non-essential down, people can cook on open fires if they need to, get these lights off…'

'We're doing it now,' she replies haughtily, 'the lights are from batteries and we're draining all the spare vehicle tanks now.'

'We've got more vehicles behind us, you can use them until we get more. Right we're going in for a wash, shout when the fuel is done.' We walk off towards the gates. Both of us stunned and silent from the news.

Breaching protocol we go straight through without being checked, heading inside to find the lads stood with their tops off and Cookey bent over holding the hose over the top of his head. Buckets have been filled which they use to soak and rinse their tops before using the hose to rinse the sweat off their skin.

We join in, stripping off as Dave and Lani jog back clutching handfuls of fresh tops from our rooms.

The water is amazing, feeling icy cold and making me yelp in delight as it rushes out down my face and onto my chest. I could stand here for hours, just letting the cold liquid spill over me.

We each take a turn, rushing through the wash and soaking our filthy clothes. Lani goes last, smiling at me and holding a towel out.

'Can you hold this up please, I've only got a bra on underneath,' the lads all turn away thoughtfully as I spread it out, holding it up high.

She yelps too as the water hits her skin, 'oh that's so nice,' she moans with pleasure. Damn I wish I could peek behind this towel, just the image of her standing there in a bra with the water pouring down her dusky skin gets me going. Shaking my head to re-focus she laughs and splashes noisily.

'Don't let it slip now,' she whispers, 'I'm just changing my bra.'

'Stop it,' I whisper back.

'Oh it's so nice to stand here with no top on, the water is lovely.'

'Oh god,' I mutter quietly.

'Are you tempted to look?' She whispers again.

'Of course I bloody am,' I reply.

'You're very restrained.'

'I won't be if you don't hurry up.'

'Get Clarence to hold it and come round here with me,' she laughs.

'I wish...but we've got to see a man about a dog.'

'What man?' she asks.

'Eh? It's a saying...you know when...'

'I know I was joking.'

'Oh, sorry.'

'I'm done, you can relax,' she steps out looking fresh as a daisy with a big grin.

'Thank god for that,' I smile back.

We join the others, Lani mentioning she needs to get

something from the Saxon and heading back out. We change into dry tops, checking our sizes and laughing when Clarence tries to put a much smaller one on.

'Mr Howie, can I show you something please?' Lani asks, stood to the side of the medical tent as the rest of us walk through towards the outside and Ted filling the Saxon from fuel cans.

'Yeah what's up?' I reply, stepping over to the side. She pauses for a second, watching the others file out the gates. Nodding her head she motions me to follow her and steps further back into the shadows.

'Lani? What's up?' I ask concerned, carefully stepping after her. I feel a tight grip on my wrist as she pulls me in and presses her body against mine.

'You're so bloody slow,' she mutters before pushing her lips against mine. The world stops spinning, time and motion is frozen as our lips touch. A stolen kiss behind a medical tent after an exhausting day and it's the best moment of my life. My hands reach up, cupping and framing her face. Our lips press gently at first, savouring the touch. My heart hammers in my chest, my legs feel shaky. The pressure between us builds as we start to kiss harder, her arms going round my neck and pulling me in tightly.

Stars explode behind my eyes, blood thunders past my ears. She feels so warm and soft, the natural scent of her hair filling my nose. Her lips so soft and inviting. Our tongues probe gently, she murmurs softly. My arms reach round her body holding her close.

Of all the things I've done in my life, of all the amazing adventures Dave and I have had, the fights, the battles...this is by far the most beautiful of them all.

'Wow,' I breathe out as we separate, our faces holding inches apart and bodies still pressing together.

'We could be in for a rough night,' she whispers, 'in case something happens…I didn't want to wait any longer…'

'I'm glad you didn't, I wish I'd done this ages ago.'

'Then why didn't you?' She asks gently.

'Too shy I guess.'

'Shy? You're Mr Howie, the fearsome killer of the undead, the leader of the living army,' she chuckles softly.

'Yeah but…' I don't finish my sentence, instead pulling her in for another kiss.

'Boss, we're ready to go,' Clarence yells from somewhere a million miles away in another dimension. His words do bring us back to reality and we slink out into the pale light, our faces flushed and grinning. Clarence stands there, a slow smile spreading across his broad face and gives a knowing wink.

'Right behind you,' I reply sheepishly. He nods, leading us back to the Saxon which gives me just enough time to regain my composure. The lads are stood round chatting, Lani heads straight for them as I climb into the driver's seat and start the engine.

'Did we get the water?' I call out as I swing the front round to head back down the lane.

'Yeah loads,' Blowers replies passing me a bottle which is surprisingly cold to the touch, 'they kept them in buckets of water in the shade,' he explains.

'Good, I think we're going to need them.'

CHAPTER THIRTY-THREE

D AY ELEVEN

He emerges into the blinding light, hand held in front of his eyes trying to shield them from the glare. The past few days have passed in a drunken blur. Going through bottle after bottle of booze, only stopping to eat, piss, shit and sleep.

For every swig he took he toasted the memory of Meredith. The sweet angel who suffered so badly because of his cowardice and lack of action. The action of killing the fat man replays in his mind, the movements were so quick and instinctive. The years of training for films had been worth it but now it's too late. She's dead and in his mind, the whole episode is his fault.

The dog watched him slip into a blur of drunkenness, staying by his side throughout every drunken action. As he sang sweet ballads, vomited from drinking too much, as he smashed round the house in violent outbursts of temper, as he sank into depression crying and sobbing, wailing pitifully as the image of her hanging from the door refuses to budge from his head.

She was glad of the rest and to stay inside away from the ever increasing heat, but still his sadness infected her. There were times when he held her close, burying his crying eyes into the soft fur of her neck. There were times when he talked to her at length, explaining about how movies were made and imparting salacious gossip about other famous actors. And there were times he sat morose, silent and brooding, staring off into the middle distance, the only movement was his arm lifting the bottle to his lips.

On the eleventh day he ran out of booze. With the food all gone he realised what a sorry state he was in. The depths of his grief had absorbed him completely. Removed him from the present.

Now, standing in the sunlight, his jaw covered in thick dark bristles, hooded eyes almost as red and bloodshot as the monsters he realises they need to leave this place. No food, no booze, nothing but water remains here. If he had booze he would quite happily drink himself to death and wait his turn to die, remembering the promise he made to take the sins of the girl.

But the dog, she had saved him time and time again and she was hungry. He had been a total douchebag already but he'd be damned if she would suffer anymore because of him. They had to move out, find food and then head back here.

The minivan was still there, he headed towards it, grateful that he didn't have to walk in this blistering head. England was meant to be cold and damp with overcast skies. This was like Hawaii or the Caribbean but without the ocean breeze.

Damn, the bodies were still there. Stinking filthy corpses covered in flies and maggots crawling in the open wounds of the skinny guy. He veered round them, covering his nose and mouth from the foul stench. Standing at the driver's door his shoulders sagged, the keys weren't in the ignition.

'Jesus guys, who's gonna steal it out here?' he asked the corpses at his feet. He chose the skinny guy first, remembering he went back for the bottle. Gingerly he plucks the material away from the bloated body, tapping his hand down the pockets and finding a bulge within. Gagging from the stench invading his throat he reaches a hand inside, plucking the keys before darting away to retch on hands and knees.

An empty stomach produces only bitter, stinging bile. He staggers to his feet, spitting the taste away and shaking his head at the misery of it all.

Slamming the rear doors closed he climbs into the driver's seat and works out how to push the chair back. The engine fires up first time as he familiarises himself with the stick shift in the middle. The dog, already seated on the small double passenger seat with her head out the window looks excited to be moving. Panting away and making small whining noises.

Pulling away he heads onto the lane, driving slowly past the field and staring at the stark mound of earth so obvious against the green grass.

The sadness plunges him back down as he faces forward. Not a flicker of emotion shows on his face now, just the spreading numbness and a sick empty feeling from too much liquor and not enough food.

They drive in silence with the dog in a state of ecstasy at holding her head outside and feeling the rush of wind against her face. Her bulk blocks the window entirely, barely keeping herself on the seat and he quickly learns to brake gently to save her slipping off.

Glancing at the fuel gauge he nods at the indicator

showing just below half a tank. Should be enough to get into the town, find food, booze and get back again. After that? Who cares? There is no place else to go, nothing else to do but sit and wait for the inevitable.

CHAPTER THIRTY-FOUR

D AY ELEVEN

The infection lost the dog some days ago, after losing yet more valuable host bodies to its sharp teeth and powerful jaws. Since then the world had moved on. The survivors had already become fewer and were more cunning. Hiding during the night and only moving in the day.

The battle of the fort had withered resources too and this area was already vastly thinned out. As small pockets of survivors were found, the infection learnt to mass and attack fast and hard. Many were wiped out, simply unable to cope with the overwhelming numbers and the increasing ferocity of the attacks. Others, Like Maddox on his council estate, had brave people like Howie coming to their rescue. Withering yet more of the hosts down and killing in quantities that were simply unacceptable.

The infection moved its hosts about slowly during the heat of the day. Shuffling them towards targets, gathering numbers, collating intelligence and all the time learning and evolving.

On this, the eleventh day, the infection sends those hosts out. Knowing there are more survivors holed up and just needing to sniff them out. Following the scent of fear, shit and piss.

A horde gathers in a wide affluent street, waiting for greater numbers to arrive before they assault the house with the old lady inside who stubbornly refuses to come out and be taken.

They turn and watch as a red minivan drives by slowly, a bearded man staring at them from behind the wheel. A big black dog growling and barking angrily out the window.

The dog. The same dog that killed so many hosts. It's back in the town. The collective intelligence buzzes with the update. The dog must be killed before it starts the killing spree again.

Leaving just two hosts to terrorise the old lady, the infection sends the others after the van heading towards the town centre.

The van's journey is tracked and picked up by many pairs of red, bloodshot eyes as it navigates the streets, driving round the corpses and abandoned vehicles.

The sun is strong and the infection knows if it moves the hosts too quickly they will weaken and die easier. But it has also been learning and evolving and has a deadly surprise just waiting to be tried out.

CHAPTER THIRTY-FIVE

DAY ELEVEN

'Dirty bastards,' Paco growls almost as deeply as the dog at seeing the monsters gathered at the side of the road. The dog reacts instantly, standing up and barking like crazy out the window. For a second he feared she would jump out and go for them, and probably get her body trapped in the small window. Instead she seemed content to voice her disapproval, telling them to fuck off.

They see more of the monsters here and there, single ones or couples shuffling along. All of them turning to stare at the passing vehicle. The dog giving voice to each and every one of them.

With the change caused from the death of Meredith, they don't seem that scary now. Whereas before he would have been flooring the gas pedal and driving off desperate to avoid them, now he slows down. Staring hard at their mutilated bodies, the gross decaying colour of their skin and the insects buzzing round them. They're not monsters. They're just dirty infected mother fuckers who ultimately caused the death of Meredith. Sure, he played a part in the final act by failing to act fast enough but it was them that made it happen. If they hadn't have done this she would have been safe at home with her folks, dating boys, doing homework and dreaming of a bright future.

After several minutes of carefully driving through the residential streets he snaps at seeing a small horde gathered by a junction. Bringing the minivan to a gradual stop he stares out the window as they start shuffling towards them.

He opens the door and climbs out, walking steadily towards them. Daring them to run at him, wanting them to run at him. His hands open and close into tight fists, anger surges through his mind. Adrenalin pumping his heart and making him breathe faster.

Again he fails to act fast enough as the dog pounds past his legs, leaping at the first one and dragging it down to the ground by its throat. Her actions spur him on, driving his legs as he sprints hard at them. His face a picture of pure seething hatred.

She's already taking the second one down as Paco reaches the horde. His strong hands grabbing the shoulders and pulling the thing into him. It bucks and writhes as Paco slams his foot down onto its knee joint at the same time as squeezing hard with his arms and twisting to the side. The neck breaks and he drops the body, deftly moving back as another one lunges at him with teeth bared. It's taken down by the dog, her teeth savaging at the neck, bright red blood spraying out.

The last one moves in, but goes for the dog instead of Paco. A fact he doesn't register due to the bloodlust. He moves in, drawing his arm back and slamming his fist into the side of the creatures head. Follow through, he remembers the constant mantra from his trainer, follow through…he does it now, sending the thing spinning off to land in a crumpled heap. Paco is on it before the thing has a chance to rise. Slamming his foot down on the head, pulverising and smashing the skull to bits.

'Fuck you,' he spits down angrily, stepping back and turning to view the bodies they took down.

'Fuck you, fuck all o'ya, you want me? YOU WANT ME?' He bellows into the air, 'YOU WANT ME…THEN COME GET ME…'

He walks off towards the van, not looking back at the death he's caused. Revelling in the strength of his arms and the new found ability he's found to fight back and kill.

Paco stretches one heavy arm across the side of the dog, pushing her into the back of the seat as he drives at the bodies. The small wheels bouncing over the squishy remains of the things and bouncing down the other side. Releasing the dog he breathes out noisily, gripping the steering wheel with such force that anymore pressure would see it pulled off in his hands.

In the next street he spots a lone monster shuffling along with a broken arm, the bone sticking out of the elbow joint. The thing looks unimpeded from the injury and soon switches its lolling gaze to Paco. He stops the van , stepping out and holding the door open for the dog to bound over, rip the thing to shreds, growl at the corpse and run back.

'Good girl,' Paco rubs her back, once more behind the wheel and continuing their journey. Every undead they see is taken down. The dog doing most of the work but Paco alighting every now and then to help, snapping necks with his powerful arms.

Before long they've left a trail of broken bodies behind them and for every death served by his hands he offers a prayer to Meredith.

They reach the town centre and head along the main road, examining the smashed in shop fronts. Bodies everywhere, old and decaying. Rancid from being out in the sun for so long. The stench in the air is thick with death and decay.

Every shop looks empty and completely destroyed, glass scattering the ground or hanging down in sharp deadly looking shards. Doors ripped off hinges, car's embedded in entrance ways, someone has even taken a digger to a cashpoint, ripping it from the wall but leaving it several metres away on the ground, the digger abandoned further along with dried blood stains on the glass of the drivers cab.

In the centre of town he parks the minivan next to a pedestrian precinct, seeing more shops further up but prevented from driving in by traffic posts. They jump down, leaving the van in situ but pocketing the keys.

'We'll try here, if no good we go for the houses,' Paco mutters to the dog. She seems nonplussed, just glad to be out of the house and killing the things again. He even joined in this time which just served to strengthen the pack instinct and bond between them.

CHAPTER THIRTY-SIX

More hosts are taken by the dog, this time it works with an adult male. The one they had tracked before who left the scent of fear everywhere he went. He, like many others, has changed. Adapted to the new way of life and become harder, tougher. Killing the host bodies with his bare hands and roaring a challenge to the infection.

It tracks their progress as they move through the quiet streets and into the town centre. The infection doesn't know if their killing spree is intended to last or if they're just killing the ones they can see. What it does know is it cannot take the risk of that dog dominating this area again.

Host bodies from every street, every house and every corner are given one simple instruction; move towards the town centre.

Chemicals are released into the systems, giving them just a slight increase in energy. The infection has learnt that the chemical they call Serotonin is produced in the brain and gives the host a feeling of well-being, an ability to rationalise and think straight. The infection has also learnt other chemicals such as Testosterone and Adrenalin. These chemicals are produced in tiny quantities and give the humans the senses and emotions, the desires and reactions they need. Mixed together, along with a perfect recipe of hormones and many other chemicals they produce the perfect being.

The infection has practised with the hosts, released Serotonin in large quantities. Watching and learning as the host body ceased the desire to feast and simply remained still or sank to the floor in a pleasurable heap of drool.

Testosterone was interesting. It sent the hosts wild with energy, giving them great strength and speed but too much made them so violent they turned on each other and more than that saw them turn on themselves. Tearing their own flesh apart to devour the meat held on their own limbs.

Adrenalin was used. It produced faster reflexes, heightened senses, made them stronger and faster, not the same as the Testosterone. Subtler and far more controllable. But the effects were fast acting and left the bodies shaky and exhausted. Pumping adrenalin continually simply caused the body to shut down unable to take it.

But all of these mixed in perfect quantities. A strong mix of Testosterone for the strength and speed, a small dose of Serotonin to enable the host to feel good about what it was doing, using it as a reward, and calculated releases of Adrenalin and it had good results.

This was a time to make use of those results. It sent the hosts towards the town. Willing to practise with these hosts and experiment with the mixtures. There were far bigger targets to go after, but the infection knew it had to evolve. And in order to evolve it must practise.

This is the perfect time.

CHAPTER THIRTY-SEVEN

DAY ELEVEN

'What a fucking dump,' Paco stares round at the measly collection of shops in the precinct. Adult fashion stores displaying styles that went out in LA like three seasons ago. He shrugs, no longer a part of that community. No longer a part of any community. Just him and the dog, booze, monsters and death.

'Bring it on,' he voices his thoughts. Longing for the blackness to swallow him up. Suicide had been in his mind since he buried the girl. The only thing that stopped him was abandoning the dog who had fought so hard to save him and Meredith.

Ah, Meredith. That sweet youthful face flashes through his mind again. The image flitting to the view of her pale thighs and the crimson blood upon them.

'Come on,' he instructs the dog after watching her take a crap next to a bench. He strolls past the windows, staring in at the smashed displays and the torn up posters. For the first time in days he becomes aware of his own self. Of the stench radiating from his body and clothes.

The self-loathing hits hard again, the state he's let himself get into. He heads into the closest clothes shop. The windows and doors smashed in but only half the stock taken. Clothing and accessories litter the floor, shelving pulled down. Dried blood smeared across the white tiled floor.

He heads to the men's section. Rooting through tops and trousers, finding a pair of blue denim jeans and a black t shirt along with underwear and socks.

Looking round for the changing room he shrugs and starts stripping off on the shop floor. Dumping his filthy clothes on the floor he goes to start dressing, realising most of the smell is coming from him, from his armpits, groin and backside.

'You coulda told me,' he tells the dog. Searching round he finds the rear door marked STAFF ONLY and heads through. More looting through here, boxes and hanging rails scattered about. He ignores the lot, heading through the stock room to the staff room and finding a toilet with a wash basin.

Soap from a plastic dispenser and cold water do the job well enough. He washes thoroughly, using paper towels to rub at the filthy parts of his body. Methodical, uncaring and for the first time in his adult life he doesn't even register the mirror above the sink. Only when he's finished washing, using the towels to dry and dressing in his new clothes does his own movements catch his eye. Shrugging the black t-shirt on he glances at himself, almost recoiling in horror at the sight. Thick stubbly beard with flecks of grey, his hair shaggy and unkempt. His permanent tan faded, he looks pale and drawn. His eyes red, puffy and swollen. When was the last time he brushed his teeth or used mouthwash? Had a shave or used moisturiser?

Meredith will never brush her teeth again, she'll never use

mouthwash or wash her hair. Why? He asks his reflection. I'll tell you why Paco, cos you failed. You cowered and hid, you killed Lucy and Meredith. He lashes out, punching the mirror and shattering it into thousands of glittering pieces that fall tinkling to the ground.

Back out in the street he spots a pharmacy up ahead and heads towards it. This has been very well looted, the entire stock of medicines from the back taken. He doesn't need medicine. He doesn't deserve it. If he gets ill now, he dies. Simple. Deserved.

Instead he finds a sealed toothbrush in a packet, and a tube of toothpaste from a scattered display now on the floor. Not for the act of hygiene, just to rid himself of the foul taste he is now acutely aware of.

Once more he heads to the rear, finding a sink in a staff room and brushing his teeth thoroughly. Relishing the minty taste and then instantly feeling guilty for feeling something that could be taken as pleasure.

He finds mouthwash, ripping the plastic film from the lid and filling his mouth as he walks round the shelves, sloshing the liquid into his cheeks and sucking it back into his mouth. His eyes fall on a hanging unit full of disposable razors. The cheap kind. He spits the mouthwash onto the floor, coating his own boots and not caring one dot.

'The beards gotta go,' he says, picking a razor from the display. Vanity screams at him. His old ways coming back, make yourself look pretty and for what? So you can hide and cower but still look good. He looks down at his arms, realising that he chose a tight fitting top without even thinking about it. His arm muscles bulge in the sleeves.

Even here, in this damned place he still looks good. His frame hardly showing the excesses of the last few days. A lifetime of physical devotion paying off. He throws the razor down and stalks out of the shop furious at himself.

The dog whines nearby. She can sense the coming darkness. Paco, not wearing a watch and having no means by which to tell the time failed to register the lateness of the day when he set out. Now, in the town centre, stomping about and avoiding seeing his own reflection in the bits of glass that remain in the shop frames he misinterprets the dogs whine. Cursing for letting her go thirsty in such high heat.

'Come on,' he motions to the dog, heading down the row of shop fronts and staring in, looking for anywhere that holds food or water.

These are too looted, too fucked up. There will be nothing of value left, and by value he means food and water. He doesn't want to go into the houses again. He doesn't want to see the remnants of the lives left behind. Humanity isn't for him anymore.

Sighing he turns back to the van, knowing the dog needs food so he must go into the houses to find it. He stops and stares up, looking at the windows above the shops. Apartments must be up there. He looks down and spots plain front doors situated between the shop fronts. They must lead into the apartments or the flats as the English call them. Why flats? They're not flat and have nothing to do with being flat. Stupid country. Stupid words.

'I say, open the bonnet and the boot,' he says to the dog in a mock posh English accent, 'we're jolly well going into the flats old boy.' He makes his way to the nearest private door, a wooden thing with several bells in a line next to the frame. Each one marked with a number.

Nodding he tries the door. Locked. He steps back and throws a well-aimed kick at the lock. It takes several attempts but the door yields, giving him access to a narrow corridor and set of stairs.

'Tally ho,' he growls, not bothering with the accent this time. This time, instead of waiting for the dog to enter first,

Paco walks straight through. Climbing the stairs and reaching the first two doors. Another set of stairs leading off to the next floor. So far no blood or stains showing signs of the things.

He tries the doors, twisting the handles down and finding them both locked. The first kick drives his foot through the cheap ply board, almost jamming his ankle and making him fall. He wrenches the foot back and kicks again, aiming towards the lock. The even cheaper lock gives instantly, the door bursting to reveal a faded red carpet leading through a small hallway. The dog pushes forward, running through the rooms with her nose down to the floor. Paco doesn't wait for her to finish but strolls through, opening doors until he finds the kitchen. Filling a ceramic bowl with water for the dog he finds a matching cup joins in with satisfying his raging thirst. They both drink deeply, the pressing heat is almost unbearable. The apartment smells musty of stale air, no circulation, no movement, no windows open.

He roots through the cupboards, finding a lone box of breakfast cereal. No tinned goods anywhere. Only rotten food in the fridge and freezer which flood the room with a foul stench as soon as he pulls the doors open.

He mixes the cornflakes with water, walking through the rooms while crunching noisily. The taste should be disgusting without milk but days of drinking and hardly touching food have left him ravenous. The bowl is emptied within minutes and dumped on the side as he heads back out and forces his way into the next apartment.

Inside he finds more tinned goods, tomato soup, beans and tuna. He splits the contents between two bowls, mixing the contents together. One is put down for the dog, the other he attacks with a dessert spoon. Shovelling the food into his mouth and again savouring the mix of tastes and textures.

The dog wolfs her serving down, licking the bowl clean

and staring up at him with tomato sauce dripping from her muzzle.

'Still hungry?' Stupid question. She's a dog, they're always hungry. He empties more food into bowls, putting them down and filling his own stomach in the process.

'No farting in the van,' he says dully, she ignores him, snuffling the bowl across the smooth linoleum covered floor.

The second apartment serves to ease their hunger but doesn't provide enough to take with them. Paco, his face expressionless, his movements robotic , his mind dark, walks back out and heads up the stairs. Two more doors on the next floor. Both the same cheap ply board which are forced in easy enough.

Inside the first he finds an old rucksack in the bedroom and uses it to fill with tins and snack food from the cupboards. The sight of the child's bedroom plummets his mood down even further. The bright yellow walls and brightly coloured plastic toys strewn about the floor. Posters of television and cartoon characters on the walls. A height chart marked with pen with the date it was done written to the side. He turns away quickly. This is exactly why he didn't want to come into the houses. The reminder of the lives lost, the suffering, the depravation. Everything swirls and comes back to Meredith.

He knows his lack of action also led to the death of Lucy, but it was her idea to enter the houses. She knew the risk and took it knowing the consequences. It doesn't make it easier to deal with but different. Meredith was tied and bound, tortured then raped. She was also young, where-as Lucy was older and clearly very confident.

The dog, learning the behaviour of the man when he enters the kitchens whines impatiently for another bowl of food. Paco obliges, finding a big mixing bowl and filling it with fish, sweet corn and, knowing he'll regret it later, more baked beans.

'The Brits love their beans,' he comments to the dog, 'I guess that's why they find farting so funny.'

In the next apartment, Paco fills the bag with yet more food. Doing a quick tour of the rooms he finds a liquor cabinet full of bottles, shoving these into the bag too which rapidly gets filled up. He pulls the bag onto his bag, adjusting the straps for his big shoulders. Finding a ladies gym back he carries on scavenging food and alcohol before heading out and climbing to the top floor.

One door this time. Stronger and sturdier than the others with far less space on the landing to get a good kick in. He dumps the bags and bracing himself with the handrail he launches kick after kick at the door. The loud bangs reverberating throughout the building, vibrating through the walls and drifting easily out into the still silent air of the town centre.

The door finally gives as Paco switches to his shoulder, ramming his body weight against the door to force the bolts and lock. A closed chain brings him to a sudden stop; realising the door was locked from within. Top floor so there can't be any other ways out.

'Hey?' He calls out. No response. He shoves the door harder, the dog squeezing through and running ahead. He follows in, his nose recognising the aroma instantly. Strong and pungent, especially in the warm stale air.

That explains why the door was so hard to force open. He walks through, carefully checking in the rooms.

'Oh hey, sorry about your door...' Paco apologises on the seeing the sleeping form on the bed. He walks in, his eyes adjusting to the gloom caused by the blackout curtains fixed to the frame.

'Oh...' Paco sighs at seeing the pale skin and open lifeless eyes. The body of a young male, maybe twenty years old, skinny guy with a wispy beard and wearing hippie clothes. A burnt out rolled cigarette still clasped between his fingers.

He backs out of the room, following the smell down the hallway to a closed door at the end. He pushes it open and smiles sadly at the sight of the bushy cannabis plants sat under inert grow lights. The pungent aroma now much stronger and he's suddenly transported through time to his college days, smoking weed in the parking lot of the drama school.

A pile of money sits on a wooden table at the side of the room. A big wedge of twenty pound notes.

'Business was good,' he mutters, 'he must have munchies, all pot heads have munchies.' He turns back to find the kitchen. Coming up trumps with large multi-bags of potato chips. No wait, what do the English call them? Crisps, yeah that's it.

Cookies, biscuits, chocolate bars, bags of popcorn and plastic tubs of Pot Noodles.

'Pringles,' Paco remarks, finally recognising one of the food stuffs. He pops the cap and pulls the silver foil back, sniffing deeply at the smell of the cheesy contents before prising one out. He stares at the thin single potato chip. The chip is gone with one munch. He leans against the counter, fingering the contents out, giving some to the dog sat next to him staring up hopefully.

'Once you pop, you just can't stop,' Paco tells her as she crunches away noisily. They finish the tube off and drink more water.

Now with three bags loaded with food and booze they traipse down the stairs, his heavy boots clumping on the wooden steps. They pass the floors in silence, the dog running ahead and pausing for him at each turn.

'Holy shit,' Paco staggers at the wall of heat that hits him as he walks out into the scorching evening. They walk slowly back towards the van. Paco looks about, checking the devastation and frowning at seeing one shop with an undamaged window, the door still intact. He stops walking and peers at the shop front, finally recognising the Interflora sign on the door. Nobody wants to loot a florist. Within two steps his mind has made the connection between florists, flowers, weddings and funerals then Meredith. She deserves something to mark her grave.

This heat would have killed all the flowers but something might remain. He wanders over, looking through the window. Everything inside is wilted and dead. Dried out flowers hanging listlessly from vases. Balloons sagging on counter tops. Nothing here.

The dog growls, her ears pricking up as she stares out of the precinct towards the van. Paco looks over, seeing nothing there but trusting the dog's instincts. He starts back to the van, his walking quicker now.

As they emerge from the precinct onto the main road he sees what the dog was growling at. A thick horde of the monsters on both sides. The two armies stand there, eyes locked on him and the dog. He stands still holding the bags, looking left and right. The road is blocked on both sides. He glances up, realising how close they are to nightfall.

He examines the front ranks of them. They stand there unmoving apart from a gentle sway back and forth. This is still daytime, they should be shuffling, slow and ungainly. Instead they stand normal, heads up. Not moving, not shuffling, not running, just standing there staring at him.

The dog moves out into the middle of the road, her hair standing on end, head low and a deep throaty growl coming from her as she flits her gaze left and right.

Paco calmly walks to the back of the van and dumps the bags inside before slamming the doors closed.

'Well here it is,' he says quietly, standing just behind the dog and equally flicking his gaze between the two solid fronts. Amazed at how many there are. All sizes and shapes, all ages, children, young, adults and the elderly all stood there watching him.

The hairs on the back of his neck prickle at the sight of them and the silence that hangs expectantly in the air.

'Say...I don't think they want me,' Paco adds, 'I think they're a bit pissed at you dog.' The realisation makes him laugh. Throwing his head back with a hearty laugh. His ego made him believe they wanted him and only him. It was the dog! She must have killed so many they came after her. He thinks back to the house, the last night they stayed in the town. Horrified at the memory of hiding in the bedroom and leaving to fend off so many of the things alone.

Well this time he's sticking by her. Right by her side no matter what happens. If that leads to death then so be it. He can pay the debt for Meredith's soul.

The stand-off continues. Two hordes facing off against one man and one dog. Shadows lengthen as the sun begins its final descent to the horizon. The only sound comes from the dog, her constant growling. Nothing else moves. No other noise. Paco stares at both sides, moving his head to take them in and expecting them to charge any second.

The sun drops out of sight, bringing much relieved light to another part of the world but here, for this day, its work is done. Night follows day. Nothing can be done to change that. And night falls here.

As one, the hordes crane their heads up and howl screaming into the night air. The sound is deafening. Paco's blood runs cold at the noise. The sheer synchronised volume of it. The feral wild sound fills the street, bouncing off the high building fronts, echoing through the precinct.

The dog ceases growling. A primal instinct kicks in as he

lifts her head, stretching her long neck up. She joins the howling. Giving her voice to the cacophony of noise. Paco feels a sudden strong sense of pride at the dog. She shows no fear at them. But instead howls back with her sweet voice howling perfectly into the night.

The hordes cease as one. Her howl continues. A lone voice of a wolf calling through the forest. Pitch perfect she carries on, expending her breath as the noise eases off gradually.

The hordes charge. One second they're stood there staring. The next second and they're moving and moving fast.

'Fuck this,' Paco shouts, 'come on dog.' They turn away, running back towards the precinct. A sudden urge to live, to try and protect the dog floods through Paco. Not a fear of being taken by them, more a desire to give her the best chance possible. Re-pay the debt. All of the debts.

They sprint easily through the bollards, heading towards the enclosed shopping area. Paco selects a shop at the far end, a big clothes store that must have a delivery door at the back.

They charge in, Paco throwing rails and mannequins behind him in a vain attempt to slow them down. He slams through the rear door, heading down the bare walled corridor and the wooden notice board filled with motivational sales messages and a Health and Safety at work poster.

Reaching the double doors at the back, Paco slams the bar down, wrenching the doors open as he hears the first of the monsters coming through the broken windows of the shop floor behind him.

They sprint off into the darkness. Not knowing the direction to take or what route to follow, just knowing they need to make distance as fast as possible.

CHAPTER THIRTY-EIGHT

DAY ELEVEN

'Not far, just stay on this road,' Clarence says, shining his torch onto the map book spread open on his lap.

'Okay, how the hell are we going to find Chris?' I ask him.

'We can use the radios when we get into the town, it doesn't look too big.'

'Ted said he's in a four wheel drive vehicle, he's got two others with him, both ex-army,' Blowers shouts down.

'Right, so we've got two vehicles with about a dozen people to find a black dog at night in a town with no street lights working...shouldn't be too hard,' I muse for the benefit of everyone.

'At least we're not going to attack a giant horde of zombies this time,' Cookey shouts.

'Ahhh Cookey! You've said it now,' Nick replies.

'Ha sorry,' Cookey laughs.

Despite the long day and incredible heat, our spirits are high from the news about the dog and the implications this has. That maybe this thing can be beaten. Just the faintest glimmer of hope, but that's all we need.

'Turn off here,' Clarence points to the junction ahead, indicating me to take the left side. The powerful headlights sweep across the dark hedgerows and fields. Slowly they give way to cottages, then houses and within a few minutes were in the town proper. Driving along residential streets with dark houses on both sides. No lights other than the headlights of the vehicle.

'Someone keep trying the radio,' I shout back. Dave picks it up, transmitting for Chris every few seconds. Static and a crackled transmission finally comes back. We keep going, trying to figure out which way to go to improve the signal.

'Dave to Chris, come in over.'

'Chris to Dave can you hear me?'

'Dave to Chris, loud and clear now, suggest you stop moving in case the signal goes.'

'Chris to Dave, roger that we are stationary.'

'Likewise Chris, what is your current location?'

'Chris to Dave, we missed the first turning and went too far north, we've turned round and just entered the town from the north. We're in, hang on....we're in Sycamore Street over.'

'He said they're in Sycamore Street,' Dave relays to Clarence.

'Yeah I heard it...on the radio...that I'm holding in my hand,' Clarence replies pointedly. *'Clarence to Chris.'*

'Go ahead Clarence.'

'I've got you on Sycamore Street, stay there, we'll come to you.'

'Roger that, remaining here out.'

Clarence directs me through the streets until we reach the right one and see a four wheel drive parked up in the middle of the road with the lights off. We head over, stopping nearby and I kill the lights and engine so we can talk quietly without attracting too much attention.

We jump down, armed up and ready. Dave directs the lads to fan out into a circle facing outwards while Clarence and I head over to Chris.

'You made good time,' he says with a quick handshake.

'Bloody right we did,' I reply.

'Chris, what's your search pattern?'

'Hello Dave, nice to see you too, we haven't established one yet but we have seen shit loads of bodies in the streets.'

'Really?' I ask.

'Yeah, first residential street we went into, bodies everywhere. Most of them had their throats ripped out, but messy…not with a knife or blade.'

'That's a good sign.'

'Yeah but they're also old. Been there for days at least. Couldn't see any fresh corpses.'

'Okay…er what do we do if we see it?'

'Take it back to the fort,' Chris replies with a puzzled expression.

'What if it doesn't want to go?' I ask, 'if it's big enough to kill so many of them…we can't exactly shoot it can we?'

'Good point, my best answer? Worry about it when it happens, we've got to find the thing first.'

'Chris, looking on the map the town centre is…believe it or not,' he grins up, 'in the centre of the town…we should head there first and work out.'

'Mr Howie,' Tom calls out.

'Yes mate.'

'I'm sure the army do the same thing but I was search-trained with the police. Clarence is right, we should start in the middle and work out in a radius, marking the streets off as we go. The biggest problem is that its night so unless the dog has reverted to wild behaviour it will probably be holed up somewhere asleep…if it's still here.'

'Alright, we do street by street for now, if that doesn't work then in the best words of the army we worry about the rest later.'

'There's more likely to be contact in the town centre,' Clarence suggests.

'Is that a good thing or not? Is the sound likely to draw the dog out or make it run away?' I ask everyone.

'Run away probably, they have to train dogs not to run from gunfire, dogs naturally don't like loud noises, ever done the vacuuming near one?' Chris answers.

'Yeah fair one, right…town centre, see you there?'

'Roger that,' Chris replies. We head back to our vehicles.

'We'll take the lead Chris,' Clarence shouts out. We have to wait for the four wheel drive to reverse back and let us get through, then we wait again while it executes a fifteen point turn using the narrowest part of the road. Clarence tutting and shaking his head at the delay.

'Chris was always a shit driver, I bet he's going nuts right now fucking it up in front of us,' he chuckles.

We get going, guided by Clarence through the street towards the centre. Nick takes the GPMG with Dave sat on the top holding a powerful searchlight powered by a cable running back into an auxiliary plug in the back of the Saxon. The beam of light sweeps across the road in front of us every few seconds as Dave makes a full methodical rotation. Blowers opens the rear doors, everyone else crammed towards the rear scanning the houses and sides as we go by.

'BODIES AHEAD,' Dave shouts down, his comments relayed by Nick. The beam of light picks up several corpses in the street.

'We're gonna have a look at them, Nick stay on the GPMG, everyone else fan out,' I bring the vehicle to a stop. Blowers leads the lads from the back doors, fanning out holding torches in one hand and staring out to the sides and front.

'They're fresh,' Clarence says, dropping down and shining his torch into the gaping ragged hole of a neck wound. Several others have the same throat wounds.

'You got something?' Chris walks up, his men joining ours in facing out to form a guard.

'These the same as you saw before?' I ask him.

'Yep, exactly the same but these are fresh. Maybe a few hours at most.'

'Look at these two, broken necks but no wounds,' Clarence lifts the head of an undead, twisting it to show the lack of resistance from the spinal column.

'A dog couldn't do that, there must be someone with it, how hard is it to do that?'

'What break a neck like that? If you do it exactly right it's not that difficult but you have to remember these things would have been fighting back and squirming....keeping hold of an adult body and doing it requires strength.'

'So we're looking for a big bastard and a dog then?'

'Not necessarily, Dave could do this easy enough, so could Lani if they knew exactly what they were doing,' Clarence explains.

'The woman said the dog was going for the throat nearly every time, and those other bodies look old enough to be the right time...and these are fresh and have the same wounds, at least we can assume the dog is still here,' Chris adds, standing up and looking about. We all do, as if the dog will come bounding over wagging its tail with a ball in its mouth.

A few minutes later and we're driving on, pulling out of a

side road into the town centre and looking at the same level of destruction as every other town centre we've seen so far.

'CONTACT,' Dave shouts down, 'DEAD AHEAD.'

Clarence and I both lean forward, staring out the window but seeing nothing moving.

'Where?' Clarence shouts.

'It was moving away to the left,' Dave replies.

'Moving away? Was it a person then?' I ask.

'Not sure, I don't think so, it ran like one of the things,' Dave shouts.

'They don't run away,' Clarence mutters as I speed up, heading down the main road.

'Stop there, next to that red van,' Dave shouts, 'it went towards those shops.'

'Clarence, let Chris know what we've got, we'll go after it and leave him here with the Saxon in case we lose it, everyone else get ready to run.' I shout out.

'Chasing zombies…great,' Nick groans.

Clarence relays the message as we jump down, quickly shrugging our rucksacks on and taking our assault rifles, we de-camp the Saxon and follow Dave as he leads us into a precinct area. His torch beam holding steady despite his running.

'Which way Dave?' I shout ahead.

'Wait,' Dave holds his hand up in a fist. We come to a halt as he scans the ground, moving from shop front to shop front.'

'Fresh dog shit here,' Tom shouts, holding his torch on a brown pile of dog mess.

'How do you know it's fresh?' Cookey asks.

'It looks fresh,' Tom replies.

'Touch it, see if it's still warm,' Cookey urges.

'Okay,' Tom bends down, his hand extending towards the pile of shit.

'Tom I was joking,' Cookey yells as Tom looks up grinning, 'twat.'

'Yeah like I was gonna stick my finger in it.'

'Blowers would, he'd stick something else in it,' Cookey laughs.

'Through here,' Dave yells. We jog over as Dave shows us the fresh looking damage through a clothes shop.

'Fresh blood,' Dave shines his torch on the ground at smeared and still glistening blood stains.

'Whoever it was cut their feet on the glass,' he continues, 'no shoes…must be the things.'

'Why was it running away?' Clarence asks, shining his torch about at the debris strewn about the shop floor.

'Not it, them,' Dave replies, 'a lot went through here, different blood marks across a wide aisle.'

'And it was running?' I ask him.

'It was Mr Howie.'

'Maybe chasing something then? Otherwise it would come for us, come on.' I take the lead with Dave, shining our torches and following the blood trails through the rear store rooms to the open back doors.

'Chris to Howie.'

'Yeah go ahead mate.'

'This van is covered in dog hair on the seat, there's fresh supplies in the back too.'

'Okay mate, we're chasing zombies…hang on there.'

'CONTACT,' Dave drops to a kneeling position, aiming down the road. He takes a single shot as the rest of us bundle out the doors, looking up to see a body dropping down. We jog up the road to the body. An adult male undead lying in a pool of blood with half its head blown off.

'Feet aren't cut,' I shine my torch down. The undead is wearing shoes.

'So he's chasing something that's chasing something else… that might be our dog?' Clarence asks, 'is that about right?'

'Just about mate,' we take off. Following the road as Dave picks out spots of blood here and there, some of it still glistening and wet looking.

'This is a weird fucking day,' Cookey mutters.

'Aren't they all?' Blowers replies.

CHAPTER THIRTY-NINE

The gunshot brings Paco to a sudden stop. Staring back over the heads of the horde still chasing after them. They don't use guns do they? Shit, that wouldn't be fair if one of them had a damn gun.

The dog barks at him, as though urging him to keep moving. That's how he interprets it anyway, she could have just been barking at the things coming after them. It's enough to get him moving and they start running again.

The long easy strides easily outstripping the monsters who run too jerkily to make gains on the distance. The only problem is the pace, Paco might be fit and strong but it's also incredibly hot and there is no way he can maintain this pace. At some point he'll have to slow down and rest, whereas the horde won't.

All this runs through his mind as he runs. He eases down to a jog, checking behind him every few seconds and making sure the distance is pretty much the same. They gain very gradually but he knows he can hold this pace for a longer period, which buys them time.

They take side streets, veering off and taking lefts and

right. Paco considered taking to the back gardens, vaulting the fences and disappearing into the darkness but the dog couldn't jump six foot fences, well maybe it could but not one after the other and then keep doing it until they lost the things.

No, for now they've no choice but to stick to the roads and maybe lead the things away from the town centre before they head back towards their van and drive off. Yeah, that's a good plan. Lead these stupid dumbfucks in a big loop and take them back to the start. A giggle escapes from his mouth at the thought of the stupid monsters being run round the block in a long line, like something from a crappy B movie.

'Easy as pie,' he laughs, reaching a hand out to pat the dog's head.

CHAPTER 40

It held the hosts in the road. Content to watch the man and dog. For a few minutes it looked like they were going to charge and attack the hosts, which would have ended the matter easily.

For every second they paused, the infection gathered numbers. Far fewer than it wanted but then it had lost so many hosts to the constant battles.

Of the town's population of tens of thousands, the infection had taken over half of them just in this area. Most of those had been lost at the fort, but these remained. And the more survivors it took out the greater the numbers grew.

The infection held them steady, watching the man and dog, the sun dropped and the infection released some of the chemicals. Making the hosts faster and stronger. The charge started. The prey ran off. The infection took off after them.

Now, as it pushed the hosts through the quiet streets it waited, waited for the heat and the distance to tire the man out. At that point it would release the chemicals it had chosen for tonight's use.

CHAPTER 41

'I can smell them,' Dave shouts from ahead of us. Him and Lani out front and scanning the ground as they lead us through the streets.

'Glad he can, I can only smell Nick's arse,' Cookey mutters.

'Wasn't me,' Nick replies.

'It was me, sorry, all this jiggling about made me fart,' Tom says.

'You sure you haven't shit yourself Tom?' Nick spits at the smell.

'Might have done mate, wanna check for me?'

'Ask Blowers, that's his bag,' Cookey quips.

'Get fucked,' Blowers swears.

We keep running, the sweat pouring down our faces and soaking our clothes. Dave urges us to speed up. We respond by lengthening our stride and trying to keep pace with him and Lani. Clarence still surprises me, how someone so big can run so well. His face looks strained and focussed at the same time. Flushed with sweat literally pouring from his bald head but he doesn't moan once, just stares ahead with complete concentration.

'Lani, stay with the group, I'm running ahead to see how far they are,' Dave shouts and moves off as Lani reluctantly drops back. We watch as Dave opens up and strides ahead to the next junction, turning to make sure we've seen the route he's taking before running out of view.

On reaching the junction we turn into the road, Dave in the distance still pulling away. We chug along breathing hard but maintaining a steady pace. Dave's voice shouts quickly followed by shots ringing out. We reach Dave standing over several bodies, his chest hardly heaving as he checks his magazine and slots it back in.

'Big group chasing something,' he explains, 'I shouted and fired into them, they didn't acknowledge me.'

'They're after something important then,' I reply.

'Darren came after us, and despite the personal connection I think he did it because we killed so many. If that dog is killing so many then maybe it's the same thing?' Dave shrugs and looks back up the road.

'Fresh dog shit, freshly killed bodies, it's worth considering, come on let's see if we can't catch them up,' we start off again. Charging down the street moving faster now.

'Dave, let Chris know what's going on, you and Lani are the only ones able to run and speak,' I gasp for breath myself at the speed were going. Dave relays our information to Dave, the fit bastard hardly speaking above a normal tone as he jogs along easily.

'Received that, where are you? We'll come round in the Saxon and see if we can get to the front.'

'Understood, we're going into Green Street now.'

'Which end you going in from?'

'Not sure, will update you when we reach the end, Dave out.'

This feels farcical and stupid. Us chasing a horde that is chasing something else through the quiet backstreets of a deserted ruined town. Still, if it is the dog then getting to the horde and finishing them off will be easy enough.

Famous last words.

CHAPTER 42

'Which way to the centre?' Paco asks the dog, not for the first time wishing she could speak. But then if dogs could speak they would rule the world and none of this would have happened. They keep jogging, maintaining roughly the same distance from the horde behind them.

The strange town isn't built on the grid format of American towns. The ancient High Street is straight enough but streets and roads have been added over the years, creating a confusing layout of twisting avenues, streets and roads that all look the damn same with the damn same construction of red brick and slate roofs. How the hell do people find their way back to their houses in this country?

He jogs on, the high level of fitness showing as he keeps a steady rate of breathing, his motion fluid and gentle.

He turns left at the next junction and waits for a couple of seconds until he knows he's out of sight before opening his stride and sprinting easily down the road to the next junction. Taking a right and sprinting again, trying to use his power and speed to lose the monsters in the twisting confusing streets.

A howling sounds behind him, he stops and twists round

to see the front of the horde now sprinting having halved the gap between them. They move as fluid as he was. Sprinting with arms pumping, faces contorted with rage and fury.

'What the...' He doesn't finish the sentence but sprints away, his mind working furiously at the change. How can they run so fast? What changed?

They gain quickly and within seconds he hears the drumming of their feet on the ground, impossibly fast and still gaining. He veers off calling for the dog and knowing he can't outrun them anymore. Crossing the road he stares at the passing houses until he sees one with an open front door.

'Dog,' he bellows, quickly turning into the front garden and charging up the path. The dog runs ahead of him, streaking into the door. Paco reaches it, leaping in and slamming it closed behind him. Gasping for breath he checks the locks, ramming security bolts home and even putting the thin chain across.

A loud thud signifies their arrival. More thuds as bodies slam themselves into the door. Smashing glass from the front room as a monster launches itself bodily through the plate glass, splintering the thin wooden frame. The dog is on it instantly, ragging the already bleeding body about. Another throws itself through, Paco reaching down as the body crumples to the floor, he grabs the neck and snaps it quickly. Shouting for the dog and heading through the dark hallway to the back door.

He wrenches the door open, bursting into the back garden and running for the back fence. He curses at the six foot fence runs over to grab the dog and launches it over the top, hearing it land with a thud and an indignant bark. The weak structure wobbles precariously under his weight as he pulls himself over and lands in a flower bed next to the dog. Howling from not far behind them sends him on, racing across the manicured lawn and vaulting the next high fence with ease.

Cursing as he hits the ground on the other side he goes to clamber back to help the dog as she hits the top and scrabbles to drop deftly by his side.

'Thank god for that,' he says hoarsely as the first fence crashes down with the combine weight of the monster bodies slamming into it.

The frantic chase continues, Paco and the dog clambering fences, falling into ponds, crashing through weak trellis and all the time hearing the things behind them. Simply powering through everything they can't go over or under.

He sees a back door open and runs for it, calling for the dog. He flees into the house, slamming the door closed behind them before running down the hallway to the open front door, skidding to a stop as it bursts open with one of them coming through. The dog leaps, driving the thing back through the door into the garden. The heavy set monster withstands the initial attack, wailing his arms about and thrashing the dog off to one side. Paco launches for him, taking him down under a flurry of hard punches. The dog recovers, surging in to sink her teeth into his exposed face. She tears his nose off, violently shaking her head and pushing her teeth into his eye sockets. Paco quickly slams his foot down onto the neck. Shouting for the dog he runs out of the front gate, cursing at seeing more of them sprinting down the road towards them.

The sprinting starts again, man and dog running fast down the dark street. Howls of rage behind them. Desperately trying to think of an escape route, of a path to take that would slow them down. Instinct takes over, just running blind and knowing that sooner or later he'll run out of steam and have to stand and fight.

A grimace spreads across his face at the thought of failing

again, causing the death of the dog through his own stupid selfish actions. Not bothering to check the time of day and leading them into danger again.

More gunshots sound out, coming from another street. Single shots fired from an assault rifle. Paco has heard more gunfire from years of action movies than most soldiers and recognises the sounds.

He thinks to shout, to try and alert whoever has the guns where they are, but his lungs can just about cope with the running, forget trying to shout at the same time.

They run wide into another junction, making use of the whole width of the road to make the turn while keeping his speed up. He glances back on the turn, amazed at the speed of the things, at the power they're displaying. Only a few metres behind him now, the rest still negotiating the corners, fences and house he came through. For a split second he thinks to stop and take these on, but that action would only give the others time to catch up.

No choice, they have to keep running. His sense of direction now gone completely, no idea which way the town centre lies so they pound on with the relentless things slowly gaining behind them.

CHAPTER 43

'Which way?' I shout at Dave as we join him at the next junction.

'I don't know, they're gone,' he replies searching the ground for blood stains.

'How can they go? I thought you had 'em in sight?' Clarence wheezes, fighting for breath.

'I did, but they've gone,' Dave shrugs, 'they must have got faster and outran us.'

'What? They don't run that fast?' Clarence replies bitterly.

'We didn't think they could speak either but they did,' Dave says flatly. We spread out, shining our torches at the ground. The sound of smashing glass reaches us but in the dark with the buildings on either side we can't tell the direction it came from, all of us spinning round and straining to listen. Howls and roars add to the noise then more smashing glass.

'This way,' Dave starts off down the street. We follow as best we can, all of us apart from Dave and Lani fighting for breath and suffering in the heat. Legs getting heavier with every passing minute. Sweat pouring from our faces and stinging our eyes.

At the end of the road we come to an abrupt halt at seeing Dave stood with his fist held up. We fight for breath, trying to gasp quietly and listen at the same time.

'Blood,' Dave spots a patch on the ground further into the next street. We start off again, Nick wheezing and starting to drop back.

'There,' Dave shines his torch onto the front of a house, the ground floor windows smashed in, some of the shards still wobbling in the frame. The front door has been forced in, now hanging from its hinges. We head inside, our beams of light picking out the blood smears in the hallway two dead bodies in the front room.

'Throat ripped out and a broken neck,' Dave calls out as he quickly checks both the bodies. We push through to the back garden, instantly seeing the route they've taken from the smashed down fence panels. In the next garden we see the same, just a straight line of destroyed fences leading through gardens as the horde have demolished everything in their path.

'Fuck me they really want that dog,' Cookey says quietly.

'So do we,' I reply. We pick our pace up hoping the ease of our run through the gardens will enable us to catch them up. The shattered fences end as the route veers into the back door of a house. In the front garden a trampled and very dead undead lies with his face ripped off. More howls sound out, we judge the direction and head off. Dave again in the lead scanning the ground to pick out the patches of blood.

'They must know...about the importance....of the dog,' I gasp out as we run after Dave and Lani. Still no visible sign of them other than the blood patches on the ground. The person and the dog are running fast and doing well to stay in front of them, but that can't last for a long time. At some point they'll tire and slow down and this horde seems hell-bent on getting that dog.

There is no choice now. We're dropping further back and just chasing signs of them through the streets. This could go on for hours. If that dog is still alive and normal after all this time, if it is the same dog as the woman said she saw then it has to be saved. Nothing else matters.

'Dave,' I shout out, he slows down and turns to face me, 'mate you have to go on, you're faster than us, find that dog and keep it alive...'

'Are you sure Mr Howie?'

'Yes, go...' He seems unsure for a second. Torn between his loyalty to us but knowing he's the best chance to help them.

'Okay, keep your radio on,' he shouts before turning and opening his stride up. He powers away easily, running like an athlete with his rifle held in one hand.

'Good call boss,' Clarence grunts. Lani takes Dave place, her breathing so much more controlled than ours as she runs ahead finding the blood patches.

CHAPTER 44

His lungs are bursting. His heart pounding to pump the blood into his muscles. He knows that a few seconds break will be enough for him to recover but they don't have a few seconds. They have no seconds.

He can hear the things breathing coarsely now, picking out the drumming of the footsteps and the low growls. He doesn't speak or look back, anything other than facing ahead will use vital energy and slow them down.

The dog runs easily at his side. She pants hard but he can sense she's coasting along just for the sake of being with him. She could easily flee these things, go places they can't go. She could run for miles back into the country and hide. He wants to shout at her to go, tell her to keep running but he knows it will do no good. She wouldn't understand and would stay by his side as the things finally caught them.

Tears prick his eyes at the thought of failing again, that again his actions have led to another death and one so pure too.

His mind fills with the image of the dog when she first

saved him. The savage violence followed instantly by the softness of her approach to him. Hiding in the bedroom while she fought all night. Letting him hug her in a drunken stupor.

His whole life has been about Paco. About Paco going to the best drama school getting the best parts, using the best gym with the best trainers. Eating only the best food and being adored by millions of people. All of it fake and worthless.

Just one chance, that's all he wants. Just one chance to show he can be worthwhile and mean something.

They're so close now. So very close. Minutes of his life left. Just minutes before they take him and the dog.

Ahead. There...a house with an open door. The windows still intact. There it is, that one chance...thank you god, thank you for giving me this chance, I will not fail again.

A roar erupts from his throat as he drives every ounce of strength into his legs, powering away and sucking huge lungful's of air in. He can make it. He can make that door. Heart bursting with the strain, pain spreading across his chest. He makes the path, gripping the wall to slow his speed down and turn quickly in. Up the front garden and there it is, the open door.

'GO ON,' he screams at the dog. She bounds ahead clearing the doorway. He stops, yanking the door closed and hearing the lock slam home.

Chest heaving he smiles as he turns back to face the front garden, the dog locked inside the house and barking like crazy at being separated from him.

His face intent he sprints back down the path and into the road, turning away from the first of the things.

'COME ON,' he screams into the air, once more driving his legs like crazy. He glances back, smiling in triumph at the sight of them following him. Just metres between them now.

CHAPTER 44

He's done his best. No man can ask for more. Every step taken now will lead them away from that house. Every foot gained is another chance for the dog to survive.

He'll take Meredith's sin. He'll stand before the judgement and look them in the eye. Send me to hell; send me down to fiery depths...but damn if he won't take a few with him.

The best shot of his life. The camera pulls back showing Paco running with the growling things gaining with every second. One last show. One last scene before the final cut. No edits, this is a one shot take.

He imagines the crew stood about watching him, the director holding his hand to his mouth. The audiences going wild in the theatre.

One more street, that's all he has left. One more corner to run round and they'll be on him. He takes the corner, his legs stumbling but recovering. Thigh muscles burning with agony, he feels vomit rising in his stomach and erupting from his mouth, spewing to the side, choking on the remains of the barely digested meal.

Paco glances round, staring in horror at the front of the horde turning the corner. They haven't slowed once, relentless and unfaltering.

This is it. The power drains from his legs, a burning pain in his head, vision blurred. He can feel himself slowing down, the body simply unable to continue.

Suddenly he's standing still with no recollection of having slowed down. Chest heaving with puke dribbling down his chin. He waits for them to take him, knowing the impact is but seconds away.

'DOWN DOWN DOWN...GET DOWN NOW,' the loudest voice Paco has ever heard booms down the street. The voice is so powerful, so commanding his body responds before his mind can question it. Face down hugging the road, eyes blurred from sweat and tears, his airways feeling rough and bitter from the vomit. A bright flash and loud bangs from ahead of him, gunshots. Even in his state he recognises the sound of the assault rifle.

'CONTACT AHEAD, MULTIPLE TARGETS,' the voice roars between shots. The bright muzzle flashes drop low, more loud bangs sound from further away. More people firing over the head of the first man.

'YOU…WHEN I SAY YOU GET UP AND RUN… CEASE FIRING…NOW RUN NOW…RUN NOW.'

The shooting ends as abruptly as it started, he heaves himself to his feet, running wildly towards the sounds of the gunfire and the bright muzzle flashes.

'WHERE IS THE DOG?' The voice screams at him. Paco can't speak, he can hardly breathe. His entire being is on autopilot, a dream sequence of hazy images

'DAVE, where is the dog?' Another voice shouts, not as loud but still full of power and authority.

'It's not here Mr Howie.'

'FIRE,' another voice shouts, someone drags him away, leading him as they fire at the things coming after them. The shots deafening his ears so close, the shouts of young voices. A woman too. Someone else with a very deep voice.

'Chris we're in John Street, multiple contacts, receive? John Street, multiple contacts.'

'Loud and clear, coming now.'

'Clarence, find out where the dog is.'

'WHERE IS THE FUCKING DOG?' The deep voice shouts in his face.

'…House…in…house…' Paco tries to speak, his head spinning.

'WHAT HOUSE?' The voice is so deep and angry. Water

gets sloshed down his face, cool and refreshing. A rough hand slaps him across the cheek, 'WHAT HOUSE?'

Paco's senses snap back, rubbing his eyes to clear his vision and shaking his head. A giant of a man with a bald head is glaring at him. Paco realises they're still moving, being half dragged and somehow still walking. His head turns slowly to see a motley collection of people firing assault rifles into the monsters as they retreat down the road.

'WHAT HOUSE?' The giant screams again, leaning his face inches from Paco, spittle flying from his lips.

'The corner...back round the corner....I got it inside a house...'

'THE STREET YOU JUST CAME FROM? IN A HOUSE IN THAT STREET?' The question is too difficult for Paco to process, his dull senses working overtime just to see and hear, his legs weak and shaky.

'WHICH STREET?'

'Er....I....' Paco thinks furiously, the last few minutes just a blank in his mind. An image of the door he closed swims into his mind. Two brass numbers were on the door, right in front of his face.

'Thirty four,' he yells back, 'it's in thirty four.'

'BOSS THE DOGS IN NUMBER THIRTY FOUR.'

'WHICH STREET CLARENCE?'

'HE'S OUT OF IT BOSS, MUST BE THAT ONE HE CAME FROM.'

'CLARENCE, YOU HOLD THEM HERE AND WAIT FOR CHRIS, DAVE YOU'RE WITH ME...WE'LL GO OVER THE GARDENS...TAKE MY BAG'

'YOU HEARD THE BOSS, KEEP FIRING AND GIVE THEM SOME COVER...*Chris where the fuck are you?*'

'Not far Clarence, hold your position we've got the GPMG ready to go.'

*'HURRY THE FUCK UP CHRIS...*KEEP FIRING, CAN YOU USE A GUN?'

Paco feels himself being pulled along, listening to the voices around him with a detachment.

'TAKE THIS,' the big man shoves a bottle into his hand, Paco lifts it to his lips expecting water but getting a syrupy liquid instead. He gulps it down greedily, the liquid cascading down his chin.

'FALL BACK....KEEP FIRING.'

Paco feels the glucose and sugar hitting him, the instant carbohydrate working wonders in snapping his mind back to reality. He's walking behind the group, not knowing he was walking but taking steps all the same. The monsters are still charging, some of them coming straight and others weaving across the road. He can see they are only just being held back and getting closer every second. Two others running across the road and climbing a fence, one of them with an axe in one hand and an assault rifle in the other, the smaller man just carrying an assault rifle.

'CAN YOU USE A GUN?' The huge man with the bald head shouts at him, firing one handed while holding a pistol towards Paco. He takes the gun, a 9mm pistol. The weight and feel is familiar to him from so many action movies. His fingers switch into auto-pilot as habit of hand kicks in, ejecting the magazine, checking the rounds before slamming it back home and sliding the top back to engage the first round.

He lifts his arm, tracking one of the monsters and firing easily. The thing drops down but he hardly notices, already raising his aim for the next one.

'CLARENCE...WE'RE GIVING TOO MUCH GROUND, WHERE 'S CHRIS?' One of the young men shouts from the front.

'ON HIS WAY.'

'HE BETTER FUCKING HURRY UP OR WE'RE FUCKED.'

Paco doesn't know who Chris is, he doesn't know who any of these people are, but suddenly he's wishing that Chris, whoever he is, hurries the fuck up.

CHAPTER 45

She makes noise at the entrance to the den. He sealed it off, preventing her from being with him. She throws herself at the door again and again. Her body weight slamming and vibrating the frame, rattling the windows.

Her head cocks slightly to the side as she hears him pounding away, the things running after him. She doesn't understand his intentions. This is a mistake. Separation of the pack is a mistake. She must be with him.

Running into the front room she leaps at the window, watching the things as they pour past the garden. So many of them. They want her man just like they wanted her little one.

She can see them but she can't get to them. An invisible wall is in her way. She backs up and throws herself at it, bouncing off from the thick frame holding the double glazed windows in place.

Through the window she can see as the last of the things stops and stares into the house. She makes noise, warning it to stay away from her pack leader, urging it to come for her, willing it to fight. The thing is joined as more of them drop back and stare into the window.

Their numbers grow outside in the street. They pause, waiting for more to drop back before moving towards the house, swarming over the low wall and pouring through the gate. She stays at the window, making noise and leaping up to try and get to them.

They attack the windows, throwing themselves bodily but bouncing back of the thick panes. They persist, slamming fists, elbows, feet and heads into the panes. They start to fracture, giving under the constant bombardment.

She hears bangs coming from the front door and barks her fury at them. Come for me, come in here and see what waits for you. I've killed many of you and I will again.

Pure instinct drives her on. She runs to the front door, nose down to the very bottom and barking constantly. The hairs on her back standing up, her feet planted wide apart. Tail curled up.

She wants to be with the man. She needs to be with her pack, protecting him. He is alone now and the things will be going for him.

The dog turns again to head for the windows of the front room, her eyes catch sight of the open back door. She bounds outside into the enclosed back garden. A six foot fence but with ivy coated trellis on the top of that making the height even higher, too high for her to jump. The fence circuits the perimeter of the garden, trapping her within. No escape, no way of getting out to her man until the things beat their way inside. Smashing noises in the house, the sounds of heavy repeated thuds at the front door.

Inside the house she runs between the front door and the lounge windows, barking and snarling as she leaps at them, her paws clawing the glass and frame.

CHAPTER 46

'You okay?' Dave asks me as I land heavily the other side of the fence, losing my balance and stumbling down into the flower bed.

'Fine, fine...keep going,' getting to my feet we run across the lawn. Dave leaps to the top of the fence, almost vaulting it. I on the other hand hit it almost full on, the fence wobbles dangerously as I scoot my arse over the top and land the other side.

'We need to get into the street and find the numbers,' I shout as Dave runs at the next fence, he swerves off and heads to the back door, trying to handle but finding it locked.

'Your axe,' he shouts. I throw it over to him. He catches it easily, dropping his rifle and slamming the heavy metal end into the pane of glass, raking it round the frame to remove the shards of glass. He reaches in, feeling for a lock to undo.

'Key locked, no key,' he calls out and climbs through the empty pane. I pass my rifle through, then the axe and finally myself. Ungainly and the polar opposite to Dave's graceful movements. Fortunately the end result is the same with both of inside the house, running towards the front door.

Dave gets there first, as expected. The key in the lock on the inside. He goes to unlock it, pausing to glance at me as we both make the connection between this door locked on the inside and the back door locked with no key.

'Who the fuck are you?' A man shouts from the top of the stairs brandishing a cricket bat.

'Sorry, emergency…we lost our dog,' I shout as Dave gets the door open. We sprint out, down the path and into the garden. The front door slams behind us a few seconds later. Feeling guilty from smashing in the back door of what must be one of the only occupied houses we move away, heading up the street.

'What number was that?' I ask Dave.

'I don't know, I thought you checked it.'

'Er…nope, what's that one?' We both run to the next house, stopping to shine our torches at the front door.

'No number,' Dave replies, our torch beams strafing the door and front walls.

'Fucking wankers,' I mutter with indignation.

We run to the next house and stop at the gate, again shining our torches at the front door.

'White Gates,' Dave reads the wooden sign on the wall, 'no number.'

'Fucking wankers!…they don't even have white gates… must be the next street if these are all named.' Jogging down the street we keep checking the front doors, finding them all to be named instead of numbered. At the junction we pause, the sound of loud thuds and shattering glass gives us direction. We head towards it, seeing a mass of bodies illuminated by the moon, assaulting the front of a house. Undead throwing themselves with unbelievable ferocity at the windows and door. As we get closer I watch as one of them stands in front of the thick double glazed glass, pulling his head back and ramming his forehead repeatedly into the panes of glass. They fracture, large spider web cracks forming. He keeps going, driving his bloodied skull into the thick glass, fracturing and smashing it bit by bit.

'We can't shoot in, we might hit the dog,' Dave says quickly.

'Round the back then, we can shoot out.'

'Roger,' he replies leading the way up a garden path a few doors down. The front door is locked and secure, a solid UPVC door. Dave drops down, kicking at the panel at mid centre of the bottom half. Sat on his arse with his feet cycling back and forth, raining blow after blow. The panel comes free, the whole of it simply falling into the house.

'How the?' I whisper as he peers inside before pulling himself through.

'Kick panel,' he replies. Again I have to pass my kit through before I squeeze through the hole, Dave standing facing away to cover me until I get through.

'I'm in.'

'This way,' he says leading us through the dark house towards the back. We find the kitchen door closed but unlocked and head out into the garden. Another six foot high fence, I throw my axe over and swing the rifle round onto my back, I back up so I can take a running jump at it.

Dave vaults it easily again like a cat. My running jump gets me most of the way up. My hands pressing down on the top to lever the rest of my body up. The fence groans with a splintering sounds them gives way, crashing down with me still on top of it.

'Sorry,' I whisper to Dave, picking myself up from the debris and pulling fence panels from the straps of my bag.

'Listen,' he stares at me. I strain my ears, hearing a dog barking furiously. The sound mixed in with the repeated thuds and bangs.

'Go!' I urge him as I run at the next fence. Thankfully this one doesn't collapse under my weight and I manage to get myself over.

'Oh fucking hell,' I mutter at the sight of the much larger fence. The barking and thuds loud and clear now.

'Must be in that one,' Dave nods at the high ivy covered fence looming over our heads. The noises suddenly escalate. Glass shattering noisily and we hear the dog snarling as it attacks something.

'They're through,' I call out, spotting a garden shed in the corner I head towards it. Using my axe to smash the door open. 'Dave take the end,' I grab the ladders inside the shed, trying to yank them free, bungee cords hold them in place and I curse with harsh language as my fingers fight to get them off.

'Got it,' Dave pulls the end, dragging the ladder from the shed and running across the lawn to prop them up against the fence. The top of the ladder slams against the fence, a foot too short. Dave scales up, levering himself over the top and dropping down the other side.

I go next, feeling the wobble as the ladder slides on the hard compacted ground underneath it. Reaching the top I straddle the edge, just weak trellis that sways and rocks underneath me. I drop my legs down, holding onto the top spoke and closing my eyes as I let go. The drop isn't that bad, just jarring more than anything.

We're in a garden with the same high fence on all sides. The back door open and the sound of fierce fighting coming from within. Both of us sprint to the back door, gaining the kitchen just as the front door bursts open and the undead start pushing through.

Dave starts firing instantly, it takes me a few more seconds to swing my rifle round from my back and take aim. The dog is out of sight in the front room but we can both hear it snarling and attacking the undead as they come through the windows.

'AIM HIGH, THE DOG MIGHT COME OUT,' Dave shouts. I take aim at head height, single shot only and aiming into mass of bodies trying to push through the now open doorway.

Heads explode, bodies flung back from the power of the rounds slamming into them. We edge forward slowly, firing quickly into the mass.

'MAGAZINE,' I shout and scrabble for the next full one in the pouch on my belt, ramming it home quickly and pulling the bolt back.

'COVER ME,' Dave shouts, he crouches down, crabbing down the hallway towards the lounge door, kneeling at an angle and firing his weapon into the room. I keep firing at the front door. Every one killed is instantly replaced. The zombies are possessed, more ferocious than I have ever seen them. Body shots go unnoticed apart from the power of the bullet forcing them back. Only head shots drop them.

Dave shouts and quickly changes his magazine, shouting that it's his last one. He picks his shots, firing into lounge. The end of the gun making tiny adjustments as he aim and fires.

'MAGAZINE, LAST ONE,' I shout, kneeling down to quickly change. Dave draws his pistol with his right hand, half turning and firing one shot at the front door with the hand weapon, then the next shot with the assault rifle into the lounge.

'GET THE DOG OUT,' I scream, pulling the bolt back and firing the last magazine of my assault rifle into the front door.

He disappears into the lounge as I move up the hallway. Shots ring out from within the room, the dog snarling and barking. I reach the doorway and glance inside just in time to see the dog leap at the smashed in window, snapping her mouth shut onto the throat of an undead clambering bodily through the gap. She grips it between her teeth, shaking her head violently and tearing a huge clump of flesh from the neck. Blood spurts out thick and fast, coating the already sodden floor. The undead struggles for a second before slumping down half in the gap. Dave shoots over the top of it as I empty my magazine into the front door. The fallen bodies again form an obstacle, giving us just a few seconds back down the hallway.

I whistle and urge the dog to come with us. The thing is massive, easily one of the biggest dogs I have ever seen. Paws like a lion, standing broad and high she looks wild and feral. Blood dripping from her panting mouth. Her lips stretched open to show the row of deadly teeth coated pink. Her hair is standing up and tail curled up over her back making her look even larger.

She looks at me, big beautiful soft brown eyes with no sign of the red bloodshot look of the undead.

'Good girl, come on...good girl,' I smile at her watching as her tail twitches which maybe a wag or a pre-cursor to ripping my head off.

Backing down the hallway I push the now useless rifle round to my back and draw my pistol. Firing at the undead as they scrabble and claw to climb over the bodies mounting up. Dave does the same, firing with ruthless precision directly into their heads.

The dog takes up her barking again, an incredibly deep noise that resonates round as much as the gunfire in the enclosed space.

'Fuck it! My radio is on my bag, did you bring yours?'

'No, sorry.'

We pull back further towards the garden. The things are pushing at the bodies now, their combined weight and utterly venomous thirst for destruction driving the corpses inside. I change magazine, ramming the new clip home and moving a couple of steps towards the door to fire into the pressing mass. My heart sinks at the number of undead behind the wall of cadavers. Too many, far too many.

One magazine left in my pistol, I ram it home and slide the top back. Dave goes forward firing individual fast shots, aiming for their heads. Each of his bullets slam home, taking the skulls off and sending the foul beast to hell. But it isn't enough.

'How many you got left?'

'Last one,' he replies, 'got knives though,' he gives me a quick smile before stepping in shooting his last magazine into them. 'I'm out.' He steps back re-holstering the gun.

'My last one now, you take it,' I hand the pistol to him which he takes without complaint.

'Get your axe into that fence Mr Howie,' he shouts before turning to fire. I run out the back door, swinging my axe into the fence. The thing isn't the cheap thin feather board fences that everyone else uses. Oh no, this wanker has had a proper fence built. Thick sturdy boards at six feet in height with that shitty trellis on the top.

'Fucking Alan Titchsmarsh,' I yell in fury as the axe bites into the boards. I hack away, hearing Dave place his shots slowly and carefully. More gunfire in the distance, the assault rifles cutting the other horde down.

This is desperate now. Even Dave might struggle to hold them back, they've changed again, evolved and become stronger and wilder. Roaring I swing the axe down, biting into the wood and wrenching it back. The boards split, slowly smashing under the blows.

'I'M OUT,' Dave bellows from inside.

'COMING,' I shout and start towards the door.

'KEEP GOING,' he shouts back. The image of him right

at that point will stay with me forever. Shoving the pistol into his waist band he pulls the knives from his back. The points of the blades down towards the floor. His wrists flicker as they're suddenly rotated and turned, the blades now pointing upwards against his forearms. The dog next to him, standing fierce and proud, her head low.

They both turn back to the door, both of them growling, quivering with anger, waiting for the attack. Wild animals full of pure killing instinct. Shit, I could probably sit down and have a cup of tea. Nothing could get through them. I've been with Dave since this started, seen him kill and kill again with such ease. But now, with that huge beast of a dog next to him…well, it's something else. The poor zombies are fucked. Then I remember why we're here in the first place and the extreme importance of that animal, the dog I mean, not Dave. That dog has pure untainted blood that we need.

The thought drives me back to the fence, the axe once more swinging down into the boards. Slowly it's beaten down, a hole through to the next garden forms slowly. I hack away making it big enough for me to squeeze through.

'INCOMING,' Dave screams from inside the house. The sounds of battle reaching me.

'WE'RE THROUGH,' I shout back as the dog appears through the door, walking backwards and lunging back in. I start forward seeing the back of Dave spinning and twisting as he fells anything that comes at him. The hallway is packed with them, deep and dense. Their drive is too much, pushing Dave and the dog back into the garden.

'GO GO,' Dave shouts, just about holding them at the doorway.

'Come on, good girl, come on…' I whistle and pull at the dog by her neck. She fights against me for a second, desperate to get at the undead. I keep shouting and pulling, she relents and turns with me, letting me guide and get her through the hole. I drop down onto all fours and start backing through it, pausing when just my head is left poking out.

'CLEAR...NOW DAVE...'he breaks free, turning to sprint across the lawn. I jerk back just in time as he dives through. Scrabbling to get his legs in. I'm already up, the axe held ready as Dave gets clear. I swing down at the first head that comes through, the blade biting deep into the skull killing it instantly. Another appears above it, clawing and thrashing through the hole. I swing in, slicing into the face and cleaving the skull open. As I free the blade the dog lunges in, savaging the remains of the skull with her teeth.

The fence vibrates as the bodies slam into it on the other side. We hold our position. The axe chopping down anything that comes through the hole.

'THE TOP,' Dave bellows as an undead launches itself from the top of the fence, the trellis crashing down with the weight of the zombies climbing up it. More bodies fall down our side. Dave and the dog moving quickly between them, killing them swiftly as I focus on the hole in the fence.

She is amazing. So quick and agile yet her strength is awesome. Days of doing this have honed her killing skill to perfection. If Dave came back as an animal he would be that dog. Swift and brutal.

She leaps between them, using her weight to slam them down and tear at their throats. If they withstand the weight of her body ramming into them she goes straight for the neck anyway. Shaking her neck and ragging them about the garden. Fully grown adults being tossed about like dolls. For once something other than Dave mesmerises me.

I slam my axe down, killing another one. The hole is now blocked by bodies. But the fence is shaking violently as the press of bodies from the other side slam and slam into it.

The fence starts to come down, slowly creaking with a loud splintering sound. I sprint across the lawn, swinging the axe into the next fence which thankfully is the cheap thin feather-board variety. The axes bites through the thin panels and I kick the rest away as Dave and the dog kill the things as they drop down onto the lawn.

The sturdy fence comes down, the first couple of ranks of the undead toppling over with it. We scoot through the hole of the next fence and keep going for the next one, Dave and I charge it bodily, our combined weight smashing clean through the middle of one panel. We both fall from the charge but we're through. We glance back as the undead regain their feet from the falling first fence and start charging across. Several of the next panels splinter and fall as they press home their attack but we're already off, charging across the garden and turning our shoulders into the middle of the next panel.

We burst through the fence, the dog charging back at the things and taking one down before running back to join us. Dave and I keep going, intent on making as much distance as possible between us and them.

The next fence panel goes down, pain in my shoulder from the impact but no damage as I can still move my arm as we sprint across for the next one. The undead are roaring and howling, a sickening sound that just drives us on faster. We hit the next fence at the same time as they impact on the one behind us. Two splintering crashing noises but their drive and speed pushes them on faster than us. They don't care about pain or position, just slamming into the fence panel's face on. Bodies dropping from the impact and being trampled only to get back up and keep charging. We don't have that luxury, we have to position and brace ourselves for the impact. Those two slight things mean they're closing the gap far quicker than either of us expected.

We crash into the final garden, my heart sinks at the sight of the wall. The solid brick wall that borders the road. The garden is lower than the road, now I understand why I fell when I jumped down, the drop being further than I expected.

Ferocious fighting is taking place the other side of that wall but it might as well be in fucking France, the distance is just too great. The wall is just too high. Dave might make it but me and the dog won't, well maybe the dog would…but that would mean it has to understand its own importance and know it must survive, it must run at the wall and leap high. There isn't time to communicate this to the dog, there isn't time to urge the dog over. The dog wants to fight, it wants to kill the undead.

These last few strides will take us to the wall, then we have no choice but to fight. Time slows as my legs make the strides. I glance at Dave as he nods at me, his eyes alight and telling me everything I need to know. The dog is running to the side of us, her ears pricked at the sounds coming from the other side of the wall.

We reach the wall and stop, quickly turning back. Four, maybe five seconds before they're on us. My axe is ready, gripped in both hands. Dave has a knife in each hand. We face the horde, the fetid dirty foul evil spawn that charge at us across a once perfectly manicured green lawn. The dog is ready, her head low and top lip crumpled showing them her teeth.

'READY DAVE?'

'YES MR HOWIE,' He bellows back, his voice loud and strong. Fury etched onto his face, his own lips pulled back, snarling. My own top lip pulls up as I roar my challenge at them. Dave gives voice, the dog glances between us. Her eyes on fire as she joins us.

We do not fear you. We ran for a reason but not through fear, never through fear. We are not cowards but warriors strong and true. We three stand before your many and we stand proud and ready. We hold weapons but we will fight you without them if we have to. Know us. Know our names. Know who we are for we will reap a vengeance on you. See us before you. Feel that power surging through our bodies and know that one of our few cannot be turned. For that you have failed and we have that one thing that will drive humanity forever onwards. We have hope. One tiny spark of hope that will keep you from our doors.

I am Howie. Son of Howard.

We have met before.

You know me.

I am your destroyer and I will end you.

The three of us charge the many. Dave goes right, I go left and the dog takes the middle. My axe swings back high and swipes forward into their ranks. The shaft with the heavy weighted double blade becomes an extension of my body, a part of me as intrinsic as my arms and legs. We are connected and it becomes alive in my hands. The blade bites and snarls with a life and heart of its own. The undead wilt and die before me. They have no power, no love. I fight for my friends, for they are my family. My axe flies and bites, slices and sweeps. It skewers and cleaves, taking heads off, destroying necks, slicing through shoulder joints. They pile in, oh they pile in with such ferocity that it should make me feel overwhelmed but instead I relish the challenge. One may get me, one bite or scratch will be all it needs but until that happens I shall not stop.

Dave is to the right fighting deep amongst them. His athletic grace is unstoppable, the power generated through his small body becomes something ethereal, magical. An ability that humans should not possess for the power it gives them must, must corrupt their soul. For Dave though it is a simply a skill he has and a task that needs doing. The more I know him, the more time I spend with him the more I see further into him. There is a spark there, something that comes alive when he does this.

I throw my head back and scream my vengeance at them, swinging out and keeping them at bay. The grass quickly becomes slick from the blood, the bodies become trip hazards in the dark of the garden. The fighting becomes dirty and close quartered, I glance over to the fence and see more pouring through. Too many. The gardens are thick with them. I catch sight of the dog leaping high and taking a throat out with her jaws.

They lunge at her, diving and frantic to take her down. She takes bites, I see it happen. One of them sinking his teeth into her shoulder. She howls and spins round, ravaging the thing to death and dragging it quickly backwards knocking more of their feet as the undead flails its arms and legs about.

The man we saved in the street roars and leaps from the top of the wall, landing feet from me and taking several down with him. He's on his feet within a second, his face is filled with pure vengeance. His thick muscular arms punch out quick and hard. Faces lunge at him, he punches fast and knocks them back. His hard knuckles breaking bones left right and centre. With his bare hands he fights them. That dog must mean the world to him, maybe he knows of her pure blood and fights for the same reasons.

'MEREDITH,' he screams with a deep voice. He lashes out, knocking one back and grabbing another. His arms quickly wrapping round the thing and snapping its neck. His movements become faster as he repeats the action, grabbing another and twisting violently.

My axe is bloodied now, the crimson foulness pours down the shaft and coats my hands. I grip harder and do the work I was made for; killing and destroying the evil things before me.

'MEREDITH,' the man bellows. He grabs another one, slamming his foot down onto the undeads knee and snapping the neck. I've seen that before, many times. Who does that move? Not Dave or Clarence.

We fight on, losing. Losing and we know it. The firing continues the other side of the wall, they must be as pinned down as we are. No hope of rescue then. Oh well, they'll have to cope for a while longer until we've finished these off. Ha! Hope Howie, there's always Hope. Our four pitted against them, we don't fight in a circle but on our own. Each beast amongst us fighting for his own reasons but for the same end.

We're going to lose. That is almost certain now. For everything wonderful that Dave can do, for the sheer destructive power of the dog, for the lunacy of that big bloke, even for the power I possess we are simply too outnumbered to win. I'm getting backed into a corner, giving ground but killing for every step back I have to take.

A huge sound fills the air, cheering erupts from the other side of the wall as the beloved, beautiful, glorious sound of the General Purpose Machine Gun fills the air. That constant beat it produces so distinctive and true.

Within a second the top of the wall is swarming with my blessed team. Every-one of them scrambling and dropping down. Rifles cast aside for fear of shooting their own.

Blowers. That brave lad always with Cookey at his side. They leap with axes drawn, landing deep in the fray. Clarence bellows with his axe held out above his head. A Viking berserker sent from ages past to rid the world of this plague. Lani, slight and deadly, meat cleaver shining in her hand. She casts her eyes, seeing me backed into the corner and surrounded by the filthy undead. Too many of them for my axe to take. Her face twists into one of pure rage, she charges at them with the scream of a banshee intent on destruction. Tom and Nick roar in with unbridled glory, they team up covering each-others backs and fighting with utter brutality. Chris drops down, his eyes ablaze as the diplomat and leader leaves to be replaced with the warrior he is. He makes for Clarence. The two big men fighting side by side. Long years spent doing the same has made them an intuitive and amazing team to behold.

See us you foul things. See my team. See who we are for now we are not few but we are many. Less than you but enough for I will take any of these against a horde a hundred times your size.

The unknown man fights towards the dog, she gets to his side and they fight out. We give voice as we do battle. They howl and scream with fury and we howl and scream back. This garden of a house of a street in a quiet town becomes to site of a furious battle. Undead stream at us and die under our weapons. Lani reaches my side and we fight out together. Her meat cleaver so deadly and accurate as she whips and charges them unafraid and fearsome.

The man snaps necks one after the other, with more of us fighting the space has evened out and he becomes deadlier than before. The dog watches him constantly, taking anything down that even looks like its heading his way. He fights with glorious beauty, screaming the name Meredith over and again.

They sense the loss and they change. Fighting harder than before with such savagery it becomes almost frightening to watch them for never before have I seen such twisted hatred, such darkness of violence driving a creature for these are creatures with nothing human about them now. Hands become claws, lashing out with deadly strength.

The dog howls as an undead sinks its teeth into her body, the hands of the zombie pummelling her side. She thrashes wildly, the man screaming and diving down onto the zombie.

His fists driving punches into its head. He breaks the things grip and snaps its neck. The dog bleeds from a wound to her side but pays no heed. On her feet and returning the gesture with her teeth. The man drives into them again. He becomes overwhelmed, hands driving at him. The dog leaps into them, using her body to slam them backwards. Dave gains the dog's side, his knives slashing and cutting deeply, his feet kicking out as he battles them away. Chris and Clarence fight in, destroying the things she knocked back.

Blowers leads the rest to the fence, screaming orders as he, Cookey, Nick and Tom form a line across the boundary. They fight out with their backs to us, trusting their comrades to protect them from the rear. Lani and I fight towards them, the battle is ferocious now. They become super charged with greater strength and unabated violence coursing through their dead systems. The man goes down, bodies of undead swarming over him. The dog leaps in amongst them, her teeth gnashing left and right ripping bodies away. Dave roars, joining the dog and fighting into them. The man is lost to view, his body covered by undead. The dog going wild with fury and bleeding from several wounds to her body, her black fur matted with the wet glistening blood. Clarence loses his axe in the head of one if the things. He kicks the undead away, lifting it from its feet as it ploughs deep into the ranks of the oncoming. He reverts to hands, his massive arms swiping and knocking them down. He scoops a broken body up, using it as a battering ram at first before grabbing the corpse by the ankles and swinging at the undead. Releasing the body to slam them against the end wall and he piles in after them. Chris at his side as they bring their own way of fighting to the zombies.

Lani and I reach the pile in the middle, hacking, kicking, punching and gouging. We beat the bodies back. The man fights under them, still alive and his face contorted with the indignation of losing his feet. His t-shirt is ripped from his body as clawed hands rake at him. Blood coats his skin, his own blood from cuts and bites to his arms, neck and body. He doesn't notice, he doesn't care. Dave stares at him for a split second before fighting out again. Chris and Clarence, having killed their end fight back towards the middle. Corpses everywhere, bits of corpse everywhere. Feet slipping and sliding and the fighting becomes the hardest in these last few minutes. They've lost but they don't care. They fight and claw, lunging and snapping their teeth without hesitation.

Lani stays at my side, Dave stays with the dog and the dog stays by the man as we fight for our lives. The line at the fence breaks as Chris roars to cover the dog. The undead are no longer coming at us, their numbers are exhausted.

The rest fall back into a slowly decreasing circle, ending the life of anything that doesn't belong on this earth.

The last seconds and the man slips, going down hard. The last few undead pile into him, covering his body. The dog reacts as quickly as before and we're there, all of us are there pulling the bodies away and ending them quickly.

As the last body has its neck snapped by Clarence and thrown casually aside we stand and stare about us. Chests heaving, weapons raised and ready.

Its' done. The battle is ours but the bloodlust is still on us. We still snarl and growl as the reality of the victory slowly trickles into our heads.

The man starts to rise, his face still flushed with battle as he gets up to fight some more. He slips and staggers, his legs giving way underneath him. The dog whines at his side, licking his face with her tail wagging, the hair on her back no longer standing on end. Her teeth no longer showing.

I rush over, dropping down next to him. The wounds are deep, too deep and too many of them. His body covered in cuts and bites. His face is familiar, a thick beard covers his jaw and suddenly the image of that move he did comes to mind.

'Paco Maguire, fuck me...' Cookey says hoarsely as he too recognises the fallen man.

'Get me up,' the man gasps for air. I try to help him to his feet but his own legs won't take his weight, he sinks back down.

'It's done, it's over...we won,' I say between lungful's of air.

'Oh,' he says simply and the fight goes out of him, he rises to sit upright. Staring at the dog and wincing as she licks at his wounds. 'I'm cut...' his deep American voice says flatly, 'I've been bit.'

He stares up at our faces, no one says anything, too out of breath and knowing what it means too.

'Are you okay?' He asks the dog, 'you've been bit too, get me water...quick.' Someone passes him a bottle which he uses to pour down her side, cleaning the wounds, 'good girl, you're gonna be okay...you know that...you're gonna be okay,' he pours the bottle on her bites. She winces but takes the pain, holding her head so close to his. She sniffs at his wounds, licking them as they try to clean each other. 'More water damn you,' the man snaps. Bottles are passed down to him. He cups his hands, telling someone to pour water into them. It's done by Lani but the man doesn't acknowledge the action, just stares at the dog as he pushes the makeshift bowl towards her. She laps at the water, her long pink tongue licking his hands in the process. He takes the bottle from Lani and holds it to her mouth, gently pouring it out as she licks the cascading liquid. He smiles and rubs her neck, 'drink, good girl, you drink it all up....clean her wounds for damn sake,' he snarls out the side of her mouth.

We dart forward, hands holding water bottles and pouring the liquid down her sides. She suffers the pain, intent on lapping at the water he pours by her mouth.

The man coughs once, then again harder. The bottle falls from his grip as he sinks onto his side, gripping his stomach and writhing in pain.

The dog whines and licks his face, her rough tongue removing the blood from his skin. He comes to, opening his eyes and smiling up at her. He rolls onto his back, his arms coming up to wrap round her neck. She sinks down onto his chest, her front legs either side of his head.

'Meredith...' he whispers softly hugging the dog. 'Meredith....I'm coming...'

I drop down to his side, the dog suddenly showing me teeth and growling. We back off, leaving them together. He clings to her neck, his face a picture of happiness and contentment. His fingers stroke her fur as he whispers soft murmurings into her ears. She licks his face again, he chuckles softly.

'You take care of her you hear me...you damn well take care of her,' he suddenly roars with power in his voice.

'We will, I promise,' I say back. My voice choking as tears sting my eyes. Glancing round I see clean streaks down the faces of most of the others. Even Clarence and Chris. Dave is the only one who doesn't show a reaction.

'Good girl....good.....girl....Meredith....good....' his voice becomes a whisper, his hands cling to the dog's neck. His breathing slows, becoming shallower with every second. His fingers slip as his hands fall down. He exhales and dies.

The dog whines, licking his face and gently moving her paws against his neck. Dave steps forward, his knife ready. She growls softly, sensing his movement, the hair on her back on end. I wave my hand at him, telling him to back away. He nods and steps back.

We stand ready, knowing the outcome. Chris slowly pulls his pistol and aims at the head, ready for the turn.

The dog whines, staring at Paco's face. Her tongue still

licking at his skin. The hair on her back settles. She whines longer, her head lifting as she howls long and sorrowfully into the night air. The piercing sound makes the tears come harder. Lani chokes and moves into my side, I wrap my arm round her shoulders. Cookey drops to his knees quietly sobbing. Nick turns away his chest heaving.

She stops the howl, looking down at her master. The howl ends as her head cocks to one side, staring with intensity at the body of Paco Maguire. Ears pricked and eyes fixed.

I glance at Chris, he shrugs almost imperceptibly. The hair on her back slowly stands up again, a low growl in her throat. She doesn't blink or look away, but slowly rises up. Her body lifting from the chest of the man she fought so bravely for. The top lip of the dog pulls back, showing the huge teeth. The growl becomes louder. Her body rigid.

The corpse twitches once, a judder of electricity running through its body. She growls louder still. Holding position with her front feet planted either side of the corpses head. Her nose inches from the face.

The hands clench and flex, the arms spasm. The corpse jolts and the eyes open. The red bloodshot eyes staring out at the face of the dog. A loud snarl erupts as her jaws clamp down, tearing the throat out.

Instinct forces my eyes closed, squeezing them shut. The wet tearing sound of flesh as the dog savages the undead body of Paco Maguire.

When I open my eyes she's stood to the side of the body, growling at it. She barks fiercely at the corpse, then backs away and lifts her head to stare at everyone stood watching her. She looks at each face, her eyes locking on mine for long seconds. She twitches and looks down at her own side, as though suddenly aware of the wounds. She twists back to sniff at them, her back end slumping down to the ground. We rush forward, hands ready to lift and carry her if need be.

More water gets poured down her wounds, washing the blood away. Nick runs off to the house, the sound of smashing glass reaches us. I crouch down at her head, stroking the broad top of her skull. Her tail wags at the attention as many voices all tell her what a good girl she is.

Torches shine onto the wounds. Nick runs back carrying a large glass mixing bowl and pulling a hose with him. He puts the bowl down, pushing the end of the hose into the bowl and filling it with water.

'JOHN CAN YOU HEAR ME?' Chris shouts at the wall.

'Yeah, you alright over there?' A voice shouts back.

'I WANT THE FIELD DRESSINGS OVER HERE.'

'Roger,' the voice shouts back.

The dog laps at the water, Nick runs back with towels and cloths from the house, using the end of the hose to soak her coat and wipe the filth away. Every hand that can get to her does something. Cleans, pats, strokes. She seems unbothered, letting her wounds be tended as she drinks and drinks. Her skin judders as the bites and cuts are cleaned and washed. The field kit is carried over by one of Chris's men. They tear the packages open, unravelling bandages and wrapping them round the dog.

'She needs to stand up,' Chris says quietly. We gently lift the dog to her feet. For such a vicious animal she takes it remarkably well. Allowing herself to be held and fussed. Her tail wagging slowly and all the time drinking water from the bowl.

Within a couple of minutes the dog is washed , rubbed dry and covered in bandages.

'Any idea what her name is?' Cookey asks.

'No mate, that bloke kept saying Meredith though,' I reply.

'Must be her name then,' Nick says.

'Bit of a weird name for a dog,' Clarence offers.

'That was Paco Maguire wasn't it?' Cookey asks.

'It was.'

'What the hell was he here doing here?' Blowers asks standing back and pouring water down his face from the hose.

'No idea, didn't really get a chance to ask him.'

'Hard bloke though, I thought all those actors were pussies,' Tom adds.

'He was proper hard, did you see him doing that thing he does from the movies, with the knee and breaking the neck?' Nick joins in.

'That was so cool, like really cool,' Cookey says taking the hose from Blowers to wash his own face off.

'Did you see the dog watching him, she knew he turned… she bloody knew it,' Chris says, 'how many bites does she have?'

'Loads,' Clarence replies.

'We need to watch her like a hawk, Dave if she even looks like she's going to turn…'

'I'm on it,' Dave cuts me off, standing close with a knife in his hand.

'You can't kill her,' Chris says.

'If she turns I bloody can.'

'She's bitten all over, look at the wounds…no sign of turning…'

'Doesn't mean she won't though Chris, could be a delayed reaction or something.'

'How we getting her back?' He asks.

'She can come with us, Dave'll be right next to her.'

'Howie she might hold the cure for this thing, you cannot kill her.'

'He's right boss,' Clarence cuts in.

'And what if she turns? What good will she be then?'

'She'll still have her blood inside her!' Chris shouts.

'Okay, Dave don't kill the dog unless you have to.'

'Okay Mr Howie.'

'Everyone else okay? Check for wounds and cuts, that was a fucking fight and a half that was...where the hell did they get that energy and power from?'

'Mutating, it must be learning to get them stronger,' Tom adds, 'the flu virus mutates and changes every year doesn't it, my nan had to go the doctors every winter to get a jab as the one from last year wouldn't protect her.'

Torches get shined onto each other's bodies as we check for cuts, using the hose to rinse the filth and gore off. The dog rests on the grass next to us, watching with interest and panting heavily with her mid-section covered in white bandages.

'All clear,' Clarence finishes checking Chris, handing me the hose so I can do Lani. I check her arms, neck and face thoroughly. Hosing her skin off and making sure none of her clothes are ripped or torn. She does me after while Nick breaks out the cigarettes and passes them round. Dave standing close to the dog with a knife still held in his hand and staring down at her intently.

She lifts her head and stares back at him. The rest of us come to a stop as we watch them lock eyes. Neither flinching or looking away. Two killers of pure instinct staring at each other. Dave cocks his head to one side, frowning. The dog closes her mouth and does the same, cocking her head and staring back. Like some fierce competition taking place. Both of them trying to judge who is the most powerful, the most deadly. It goes on for a few seconds, silence from the rest of us as we watch with interest.

Then the spell is broken as the dog turns away to sniff at the bandages, Dave shrugs and looks up, surprised to see us all watching him.

'What?' He asks.

'Nothing,' Clarence replies for us as we all turn away quickly and find something else to do.

'Can she walk?' I ask as we get ready to go.

'Yes,' Dave replies, 'come on,' he speaks flatly to the dog. She gets to her feet and follows behind him into the house, walking straight through the rest of us with barely a glance.

'Fuck, you wouldn't pick a fight with them two would you,' Chris whispers.

'Let's go,' I say in reply We file out of the garden, stepping over the corpses of the undead. I spare a few seconds to look down at the remains of Paco. Wondering why he was here but giving thanks for his bravery in protecting the dog. If he hadn't come over that wall when he did this would have ended badly. Hard man, I always thought his movies were good but never realised he could do that stuff in real-life too. Pity, he would have been a great asset in our team.

Shaking my head I walk through the house and into the street, following the others as we file back to the Saxon. Dave and the dog already stood by the open back doors.

'Ready for that swim?' I call out.

'Too bloody right,' Clarence laughs.

'What swim?' Chris asks.

'Mr Howie has been promising us a swim all day..' Cookey explains.

'And a cold beer,' Blowers adds.

'And a take-away,' Nick joins in.

'I never said anything about a take-away,' I laugh back at them.

'Well I reckon you've earned it,' Chris says.

'Yeah right,' Cookey laughs, 'you say that now but something else will happen...'

'Always bloody does,' Blowers chuckles.

'Every half hour isn't it Mr Howie?' Nick asks.

'Fact,' I reply with a smile.

We load up slowly, the heat and exhaustion making us sluggish. The back doors are left open, the dog settling down on the floor and sleeping as Dave rests next to her, his eyes never leaving her face.

Clarence takes the front with me as we pull away, leading the way through the town back to our fort.

I don't think I have ever felt this tired before. My eyes sting from exhaustion, my limbs feel detached. Clarence is already dozing off, Nick up top on the GPMG.

'You look like you need this,' Lani says behind me, passing me another sugary energy drink.

'What a night,' I reply with a yawn.

'It's not over yet,' she whispers softly in my ear as her hand rests on my shoulder. A huge grin spreads across my face and suddenly I don't feel quite so sleepy.

CHAPTER 47

She rests in the big thing, her eyes closed but ears pricked. The loss of another pack leader was hard. She felt the love coming from the man at the end. She'd watched him change in those few days. Full of fear and panic but he became a man, a leader, strong and true and someone she would follow.

She felt his life cease. The heartbeat that ended and the energy that expired. What came back wasn't the man. It was one of the things and it had to be destroyed. There was no confusion about this, no mixed feeling.

The pack around her was strong. She sensed their unity and strength. They fought and moved like a pack. Sensing each other with instinct. Her own pack ceased when the man died but they were quickly upon her. Giving her water, stroking and fussing her. They made noises like her first pack, they tended her wounds which hurt but she was thirsty she didn't care for the pain. At the centre of attention from this pack she felt a strange connection developing. The way they moved around her, they were showing her they wanted her in their pack.

She rested on the grass, watching and listening to them around her. One stood close. He was smaller than the others but the energy he gave off was incredible. Primal without an ounce of fear. She stared at his eyes, staring into his soul. Not a flicker of reaction. Pure positive energy emanating from him. No confusion of emotions that the people so often show.

Only he wasn't the pack leader. His energy poured towards the other man. The one with the dark eyes. The one that the others listened to and watched so intently.

She felt his presence during the fight and she wasn't the only one. The things felt his presence too. They feared him. They didn't show it but she could sense it.

The things feared him.

He was the leader.

Printed in Great Britain
by Amazon